The Professor

The Professor

Charlotte Brontë

ALMA CLASSICS

ALMA CLASSICS
an imprint of

ALMA BOOKS LTD
3 Castle Yard
Richmond
Surrey TW10 6TF
United Kingdom
www.almaclassics.com

The Professor first published in 1857
This edition first published by Alma Books Ltd in 2018

Cover design by Will Dady

Extra Material © Alma Books Ltd

Printed in Great Britain by CPI Group (UK) Ltd, Croydon CR0 4YY

ISBN: 978-1-84749-717-8

Contents

Charlotte Brontë (1816–55)

Revd Patrick Brontë,
Charlotte's father

Maria Branwell,
Charlotte's mother

Emily Brontë

Anne Brontë

The Brontë Parsonage in Haworth (above) and
Haworth's parish church and cemetery (below)

The Clergy Daughters' School at Cowan Bridge,
attended by the young Brontës

Miss Woolers' school at Roe Head, where Charlotte
was first a pupil and later a teacher

The Professor

Preface

This little book was written before either *Jane Eyre* or *Shirley*, and yet no indulgence can be solicited for it on the plea of a first attempt. A first attempt it certainly was not, as the pen which wrote it had been previously worn a good deal in a practice of some years. I had not indeed published anything before I commenced *The Professor*, but in many a crude effort, destroyed almost as soon as composed, I had got over any such taste as I might once have had for ornamented and redundant composition, and come to prefer what was plain and homely. At the same time I had adopted a set of principles on the subject of incident etc., such as would be generally approved in theory, but the result of which, when carried out into practice, often procures for an author more surprise than pleasure.

I said to myself that my hero should work his way through life as I had seen real living men work theirs – that he should never get a shilling he had not earned – that no sudden turns should lift him in a moment to wealth and high station; that whatever small competency he might gain should be won by the sweat of his brow; that, before he could find so much as an arbour to sit down in, he should master at least half the ascent of "the Hill of Difficulty";* that he should not even marry a beautiful girl or a lady of rank. As Adam's son he should share Adam's doom,* and drain throughout life a mixed and moderate cup of enjoyment.

In the sequel, however, I find that publishers in general scarcely approved of this system, but would have liked something more imaginative and poetical – something more consonant with a highly wrought fancy, with a taste for pathos, with sentiments more tender, elevated, unworldly. Indeed, until an author has tried to dispose of a manuscript of this kind, he can never know what stores of romance and sensibility lie hidden in breasts he would not have suspected of casketing such treasures. Men in business are usually thought to prefer the real; on trial the idea will be often found fallacious: a passionate preference for the wild, wonderful and thrilling – the strange, startling and harrowing – agitates divers souls that show a calm and sober surface.

Such being the case, the reader will comprehend that to have reached him in the form of a printed book, this brief narrative must have gone through some struggles – which indeed it has. And after all, its worst struggle and strongest ordeal is yet to come; but it takes comfort – subdues fear – leans on the staff of a moderate expectation – and mutters under its breath, while lifting its eye to that of the public.

He that is low need fear no fall.

CURRER BELL

The foregoing preface was written by my wife with a view to the publication of *The Professor*, shortly after the appearance of *Shirley*. Being dissuaded from her intention, the authoress made some use of the materials in a subsequent work – *Villette*. As, however, these two stories are in most respects unlike, it has been represented to me that I ought not to withhold *The Professor* from the public. I have therefore consented to its publication.

A.B. NICHOLLS
Haworth Parsonage,
September 22nd, 1856

Chapter 1

INTRODUCTORY

THE OTHER DAY, IN LOOKING OVER MY PAPERS, I found in my desk the following copy of a letter, sent by me a year since to an old school acquaintance:

Dear Charles,
I think when you and I were at Eton together, we were neither of us what could be called popular characters: you were a sarcastic, observant, shrewd, cold-blooded creature; my own portrait I will not attempt to draw, but I cannot recollect that it was a strikingly attractive one – can you? What animal magnetism drew thee and me together I know not; certainly I never experienced anything of the "Pylades and Orestes"* sentiment for you, and I have reason to believe that you, on your part, were equally free from all romantic regard to me. Still, out of school hours we walked and talked continually together; when the theme of conversation was our companions or our masters, we understood each other, and when I recurred to some sentiment of affection, some vague love of an excellent or beautiful object, whether in animate or in inanimate nature, your sardonic coldness did not move me. I felt myself superior to that check then as I do now.

It is a long time since I wrote to you, and a still longer time since I saw you. Chancing to take up a newspaper of your county the other day, my eye fell on your name. I began to think of old times, to run over the events which have transpired since we separated, and I sat down and commenced this letter. What you have been doing I know not, but you shall hear, if you choose to listen, how the world has wagged with me.

First, after leaving Eton, I had an interview with my maternal uncles, Lord Tynedale and the Hon. John Seacombe. They asked me if I would enter the Church, and my uncle the nobleman offered me the living of Seacombe, which is in his gift, if I would; then my other uncle, Mr Seacombe, hinted that when I became Rector of Seacombe-cum-Scaife, I might perhaps be allowed to take, as mistress of my house and head of my parish, one of my six cousins, his daughters, all of whom I greatly dislike.

I declined both the Church and matrimony. A good clergyman is a good thing, but I should have made a very bad one. As to the wife – oh, how like a nightmare is the thought of being bound for life to one of my cousins! No doubt they are accomplished and pretty, but not an accomplishment, not a charm of theirs, touches a chord in my bosom. To think of passing the winter evenings by the parlour fireside of Seacombe Rectory alone with one of them – for instance, the large and well-modelled statue, Sarah – no; I should be a bad husband, under such circumstances, as well as a bad clergyman.

When I had declined my uncles' offers, they asked me what I intended to do. I said I should reflect. They reminded me that I had no fortune, and no expectation of any, and, after a considerable pause, Lord Tynedale demanded sternly whether I had thoughts of following my father's steps and engaging in trade. Now, I had had no thoughts of the sort. I do not think that my turn of mind qualifies me to make a good tradesman; my taste, my ambition does not lie in that way; but such was the scorn expressed in Lord Tynedale's countenance as he pronounced the word trade – such the contemptuous sarcasm of his tone – that I was instantly decided. My father was but a name to me, yet that name I did not like to hear mentioned with a sneer to my very face. I answered then, with haste and warmth, "I cannot do better than follow in my father's steps; yes, I will be a tradesman." My uncles did not remonstrate; they and I parted with mutual disgust. In reviewing this transaction, I find that I was quite right to shake off the burden of Tynedale's patronage, but a fool to offer my shoulders instantly for the reception of another burden – one which might be more intolerable, and which certainly was yet untried.

I wrote instantly to Edward – you know Edward – my only brother, ten years my senior, married to a rich mill owner's daughter, *and now possessor of the mill and business which was my father's before he failed. You are aware that my father – once reckoned a Croesus* of wealth – became bankrupt a short time previous to his death, and that my mother lived in destitution for some six months after him, unhelped by her aristocratical brothers, whom she had mortally offended by her union with Crimsworth, the —shire manufacturer. At the end of the six months she brought me into the world, and then herself left it without, I should think, much regret, as it contained little hope or comfort for her.*

My father's relations took charge of Edward, as they did of me, till I was nine years old. At that period it chanced that the representation of an important borough in our county fell vacant; Mr Seacombe stood for it. My Uncle Crimsworth, an astute mercantile man, took the opportunity of writing a fierce letter to the candidate, stating that if he and Lord Tynedale did not consent to do something towards the support of their sister's orphan children, he would expose their relentless and malignant conduct towards that sister, and do his best to turn the circumstances against Mr Seacombe's election. That gentleman and Lord T. knew well enough that the Crimsworths were an unscrupulous and determined race; they knew also that they had influence in the borough of X—; and, making a virtue of necessity, they consented to defray the expenses of my education. I was sent to Eton, where I remained ten years, during which space of time Edward and I never met. He, when he grew up, entered into trade, and pursued his calling with such diligence, ability and success that now, in his thirtieth year, he was fast making a fortune. Of this I was apprised by the occasional short letters I received from him, some three or four times a year; which said letters never concluded without some expression of determined enmity against the house of Seacombe, and some reproach to me for living, as he said, on the bounty of that house. At first, while still in boyhood, I could not understand why, as I had no parents, I should not be indebted to my uncles Tynedale and Seacombe for my education; but as I grew up and heard by degrees of the persevering hostility, the hatred till death evinced by them against my father – of the sufferings of my mother – of all the wrongs, in short, of our house – then did I conceive shame of the dependence in which I lived, and form a resolution

7

no more to take bread from hands which had refused to minister to the necessities of my dying mother. It was by these feelings I was influenced when I refused the Rectory of Seacombe, and the union with one of my patrician cousins.

An irreparable breach thus being effected between my uncles and myself, I wrote to Edward, told him what had occurred and informed him of my intention to follow his steps and be a trades-man. I asked, moreover, if he could give me employment. His answer expressed no approbation of my conduct, but he said I might come down to —shire, if I liked, and he would "see what could be done in the way of furnishing me with work". I repressed all – even mental *– comment on his note, packed my trunk and carpet bag, and started for the North directly.*

After two days' travelling (railroads were not then in existence) I arrived, one wet October afternoon, in the town of X—. I had always understood that Edward lived in this town, but on enquiry I found that it was only Mr Crimsworth's mill and warehouse which were situated in the smoky atmosphere of Bigben Close; his residence *lay four miles out, in the country.*

It was late in the evening when I alighted at the gates of the habita-tion designated to me as my brother's. As I advanced up the avenue, I could see through the shades of twilight, and the dank gloomy mists which deepened those shades, that the house was large, and the grounds surrounding it sufficiently spacious. I paused a moment on the lawn in front and, leaning my back against a tall tree which rose in the centre, I gazed with interest on the exterior of Crimsworth Hall.

"Edward is rich," thought I to myself. "I believed him to be doing well – but I did not know he was master of a mansion like this." Cutting short all marvelling, speculation, conjecture, etc., I advanced to the front door and rang. A manservant opened it – I announced myself – he relieved me of my wet cloak and carpet bag, and ushered me into a room furnished as a library, where there was a bright fire, and candles burning on the table; he informed me that his master was not yet returned from X— market, but that he would certainly be at home in the course of half an hour.

Being left to myself, I took the stuffed easy chair, covered with red morocco, which stood by the fireside, and while my eyes watched the flames dart from the glowing coals, and the cinders fall at intervals on the hearth, my mind busied itself in conjectures concerning the meeting about to take place. Amidst much that was doubtful in the subject of these conjectures, there was one thing tolerably certain: I was in no danger of encountering severe disappointment; from this, the moderation of my expectations guaranteed me. I anticipated no overflowings of fraternal tenderness; Edward's letters had always been such as to prevent the engendering or harbouring of delusions of this sort. Still, as I sat awaiting his arrival, I felt eager – very eager – I cannot tell you why; my hand, so utterly a stranger to the grasp of a kindred hand, clenched itself to repress the tremor with which impatience would fain have shaken it.

I thought of my uncles; and as I was engaged in wondering whether Edward's indifference would equal the cold disdain I had always experienced from them, I heard the avenue gates open; wheels approached the house; Mr Crimsworth had arrived; and after the lapse of some minutes, and a brief dialogue between himself and the servant in the hall, his tread drew near the library door – that tread alone announced the master of the house.

I still retained some confused recollection of Edward as he was ten years ago – a tall, wiry, raw youth; now, as I rose from my seat and turned towards the library door, I saw a fine-looking and powerful man, light-complexioned, well-made, and of athletic proportions; the first glance made me aware of an air of promptitude and sharpness, shown as well in his movements as in his port, his eye and the general expression of his face. He greeted me with brevity, and, in the moment of shaking hands, scanned me from head to foot; he took his seat in the morocco-covered armchair and motioned me to another seat.

"I expected you would have called at the counting house in the Close," said he; and his voice, I noticed, had an abrupt accent, probably habitual to him; he spoke also with a guttural northern tone, which sounded harsh in my ears, accustomed to the silvery utterance of the South.

"The landlord of the inn, where the coach stopped, directed me here," said I. "I doubted at first the accuracy of his information, not being aware that you had such a residence as this."

"Oh, it is all right!" he replied. "Only I was kept half an hour behind time, waiting for you – that is all. I thought you must be coming by the eight-o'clock coach."

I expressed regret that he had had to wait; he made no answer, but stirred the fire, as if to cover a moment of impatience; then he scanned me again.

I felt an inward satisfaction that I had not, in the first moment of meeting, betrayed any warmth, any enthusiasm; that I had saluted this man with a quiet and steady phlegm.

"Have you quite broken with Tynedale and Seacombe?" he asked hastily.

"I do not think I shall have any further communication with them; my refusal of their proposals will, I fancy, operate as a barrier against all future intercourse."

"Why," said he, "I may as well remind you at the very outset of our connection, that 'no man can serve two masters'.* Acquaintance with Lord Tynedale will be incompatible with assistance from me." There was a kind of gratuitous menace in his eye as he looked at me in finishing this observation.

Feeling no disposition to reply to him, I contented myself with an inward speculation on the differences which exist in the constitution of men's minds. I do not know what inference Mr Crimsworth drew from my silence – whether he considered it a symptom of contumacity or an evidence of my being cowed by his peremptory manner. After a long and hard stare at me, he rose sharply from his seat.

"Tomorrow," said he, "I shall call your attention to some other points; but now it is supper time, and Mrs Crimsworth is probably waiting; will you come?"

He strode from the room, and I followed. In crossing the hall, I wondered what Mrs Crimsworth might be. "Is she," thought I, "as alien to what I like as Tynedale, Seacombe, the Misses Seacombe – as the affectionate relative now striding before me? Or is she better than these? Shall I, in conversing with her, feel free to show something of my real nature; or—" Further conjectures were arrested by my entrance into the dining room.

A lamp, burning under a shade of ground glass, showed a handsome apartment, wainscoted with oak; supper was laid on the table;

by the fireplace, standing as if waiting our entrance, appeared a lady; she was young, tall and well shaped; her dress was handsome and fashionable: so much my first glance sufficed to ascertain. A gay salutation passed between her and Mr Crimsworth; she chid him, half playfully, half poutingly, for being late; her voice (I always take voices into the account in judging of character) was lively – it indicated, I thought, good animal spirits. Mr Crimsworth soon checked her animated scolding with a kiss – a kiss that still told of the bridegroom (they had not yet been married a year); she took her seat at the supper table in first-rate spirits. Perceiving me, she begged my pardon for not noticing me before, and then shook hands with me, as ladies do when a flow of good humour disposes them to be cheerful to all, even the most indifferent of their acquaintance. It was now further obvious to me that she had a good complexion, and features sufficiently marked but agreeable; her hair was red – quite red. She and Edward talked much, always in a vein of playful contention; she was vexed, or pretended to be vexed, that he had that day driven a vicious horse in the gig, and he made light of her fears. Sometimes she appealed to me.

"Now, Mr William, isn't it absurd in Edward to talk so? He says he will drive Jack and no other horse, and the brute has thrown him twice already."

She spoke with a kind of lisp – not disagreeable, but childish. I soon saw also that there was more than girlish – a somewhat infantine expression in her by no means small features; this lisp and expression were, I have no doubt, a charm in Edward's eyes, and would be so to those of most men, but they were not to mine. I sought her eye, desirous to read there the intelligence which I could not discern in her face or hear in her conversation; it was merry, rather small; by turns I saw vivacity, vanity, coquetry look out through its irid, but I watched in vain for a glimpse of soul. I am no Oriental; white necks, carmine lips and cheeks, clusters of bright curls do not suffice for me without that Promethean spark which will live after the roses and lilies are faded, the burnished hair grown grey. In sunshine, in prosperity, the flowers are very well, but how many wet days are there in life – November seasons of disaster, when a man's hearth and home would be cold indeed without the clear, cheering gleam of intellect.

Having perused the fair page of Mrs Crimsworth's face, a deep, involuntary sigh announced my disappointment; she took it as a homage to her beauty, and Edward, who was evidently proud of his rich and handsome young wife, threw on me a glance – half ridicule, half ire.

I turned from them both and, gazing wearily round the room, I saw two pictures set in the oak panelling – one on each side of the mantelpiece. Ceasing to take part in the bantering conversation that flowed on between Mr and Mrs Crimsworth, I bent my thoughts to the examination of these pictures. They were portraits – a lady and a gentleman, both costumed in the fashion of twenty years ago. The gentleman was in the shade. I could not see him well. The lady had the benefit of a full beam from the softly shaded lamp. I presently recognized her; I had seen this picture before in childhood; it was my mother; that and the companion picture being the only heirlooms saved out of the sale of my father's property.

The face, I remembered, had pleased me as a boy, but then I did not understand it; now I knew how rare that class of face is in the world, and I appreciated keenly its thoughtful, yet gentle expression. The serious grey eye possessed for me a strong charm, as did certain lines in the features indicative of most true and tender feeling. I was sorry it was only a picture.

I soon left Mr and Mrs Crimsworth to themselves; a servant conducted me to my bedroom; in closing my chamber door, I shut out all intruders – you, Charles, as well as the rest. Goodbye for the present,

WILLIAM CRIMSWORTH

To this letter I never got an answer; before my old friend received it, he had accepted a Government appointment in one of the colonies, and was already on his way to the scene of his official labours. What has become of him since, I know not.

The leisure time I have at command, and which I intended to employ for his private benefit, I shall now dedicate to that of the public at large. My narrative is not exciting – and, above all, not marvellous – but it may interest some individuals who, having toiled in the same vocation as myself, will find in my experience frequent reflections of their own. The above letter will serve as an introduction. I now proceed.

Chapter 2

A FINE OCTOBER MORNING SUCCEEDED to the foggy evening that had witnessed my first introduction to Crimsworth Hall. I was early up and walking in the large, park-like meadow surrounding the house. The autumn sun, rising over the —shire hills, disclosed a pleasant country: woods brown and mellow varied the fields from which the harvest had been lately carried; a river, gliding between the woods, caught on its surface the somewhat cold gleam of the October sun and sky; at frequent intervals along the banks of the river, tall, cylindrical chimneys, almost like slender round towers, indicated the factories which the trees half concealed; here and there mansions, similar to Crimsworth Hall, occupied agreeable sites on the hillside; the country wore, on the whole, a cheerful, active, fertile look. Steam, trade, machinery had long banished from it all romance and seclusion. At a distance of five miles, a valley, opening between the low hills, held in its cup the great town of X—. A dense, permanent vapour brooded over this locality: there lay Edward's "Concern".

I forced my eye to scrutinize this prospect; I forced my mind to dwell on it for a time, and when I found that it communicated no pleasurable emotion to my heart – that it stirred in me none of the hopes a man ought to feel when he sees laid before him the scene of his life's career – I said to myself, "William, you are a rebel against circumstances; you are a fool, and know not what you want; you have chosen trade and you shall be a tradesman. Look!" – I continued mentally – "Look at the sooty smoke in that hollow, and know that there is your post! There you cannot dream, you cannot speculate and theorize – there you shall out and work!"

Thus self-schooled, I returned to the house. My brother was in the breakfast room. I met him collectedly – I could not meet him cheerfully; he was standing on the rug, his back to the fire – how much did I read in the expression of his eye as my glance encountered his, when I advanced to bid him good morning – how much that was contradictory to my nature! He said "Good morning" abruptly and nodded, and then he snatched, rather than took, a newspaper from the table, and began to read it with the air of a master who seizes a pretext to escape the bore of conversing with an underling. It was well I had taken a resolution to endure for a time, or his manner would have gone far to render insupportable the disgust I had just been endeavouring to subdue. I looked at him: I measured his robust frame and powerful proportions; I saw my own reflection in the mirror over the mantelpiece; I amused myself with comparing the two pictures. In fact I resembled him, though I was not so handsome; my features were less regular; I had a darker eye, and a broader brow – in form I was greatly inferior – thinner, slighter, not so tall. As an animal, Edward excelled me far; should he prove as paramount in mind as in person I must be a slave – for I must expect from him no lion-like generosity to one weaker than himself; his cold, avaricious eye, his stern, forbidding manner told me he would not spare. Had I then force of mind to cope with him? I did not know; I had never been tried.

Mrs Crimsworth's entrance divided my thoughts for a moment. She looked well, dressed in white, her face and her attire shining in morning and bridal freshness. I addressed her with the degree of ease her last night's careless gaiety seemed to warrant, but she replied with coolness and restraint: her husband had tutored her; she was not to be too familiar with his clerk.

As soon as breakfast was over, Mr Crimsworth intimated to me that they were bringing the gig round to the door, and that in five minutes he should expect me to be ready to go down with him to X—. I did not keep him waiting; we were soon dashing at a rapid rate along the road. The horse he drove was the same vicious animal about which Mrs Crimsworth had expressed her fears the night before. Once or twice Jack seemed disposed to turn restive, but a vigorous and determined application of the whip from the ruthless hand of his master soon compelled him to submission, and Edward's dilated nostril expressed his triumph in the result of the contest; he scarcely spoke to me during the whole of the brief drive, only opening his lips at intervals to damn his horse.

X— was all stir and bustle when we entered it; we left the clean streets where there were dwelling-houses and shops, churches and public buildings; we left all these, and turned down to a region of mills and warehouses; thence we passed through two massive gates into a great paved yard, and we were in Bigben Close, and the mill was before us, vomiting soot from its long chimney, and quivering through its thick brick walls with the commotion of its iron bowels. Workpeople were passing to and fro; a wagon was being laden with pieces.* Mr Crimsworth looked from side to side, and seemed at one glance to comprehend all that was going on; he alighted and, leaving his horse and gig to the care of a man who hastened to take the reins from his hand, he bid me follow him to the counting house. We entered it; a very different place from the parlours of Crimsworth Hall – a place for business, with a bare, planked floor, a safe, two high desks and stools and some chairs. A person was seated at one of the desks, who took off his square cap when Mr Crimsworth entered, and in an instant was again absorbed in his occupation of writing or calculating – I know not which.

Mr Crimsworth, having removed his mackintosh, sat down by the fire. I remained standing near the hearth; he said presently,

"Steighton, you may leave the room; I have some business to transact with this gentleman. Come back when you hear the bell."

The individual at the desk rose and departed, closing the door as he went out. Mr Crimsworth stirred the fire, then folded his arms and sat a moment thinking, his lips compressed, his brow knit. I had nothing to do but to watch him – how well his features were cut! What a handsome man he was! Whence, then, came that air of contraction – that narrow and hard aspect on his forehead, in all his lineaments?

Turning to me he began abruptly:

"You are come down to —shire to learn to be a tradesman?"

"Yes, I am."

"Have you made up your mind on the point? Let me know that at once."

"Yes."

"Well, I am not bound to help you, but I have a place here vacant, if you are qualified for it. I will take you on trial. What can you do?

Do you know anything besides that useless trash of college learning – Greek, Latin and so forth?"

"I have studied mathematics."

"Stuff! I dare say you have."

"I can read and write French and German."

"Hum!" He reflected a moment, then, opening a drawer in a desk near him, took out a letter and gave it to me.

"Can you read that?" he asked.

It was a German commercial letter; I translated it; I could not tell whether he was gratified or not – his countenance remained fixed.

"It is well," he said, after a pause, "that you are acquainted with something useful – something that may enable you to earn your board and lodging. Since you know French and German, I will take you as second clerk to manage the foreign correspondence of the house. I shall give you a good salary – £90 a year – and now," he continued, raising his voice, "hear once for all what I have to say about our relationship, and all that sort of humbug! I must have no nonsense on that point; it would never suit me. I shall excuse you nothing on the plea of being my brother; if I find you stupid, negligent, dissipated, idle or possessed of any faults detrimental to the interests of the house, I shall dismiss you as I would any other clerk. Ninety pounds a year are good wages, and I expect to have the full value of my money out of you; remember, too, that things are on a practical footing in my establishment – businesslike habits, feelings and ideas suit me best. Do you understand?"

"Partly," I replied. "I suppose you mean that I am to do my work for my wages; not to expect favour from you, and not to depend on you for any help but what I earn; that suits me exactly, and on these terms I will consent to be your clerk."

I turned on my heel and walked to the window; this time I did not consult his face to learn his opinion: what it was I do not know, nor did I then care. After a silence of some minutes he recommenced:

"You perhaps expect to be accommodated with apartments at Crimsworth Hall, and to go and come with me in the gig. I wish you, however, to be aware that such an arrangement would be quite inconvenient to me. I like to have the seat in my gig at liberty for any gentleman whom for business reasons I may wish to take down to the Hall for a night or so. You will seek out lodgings in X——."

Quitting the window, I walked back to the hearth.

"Of course I shall seek out lodgings in X——," I answered. "It would not suit me either to lodge at Crimsworth Hall."

My tone was quiet. I always speak quietly. Yet Mr Crimsworth's blue eye became incensed; he took his revenge rather oddly. Turning to me he said bluntly,

"You are poor enough, I suppose; how do you expect to live till your quarter's salary becomes due?"

"I shall get on," said I.

"How do you expect to live?" he repeated in a louder voice.

"As I can, Mr Crimsworth."

"Get into debt at your peril! That's all," he answered. "For aught I know you may have extravagant aristocratic habits: if you have, drop them. I tolerate nothing of the sort here, and I will never give you a shilling extra, whatever liabilities you may incur – mind that."

"Yes, Mr Crimsworth, you will find I have a good memory."

I said no more. I did not think the time was come for much parley. I had an instinctive feeling that it would be folly to let one's temper effervesce often with such a man as Edward. I said to myself, "I will place my cup under this continual dropping; it shall stand there still and steady; when full, it will run over of itself* – meantime patience. Two things are certain. I am capable of performing the work Mr Crimsworth has set me; I can earn my wages conscientiously, and those wages are sufficient to enable me to live. As to the fact of my brother assuming towards me the bearing of a proud, harsh master, the fault is his, not mine, and shall his injustice, his bad feeling, turn me at once aside from the path I have chosen? No; at least, ere I deviate, I will advance far enough to see whither my career tends. As yet I am only pressing in at the entrance – a strait gate enough;* it ought to have a good terminus." While I thus reasoned, Mr Crimsworth rang a bell; his first clerk, the individual dismissed previously to our conference, re-entered.

"Mr Steighton," said he, "show Mr William the letters from Voss Brothers, and give him English copies of the answers; he will translate them."

Mr Steighton, a man of about thirty-five, with a face at once sly and heavy, hastened to execute this order. He laid the letters on the desk, and I was soon seated at it, and engaged in rendering the English answers into German. A sentiment of keen pleasure accompanied this first effort to earn my own living – a sentiment neither poisoned nor weakened by the presence of the taskmaster, who stood and watched me for some time as I wrote. I thought he was trying to read my character, but I felt as secure against his scrutiny as if I had had on a casque with the visor down – or rather I showed him my countenance with the confidence that one would show an unlearned man a letter written in Greek; he might see lines, and trace characters, but he could make nothing of them; my nature was not his nature, and its signs were to him like the words of an unknown tongue. Ere long he turned away abruptly, as if baffled, and left the counting house. He returned to it but twice in the course of that day; each time he mixed and swallowed a glass of brandy-and-water, the materials for making which he extracted from a cupboard on one side of the fireplace; having glanced at my translations – he could read both French and German – he went out again in silence.

Chapter 3

I SERVED EDWARD AS HIS SECOND CLERK FAITHFULLY, punctually, diligently. What was given me to do I had the power and the determination to do well. Mr Crimsworth watched sharply for defects, but found none; he set Timothy Steighton, his favourite and headman, to watch also. Tim was baffled; I was as exact as himself, and quicker. Mr Crimsworth made enquiries as to how I lived, whether I got into debt – no, my accounts with my landlady were always straight. I had hired small lodgings, which I contrived to pay for out of a slender fund – the accumulated savings of my Eton pocket money; for, as it had ever been abhorrent to my nature to ask pecuniary assistance, I had early acquired habits of self-denying economy, husbanding my monthly allowance with anxious care, in order to obviate the danger of being forced, in some moment of future exigency, to beg additional aid. I remember many called me miser at the time, and I used to couple the reproach with this consolation: better to be misunderstood now than repulsed hereafter. At this day I had my reward; I had had it before, when on parting with my irritated uncles one of them threw down on the table before me a five-pound note, which I was able to leave there, saying that my travelling expenses were already provided for. Mr Crimsworth employed Tim to find out whether my landlady had any complaint to make on the score of my morals; she answered that she believed I was a very religious man, and asked Tim, in her turn, if he thought I had any intention of going into the Church some day; for, she said, she had had young curates to lodge in her house who were nothing equal to me for steadiness and quietness. Tim was "a religious man" himself; indeed, he was "a joined Methodist", which did not (be it understood) prevent him from being at the same time an ingrained rascal, and he came away much posed* at hearing this account of my piety. Having imparted it to Mr Crimsworth, that gentleman, who himself frequented no place of worship, and owned no god but Mammon, turned the information into a weapon of attack against the equability of my temper. He commenced a series of covert sneers, of which I did not at first perceive the drift, till my landlady happened to relate the conversation she had had with Mr Steighton; this enlightened me; afterwards I came to the counting house prepared, and managed to receive the mill owner's blasphemous sarcasms, when next levelled at me, on a buckler of impenetrable indifference. Ere long he tired of wasting his ammunition on a statue, but he did not throw away the shafts – he only kept them quiet in his quiver.

Once during my clerkship I had an invitation to Crimsworth Hall; it was on the occasion of a large party given in honour of the master's birthday; he had always been accustomed to invite his clerks on similar anniversaries, and could not well pass me over; I was, however, kept strictly in the background. Mrs Crimsworth, elegantly dressed in satin and lace, blooming in youth and health, vouchsafed me no more notice than was expressed by a distant move; Crimsworth, of course, never spoke to me; I was introduced to none of the band of young ladies who, enveloped in silvery clouds of white gauze and muslin, sat in array against me on the opposite side of a long and large room; in fact, I was fairly isolated, and could but contemplate the shining ones from afar and, when weary of such a dazzling scene, turn for a change to the consideration of the carpet pattern. Mr Crimsworth, standing on the rug, his elbow supported by the marble mantelpiece, and about him a group of very pretty girls, with whom he conversed gaily – Mr Crimsworth, thus placed, glanced at me; I looked weary, solitary, kept down like some desolate tutor or governess; he was satisfied.

Dancing began; I should have liked well enough to be introduced to some pleasing and intelligent girl, and to have freedom and opportunity to show that I could both feel and communicate the pleasure of social intercourse – that I was not, in short, a block, or a piece of furniture, but an acting, thinking, sentient man. Many smiling faces and graceful figures glided past me, but the smiles were lavished on other eyes, the figures sustained by other hands than mine. I turned away tantalized, left the dancers and wandered into the oak-panelled dining room. No fibre of sympathy united me to any living thing in this house; I looked for and found my mother's picture. I took a wax taper from a stand and held it up. I gazed long, earnestly; my heart grew to the image. My mother, I perceived, had bequeathed to me much of her features and countenance – her forehead, her eyes, her complexion. No regular beauty pleases egotistical human beings so much as a softened and refined likeness of themselves; for this reason, fathers regard with complacency the lineaments of their daughters' faces, where frequently their own similitude is found flatteringly associated with softness of hue and delicacy of outline. I was just wondering how that picture, to me so interesting, would strike an impartial spectator, when a voice close behind me pronounced the words,

"Humph! There's some sense in that face."

I turned; at my elbow stood a tall man, young, though probably five or six years older than I – in other respects, of an appearance the opposite to commonplace; though just now, as I am not disposed to paint his portrait in detail, the reader must be content with the silhouette I have just thrown off; it was all I myself saw of him for the moment: I did not investigate the colour of his eyebrows, nor of his eyes either; I saw his stature, and the outline of his shape; I saw, too, his fastidious-looking *retroussé* nose; these observations, few in number, and general in character (the last excepted), sufficed, for they enabled me to recognize him.

"Good evening, Mr Hunsden," muttered I with a bow, and then, like a shy noodle as I was, I began moving away – and why? Simply because Mr Hunsden was a manufacturer and a mill owner, and I was only a clerk, and my instinct propelled me from my superior. I had frequently seen Hunsden in Bigben Close, where he came almost weekly to transact business with Mr Crimsworth, but I had never spoken to him, nor he to me, and I owed him a sort of involuntary grudge because he had more than once been the tacit witness of insults offered by Edward to me. I had the conviction that he could only regard me as a poor-spirited slave, wherefore I now went about to shun his presence and eschew his conversation.

"Where are you going?" asked he, as I edged off sideways. I had already noticed that Mr Hunsden indulged in abrupt forms of speech, and I perversely said to myself,

"He thinks he may speak as he likes to a poor clerk; but my mood is not, perhaps, so supple as he deems it, and his rough freedom pleases me not at all."

I made some slight reply, rather indifferent than courteous, and continued to move away. He coolly planted himself in my path.

"Stay here awhile," said he. "It is so hot in the dancing room; besides, you don't dance; you have not had a partner tonight."

He was right, and as he spoke neither his look, tone nor manner displeased me; my *amour-propre* was propitiated; he had not addressed me out of condescension, but because, having repaired to the cool dining room for refreshment, he now wanted someone to talk to, by way of temporary amusement. I hate to be condescended to, but I like well enough to oblige. I stayed.

"That is a good picture," he continued, recurring to the portrait.

"Do you consider the face pretty?" I asked.

"Pretty! No – how can it be pretty, with sunk eyes and hollow cheeks? But it is peculiar; it seems to think. You could have a talk with that woman, if she were alive, on other subjects than dress, visiting and compliments."

I agreed with him, but did not say so. He went on.

"Not that I admire a head of that sort; it wants character and force; there's too much of the sen-si-tive (so he articulated it, curling his lip at the same time) in that mouth; besides, there is 'aristocrat' written on the brow and defined in the figure; I hate your aristocrats."

"You think, then, Mr Hunsden, that patrician descent may be read in a distinctive cast of form and features?"

"Patrician descent be hanged! Who doubts that your lordlings may have their 'distinctive cast of form and features' as much as we —shire tradesmen have ours? But which is the best? Not theirs, assuredly. As to their women, it is a little different: they cultivate beauty from childhood upwards, and may by care and training attain to a certain degree of excellence in that point, just like the oriental odalisques. Yet even this superiority is doubtful. Compare the figure in that frame with Mrs Edward Crimsworth – which is the finer animal?"

I replied quietly: "Compare yourself and Mr Edward Crimsworth, Mr Hunsden."

"Oh, Crimsworth is better filled up than I am, I know; besides, he has a straight nose, arched eyebrows and all that; but these advantages – if they are advantages – he did not inherit from his mother, the patrician, but from his father, old Crimsworth, who, *my* father says, was as veritable a —shire blue-dyer as ever put indigo in a vat; yet withal the handsomest man in the three Ridings. It is you, William, who are the aristocrat of your family, and you are not as fine a fellow as your plebeian brother by a long chalk."

There was something in Mr Hunsden's point-blank mode of speech which rather pleased me than otherwise, because it set me at my ease. I continued the conversation with a degree of interest.

"How do you happen to know that I am Mr Crimsworth's brother? I thought you and everybody else looked upon me only in the light of a poor clerk."

"Well, and so we do; and what are you but a poor clerk? You do Crimsworth's work, and he gives you wages – shabby wages they are, too."

I was silent. Hunsden's language now bordered on the impertinent; still his manner did not offend me in the least – it only piqued my curiosity; I wanted him to go on, which he did in a little while.

"This world is an absurd one," said he.

"Why so, Mr Hunsden?"

"I wonder you should ask: you are yourself a strong proof of the absurdity I allude to."

I was determined he should explain himself of his own accord, without my pressing him to do so – so I resumed my silence.

"Is it your intention to become a tradesman?" he enquired presently.

"It was my serious intention three months ago."

"Humph! The more fool you – you look like a tradesman! What a practical, businesslike face you have!"

"My face is as the Lord made it, Mr Hunsden."

"The Lord never made either your face or head for X—. What good can your bumps of ideality, comparison, self-esteem, conscientiousness do you here?* But if you like Bigben Close, stay there; it's your own affair, not mine."

"Perhaps I have no choice."

"Well, I care naught about it – it will make little difference to me what you do or where you go; but I'm cool now – I want to dance again; and I see such a fine girl sitting in the corner of the sofa there by her mamma; see if I don't get her for a partner in a jiffy! There's Waddy – Sam Waddy making up to her; won't I cut him out?"

And Mr Hunsden strode away. I watched him through the open folding doors; he outstripped Waddy, applied for the hand of the fine girl and led her off triumphant. She was a tall, well-made, full-formed, dashingly dressed young woman much in the style of Mrs E. Crimsworth; Hunsden whirled her through the waltz with spirit; he kept at her side during the remainder of the evening, and I read in her animated and gratified countenance that he succeeded in making himself perfectly agreeable. The mamma too (a stout person in a turban* – Mrs Lupton by name) looked well pleased; prophetic visions probably flattered her inward eye. The Hunsdens were of an old stem; and scornful as Yorke (such was my late interlocutor's name) professed to be of the advantages of birth, in his secret heart he knew well and fully appreciated the distinction his ancient, if not high lineage conferred on him in a mushroom-place like X—, concerning whose inhabitants it was proverbially said that not one in a thousand knew his own grand-father.* Moreover, the Hunsdens, once rich, were still independent; and report affirmed that Yorke bade fair, by his success in business, to restore to pristine prosperity the partially decayed fortunes of his house. These circumstances considered, Mrs Lupton's broad face might well wear a smile of complacency as she contemplated the heir of Hunsden Wood occupied in paying assiduous court to her darling Sarah Martha. I, however, whose observations, being less anxious, were likely to be more accurate, soon saw that the grounds for maternal self-congratulation were slight indeed: the gentleman appeared to me much more desirous of making, than susceptible of receiving, an impression. I know not what it was in Mr Hunsden that, as I watched him (I had nothing better to do), suggested to me, every now and then, the idea of a foreigner. In form and features he might be pronounced English, though even there one caught a dash of something Gallic; but he had no English shyness: he had learnt somewhere, somehow, the art of setting himself quite at his ease, and of allowing no insular timidity to intervene as a barrier between him and his convenience or pleasure. Refinement he did not affect, yet vulgar he could not be called; he was not odd – no quiz* – yet he resembled no one else I had ever seen before; his general bearing intimated complete, sovereign satisfaction with himself; yet, at times, an indescribable shade passed like an eclipse over his countenance, and seemed to me like the sign of a sudden and strong inward doubt of himself, his words and actions – an energetic discontent at his life or his social position, his future prospects or his mental attainments – I know not which; perhaps, after all, it might only be a bilious caprice.

Chapter 4

N O MAN LIKES TO ACKNOWLEDGE that he has made a mistake in the choice of his profession, and every man worthy of the name will row long against wind and tide before he allows himself to cry out, "I am baffled!" and submits to be floated passively back to land. From the first week of my residence in X— I felt my occupation irksome. The thing itself – the work of copying and translating business letters – was a dry and tedious task enough, but had that been all, I should long have borne with the nuisance. I am not of an impatient nature and, influenced by the double desire of getting my living and justifying to myself and others the resolution I had taken to become a tradesman, I should have endured in silence the rust and cramp of my best faculties; I should not have whispered, even inwardly, that I longed for liberty; I should have pent in every sigh by which my heart might have ventured to intimate its distress under the closeness, smoke, monotony and joyless tumult of Bigben Close, and its panting desire for freer and fresher scenes; I should have set up the image of Duty, the fetish of Perseverance, in my small bedroom at Mrs King's lodgings, and they two should have been my household gods, from which my darling, my cherished-in-secret Imagination, the tender and the mighty, should never, either by softness or strength, have severed me. But this was not all; the antipathy which had sprung up between myself and my employer, striking deeper root and spreading denser shade daily, excluded me from every glimpse of the sunshine of life; and I began to feel like a plant growing in humid darkness out of the slimy walls of a well.

Antipathy is the only word which can express the feeling Edward Crimsworth had for me – a feeling, in a great measure, involuntary, and which was liable to be excited by every, the most trifling movement, look or word of mine. My southern accent annoyed him; the degree of education evinced in my language irritated him; my punctuality, industry and accuracy fixed his dislike, and gave it the high flavour and poignant relish of envy; he feared that I too should one day make a successful tradesman. Had I been in anything inferior to him, he would not have hated me so thoroughly, but I knew all that he knew – and, what was worse, he suspected that I kept the padlock of silence on mental wealth in which he was no sharer. If he could have once placed me in a ridiculous or mortifying position, he would have forgiven me much, but I was guarded by three faculties – Caution, Tact, Observation; and prowling and prying as was Edward's malignity, it could never baffle the lynx eyes of these, my natural sentinels. Day by day did his malice watch my tact, hoping it would sleep, and prepared to steal snake-like on its slumber; but tact, if it be genuine, never sleeps.

I had received my first quarter's wages, and was returning to my lodgings, possessed heart and soul with the pleasant feeling that the master who had paid me grudged every penny of that hard-earned pittance (I had long ceased to regard Mr Crimsworth as my brother – he was a hard, grinding master; he wished to be an inexorable tyrant: that was all). Thoughts, not varied but strong, occupied my mind; two voices spoke within me; again and again they uttered the same monotonous phrases. One said, "William, your life is intolerable." The other: "What can you do to alter it?" I walked fast, for it was a cold, frosty night in January. As I approached my lodgings, I turned from a general view of my affairs to the particular speculation as to whether my fire would be out. Looking towards the window of my sitting room, I saw no cheering red gleam.

"That slut of a servant has neglected it as usual," said I, "and I shall see nothing but pale ashes if I go in; it is a fine starlight night – I will walk a little farther."

It *was* a fine night, and the streets were dry and even clean for X—; there was a crescent curve of moonlight to be seen by the parish-church tower, and hundreds of stars shone keenly bright in all quarters of the sky.

Unconsciously I steered my course towards the country; I had got into Grove Street, and began to feel the pleasure of seeing dim trees at the extremity, round a suburban house, when a person leaning over the iron gate of one of the small gardens which front the neat dwelling-houses in this street addressed me as I was hurrying with quick stride past.

"What the deuce is the hurry? Just so must Lot have left Sodom when he expected fire to pour down upon it out of burning brass clouds."*

I stopped short, and looked towards the speaker. I smelt the fragrance and saw the red spark of a cigar; the dusk outline of a man, too, bent towards me over the wicket.

"You see I am meditating in the field at eventide," continued this shade. "God knows it's cool work! Especially as instead of Rebecca on a camel's hump,* with bracelets on her arms and a ring in her nose, Fate sends me only a counting-house clerk, in a grey tweed wrapper."

The voice was familiar to me – its second utterance enabled me to seize the speaker's identity.

"Mr Hunsden! Good evening."

"Good evening, indeed! Yes, but you would have passed me without recognition if I had not been so civil as to speak first."

"I did not know you."

"A famous excuse! You ought to have known me; I knew you, though you were going ahead like a steam engine. Are the police after you?"

"It wouldn't be worth their while; I'm not of consequence enough to attract them."

"Alas, poor shepherd! Alack and welladay! What a theme for regret, and how down in the mouth you must be, judging from the sound of your voice! But since you're not running from the police, from whom are you running? The Devil?"

"On the contrary, I am going post to him."

"That is well – you're just in luck: this is Tuesday evening; there are scores of market gigs and carts returning to Dinneford tonight; and he, or some of his, have a seat in all regularly; so if you'll step in and sit half an hour in my bachelor's parlour, you may catch him as he passes without much trouble. I think though you'd better let him alone tonight: he'll have so many customers to serve; Tuesday is his busy day in X— and Dinneford; come in, at all events."

He swung the wicket open as he spoke.

"Do you really wish me to go in?" I asked.

"As you please – I'm alone; your company for an hour or two would be agreeable to me; but, if you don't choose to favour me so far, I'll not press the point. I hate to bore anyone."

It suited me to accept the invitation as it suited Hunsden to give it. I passed through the gate, and followed him to the front door, which he opened; thence we traversed a passage and entered his parlour; the door being shut, he pointed me to an armchair by the hearth; I sat down and glanced round me.

It was a comfortable room, at once snug and handsome; the bright grate was filled with a genuine —shire fire, red, clear and generous, no penurious south of England ember happed* in the corner of a grate. On the table a shaded lamp diffused around a soft, pleasant and equal light; the furniture was almost luxurious for a young bachelor, comprising a couch and two very easy chairs; bookshelves filled the recesses on each side of the mantelpiece; they were well furnished, and arranged with perfect order. The neatness of the room suited my taste; I hate irregular and slovenly habits. From what I saw I concluded that Hunsden's ideas on that point corresponded with my own. While he removed from the centre table to the sideboard a few pamphlets and periodicals, I ran my eye along the shelves of the bookcase nearest me. French and German works predominated, the old French dramatists, sundry modern authors, Thiers, Villemain, Paul de Kock, George Sand, Eugène Sue; in German – Goethe, Schiller, Zschokke, Jean Paul Richter;* in English there were works on political economy. I examined no further, for Mr Hunsden himself recalled my attention.

"You shall have something," said he, "for you ought to feel disposed for refreshment after walking nobody knows how far on such a Canadian night as this; but it shall not be brandy and water, and it shall not be a bottle of port, nor ditto of sherry. I keep no such poison. I have Rheinwein for my own drinking, and you may choose between that and coffee."

Here again Hunsden suited me: if there was one generally received practice I abhorred more than another, it was the habitual imbibing of spirits and strong wines. I had, however, no fancy for his acid German nectar, but I liked coffee, so I responded,

"Give me some coffee, Mr Hunsden."

I perceived my answer pleased him; he had doubtless expected to
see a chilling effect produced by his steady announcement that he
would give me neither wine nor spirits; he just shot one searching
glance at my face to ascertain whether my cordiality was genuine or
a mere feint of politeness. I smiled, because I quite understood him;
and, while I honoured his conscientious firmness, I was amused at
his mistrust. He seemed satisfied, rang the bell and ordered coffee,
which was presently brought; for himself, a bunch of grapes and half
a pint of something sour sufficed. My coffee was excellent; I told him
so, and expressed the shuddering pity with which his anchorite fare
inspired me. He did not answer, and I scarcely think heard my remark.
At that moment one of those momentary eclipses I before alluded
to had come over his face, extinguishing his smile and replacing, by
an abstracted and alienated look, the customarily shrewd, bantering
glance of his eye. I employed the interval of silence in a rapid scrutiny
of his physiognomy. I had never observed him closely before; and,
as my sight is very short, I had gathered only a vague, general idea
of his appearance. I was surprised now, on examination, to perceive
how small, and even feminine, were his lineaments; his tall figure,
long and dark locks, his voice and general bearing, had impressed
me with the notion of something powerful and massive; not at all:
my own features were cast in a harsher and squarer mould than his.
I discerned that there would be contrasts between his inward and
outward man; contentions too, for I suspected his soul had more of
will and ambition than his body had of fibre and muscle. Perhaps in
these incompatibilities of the "physique" with the "morale" lay the
secret of that fitful gloom; he *would* but *could* not, and the athletic
mind scowled scorn on its more fragile companion. As to his good
looks, I should have liked to have a woman's opinion on that subject;
it seemed to me that his face might produce the same effect on a lady
that a very piquant and interesting, though scarcely pretty, female face
would on a man. I have mentioned his dark locks – they were brushed
sideways above a white and sufficiently expansive forehead; his cheek
had a rather hectic freshness; his features might have done well on
canvas, but indifferently in marble: they were plastic; character had
set a stamp upon each; expression recast them at her pleasure, and
strange metamorphoses she wrought, giving him now the mien of

a morose bull, and anon that of an arch and mischievous girl; more frequently, the two semblances were blended, and a queer composite countenance they made.

Starting from his silent fit, he began,

"William! What a fool you are to live in those dismal lodgings of Mrs King's when you might take rooms here in Grove Street and have a garden like me!"

"I should be too far from the mill."

"What of that? It would do you good to walk there and back two or three times a day; besides, are you such a fossil that you never wish to see a flower or a green leaf?"

"I am no fossil."

"What are you then? You sit at that desk in Crimsworth's counting house day by day and week by week, scraping with a pen on paper, just like an automaton; you never get up; you never say you are tired; you never ask for a holiday; you never take change or relaxation; you give way to no excess of an evening; you neither keep wild company, nor indulge in strong drink."

"Do you, Mr Hunsden?"

"Don't think to pose me with short questions; your case and mine are diametrically different, and it is nonsense attempting to draw a parallel. I say that when a man endures patiently what ought to be unendurable, he is a fossil."

"Whence do you acquire the knowledge of my patience?"

"Why, man, do you suppose you are a mystery? The other night you seemed surprised at my knowing to what family you belonged; now you find subject for wonderment in my calling you patient. What do you think I do with my eyes and ears? I've been in your counting house more than once when Crimsworth has treated you like a dog; called for a book, for instance, and when you gave him the wrong one, or what he chose to consider the wrong one, flung it back almost in your face; desired you to shut or open the door as if you had been his flunkey; to say nothing of your position at the party about a month ago, where you had neither place nor partner, but hovered about like a poor, shabby hanger-on; and how patient you were under each and all of these circumstances!"

"Well, Mr Hunsden, what then?"

"I can hardly tell you what then. The conclusion to be drawn as to your character depends upon the nature of the motives which guide your conduct; if you are patient because you expect to make something eventually out of Crimsworth, notwithstanding his tyranny, or perhaps by means of it, you are what the world calls an interested* and mercenary, but maybe a very wise fellow; if you are patient because you think it a duty to meet insult with submission, you are an essential sap, and in no shape the man for my money; if you are patient because your nature is phlegmatic, flat, unexcitable, and that you cannot get up to the pitch of resistance, why, God made you to be crushed; and lie down by all means, and lie flat, and let Juggernaut* ride well over you."

Mr Hunsden's eloquence was not, it will be perceived, of the smooth and oily order. As he spoke, he pleased me ill. I seemed to recognize in him one of those characters who, sensitive enough themselves, are selfishly relentless towards the sensitiveness of others. Moreover, though he was neither like Crimsworth nor Lord Tynedale, yet he was acrid and, I suspected, overbearing in his way: there was a tone of despotism in the urgency of the very reproaches by which he aimed at goading the oppressed into rebellion against the oppressor. Looking at him still more fixedly than I had yet done, I saw written in his eye and mien a resolution to arrogate to himself a freedom so unlimited that it might often trench on the just liberty of his neighbours. I rapidly ran over these thoughts, and then I laughed a low and involuntary laugh, moved thereto by a slight inward revelation of the inconsistency of man. It was as I thought: Hunsden had expected me to take with calm his incorrect and offensive surmises, his bitter and haughty taunts, and himself was chafed by a laugh scarce louder than a whisper.

His brow darkened, his thin nostril dilated a little.

"Yes," he began, "I told you that you were an aristocrat, and who but an aristocrat would laugh such a laugh as that, and look such a look? A laugh frigidly jeering; a look lazily mutinous; gentleman-like irony, patrician resentment. What a nobleman you would have

made, William Crimsworth! You are cut out for one; pity Fortune
has baulked Nature! Look at the features, figure, even to the hands
– distinction all over – ugly distinction! Now, if you'd only an estate
and a mansion, and a park, and a title, how you could play the
exclusive, maintain the rights of your class, train your tenantry in
habits of respect to the peerage, oppose at every step the advancing power of the people, support your rotten order, and be ready
for its sake to wade knee-deep in churls' blood! As it is, you've no
power; you can do nothing; you're wrecked and stranded on the
shores of commerce; forced into collision with practical men, with
whom you cannot cope, for *you'll never be a tradesman.*"

The first part of Hunsden's speech moved me not at all – or, if it
did, it was only to wonder at the perversion into which prejudice
had twisted his judgement of my character; the concluding sentence,
however, not only moved, but shook me; the blow it gave was a severe
one, because Truth wielded the weapon. If I smiled now, it was only
in disdain of myself.

Hunsden saw his advantage; he followed it up.

"You'll make nothing by trade," continued he, "nothing more than
the crust of dry bread and the draught of fair water on which you
now live; your only chance of getting a competency lies in marrying
a rich widow, or running away with an heiress."

"I leave such shifts to be put in practice by those who devise them,"
said I, rising.

"And even that is hopeless," he went on coolly. "What widow would
have you? Much less, what heiress? You're not bold and venturesome
enough for the one, nor handsome and fascinating enough for the
other. You think perhaps you look intelligent and polished; carry
your intellect and refinement to market, and tell me in a private note
what price is bid for them."

Mr Hunsden had taken his tone for the night; the string he struck
was out of tune, he would finger no other. Averse to discord, of
which I had enough every day and all day long, I concluded, at last,
that silence and solitude were preferable to jarring converse. I bade
him a goodnight.

"What! Are you going, lad? Well, goodnight; you'll find the door."
And he sat still in front of the fire, while I left the room and the

house. I had got a good way on my return to my lodgings before I found out that I was walking very fast and breathing very hard, and that my nails were almost stuck into the palms of my clenched hands, and that my teeth were set fast. On making this discovery, I relaxed both my pace, fists and jaws, but I could not so soon cause the regrets rushing rapidly through my mind to slacken their tide. Why did I make myself a tradesman? Why did I enter Hunsden's house this evening? Why, at dawn tomorrow, must I repair to Crimsworth's mill? All that night did I ask myself these questions, and all that night fiercely demanded of my soul an answer. I got no sleep; my head burned, my feet froze; at last the factory bells rang, and I sprang from my bed with other slaves.

Chapter 5

T HERE IS A CLIMAX TO EVERYTHING, to every state of feeling as well as to every position in life. I turned this truism over in my mind as, in the frosty dawn of a January morning, I hurried down the steep and now icy street which descended from Mrs King's to the Close. The factory workpeople had preceded me by nearly an hour, and the mill was all lighted up and in full operation when I reached it. I repaired to my post in the counting house as usual; the fire there, but just lit, as yet only smoked; Steighton was not yet arrived. I shut the door and sat down at the desk; my hands, recently washed in half-frozen water, were still numb; I could not write till they had regained vitality, so I went on thinking, and still the theme of my thoughts was the "climax". Self-dissatisfaction troubled exceedingly the current of my meditations.

"Come, William Crimsworth," said my conscience, or whatever it is that within ourselves takes ourselves to task – "Come, get a clear notion of what you would have, or what you would not have. You talk of a climax; pray, has your endurance reached its climax? It is not four months old. What a fine resolute fellow you imagined yourself to be when you told Tynedale you would tread in your father's steps, and a pretty treading you are likely to make of it! How well you like X—! Just at this moment how redolent of pleasant associations are its streets, its shops, its warehouses, its factories! How the prospect of this day cheers you! Letter-copying till noon, solitary dinner at your lodgings, letter-copying till evening, solitude; for you neither find pleasure in Brown's, nor Smith's, nor Nicholl's, nor Eccles's company; and as to Hunsden, you fancied there was pleasure to be derived from his society – he! He! How did you like the taste you had of him last night? Was it sweet? Yet he is a talented, an original-minded man, and even he does not like you; your self-respect defies you to like him; he has always seen you to disadvantage; he always will see you to disadvantage; your positions are unequal and, were they on the same level, your minds could not assimilate; never hope, then, to gather the honey of friendship out of that thorn-guarded plant. Hollo, Crimsworth! Where are your thoughts tending? You leave the recollection of Hunsden as a bee would a rock, as a bird a desert; and your aspirations spread eager wings towards a land of visions where, now in advancing daylight – in X— daylight – you dare to dream of congeniality, repose, union. Those three you will never meet in this world; they are angels. The souls of just men made perfect* may encounter them in heaven, but your soul will never be made perfect. Eight o'clock strikes! Your hands are thawed, get to work!"

"Work? Why should I work?" said I sullenly. "I cannot please, though I toil like a slave." "Work, work!" reiterated the inward voice. "I may work, it will do no good," I growled, but nevertheless I drew out a packet of letters and commenced my task – task thankless and bitter as that of the Israelite crawling over the sun-baked fields of Egypt in search of straw and stubble wherewith to accomplish his tale of bricks.*

About ten o'clock I heard Mr Crimsworth's gig turn into the yard, and in a minute or two he entered the counting house. It was his custom to glance his eye at Steighton and myself, to hang up his mackintosh, stand a minute with his back to the fire and then walk out. Today he did not deviate from his usual habits; the only difference was that when he looked at me, his brow, instead of being merely hard, was surly; his eye, instead of being cold, was fierce. He studied me a minute or two longer than usual, but went out in silence.

Twelve o'clock arrived; the bell rang for a suspension of labour; the workpeople went off to their dinners; Steighton, too, departed, desiring me to lock the counting-house door and take the key with me. I was tying up a bundle of papers and putting them in their place, preparatory to closing my desk, when Crimsworth reappeared at the door and, entering, closed it behind him.

"You'll stay here a minute," said he, in a deep, brutal voice, while his nostrils distended and his eye shot a spark of sinister fire.

Alone with Edward I remembered our relationship, and remembering that forgot the difference of position. I put away deference and careful forms of speech; I answered with simple brevity.

"It is time to go home," I said, turning the key in my desk.

"You'll stay here!" he reiterated. "And take your hand off that key! Leave it in the lock!"

"Why?" asked I. "What cause is there for changing my usual plans?"

"Do as I order," was the answer, "and no questions! You are my servant; obey me! What have you been about—" He was going on in the same breath when an abrupt pause announced that rage had for the moment got the better of articulation.

"You may look, if you wish to know," I replied. "There is the open desk, there are the papers."

"Confound your insolence! What have you been about?"

"Your work, and have done it well."

"Hypocrite and twaddler! Smooth-faced, snivelling grease-horn!' (this last term is, I believe, purely —shire, and alludes to the horn of black, rancid whale oil, usually to be seen suspended to cartwheels, and employed for greasing the same).

"Come, Edward Crimsworth, enough of this. It is time you and I wound up accounts. I have now given your service three months' trial, and I find it the most nauseous slavery under the sun. Seek another clerk. I stay no longer."

"What! Do you dare to give me notice? Stop at least for your wages." He took down the heavy gig whip hanging beside his mackintosh.

I permitted myself to laugh with a degree of scorn I took no pains to temper or hide. His fury boiled up, and when he had sworn half a dozen vulgar, impious oaths – without, however, venturing to lift the whip – he continued,

"I've found you out and know you thoroughly, you mean, whining lickspittle! What have you been saying all over X— about me? Answer me that!"

"You? I have neither inclination nor temptation to talk about you."

"You lie! It is your practice to talk about me. It is your constant habit to make public complaint of the treatment you receive at my hands. You have gone and told it far and near that I give you low wages and knock you about like a dog. I wish you were a dog! I'd set to this minute, and never stir from the spot till I'd cut every strip of flesh from your bones with this whip."

He flourished this tool. The end of the lash just touched my forehead. A warm excited thrill ran through my veins; my blood seemed to give a bound, and then raced fast and hot along its channels. I got up nimbly, came round to where he stood and faced him.

"Down with your whip!" said I, "and explain this instant what you mean."

"Sirrah! To whom are you speaking?"

"To you. There is no one else present, I think. You say I have been calumniating you – complaining of your low wages and bad treatment. Give your grounds for these assertions."

Crimsworth had no dignity, and when I sternly demanded an explanation, he gave one in a loud, scolding voice.

"Grounds! You shall have them; and turn to the light that I may see your brazen face blush black when you hear yourself proved to be a liar and a hypocrite. At a public meeting in the town hall yesterday, I had the pleasure of hearing myself insulted by the speaker opposed to me in the question under discussion by allusions to my private affairs; by cant about monsters without natural affection, family despots and such trash; and when I rose to answer, I was met by a shout from the filthy mob, where the mention of your name enabled me at once to detect the quarter in which this base attack had originated. When I looked round, I saw that treacherous villain Hunsden acting as fugleman.* I detected you in close conversation with Hunsden at my house a month ago, and I know that you were at Hunsden's rooms last night. Deny it if you dare."

"Oh, I shall not deny it! And if Hunsden hounded on the people to hiss you, he did quite right. You deserve popular execration; for a worse man, a harder master, a more brutal brother than you are has seldom existed."

"Sirrah! Sirrah!" reiterated Crimsworth; and to complete his apostrophe, he cracked the whip straight over my head.

A minute sufficed to wrest it from him, break it in two pieces and throw it under the grate. He made a headlong rush at me, which I evaded, and said,

"Touch me, and I'll have you up before the nearest magistrate."

Men like Crimsworth, if firmly and calmly resisted, always abate something of their exorbitant insolence. He had no mind to be brought before a magistrate, and I suppose he saw I meant what I said. After an odd and long stare at me, at once bull-like and amazed, he seemed to bethink himself that, after all, his money gave him sufficient superiority over a beggar like me, and that he had in his hands a surer and more dignified mode of revenge than the somewhat hazardous one of personal chastisement.

"Take your hat," said he. "Take what belongs to you, and go out at that door; get away to your parish, you pauper: beg, steal, starve, get transported, do what you like, but at your peril venture again into my sight! If ever I hear of your setting foot on an inch of ground belonging to me, I'll hire a man to cane you."

"It is not likely you'll have the chance. Once off your premises, what temptation can I have to return to them? I leave a prison; I leave a tyrant; I leave what is worse than the worst that can lie before me, so no fear of my coming back."

"Go, or I'll make you!" exclaimed Crimsworth.

I walked deliberately to my desk, took out such of its contents as were my own property, put them in my pocket, locked the desk and placed the key on the top.

"What are you abstracting from that desk?" demanded the mill owner. "Leave all behind in its place, or I'll send for a policeman to search you."

"Look sharp about it, then," said I, and I took down my hat, drew on my gloves and walked leisurely out of the counting house – walked out of it to enter it no more.

I recollect that when the mill bell rang the dinner hour, before Mr Crimsworth entered and the scene above related took place, I had had rather a sharp appetite, and had been waiting somewhat impatiently to hear the signal of feeding time. I forgot it now, however; the images of potatoes and roast mutton were effaced from my mind by the stir and tumult which the transaction of the last half-hour had there excited. I only thought of walking, that the action of my muscles might harmonize with the action of my nerves; and walk I did, fast and far. How could I do otherwise? A load was lifted off my heart; I felt light and liberated. I had got away from Bigben Close without a breach of resolution – without injury to my self-respect. I had not forced circumstances; circumstances had freed me. Life was again open to me; no longer was its horizon limited by the high black wall surrounding Crimsworth's mill. Two hours had elapsed before my sensations had so far subsided as to leave me calm enough to remark for what wider and clearer boundaries I had exchanged that sooty girdle. When I did look up, lo! Straight before me lay Grovetown, a village of villas about five miles out of X—. The short winter day, as I perceived from the far-declined sun, was already approaching its close. A chill frost-mist was rising from the river on which X— stands – and along whose banks the road I had taken lay. It dimmed the earth, but did not obscure the clear icy blue of the January sky. There was a great stillness near and far; the time of the day favoured tranquillity, as the people were all employed within doors, the hour of evening release from the factories not being yet arrived; a sound of full-flowing water alone pervaded the air, for the river was deep and abundant, swelled by the melting of a late snow. I stood awhile, leaning over a wall; and looking down at the current, I watched the rapid rush of its waves. I desired memory to take a clear and permanent impression of the scene, and treasure it for future years. Grovetown church clock struck four. Looking up, I beheld the last of that day's sun, glinting red through the leafless boughs of some very old oak trees surrounding the church – its light coloured and characterized the picture as I wished. I paused yet a moment, till the sweet, slow sound of the bell had quite died out of the air; then ear, eye and feeling satisfied, I quitted the wall and once more turned my face towards X—.

Chapter 6

I RE-ENTERED THE TOWN A HUNGRY MAN; the dinner I had forgotten recurred seductively to my recollection; and it was with a quick step and sharp appetite I ascended the narrow street leading to my lodgings. It was dark when I opened the front door and walked into the house. I wondered how my fire would be; the night was cold, and I shuddered at the prospect of a grate full of sparkless cinders. To my joyful surprise, I found, on entering my sitting room, a good fire and a clean hearth. I had hardly noticed this phenomenon when I became aware of another subject for wonderment: the chair I usually occupied near the hearth was already filled; a person sat there with his arms folded on his chest and his legs stretched out on the rug. Short-sighted as I am, doubtful as was the gleam of the firelight, a moment's examination enabled me to recognize in this person my acquaintance Mr Hunsden. I could not of course be much pleased to see him, considering the manner in which I had parted from him the night before; and as I walked to the hearth, stirred the fire and said coolly, "Good evening," my demeanour evinced as little cordiality as I felt. Yet I wondered in my own mind what had brought him there; and I wondered, also, what motives had induced him to interfere so actively between me and Edward. It was to him, it appeared, that I owed my welcome dismissal; still I could not bring myself to ask him questions, to show any eagerness of curiosity; if he chose to explain, he might, but the explanation should be a perfectly voluntary one on his part; I thought he was entering upon it.

"You owe me a debt of gratitude," were his first words.

"Do I?" said I. "I hope it is not a large one, for I am much too poor to charge myself with heavy liabilities of any kind."

"Then declare yourself bankrupt at once, for this liability is a ton weight at least. When I came in I found your fire out, and I had it lit again, and made that sulky drab of a servant stay and blow at it with the bellows till it had burnt up properly. Now, say 'Thank you!'."

"Not till I have had something to eat. I can thank nobody while I am so famished."

I rang the bell and ordered tea and some cold meat.

"Cold meat!" exclaimed Hunsden, as the servant closed the door. "What a glutton you are, man! Meat with tea! You'll die of eating too much."

"No, Mr Hunsden, I shall not." I felt a necessity for contradicting him: I was irritated with hunger, and irritated at seeing him there, and irritated at the continued roughness of his manner.

"It is overeating that makes you so ill-tempered," said he.

"How do you know?" I demanded. "It is like you to give a pragmatical opinion without being acquainted with any of the circumstances of the case. I have had no dinner."

What I said was petulant and snappish enough, and Hunsden only replied by looking in my face and laughing.

"Poor thing!" he whined after a pause. "It has had no dinner, has it? What! I suppose its master would not let it come home. Did Crimsworth order you to fast by way of punishment, William?"

"No, Mr Hunsden." Fortunately, at this sulky juncture, tea was brought in, and I fell to upon some bread and butter and cold beef directly. Having cleared a plateful, I became so far humanized as to intimate to Mr Hunsden "that he need not sit there staring, but might come to the table and do as I did, if he liked".

"But I don't like in the least," said he, and therewith he summoned the servant by a fresh pull of the bell rope, and intimated a desire to have a glass of toast-and-water.* "And some more coal," he added. "Mr Crimsworth shall keep a good fire while I stay."

His orders being executed, he wheeled his chair round to the table so as to be opposite me.

"Well," he proceeded. "You are out of work, I suppose."

"Yes," said I; and not disposed to show the satisfaction I felt on this point, I, yielding to the whim of the moment, took up the subject as though I considered myself aggrieved rather than benefited by what had been done. "Yes – thanks to you, I am. Crimsworth turned me off at a minute's notice, owing to some interference of yours at a public meeting, I understand."

"Ah! What! He mentioned that! He observed me signalling the lads, did he? What had he to say about his friend Hunsden – anything sweet?"

"He called you a treacherous villain."

"Oh, he hardly knows me yet! I'm one of those shy people who don't come out all at once, and he is only just beginning to make my acquaintance, but he'll find I've some good qualities – excellent ones! The Hunsdens were always unrivalled at tracking a rascal; a downright, dishonourable villain is their natural prey – they could not keep off him wherever they met him; you used the word pragmatical just now – that word is the property of our family; it has been applied to us from generation to generation; we have fine noses for abuses; we scent a scoundrel a mile off; we are reformers born, radical reformers; and it was impossible for me to live in the same town as Crimsworth, to come into weekly contact with him, to witness some of his conduct to you (for whom personally I care nothing; I only consider the brutal injustice with which he violated your natural claim to equality) – I say it was impossible for me to be thus situated and not feel the angel or the demon of my race at work within me. I followed my instinct, opposed a tyrant and broke a chain."

Now, this speech interested me much, both because it brought out Hunsden's character, and because it explained his motives. It interested me so much that I forgot to reply to it, and sat silent, pondering over a throng of ideas it had suggested.

"Are you grateful to me?" he asked, presently.

In fact I was grateful, or almost so, and I believe I half liked him at the moment, notwithstanding his proviso that what he had done was not out of regard for me. But human nature is perverse. Impossible to answer his blunt question in the affirmative, so I disclaimed all tendency to gratitude, and advised him, if he expected any reward for his championship, to look for it in a better world, as he was not likely to meet with it here. In reply he termed me "a dry-hearted, aristocratic scamp", whereupon I again charged him with having taken the bread out of my mouth.

"Your bread was dirty, man!" cried Hunsden. "Dirty and unwholesome! It came through the hands of a tyrant, for I tell you Crimsworth is a tyrant – a tyrant to his workpeople, a tyrant to his clerks, and will some day be a tyrant to his wife."

"Nonsense! Bread is bread, and a salary is a salary. I've lost mine, and through your means."

"There's sense in what you say, after all," rejoined Hunsden. "I must say I am rather agreeably surprised to hear you make so practical an observation as that last. I had imagined now, from my previous observation of your character, that the sentimental delight you would have taken in your newly regained liberty would, for a while at least, have effaced all ideas of forethought and prudence. I think better of you for looking steadily to the needful."

"Looking steadily to the needful! How can I do otherwise? I must live, and to live I must have what you call 'the needful', which I can only get by working. I repeat it, you have taken my work from me."

"What do you mean to do?" pursued Hunsden coolly. "You have influential relations; I suppose they'll soon provide you with another place."

"Influential relations? Who? I should like to know their names."

"The Seacombes."

"Stuff! I have cut them."

Hunsden looked at me incredulously.

"I have," said I, "and that definitively."

"You must mean they have cut you, William."

"As you please. They offered me their patronage on condition of my entering the Church. I declined both the terms and the recompense; I withdrew from my cold uncles, and preferred throwing myself into my elder brother's arms, from whose affectionate embrace I am now torn by the cruel intermeddling of a stranger – of yourself, in short."

I could not repress a half-smile as I said this; a similar demi-manifestation of feeling appeared at the same moment on Hunsden's lips.

"Oh, I see!" said he, looking into my eyes, and it was evident he *did* see right down into my heart. Having sat a minute or two with his chin resting on his hand, diligently occupied in the continued perusal of my countenance, he went on:

"Seriously, have you then nothing to expect from the Seacombes?"

"Yes, rejection and repulsion. Why do you ask me twice? How can hands stained with the ink of a counting house, soiled with the grease of a wool warehouse, ever again be permitted to come into contact with aristocratic palms?"

"There would be a difficulty, no doubt. Still, you are such a complete Seacombe in appearance, feature, language, almost manner, I wonder they should disown you."

"They have disowned me, so talk no more about it."

"Do you regret it, William?"

"No."

"Why not, lad?"

"Because they are not people with whom I could ever have had any sympathy."

"I say you are one of them."

"That merely proves that you know nothing at all about it. I am my mother's son, but not my uncle's nephew."

"Still – one of your uncles is a lord, though rather an obscure and not a very wealthy one, and the other a right honourable: you should consider worldly interest."

"Nonsense, Mr Hunsden. You know or may know that even had I desired to be submissive to my uncles, I could not have stooped with a good enough grace ever to have won their favour. I should have sacrificed my own comfort and not have gained their patronage in return."

"Very likely – so you calculated your wisest plan was to follow your own devices at once?"

"Exactly. I must follow my own devices – I must till the day of my death; because I can neither comprehend, adopt nor work out those of other people."

Hunsden yawned. "Well," said he, "in all this, I see but one thing clearly – that is, that the whole affair is no business of mine." He stretched himself and again yawned. "I wonder what time it is?" he went on. "I have an appointment for seven o'clock."

"Three quarters past six by my watch."

"Well, then, I'll go." He got up. "You'll not meddle with trade again?" said he, leaning his elbow on the mantelpiece.

"No, I think not."

"You would be a fool if you did. Probably, after all, you'll think better of your uncles' proposal and go into the Church."

"A singular regeneration must take place in my whole inner and outer man before I do that. A good clergyman is one of the best of men."

"Indeed! Do you think so?" interrupted Hunsden, scoffingly.

"I do, and no mistake. But I have not the peculiar points which go to make a good clergyman; and rather than adopt a profession for which I have no vocation, I would endure extremities of hardship from poverty."

"You're a mighty difficult customer to suit. You won't be a tradesman or a parson; you can't be a lawyer, or a doctor, or a gentleman, because you've no money. I'd recommend you to travel."

"What! Without money?"

"You must travel in search of money, man. You can speak French – with a vile English accent, no doubt – still, you can speak it. Go on to the Continent, and see what will turn up for you there."

"God knows I should like to go!" exclaimed I with involuntary ardour.

"Go: what the deuce hinders you? You may get to Brussels, for instance, for five or six pounds, if you know how to manage with economy."

"Necessity would teach me if I didn't."

"Go, then, and let your wits make a way for you when you get there. I know Brussels almost as well as I know X—, and I am sure it would suit such a one as you better than London."

"But occupation, Mr Hunsden! I must go where occupation is to be had, and how could I get recommendation, or introduction, or employment at Brussels?"

"There speaks the organ of caution.* You hate to advance a step before you know every inch of the way. You haven't a sheet of paper and a pen and ink?"

"I hope so," and I produced writing materials with alacrity, for I guessed what he was going to do. He sat down, wrote a few lines, folded, sealed and addressed a letter, and held it out to me.

"There, Prudence, there's a pioneer to hew down the first rough difficulties of your path. I know well enough, lad, you are not one of those who will run their neck into a noose without seeing how they are to get it out again, and you're right there. A reckless man is my aversion, and nothing should ever persuade me to meddle with the concerns of such a one. Those who are reckless for themselves are generally ten times more so for their friends."

"This is a letter of introduction, I suppose?" said I, taking the epistle.

"Yes. With that in your pocket you will run no risk of finding yourself in a state of absolute destitution – which, I know, you would regard as a degradation; so should I, for that matter. The person to whom you will present it generally has two or three respectable places depending upon his recommendation."

"That will just suit me," said I.

"Well, and where's your gratitude?" demanded Mr Hunsden. "Don't you know how to say 'Thank you'?"

"I've fifteen pounds and a watch, which my godmother, whom I never saw, gave me eighteen years ago," was my rather irrelevant answer; and I further avowed myself a happy man, and professed that I did not envy any being in Christendom.

"And your gratitude?"

"I shall be off presently, Mr Hunsden – tomorrow, if all be well: I'll not stay a day longer in X— than I'm obliged."

"Very good – but it will be decent to make due acknowledgement for the assistance you have received; be quick! It is just going to strike seven; I'm waiting to be thanked."

"Just stand out of the way, will you, Mr Hunsden? I want a key that is on the corner of the mantelpiece. I'll pack my portmanteau before I go to bed."

The house clock struck seven.

"The lad is a heathen," said Hunsden and, taking his hat from a sideboard, he left the room, laughing to himself. I had half an inclination to follow him: I really intended to leave X— the next morning, and should certainly not have another opportunity of bidding him goodbye. The front door banged to.

"Let him go," said I, "we shall meet again some day."

Chapter 7

R EADER, PERHAPS YOU WERE NEVER IN BELGIUM? Haply you don't know the physiognomy of the country? You have not its lineaments defined upon your memory, as I have them on mine?

Three – nay, four – pictures line the four-walled cell where are stored for me the records of the past. First, Eton. All in that picture is in far perspective, receding, diminutive, but freshly coloured, green, dewy, with a spring sky, piled with glittering yet showery clouds; for my childhood was not all sunshine – it had its overcast, its cold, its stormy hours. Second, X—, huge, dingy; the canvas cracked and smoked; a yellow sky, sooty clouds; no sun, no azure; the verdure of the suburbs blighted and sullied – a very dreary scene.

Third, Belgium; and I will pause before this landscape. As to the fourth, a curtain covers it, which I may hereafter withdraw, or may not, as suits my convenience and capacity. At any rate, for the present it must hang undisturbed. Belgium! Name unromantic and unpoetic, yet name that whenever uttered has in my ear a sound, in my heart an echo, such as no other assemblage of syllables, however sweet or classic, can produce. Belgium! I repeat the word, now as I sit alone near midnight. It stirs my world of the past like a summons to resurrection; the graves unclose, the dead are raised; thoughts, feelings, memories that slept are seen by me ascending from the clods – haloed most of them – but while I gaze on their vapoury forms, and strive to ascertain definitely their outline, the sound which wakened them dies, and they sink, each and all, like a light wreath of mist, absorbed in the mould, recalled to urns, resealed in monuments. Farewell, luminous phantoms!

This is Belgium, reader. Look! Don't call the picture a flat or a dull one – it was neither flat nor dull to me when I first beheld it. When I left Ostend on a mild February morning and found myself on the road to Brussels, nothing could look vapid to me. My sense of enjoyment possessed an edge whetted to the finest, untouched, keen, exquisite. I was young; I had good health; pleasure and I had never met; no indulgence of hers had enervated or sated one faculty of my nature. Liberty I clasped in my arms for the first time, and the influence of her smile and embrace revived my life like the sun and the west wind. Yes, at that epoch I felt like a morning traveller who doubts not that from the hill he is ascending he shall behold a glorious sunrise; what if the track be strait, steep and stony? He sees it not; his eyes are fixed on that summit, flushed already, flushed and gilded, and having gained it he is certain of the scene beyond. He knows that the sun will face him, that his chariot is even now coming over the eastern horizon and that the herald breeze he feels on his cheek is opening for the god's career a clear, vast path of azure amidst clouds soft as pearl and warm as flame. Difficulty and toil were to be my lot, but sustained by energy, drawn on by hopes as bright as vague, I deemed such a lot no hardship. I mounted now the hill in shade; there were pebbles, inequalities, briars in my path, but my eyes were fixed on the crimson peak above; my imagination was with the refulgent firmament beyond, and I thought nothing of the stones turning under my feet, or of the thorns scratching my face and hands.

I gazed often, and always with delight, from the window of the diligence* (these, be it remembered, were not the days of trains and railroads). Well! And what did I see? I will tell you faithfully. Green, reedy swamps; fields fertile but flat, cultivated in patches that made them look like magnified kitchen gardens; belts of cut trees, formal as pollard willows, skirting the horizon; narrow canals, gliding slow by the roadside; painted Flemish farmhouses; some very dirty hovels; a grey, dead sky; wet road, wet fields, wet housetops: not a beautiful, scarcely a picturesque object met my eye along the whole route; yet to me all was beautiful, all was more than picturesque. It continued fair so long as daylight lasted, though the moisture of many preceding damp days had sodden the whole country; as it grew dark, however, the rain recommenced, and it was through streaming and starless darkness my eye caught the first gleam of the lights of Brussels. I saw little of the city but its lights that night. Having alighted from the diligence, a fiacre* conveyed me to the

Hôtel de —, where I had been advised by a fellow traveller to put up. Having eaten a traveller's supper, I retired to bed, and slept a traveller's sleep.

Next morning I awoke from prolonged and sound repose with the impression that I was yet in X—, and perceiving it to be broad daylight I started up, imagining that I had overslept myself and should be behind time at the counting house. The momentary and painful sense of restraint vanished before the revived and reviving consciousness of freedom, as, throwing back the white curtains of my bed, I looked forth into a wide, lofty foreign chamber. How different from the small and dingy, though not uncomfortable, apartment I had occupied for a night or two at a respectable inn in London while waiting for the sailing of the packet! Yet, far be it from me to profane the memory of that dingy little room! It, too, is dear to my soul, for there, as I lay in quiet and darkness, I first heard the great bell of St Paul's telling London it was midnight, and well do I recall the deep, deliberate tones, so full-charged with colossal phlegm and force. From the small, narrow window of that room, I first saw *the* dome, looming through a London mist. I suppose the sensations, stirred by those first sounds, first sights, are felt but once; treasure them, Memory; seal them in urns, and keep them in safe niches! Well – I rose. Travellers talk of the apartments in foreign dwellings being bare and uncomfortable; I thought my chamber looked stately and cheerful. It had such large windows – *croisées** that opened like doors, with such broad, clear panes of glass; such a great looking glass stood on my dressing table – such a fine mirror glittered over the mantelpiece – the painted floor looked so clean and glossy; when I had dressed and was descending the stairs, the broad marble steps almost awed me, and so did the lofty hall into which they conducted. On the first landing I met a Flemish housemaid: she had wooden shoes, a short red petticoat, a printed cotton bedgown; her face was broad, her physiognomy eminently stupid; when I spoke to her in French, she answered me in Flemish, with an air the reverse of civil; yet I thought her charming; if she was not pretty or polite, she was, I conceived, very picturesque; she reminded me of the female figures in certain Dutch paintings I had seen in other years at Seacombe Hall.

I repaired to the public room; that, too, was very large and very lofty, and warmed by a stove; the floor was black, and the stove was black, and most of the furniture was black; yet I never experienced a freer sense of exhilaration than when I sat down at a very long, black table (covered, however, in part by a white cloth) and, having ordered breakfast, began to pour out my coffee from a little black coffee pot. The stove might be dismal-looking to some eyes, not to mine, but it was indisputably very warm, and there were two gentlemen seated by it talking in French; impossible to follow their rapid utterance, or comprehend much of the purport of what they said – yet French, in the mouths of Frenchmen, or Belgians (I was not then sensible of the horrors of the Belgian accent), was as music to my ears. One of these gentlemen presently discerned me to be an Englishman – no doubt from the fashion in which I addressed the waiter; for I would persist in speaking French in my execrable south-of-England style, though the man understood English. The gentleman, after looking towards me once or twice, politely accosted me in very good English. I remember I wished to God that I could speak French as well; his fluency and correct pronunciation impressed me for the first time with a due notion of the cosmopolitan character of the capital I was in; it was my first experience of that skill in living languages I afterwards found to be so general in Brussels.

I lingered over my breakfast as long as I could. While it was there on the table, and while that stranger continued talking to me, I was a free, independent traveller; but at last the things were removed, the two gentlemen left the room; suddenly the illusion ceased: reality and business came back. I, a bondsman just released from the yoke, freed for one week from twenty-one years of constraint, must, of necessity, resume the fetters of dependency. Hardly had I tasted the delight of being without a master when duty issued her stern mandate: "Go forth and seek another service." I never linger over a painful and necessary task; I never take pleasure before business: it is not in my nature to do so; impossible to enjoy a leisurely walk over the city, though I perceived the morning was very fine, until I had presented Mr Hunsden's letter of introduction, and got fairly onto the track of a new situation. Wrenching my mind from liberty and delight, I seized my hat and forced my reluctant body out of the Hôtel de — into the foreign street.

It was a fine day, but I would not look at the blue sky nor at the stately houses round me; my mind was bent on one thing: finding out "Mr Brown, Numero —, Rue Royale", for so my letter was addressed. By dint of enquiry I succeeded; I stood at last at the desired door, knocked, asked for Mr Brown and was admitted.

Being shown into a small breakfast room, I found myself in the presence of an elderly gentleman – very grave, businesslike and respectable-looking. I presented Mr Hunsden's letter; he received me very civilly. After a little desultory conversation, he asked me if there was anything in which his advice or experience could be of use. I said, "Yes," and then proceeded to tell him that I was not a gentleman of fortune, travelling for pleasure, but an ex-counting-house clerk, who wanted employment of some kind, and that immediately too. He replied that as a friend of Mr Hunsden's he would be willing to assist me as well as he could. After some meditation he named a place in a mercantile house at Liège, and another in a bookseller's shop at Louvain.

"Clerk and shopman!" murmured I to myself. "No." I shook my head. I had tried the high stool; I hated it; I believed there were other occupations that would suit me better; besides, I did not wish to leave Brussels.

"I know of no place in Brussels," answered Mr Brown, "unless indeed you were disposed to turn your attention to teaching. I am acquainted with the director of a large establishment who is in want of a professor of English and Latin."

I thought two minutes, then I seized the idea eagerly.

"The very thing, sir!" said I.

"But," asked he, "do you understand French well enough to teach Belgian boys English?"

Fortunately I could answer this question in the affirmative; having studied French under a Frenchman, I could speak the language intelligibly, though not fluently. I could also read it well and write it decently.

"Then," pursued Mr Brown, "I think I can promise you the place, for Monsieur Pelet will not refuse a professor recommended by me; but come here again at five o'clock this afternoon, and I will introduce you to him."

The word "professor" struck me. "I am not a professor," said I.

"Oh," returned Mr Brown, "professor, here in Belgium, means a teacher, that is all."

My conscience thus quieted, I thanked Mr Brown and, for the present, withdrew. This time I stepped out into the street with a relieved heart; the task I had imposed on myself for that day was executed. I might now take some hours of holiday. I felt free to look up. For the first time I remarked the sparkling clearness of the air, the deep blue of the sky, the gay, clean aspect of the whitewashed or painted houses; I saw what a fine street was the Rue Royale, and, walking leisurely along its broad pavement, I continued to survey its stately hotels, till the palisades, the gates and trees of the park, appearing in sight, offered to my eye a new attraction. I remember, before entering the park, I stood awhile to contemplate the statue of General Belliard,* and then I advanced to the top of the great staircase just beyond, and I looked down into a narrow backstreet, which I afterwards learnt was called the Rue d'Isabelle. I well recollect that my eye rested on the green door of a rather large house opposite, where, on a brass plate, was inscribed, "*Pensionnat de Demoiselles*". *Pensionnat*! The word excited an uneasy sensation in my mind; it seemed to speak of restraint. Some of the *demoiselles*, *externats** no doubt, were at that moment issuing from the door. I looked for a pretty face amongst them, but their close little French bonnets hid their features; in a moment they were gone.

I had traversed a good deal of Brussels before five o'clock arrived, but punctually as that hour struck I was again in the Rue Royale. Readmitted to Mr Brown's breakfast room, I found him as before, seated at the table, and he was not alone – a gentleman stood by the hearth. Two words of introduction designated him as my future master. "M. Pelet, Mr Crimsworth; Mr Crimsworth, M. Pelet." A bow on each side finished the ceremony. I don't know what sort of a bow I made; an ordinary one, I suppose, for I was in a tranquil, commonplace frame of mind; I felt none of the agitation which had troubled my first interview with Edward Crimsworth. M. Pelet's bow was extremely polite, yet not theatrical, scarcely French; he and I were presently seated opposite to each other. In a pleasing voice – low and, out of consideration to my foreign ears, very distinct and deliberate

– M. Pelet intimated that he had just been receiving from "le respectable M. Brown" an account of my attainments and character, which relieved him from all scruple as to the propriety of engaging me as professor of English and Latin in his establishment. Nevertheless, for form's sake, he would put a few questions to test my powers. He did, and expressed in flattering terms his satisfaction at my answers. The subject of salary next came on; it was fixed at one thousand francs per annum, besides board and lodging. "And in addition," suggested M. Pelet, "as there will be some hours in each day during which your services will not be required in my establishment, you may, in time, obtain employment in other seminaries, and thus turn your vacant moments to profitable account."

I thought this very kind, and indeed I found afterwards that the terms on which M. Pelet had engaged me were really liberal for Brussels, instruction being extremely cheap there on account of the number of teachers. It was further arranged that I should be installed in my new post the very next day, after which M. Pelet and I parted.

Well, and what was he like? And what were my impressions concerning him? He was a man of about forty years of age, of middle size and rather emaciated figure; his face was pale, his cheeks were sunk, and his eyes hollow; his features were pleasing and regular, they had a French turn (for M. Pelet was no Fleming, but a Frenchman both by birth and parentage), yet the degree of harshness inseparable from Gallic lineaments was, in his case, softened by a mild blue eye and a melancholy, almost suffering, expression of countenance; his physiognomy was *fine et spirituelle*. I use two French words because they define better than any English terms the species of intelligence with which his features were imbued. He was altogether an interesting and prepossessing personage. I wondered only at the utter absence of all the ordinary characteristics of his profession, and almost feared he could not be stern and resolute enough for a schoolmaster. Externally at least, M. Pelet presented an absolute contrast to my late master Edward Crimsworth.

Influenced by the impression I had received of his gentleness, I was a good deal surprised when, on arriving the next day at my new employer's house, and being admitted to a first view of what was to be the sphere of my future labours – namely, the large, lofty and well-lighted schoolrooms – I beheld a numerous assemblage of pupils, boys of course, whose collective appearance showed all the signs of a full, flourishing and well-disciplined seminary. As I traversed the classes in company with M. Pelet, a profound silence reigned on all sides, and if by chance a murmur or a whisper arose, one glance from the pensive eye of this most gentle pedagogue stilled it instantly. It was astonishing, I thought, how so mild a check could prove so effectual. When I had perambulated the length and breadth of the classes, M. Pelet turned and said to me:

"Would you object to taking the boys as they are, and testing their proficiency in English?"

The proposal was unexpected. I had thought I should have been allowed at least a day to prepare; but it is a bad omen to commence any career by hesitation, so I just stepped to the professor's desk near which we stood and faced the circle of my pupils. I took a moment to collect my thoughts, and likewise to frame in French the sentence by which I proposed to open business. I made it as short as possible:

"*Messieurs, prenez vos livres de lecture.*"*

"*Anglais ou Français, monsieur?*" demanded a thickset, moon-faced young *Flamand* in a blouse. The answer was fortunately easy:

"*Anglais.*"

I determined to give myself as little trouble as possible in this lesson; it would not do yet to trust my unpractised tongue with the delivery of explanations; my accent and idiom would be too open to the criticisms of the young gentlemen before me, relative to whom I felt it would be necessary at once to take up an advantageous position, and I proceeded to employ means accordingly.

"*Commencez!*" cried I, when they had all produced their books. The moon-faced youth (by name Jules Vanderkelkov, as I afterwards learnt) took the first sentence. The *livre de lecture* was *The Vicar of Wakefield*,* much used in foreign schools because it is supposed to contain prime samples of conversational English; it might, however, have been a runic scroll for any resemblance the words, as enunciated by Jules, bore to the language in ordinary use amongst the natives of Great Britain. My God! How he did snuffle, snort and wheeze! All he said was said in his throat and nose, for it is thus the *Flamands* speak, but I heard him to the end of his paragraph without proffering a word of correction, whereat he looked vastly self-complacent, convinced, no doubt, that he had acquitted himself like a real born-and-bred *Anglais*. In the same unmoved silence I listened to a dozen in rotation, and when the twelfth had concluded with splutter, hiss and mumble, I solemnly laid down the book.

"*Arrêtez!*" said I. There was a pause, during which I regarded them all with a steady and somewhat stern gaze; a dog, if stared at hard enough and long enough, will show symptoms of embarrassment, and so at length did my bench of Belgians. Perceiving that some of the faces before me were beginning to look sullen, and others ashamed, I slowly joined my hands and ejaculated in a deep *voix de poitrine*:*

"*Comme c'est affreux!*"*

They looked at each other, pouted, coloured, swung their heels; they were not pleased, I saw, but they were impressed, and in the way I wished them to be. Having thus taken them down a peg in their self-conceit, the next step was to raise myself in their estimation; not a very easy thing considering that I hardly dared to speak for fear of betraying my own deficiencies.

"*Écoutez, messieurs!*" said I, and I endeavoured to throw into my accents the compassionate tone of a superior being, who, touched by the extremity of the helplessness, which at first only excited his scorn, deigns at length to bestow aid. I then began at the very beginning of *The Vicar of Wakefield*, and read, in a slow, distinct voice, some twenty pages, they all the while sitting mute and listening with fixed attention; by the time I had done, nearly an hour had elapsed. I then rose and said:

"*C'est assez pour aujourd'hui, messieurs; demain nous recommencerons, et j'espère que tout ira bien.*"*

With this oracular sentence I bowed, and in company with M. Pelet quitted the schoolroom.

"*C'est bien! c'est très bien!*" said my principal as we entered his parlour. "*Je vois que monsieur a de l'adresse; cela me plaît, car, dans l'instruction, l'adresse fait tout autant que le savoir.*"*

From the parlour M. Pelet conducted me to my apartment – my *chambre*, as Monsieur said with a certain air of complacency. It was a very small room, with an excessively small bed, but M. Pelet gave me to understand that I was to occupy it quite alone, which was of course a great comfort. Yet, though so limited in dimensions, it had two windows. Light not being taxed in Belgium, the people never grudge its admission into their houses;* just here, however, this observation is not very apropos, for one of these windows was boarded up; the open window looked into the boys' playground. I glanced at the other, as wondering what aspect it would present if disencumbered of the boards. M. Pelet read, I suppose, the expression of my eye; he explained,

"*La fenêtre fermée donne sur un jardin appartenant à un pensionnat de demoiselles,*" said he, "*et les convenances exigent... enfin, vous comprenez... n'est-ce pas, monsieur?*"*

"*Oui, oui,*" was my reply, and I looked of course quite satisfied; but when M. Pelet had retired and closed the door after him, the first thing I did was to scrutinize closely the nailed boards, hoping to find some chink or crevice which I might enlarge, and so get a peep at the consecrated ground. My researches were vain, for the boards were well joined and strongly nailed. It is astonishing how disappointed I felt. I thought it would have been so pleasant to have looked out upon a garden planted with flowers and trees, so amusing to have watched the *demoiselles* at their play; to have studied female character in a variety of phases, myself the while sheltered from view by a modest muslin curtain – whereas, owing doubtless to the absurd scruples of some old duenna of a directress, I had now only the option of looking at a bare gravelled court, with an enormous *pas de géant** in the middle, and the monotonous walls and windows of a boys' schoolhouse round. Not only then, but many a time after, especially in moments of weariness and low spirits, did I look with dissatisfied eyes on that most tantalizing board, longing to tear it away and get a glimpse of the green region which I imagined to lie beyond. I knew a tree grew close up to the window, for though there were as yet no leaves to rustle, I often heard at night the tapping of branches against the panes. In the daytime, when I listened attentively, I could hear, even through the boards, the voices of the *demoiselles* in their hours of recreation, and, to speak the honest truth, my sentimental reflections were occasionally a trifle disarranged by the not quite silvery, in fact the too often brazen sounds, which, rising from the unseen paradise below, penetrated clamorously into my solitude.

Not to mince matters, it really seemed to me a doubtful case whether the lungs of Mlle Reuter's girls or those of M. Pelet's boys were the strongest, and when it came to shrieking the girls indisputably beat the boys hollow. I forgot to say, by the by, that Reuter was the name of the old lady who had had my window boarded up. I say old, for such I, of course, concluded her to be, judging from her cautious chaperone-like proceedings; besides, nobody ever spoke of her as young. I remember I was very much amused when I first heard her Christian name; it was Zoraïde – Mademoiselle Zoraïde Reuter.* But the Continental nations do allow themselves vagaries in the choice of names, such as we sober English never run into. I think, indeed, we have too limited a list to choose from.

Meantime my path was gradually growing smooth before me. I, in a few weeks, conquered the teasing difficulties inseparable from the commencement of almost every career. Ere long I had acquired as much facility in speaking French as set me at my ease with my pupils: and as I had encountered them on a right footing at the very beginning, and continued tenaciously to retain the advantage I had early gained, they never attempted mutiny – which circumstance, all who are in any degree acquainted with the ongoings of Belgian schools and who know the relation in which professors and pupils too frequently stand towards each other in those establishments, will consider an important and uncommon one. Before concluding this chapter, I will say a word on the system I pursued with regard to my classes: my experience may possibly be of use to others.

It did not require very keen observation to detect the character of the youth of Brabant,* but it needed a certain degree of tact to adapt one's measures to their capacity. Their intellectual faculties were generally weak, their animal propensities strong; thus there was at once an impotence and a kind of inert force in their natures; they were dull, but they were also singularly stubborn, heavy as lead and, like lead, most difficult to move. Such being the case, it would have been truly absurd to exact from them much in the way of mental exertion; having short memories, dense intelligence, feeble reflective powers, they recoiled with repugnance from any occupation that demanded close study or deep thought. Had the abhorred effort been extorted from them by injudicious and arbitrary measures on the part of the professor, they would have resisted as obstinately, as clamorously, as desperate swine; and though not brave singly, they were relentless acting en masse.

I understood that, before my arrival in M. Pelet's establishment, the combined insubordination of the pupils had effected the dismissal of more than one English master. It was necessary, then, to exact only the most moderate application from natures so little qualified to apply – to assist, in every practicable way, understandings so opaque and contracted – to be ever gentle, considerate, yielding even, to a certain point, with dispositions so irrationally perverse; but, having reached that culminating point of indulgence, you must fix your foot, plant it, root it in rock – become immutable as the towers of Sainte-Gudule;* for a step – but half a step farther, and you would plunge headlong into the gulf of imbecility; there lodged, you would speedily receive proofs of Flemish gratitude and magnanimity in showers of Brabant saliva and handfuls of Low Country mud. You might smooth to the utmost the path of learning, remove every pebble from the track, but then you must finally insist with decision on the pupil taking your arm and allowing himself to be led quietly along the prepared road. When I had brought down my lesson to the lowest level of my dullest pupil's capacity – when I had shown myself the mildest, the most tolerant of masters – a word of impertinence, a movement of disobedience, changed me at once into a despot. I offered them but one alternative: submission and acknowledgement of error, or ignominious expulsion. This system answered, and my influence, by degrees, became established on a firm basis. "The boy is father to the man,"* it is said, and so I often thought when I looked at my boys and remembered the political history of their ancestors.* Pelet's school was merely an epitome of the Belgian nation.

Chapter 8

A ND PELET HIMSELF? How did I continue to like him? Oh, extremely well! Nothing could be more smooth, gentlemanlike and even friendly than his demeanour to me. I had to endure from him neither cold neglect, irritating interference nor pretentious assumption of superiority. I fear, however, two poor, hard-worked Belgian ushers in the establishment could not have said as much; to them the director's manner was invariably dry, stern and cool. I believe he perceived once or twice that I was a little shocked at the difference he made between them and me, and accounted for it by saying, with a quiet, sarcastic smile,

*"Ce ne sont que des Flamands – allez!"**

And then he took his cigar gently from his lips and spat on the painted floor of the room in which we were sitting. *Flamands* certainly they were, and both had the true *Flamand* physiognomy, where intellectual inferiority is marked in lines none can mistake. Still they were men, and, in the main, honest men; and I could not see why their being aboriginals of the flat, dull soil should serve as a pretext for treating them with perpetual severity and contempt. This idea of injustice somewhat poisoned the pleasure I might otherwise have derived from Pelet's soft, affable manner to myself. Certainly it was agreeable, when the day's work was over, to find one's employer an intelligent and cheerful companion; and if he was sometimes a little sarcastic and sometimes a little too insinuating, and if I did discover that his mildness was more a matter of appearance than of reality – if I did occasionally suspect the existence of flint or steel under an external covering of velvet – still we are none of us perfect; and weary as I was of the atmosphere of brutality and insolence in which I had constantly lived at X—, I had no inclination now, on casting anchor in calmer regions, to institute at once a prying search after defects that were scrupulously withdrawn and carefully veiled from my view. I was willing to take Pelet for what he seemed – to believe him benevolent and friendly until some untoward event should prove him otherwise. He was not married, and I soon perceived he had all a Frenchman's, all a Parisian's notions about matrimony and women. I suspected a degree of laxity in his code of morals: there was something so cold and blasé in his tone whenever he alluded to what he called "*le beau sexe*"; but he was too gentlemanlike to intrude topics I did not invite, and as he was really intelligent and really fond of intellectual subjects of discourse, he and I always found enough to talk about, without seeking themes in the mire. I hated his fashion of mentioning love; I abhorred, from my soul, mere licentiousness. He felt the difference of our notions, and, by mutual consent, we kept off ground debatable.

Pelet's house was kept and his kitchen managed by his mother, a real old Frenchwoman. She had been handsome – at least she told me so, and I strove to believe her. She was now ugly, as only Continental old women can be; perhaps, though, her style of dress made her look uglier than she really was. Indoors she would go about without cap, her grey hair strangely dishevelled; then, when at home, she seldom wore a gown – only a shabby cotton camisole; shoes, too, were strangers to her feet, and in lieu of them she sported roomy slippers, trodden down at the heels. On the other hand, whenever it was her pleasure to appear abroad, as on Sundays and fête days, she would put on some very brilliant-coloured dress, usually of thin texture, a silk bonnet with a wreath of flowers and a very fine shawl. She was not, in the main, an ill-natured old woman, but an incessant and most indiscreet talker; she kept chiefly in and about the kitchen, and seemed rather to avoid her son's august presence; of him, indeed, she evidently stood in awe. When he reproved her, his reproofs were bitter and unsparing; but he seldom gave himself that trouble.

Madame Pelet had her own society, her own circle of chosen visitors – whom, however, I seldom saw, as she generally entertained them in what she called her "cabinet", a small den of a place adjoining the kitchen, and descending into it by one or two steps. On these steps, by the by, I have not unfrequently seen Madame Pelet seated with a trencher on her knee, engaged in the threefold employment of eating her dinner, gossiping with her favourite servant, the housemaid, and scolding her antagonist, the cook; she never dined, and seldom indeed took any meal with her son; and as to showing her face at the boys' table, that was quite out of the question. These details will sound very odd in English ears, but Belgium is not England, and its ways are not our ways.

Madame Pelet's habits of life, then, being taken into consideration, I was a good deal surprised when, one Thursday evening (Thursday was always a half-holiday), as I was sitting all alone in my apartment, correcting a huge pile of English and Latin exercises, a servant tapped at the door, and, on its being opened, presented Madame Pelet's compliments – and she would be happy to see me to take my *goûter* (a meal which answers to our English tea) with her in the dining room.

"*Plaît-il?*"* said I, for I thought I must have misunderstood: the message and invitation were so unusual; the same words were repeated. I accepted, of course, and as I descended the stairs, I wondered what whim had entered the old lady's brain; her son was out – gone to pass the evening at the *Salle* of the Grande Harmonie* or some other club of which he was a member. Just as I laid my hand on the handle of the dining-room door, a queer idea glanced across my mind.

"Surely she's not going to make love to me," said I. "I've heard of old Frenchwomen doing odd things in that line; and the *goûter*? They generally begin such affairs with eating and drinking, I believe."

There was a fearful dismay in this suggestion of my excited imagination, and if I had allowed myself time to dwell upon it, I should no doubt have cut there and then, rushed back to my chamber and bolted myself in. But whenever a danger or a horror is veiled with uncertainty, the primary wish of the mind is to ascertain first the naked truth, reserving the expedient of flight for the moment when its dread anticipation shall be realized. I turned the door handle, and in an instant had crossed the fatal threshold, closed the door behind me and stood in the presence of Madame Pelet.

Gracious Heavens! The first view of her seemed to confirm my worst apprehensions. There she sat, dressed out in a light-green muslin gown, on her head a lace cap with flourishing red roses in the frill; her table was carefully spread; there were fruit, cakes and coffee, with a bottle of something – I did not know what. Already the cold sweat started on my brow, already I glanced back over my shoulder at the closed door, when, to my unspeakable relief, my eye, wandering wildly in the direction of the stove, rested upon a second figure, seated in a large *fauteuil** beside it. This was a woman, too, and, moreover, an old woman, and as fat and as rubicund as Madame Pelet was meagre and yellow; her attire was likewise very fine, and spring flowers of different hues circled in a bright wreath the crown of her violet-coloured velvet bonnet.

I had only time to make these general observations when Madame Pelet, coming forward with what she intended should be a graceful and elastic step, thus accosted me:

"Monsieur is indeed most obliging to quit his books, his studies, at the request of an insignificant person like me – will monsieur complete his kindness by allowing me to present him to my dear friend Madame Reuter, who resides in the neighbouring house – the young ladies' school?"

"Ah!" thought I. "I knew she was old," and I bowed and took my seat. Madame Reuter placed herself at the table opposite to me.

"How do you like Belgium, monsieur?" asked she, in an accent of the broadest *Bruxellois*. I could now well distinguish the difference between the fine and pure Parisian utterance of M. Pelet, for instance, and the guttural enunciation of the *Flamands*. I answered politely, and then wondered how so coarse and clumsy an old woman as the one before me should be at the head of a ladies' seminary which I had always heard spoken of in terms of high commendation. In truth there was something to wonder at. Madame Reuter looked more like a joyous, free-living Flemish *fermière,** or even a *maîtresse d'auberge,** than a staid, grave, rigid *directrice de pensionnat.** In general the Continental, or at least the Belgian old women, permit themselves a licence of manners, speech and aspect, such as our venerable grandams would recoil from as absolutely disreputable, and Madame Reuter's jolly face bore evidence that she was no exception to the rule of her country. There was a twinkle and leer in her left eye; her right she kept habitually half shut, which I thought very odd indeed. After several vain attempts to comprehend the motives of these two droll old creatures for inviting me to join them at their *goûter*, I at last fairly gave it up and, resigning myself to inevitable mystification, I sat and looked first at one, then at the other, taking care meantime to do justice to the confitures, cakes and coffee with which they amply supplied me. They, too, ate, and that with no delicate appetite, and having demolished a large portion of the solids, they proposed a *petit verre*.* I declined. Not so Mesdames Pelet and Reuter; each mixed herself what I thought rather a stiff tumbler of punch, and, placing it on a stand near the stove, they drew up their chairs to that convenience, and invited me to do the same. I obeyed; and being seated fairly between them, I was thus addressed first by Madame Pelet, then by Madame Reuter.

"We will now speak of business," said Madame Pelet, and she went on to make an elaborate speech, which, being interpreted, was to the effect that she had asked for the pleasure of my company that evening in order to give her friend Madame Reuter an opportunity of broaching an important proposal, which might turn out greatly to my advantage.

"*Pourvu que vous soyez sage,*" said Madame Reuter, "*et à vrai dire, vous en avez bien l'air.** Take one drop of the punch" – or "ponche", as she pronounced it – "it is an agreeable and wholesome beverage after a full meal."

I bowed, but again declined it. She went on:

"I feel," said she, after a solemn sip, "I feel profoundly the importance of the commission with which my dear daughter has entrusted me, for you are aware, monsieur, that it is my daughter who directs the establishment in the next house?"

"Ah! I thought it was yourself, madame?" Though, indeed, at that moment I recollected that it was called Mademoiselle, not Madame Reuter's *pensionnat*.

"I! Oh, no! I manage the house and look after the servants, as my friend Madame Pelet does for monsieur her son – nothing more. Ah! You thought I gave lessons in class – did you?"

And she laughed loud and long, as though the idea tickled her fancy amazingly.

"Madame is in the wrong to laugh," I observed. "If she does not give lessons, I am sure it is not because she cannot," and I whipped out a white pocket handkerchief and wafted it, with a French grace, past my nose, bowing at the same time.

"*Quel charmant jeune homme!*"* murmured Madame Pelet in a low voice. Madame Reuter, being less sentimental, as she was *Flamand* and not French, only laughed again.

"You are a dangerous person, I fear," said she. "If you can forge compliments at that rate, Zoraïde will positively be afraid of you; but if you are good, I will keep your secret, and not tell her how well you can flatter. Now, listen what sort of a proposal she makes to you. She has heard that you are an excellent professor, and as she wishes to get the very best masters for her school (*car Zoraïde fait tout comme une reine, c'est une véritable maîtresse-femme*),* she has commissioned me to step over this afternoon and sound Madame Pelet as to the possibility of engaging you. Zoraïde is a wary general; she never advances without first examining well her ground. I don't think she would be pleased if she knew I had already disclosed her intentions to you; she did not order me to go so far, but I thought there would be no harm in letting you into the secret, and Madame Pelet was of the same opinion. Take care, however, you don't betray either of us to Zoraïde – to my daughter, I mean – she is so discreet and circumspect herself she cannot understand that one should find pleasure in gossiping a little—"

"*C'est absolument comme mon fils!*"* cried Madame Pelet.

"All the world is so changed since our girlhood!" rejoined the other. "Young people have such old heads now. But to return, monsieur. Madame Pelet will mention the subject of your giving lessons in my daughter's establishment to her son, and he will speak to you; and then tomorrow you will step over to our house and ask to see my daughter, and you will introduce the subject as if the first intimation of it had reached you from M. Pelet himself, and be sure you never mention my name, for I would not displease Zoraïde on any account."

"*Bien! Bien!*" interrupted I – for all this chatter and circumlocution began to bore me very much. "I will consult M. Pelet, and the thing shall be settled as you desire. Good evening, *mesdames* – I am infinitely obliged to you."

"*Comment! Vous vous en allez déjà?*"* exclaimed Madame Pelet.

"*Prenez encore quelque chose, monsieur; une pomme cuite, des biscuits, encore une tasse de café?*"*

"*Merci, merci, madame – au revoir.*" And I backed at last out of the apartment.

Having regained my own room, I set myself to turn over in my mind the incident of the evening. It seemed a queer affair altogether, and queerly managed; the two old women had made quite a little intricate mess of it. Still, I found that the uppermost feeling in my mind on the subject was one of satisfaction. In the first place, it would be a change to give lessons in another seminary, and then to teach young ladies would be an occupation so interesting – to be admitted at all into a ladies' boarding school would be an incident so new in my life. "Besides," thought I, as I glanced at the boarded window, "I shall now at last see the mysterious garden: I shall gaze both on the angels and their Eden."

Chapter 9

M. PELET COULD NOT OF COURSE OBJECT to the proposal made by Mlle Reuter; permission to accept such additional employment, should it offer, having formed an article of the terms on which he had engaged me. It was, therefore, arranged in the course of the next day that I should be at liberty to give lessons in Mlle Reuter's establishment four afternoons in every week.

When evening came, I prepared to step over in order to seek a conference with Mademoiselle herself on the subject; I had not had time to pay the visit before, having been all day closely occupied in class. I remember very well that before quitting my chamber, I held a brief debate with myself as to whether I should change my ordinary attire for something smarter. At last I concluded it would be a waste of labour. "Doubtless," thought I, "she is some stiff old maid; for though the daughter of Madame Reuter, she may well number upwards of forty winters; besides, if it were otherwise, if she be both young and pretty, I am not handsome, and no dressing can make me so, therefore I'll go as I am." And off I started, cursorily glancing sideways as I passed the toilet table, surmounted by a looking glass: a thin irregular face I saw, with sunk, dark eyes under a large, square forehead, complexion destitute of bloom or attraction; something young, but not youthful, no object to win a lady's love, no butt for the shafts of Cupid.

I was soon at the entrance of the *pensionnat*; in a moment I had pulled the bell; in another moment the door was opened, and within appeared a passage paved alternately with black and white marble; the walls were painted in imitation of marble also; and at the far end opened a glass door, through which I saw shrubs and grass-plat, looking pleasant in the sunshine of the mild spring evening – for it was now the middle of April.

This, then, was my first glimpse of *the* garden; but I had not time to look long: the portress, after having answered in the affirmative my question as to whether her mistress was at home, opened the folding doors of a room to the left and, having ushered me in, closed them behind me. I found myself in a salon with a very well-painted, highly varnished floor; chairs and sofas covered with white draperies, a green porcelain stove, walls hung with pictures in gilt frames, a gilt pendule* and other ornaments on the mantelpiece, a large lustre pendent from the centre of the ceiling, mirrors, consoles, muslin curtains and a handsome centre table completed the inventory of furniture. All looked extremely clean and glittering, but the general effect would have been somewhat chilling had not a second large pair of folding doors, standing wide open – and disclosing another and smaller salon, more snugly furnished – offered some relief to the eye. This room was carpeted, and therein was a piano, a couch, a *chiffonnière** – above all, it contained a lofty window with a crimson curtain, which, being undrawn, afforded another glimpse of the garden through the large, clear panes, round which some leaves of ivy, some tendrils of vine were trained.

"*Monsieur Creemsvort, n'est-ce pas?*"* said a voice behind me; and, starting involuntarily, I turned. I had been so taken up with the contemplation of the pretty little salon that I had not noticed the entrance of a person into the larger room. It was, however, Mlle Reuter who now addressed me and stood close beside me; and when I had bowed with instantaneously recovered sangfroid – for I am not easily embarrassed – I commenced the conversation by remarking on the pleasant aspect of her little cabinet, and the advantage she had over M. Pelet in possessing a garden.

Yes, she said, she often thought so, and added, "It is my garden, monsieur, which makes me retain this house; otherwise, I should probably have removed to larger and more commodious premises long since; but you see I could not take my garden with me, and I should scarcely find one so large and pleasant anywhere else in town."

I approved her judgement.

"But you have not seen it yet," said she, rising. "Come to the window and take a better view." I followed her; she opened the sash, and leaning out I saw in full the enclosed demesne which had hitherto been to me an unknown region. It was a long, not very broad strip of cultured ground, with an alley bordered by enormous old fruit trees down the middle; there was a sort of lawn, a parterre of rose trees, some flower borders and, on the far side, a thickly planted copse of lilacs, laburnums and acacias. It looked pleasant, to me – very pleasant, so long a time had elapsed since I had seen a garden of any sort. But it was not only on Mlle Reuter's garden that my eyes dwelt; when I had taken a view of her well-trimmed beds and budding shrubberies, I allowed my glance to come back to herself, nor did I hastily withdraw it.

I had thought to see a tall, meagre, yellow, conventual image in black, with a close white cap, bandaged under the chin like a nun's headgear; whereas there stood by me a little and roundly formed woman who might indeed be older than I, but was still young; she could not, I thought, be more than six-or seven-and-twenty; she was as fair as a fair Englishwoman; she had no cap; her hair was nut-brown, and she wore it in curls; pretty her features were not, nor very soft, nor very regular, but neither were they in any degree plain, and I already saw cause to deem them expressive. What was their predominant cast? Was it sagacity? Sense? Yes, I thought so, but I could scarcely as yet be sure. I discovered, however, that there was a certain serenity of eye and freshness of complexion, most pleasing to behold. The colour on her cheek was like the bloom on a good apple, which is as sound at the core as it is red on the rind.

Mlle Reuter and I entered upon business. She said she was not absolutely certain of the wisdom of the step she was about to take, because I was so young, and parents might possibly object to a professor like me for their daughters: "But it is often well to act on one's own judgement," said she, "and to lead parents, rather than be led by them. The fitness of a professor is not a matter of age; and, from what I have heard, and from what I observe myself, I would much rather trust you than M. Ledru, the music master, who is a married man of near fifty."

I remarked that I hoped she would find me worthy of her good opinion; that if I knew myself, I was incapable of betraying any confidence reposed in me. "*Du reste*,"* said she, "the surveillance will be strictly attended to." And then she proceeded to discuss the subject of terms. She was very cautious, quite on her guard; she did not absolutely bargain, but she warily sounded me to find out what my expectations might be; and when she could not get me to name a sum, she reasoned and reasoned with a fluent yet quiet circumlocution of speech, and at last nailed me down to five hundred francs per annum – not too much, but I agreed. Before the negotiation was completed, it began to grow a little dusk. I did not hasten it, for I liked well enough to sit and hear her talk. I was amused with the sort of business talent she displayed. Edward could not have shown himself more practical, though he might have evinced more coarseness and urgency; and then she had so many reasons, so many explanations; and, after all, she succeeded in proving herself quite disinterested and even liberal. At last she concluded, she could say no more, because, as I acquiesced in all things, there was no further ground for the exercise of her parts of speech. I was obliged to rise. I would rather have sat a little longer; what had I to return to but my small empty room? And my eyes had a pleasure in looking at Mlle Reuter, especially now, when the twilight softened her features a little and, in the doubtful dusk, I could fancy her forehead as open as it was really elevated, her mouth touched with turns of sweetness as well as defined in lines of sense. When I rose to go, I held out my hand, on purpose, though I knew it was contrary to the etiquette of foreign habits; she smiled, and said,

"*Ah! C'est comme tous les Anglais,*"* but gave me her hand very kindly.

"It is the privilege of my country, mademoiselle," said I, "and, remember, I shall always claim it."

She laughed a little, quite good-naturedly, and with the sort of tranquillity obvious in all she did – a tranquillity which soothed and suited me singularly, at least I thought so that evening. Brussels seemed a very pleasant place to me when I got out again into the street, and it appeared as if some cheerful, eventful, upward-tending career were even then opening to me on that selfsame mild, still April night. So impressionable a being is man, or at least such a man as I was in those days.

Chapter 10

NEXT DAY, THE MORNING HOURS SEEMED TO PASS very slowly at M. Pelet's. I wanted the afternoon to come, that I might go again to the neighbouring *pensionnat* and give my first lesson within its pleasant precincts; for pleasant they appeared to me. At noon the hour of recreation arrived; at one o'clock we had lunch; this got on the time, and at last Sainte-Gudule's deep bell, tolling slowly two, marked the moment for which I had been waiting.

At the foot of the narrow backstairs that descended from my room, I met M. Pelet.

"*Comme vous avez l'air rayonnant!*" said he. "*Je ne vous ai jamais vu aussi gai. Que s'est-il donc passé?*"*

"*Apparemment que j'aime les changements,*"* replied I.

"*Ah! Je comprends – c'est cela – soyez sage seulement. Vous êtes bien jeune – trop jeune pour le rôle que vous allez jouer; il faut prendre garde – savez-vous?*"*

"*Mais quel danger y a-t-il?*"*

"*Je n'en sais rien – ne vous laissez pas aller à de vives impressions – voilà tout.*"*

I laughed: a sentiment of exquisite pleasure played over my nerves at the thought that "*vives impressions*" were likely to be created; it was the deadness, the sameness of life's daily ongoings that had hitherto been my bane; my blouse-clad élèves in the boys' seminary never stirred in me any "*vives impressions*", except it might be occasionally some of anger. I broke from M. Pelet and, as I strode down the passage, he followed me with one of his laughs – a very French, rakish, mocking sound.

Again I stood at the neighbouring door, and soon was readmitted into the cheerful passage with its clear dove-colour, imitation-marble walls. I followed the portress and, descending a step and making a turn, I found myself in a sort of corridor; a side door opened: Mlle

Reuter's little figure, as graceful as it was plump, appeared. I could now see her dress in full daylight: a neat, simple *mousseline-de-laine** gown fitted her compact round shape to perfection – delicate little collar and *manchettes** of lace, trim Parisian *brodequins** showed her neck, wrists and feet to complete advantage; but how grave was her face as she came suddenly upon me! Solicitude and business were in her eye – on her forehead; she looked almost stern. Her "*Bonjour, monsieur*" was quite polite, but so orderly, so commonplace, it spread directly a cool, damp towel over my "*vives impressions*". The servant turned back when her mistress appeared, and I walked slowly along the corridor, side by side with Mlle Reuter.

"Monsieur will give a lesson in the first class today," said she. "Dictation or reading will perhaps be the best thing to begin with, for those are the easiest forms of communicating instruction in a foreign language; and, at the first, a master naturally feels a little unsettled."

She was quite right, as I had found from experience. It only remained for me to acquiesce. We proceeded now in silence. The corridor terminated in a hall – large, lofty and square; a glass door on one side showed within a long, narrow refectory, with tables, an armoire and two lamps; it was empty; large glass doors, in front, opened on the playground and garden; a broad staircase ascended spirally on the opposite side; the remaining wall showed a pair of great folding doors, now closed, and admitting, doubtless, to the classes.

Mlle Reuter turned her eye laterally on me, to ascertain, probably, whether I was collected enough to be ushered into her *sanctum sanctorum.** I suppose she judged me to be in a tolerable state of self-government, for she opened the door, and I followed her through. A rustling sound of uprising greeted our entrance; without looking to the right or left, I walked straight up the lane between two sets of benches and desks, and took possession of the empty chair and isolated desk raised on an *estrade,** of one step high, so as to command one division; the other division being under the surveillance of a *maîtresse* similarly elevated. At the back of the *estrade*, and attached to a movable partition dividing this schoolroom from another beyond, was a large tableau of wood painted black and varnished; a thick crayon of white chalk lay on my desk for the convenience of elucidating any grammatical or verbal obscurity which might occur in my lessons by writing it upon the tableau; a wet sponge appeared beside the chalk, to enable me to efface the marks when they had served the purpose intended.

I carefully and deliberately made these observations before allowing myself to take one glance at the benches before me. Having handled the crayon, looked back at the tableau, fingered the sponge in order to ascertain that it was in a right state of moisture, I found myself cool enough to admit of looking calmly up and gazing deliberately round me.

At first I observed that Mlle Reuter had already glided away; she was nowhere visible. A *maîtresse* or teacher, the one who occupied the corresponding *estrade* to my own, alone remained to keep guard over me; she was a little in the shade, and, with my short sight, I could only see that she was of a thin, bony figure and rather tallowy complexion, and that her attitude, as she sat, partook equally of listlessness and affectation. More obvious, more prominent, shone on by the full light of the large window, were the occupants of the benches just before me, of whom some were girls of fourteen, fifteen, sixteen, some young women from eighteen (as it appeared to me) up to twenty; the most modest attire, the simplest fashion of wearing the hair, were apparent in all; and good features , ruddy, blooming complexions, large and brilliant eyes, forms full, even to solidity, seemed to abound. I did not bear the first view like a stoic: I was dazzled; my eyes fell and in a voice somewhat low I murmured:

"*Prenez vos cahiers de dictée, mesdemoiselles.*"*

Not so had I bid the boys at Pelet's take their reading books. A rustle followed, and an opening of desks; behind the lifted lids which momentarily screened the heads bent down to search for exercise books, I heard tittering and whispers.

"*Eulalie, je suis prête à pâmer de rire,*"* observed one.

"*Comme il a rougi en parlant!*"*

"*Oui, c'est un véritable blanc-bec.*"*

"*Tais-toi, Hortense – il nous écoute.*"*

And now the lids sank and the heads reappeared; I had marked three, the whisperers, and I did not scruple to take a very steady look at them as they emerged from their temporary eclipse. It is astonishing what ease and courage their little phrases of flippancy had given me; the idea by which I had been awed was that the youthful beings before me, with their dark nun-like robes and softly braided hair, were a kind of half-angels. The light titter, the giddy whisper, had already in some measure relieved my mind of that fond and oppressive fancy.

The three I allude to were just in front, within half a yard of my *estrade*, and were among the most womanly-looking present. Their names I knew afterwards, and may as well mention now; they were Eulalie, Hortense, Caroline. Eulalie was tall, and very finely shaped: she was fair, and her features were those of a Low Country Madonna; many a *figure de Vierge** have I seen in Dutch pictures exactly resembling hers; there were no angles in her shape or in her face, all was curve and roundness – neither thought, sentiment nor passion disturbed by line or flush the equality of her pale, clear skin; her noble bust heaved with her regular breathing, her eyes moved a little – by these evidences of life alone could I have distinguished her from some large handsome figure moulded in wax. Hortense was of middle size and stout; her form was ungraceful, her face striking, more alive and brilliant than Eulalie's; her hair was dark brown, her complexion richly coloured; there were frolic and mischief in her eye: consistency and good sense she might possess, but none of her features betokened those qualities.

Caroline was little, though evidently full grown; raven-black hair, very dark eyes, absolutely regular features, with a colourless olive complexion, clear as to the face and sallow about the neck, formed in her that assemblage of points whose union many persons regard as the perfection of beauty. How, with the tintless pallor of her skin and the classic straightness of her lineaments, she managed to look sensual, I don't know. I think her lips and eyes contrived the affair between them, and the result left no uncertainty on the beholder's mind. She was sensual now, and in ten years' time she would be coarse – promise plain was written in her face of much future folly.

If I looked at these girls with little scruple, they looked at me with still less. Eulalie raised her unmoved eye to mine, and seemed to expect, passively but securely, an impromptu tribute to her majestic charms. Hortense regarded me boldly, and giggled at the same time, while she said, with an air of impudent freedom:

"*Dictez-nous quelque chose de facile pour commencer, monsieur.*"*

Caroline shook her loose ringlets of abundant but somewhat coarse hair over her rolling black eyes; parting her lips, as full as those of a hot-blooded Maroon, she showed her well-set teeth sparkling between them, and treated me at the same time to a smile *de sa façon.**

Beautiful as Pauline Borghese,* she looked at the moment scarcely purer than Lucrèce de Borgia.* Caroline was of noble family. I heard her lady mother's character afterwards, and then I ceased to wonder at the precocious accomplishments of the daughter. These three, I at once saw, deemed themselves the queens of the school, and conceived that by their splendour they threw all the rest into the shade. In less than five minutes, they had thus revealed to me their characters, and in less than five minutes I had buckled on a breastplate of steely indifference, and let down a visor of impassable austerity.

"Take your pens and commence writing," said I, in as dry and trite a voice as if I had been addressing only Jules Vanderkelkov and Co.

The *dictée* now commenced. My three belles interrupted me perpetually with little silly questions and uncalled-for remarks, to some of which I made no answer, and to others replied very quietly and briefly.

"*Comment dit-on point et virgule en Anglais, monsieur?*"*

"Semicolon, mademoiselle."

"*Simi-collong? Ah, comme c'est drôle!*"* (giggle).

"*J'ai une si mauvaise plume – impossible d'écrire!*"*

"*Mais, monsieur – je ne sais pas suivre – vous allez si vite.*"*

"*Je n'ai rien compris, moi!*"*

Here a general murmur arose, and the teacher, opening her lips for the first time, ejaculated:

"*Silence, mesdemoiselles!*"

No silence followed – on the contrary, the three ladies in front began to talk more loudly.

"*C'est si difficile, l'Anglais!*"*

"*Je déteste la dictée.*"*

"*Quel ennui d'écrire quelque chose que l'on ne comprend pas!*"*

Some of those behind laughed: a degree of confusion began to pervade the class; it was necessary to take prompt measures.

"*Donnez-moi votre cahier,*"* said I to Eulalie in an abrupt tone; and, bending over, I took it before she had time to give it.

"*Et vous, mademoiselle – donnez-moi le vôtre,*"* continued I, more mildly, addressing a little pale, plain-looking girl who sat in the first row of the other division, and whom I had remarked as being at once the ugliest and the most attentive in the room. She rose up, walked over to me and delivered her book with a grave, modest curtsy. I glanced over the two dictations; Eulalie's was slurred, blotted and full of silly mistakes – Sylvie's (such was the name of the ugly little girl) was clearly written; it contained no error against sense, and but few faults of orthography. I coolly read aloud both exercises, marking the faults – then I looked at Eulalie.

"*C'est honteux!*"* said I, and I deliberately tore her dictation in four parts, and presented her with the fragments. I returned Sylvie her book with a smile, saying,

"*C'est bien – je suis content de vous.*"*

Sylvie looked calmly pleased; Eulalie swelled like an incensed turkey, but the mutiny was quelled: the conceited coquetry and futile flirtation of the first bench were exchanged for a taciturn sullenness, much more convenient to me, and the rest of my lesson passed without interruption.

A bell clanging out in the yard announced the moment for the cessation of school labours. I heard our own bell at the same time, and that of a certain public college immediately after. Order dissolved instantly; up started every pupil; I hastened to seize my hat, bow to the *maîtresse* and quit the room before the tide of *externats* should pour from the inner class, where I knew near a hundred were prisoned, and whose rising tumult I already heard.

I had scarcely crossed the hall and gained the corridor, when Mlle Reuter came again upon me.

"Step in here a moment," said she, and she held open the door of the side room from whence she had issued on my arrival; it was a *salle à manger,** as appeared from the *beaufet* and the *armoire vitrée,** filled with glass and china, which formed part of its furniture. Ere she had closed the doors on me and herself, the corridor was already filled with day pupils, tearing down their cloaks, bonnets and *cabas** from the wooden pegs on which they were suspended; the shrill voice of a *maîtresse* was heard at intervals vainly endeavouring to enforce some sort of order; vainly, I say: discipline there was none in these rough ranks, and yet this was considered one of the best-conducted schools in Brussels.

"Well, you have given your first lesson," began Mlle Reuter in the most calm, equable voice, as though quite unconscious of the chaos from which we were separated only by a single wall. "Were you satisfied with your pupils, or did any circumstance in their conduct give you cause for complaint? Conceal nothing from me; repose in me entire confidence."

Happily, I felt in myself complete power to manage my pupils without aid; the enchantment, the golden haze which had dazzled my perspicacity at first, had been a good deal dissipated. I cannot say I was chagrined or downcast by the contrast which the reality of a *pensionnat de demoiselles* presented to my vague ideal of the same community; I was only enlightened and amused; consequently, I felt in no disposition to complain to Mlle Reuter, and I received her considerate invitation to confidence with a smile.

"A thousand thanks, mademoiselle, all has gone very smoothly."

She looked more than doubtful.

"*Et les trois demoiselles du premier banc?*"* said she.

"*Ah! Tout va au mieux!*"* was my answer, and Mlle Reuter ceased to question me; but her eye – not large, not brilliant, not melting or kindling, but astute, penetrating, practical – showed she was even with me; it let out a momentary gleam, which said plainly, "Be as close as you like – I am not dependent on your candour; what you would conceal I already know."

By a transition so quiet as to be scarcely perceptible, the directress's manner changed; the anxious business air passed from her face, and she began chatting about the weather and the town, and asking in neighbourly wise after M. and Madame Pelet. I answered all her little questions; she prolonged her talk; I went on following its many little windings; she sat so long, said so much, varied so often the topics of discourse, that it was not difficult to perceive she had a particular aim in thus detaining me. Her mere words could have afforded no clue to this aim, but her countenance aided; while her lips uttered only affable commonplaces, her eyes reverted continually to my face.

Her glances were not given in full, but out of the corners, so quietly, so stealthily, yet I think I lost not one. I watched her as keenly as she watched me; I perceived soon that she was feeling after my real character; she was searching for salient points and weak points, and eccentric points; she was applying now this test, now that, hoping in the end to find some chink, some niche, where she could put in her little firm foot and stand upon my neck – mistress of my nature. Do not mistake me, reader, it was no amorous influence she wished to gain – at that time it was only the power of the politician to which she aspired; I was now installed as a professor in her establishment, and she wanted to know where her mind was superior to mine – by what feeling or opinion she could lead me.

I enjoyed the game much, and did not hasten its conclusion; sometimes I gave her hopes, beginning a sentence rather weakly, when her shrewd eye would light up – she thought she had me; having led her a little way, I delighted to turn round and finish with sound, hard sense, whereat her countenance would fall. At last a servant entered to announce dinner; the conflict being thus necessarily terminated, we parted without having gained any advantage on either side: Mlle Reuter had not even given me an opportunity of attacking her with feeling, and I had managed to baffle her little schemes of craft. It was a regular drawn battle. I again held out my hand when I left the room; she gave me hers: it was a small and white hand, but how cool! I met her eye too in full – obliging her to give me a straightforward look; this last test went against me: it left her as it found her – moderate, temperate, tranquil; me it disappointed.

"I am growing wiser," thought I, as I walked back to M. Pelet's. "Look at this little real woman; is she like the women of novelists and romancers? To read of female character as depicted in poetry and fiction, one would think it was made up of sentiment, either for good or bad – here is a specimen, and a most sensible and respectable specimen, too, whose staple ingredient is abstract reason. No Talleyrand* was ever more passionless than Zoraïde Reuter!" So I thought then; I found afterwards that blunt susceptibilities are very consistent with strong propensities.

Chapter 11

I HAD INDEED HAD A VERY LONG TALK with the crafty little politician, and on regaining my quarters I found that dinner was half over. To be late at meals was against a standing rule of the establishment and, had it been one of the Flemish ushers who thus entered after the removal of the soup and the commencement of the first course, M. Pelet would probably have greeted him with a public rebuke, and would certainly have mulcted him both of soup and fish; as it was, that polite though partial gentleman only shook his head, and as I took my place, unrolled my napkin and said my heretical grace to myself, he civilly dispatched a servant to the kitchen, to bring me a plate of *purée aux carottes* (for this was a maigre day),* and before sending away the first course, reserved for me a portion of the stockfish of which it consisted. Dinner being over, the boys rushed out for their evening play; Kint and Vandam (the two ushers) of course followed them. Poor fellows! If they had not looked so very heavy, so very soulless, so very indifferent to all things in heaven above or in the earth beneath, I could have pitied them greatly for the obligation they were under to trail after those rough lads everywhere and at all times; even as it was, I felt disposed to scout myself as a privileged prig when I turned to ascend to my chamber, sure to find there, if not enjoyment, at least liberty; but this evening (as had often happened before) I was to be still further distinguished.

"*Eh bien, mauvais sujet!*" said the voice of M. Pelet behind me, as I set my foot on the first step of the stair. "*Où allez-vous? Venez à la salle-à-manger, que je vous gronde un peu.*"*

"I beg pardon, monsieur," said I, as I followed him to his private sitting room, "for having returned so late – it was not my fault."

"That is just what I want to know," rejoined M. Pelet, as he ushered me into the comfortable parlour with a good wood fire – for the stove had now been removed for the season. Having rung the bell he ordered "Coffee for two", and presently he and I were seated, almost in English comfort, one on each side of the hearth, a little round table between us, with a coffee pot, a sugar basin and two large white china cups. While M. Pelet employed himself in choosing a cigar from a box, my thoughts reverted to the two outcast ushers, whose voices I could hear even now crying hoarsely for order in the playground.

"*C'est une grande responsabilité, que la surveillance,*"* observed I.

"*Plaît-il?*"* dit M. Pelet.

I remarked that I thought Messieurs Vandam and Kint must sometimes be a little fatigued with their labours.

"*Des bêtes de somme – des bêtes de somme,*"* murmured scornfully the director. Meantime I offered him his cup of coffee.

"*Servez-vous, mon garçon,*"* said he blandly, when I had put a couple of huge lumps of Contintental sugar into his cup. "And now tell me why you stayed so long at Mlle Reuter's. I know that lessons conclude, in her establishment as in mine, at four o'clock, and when you returned it was past five."

"Mademoiselle wished to speak with me, monsieur."

"Indeed! On what subject? If one may ask."

"Mademoiselle talked about nothing, monsieur."

"A fertile topic! And did she discourse thereon in the schoolroom, before the pupils?"

"No; like you, monsieur, she asked me to walk into her parlour."

"And Madame Reuter – the old duenna – my mother's gossip, was there, of course?"

"No, monsieur; I had the honour of being quite alone with mademoiselle."

"*C'est joli – cela,*"* observed M. Pelet, and he smiled and looked into the fire.

"*Honi soit qui mal y pense,*"* murmured I, significantly.

"*Je connais un peu ma petite voisine – voyez-vous?*"*

"In that case, monsieur will be able to aid me in finding out what was mademoiselle's reason for making me sit before her sofa one mortal hour, listening to the most copious and fluent dissertation on the merest frivolities."

"She was sounding your character."

"I thought so, monsieur."

CHAPTER II

"Did she find out your weak point?"

"What is my weak point?"

"Why, the sentimental. Any woman sinking her shaft deep enough will at last reach a fathomless spring of sensibility in thy breast, Crimsworth."

I felt the blood stir about my heart and rise warm to my cheek.

"Some women might, monsieur."

"Is Mlle Reuter of the number? Come, speak frankly, *mon fils*; *elle est encore jeune, plus âgée que toi peut-être, mais juste assez pour unir la tendresse d'une petite maman à l'amour d'une épouse dévouée; n'est-ce pas que cela t'irait supérieurement?*"*

"No, monsieur; I should like my wife to be my wife, and not my half-mother."

"She is then a little too old for you?"

"No, monsieur, not a day too old if she suited me in other things."

"In what does she not suit you, William? She is personally agreeable, is she not?"

"Very; her hair and complexion are just what I admire; and her turn of form, though quite Belgian, is full of grace."

"Bravo! And her face? Her features? How do you like them?"

"A little harsh, especially her mouth."

"Ah, yes! Her mouth," said M. Pelet, and he chuckled inwardly. "There is character about her mouth – firmness – but she has a very pleasant smile; don't you think so?"

"Rather crafty."

"True, but that expression of craft is owing to her eyebrows; have you remarked her eyebrows?"

I answered that I had not.

"You have not seen her looking down then?" said he.

"No."

"It is a treat, notwithstanding. Observe her when she has some knitting, or some other woman's work in hand, and sits the image of peace, calmly intent on her needles and her silk, some discussion meantime going on around her, in the course of which peculiarities of character are being developed, or important interests canvassed; she takes no part in it; her humble, feminine mind is wholly with her knitting; none of her features move; she neither presumes to smile approval, nor frown disapprobation; her little hands assiduously ply their unpretending task; if she can only get this purse finished, or this *bonnet-grec** completed, it is enough for her. If gentlemen approach her chair, a deeper quiescence, a meeker modesty settles on her features and clothes her general mien; observe then her eyebrows, *et dîtes-moi s'il n'y a pas du chat dans l'un et du renard dans l'autre.*"*

"I will take careful notice the first opportunity," said I.

"And then," continued M. Pelet, "the eyelid will flicker, the light-coloured lashes be lifted a second, and a blue eye, glancing out from under the screen, will take its brief, sly, searching survey, and retreat again."

I smiled, and so did Pelet, and after a few minutes' silence, I asked:

"Will she ever marry, do you think?"

"Marry! Will birds pair? Of course it is both her intention and resolution to marry when she finds a suitable match; and no one is better aware than herself of the sort of impression she is capable of producing; no one likes better to captivate in a quiet way. I am mistaken if she will not yet leave the print of her stealing steps on thy heart, Crimsworth."

"Of her steps? Confound it, no! My heart is not a plank to be walked on."

"But the soft touch of a *patte de velours** will do it no harm."

"She offers me no *patte de velours*; she is all form and reserve with me."

"That to begin with; let respect be the foundation, affection the first floor, love the superstructure; Mlle Reuter is a skilful architect."

"And interest, M. Pelet – interest? Will not mademoiselle consider that point?"

"Yes, yes, no doubt; it will be the cement between every stone. And now we have discussed the directress, what of the pupils? *N'y a-t-il pas de belles études parmi ces jeunes têtes?*"*

"Studies of character? Yes; curious ones, at least, I imagine; but one cannot divine much from a first interview."

"Ah, you affect discretion; but tell me, now, were you not a little abashed before those blooming young creatures?"

CHAPTER 11

"At first, yes, but I rallied and got through with all due sangfroid."

"I don't believe you."

"It is true, notwithstanding. At first I thought them angels, but they did not leave me long under that delusion; three of the eldest and handsomest undertook the task of setting me right, and they managed so cleverly that in five minutes I knew *them*, at least, for what they were – three arrant coquettes."

"*Je les connais!*" exclaimed M. Pelet. "*Elles sont toujours au premier rang à l'église et à la promenade; une blonde superbe, une jolie espiègle, une belle brune.*"*

"Exactly."

"Lovely creatures, all of them – heads for artists; what a group they would make, taken together! Eulalie (I know their names), with her smooth braided hair and calm ivory brow. Hortense, with her rich chestnut locks so luxuriantly knotted, plaited, twisted, as if she did not know how to dispose of all their abundance, with her vermilion lips, damask cheek and roguish, laughing eye. And Caroline de Blémont! Ah, there is beauty! Beauty in perfection. What a cloud of sable curls about the face of a houri! What fascinating lips! What glorious black eyes! Your Byron would have worshipped her, and you – you cold, frigid islander! You played the austere, the insensible in the presence of an Aphrodite so exquisite?"

I might have laughed at the director's enthusiasm had I believed it real, but there was something in his tone which indicated got-up raptures. I felt he was only affecting fervour in order to put me off my guard, to induce me to come out in return, so I scarcely even smiled. He went on:

"Confess, William, do not the mere good looks of Zoraïde Reuter appear dowdyish and commonplace compared with the splendid charms of some of her pupils?"

The question discomposed me, but I now felt plainly that my principal was endeavouring (for reasons best-known to himself – at that time I could not fathom them) to excite ideas and wishes in my mind alien to what was right and honourable. The iniquity of the instigation proved its antidote, and when he further added,

"Each of those three beautiful girls will have a handsome fortune; and with a little address, a gentlemanlike, intelligent young fellow like you might make himself master of the hand, heart and purse of any one of the trio."

I replied by a look and an interrogative "Monsieur?" which startled him.

He laughed a forced laugh, affirmed that he had only been joking and demanded whether I could possibly have thought him in earnest. Just then the bell rang; the play hour was over; it was an evening on which M. Pelet was accustomed to read passages from the drama and the belles-lettres to his pupils. He did not wait for my answer but, rising, left the room, humming as he went some gay strain of Béranger's.*

Chapter 12

D AILY, AS I CONTINUED MY ATTENDANCE at the seminary
of Mlle Reuter, did I find fresh occasions to compare the ideal
with the real. What had I known of female character previously to
my arrival at Brussels? Precious little. And what was my notion of it?
Something vague, slight, gauzy, glittering; now when I came in contact
with it I found it to be a palpable substance enough; very hard, too,
sometimes, and often heavy; there was metal in it, both lead and iron.

Let the idealists, the dreamers about earthly angels and human
flowers, just look here while I open my portfolio and show them
a sketch or two, pencilled after nature. I took these sketches in the
second-class schoolroom of Mlle Reuter's establishment, where
about a hundred specimens of the genus *jeune fille* collected together
offered a fertile variety of subject. A miscellaneous assortment they
were, differing both in caste and country: as I sat on my *estrade* and
glanced over the long range of desks, I had under my eye French,
English, Belgians, Austrians and Prussians. The majority belonged
to the class bourgeois; but there were many countesses, there were
the daughters of two generals and of several colonels, captains and
government *employés*; these ladies sat side by side with young females
destined to be *demoiselles de magasins*,* and with some *Flamandes*,
genuine aborigines of the country. In dress all were nearly similar, and
in manners there was small difference; exceptions there were to the
general rule, but the majority gave the tone to the establishment, and
that tone was rough, boisterous, marked by a point-blank disregard of
all forbearance towards each other or their teachers; an eager pursuit
by each individual of her own interest and convenience; and a coarse
indifference to the interest and convenience of everyone else. Most of
them could lie with audacity when it appeared advantageous to do so.
All understood the art of speaking fair when a point was to be gained,
and could with consummate skill and at a moment's notice turn the

cold shoulder the instant civility ceased to be profitable. Very little open quarrelling ever took place amongst them, but backbiting and tale-bearing were universal. Close friendships were forbidden by the rules of the school, and no one girl seemed to cultivate more regard for another than was just necessary to secure a companion when solitude would have been irksome. They were each and all supposed to have been reared in utter unconsciousness of vice. The precautions used to keep them ignorant, if not innocent, were innumerable. How was it, then, that scarcely one of those girls having attained the age of fourteen could look a man in the face with modesty and propriety? An air of bold, impudent flirtation, or a loose, silly leer, was sure to answer the most ordinary glance from a masculine eye. I know nothing of the arcana of the Roman Catholic religion, and I am not a bigot in matters of theology, but I suspect the root of this precocious impurity, so obvious, so general in popish countries, is to be found in the discipline, if not the doctrines, of the Church of Rome. I record what I have seen: these girls belonged to what are called the respectable ranks of society; they had all been carefully brought up, yet was the mass of them mentally depraved. So much for the general view: now for one or two selected specimens.

The first picture is a full-length of Aurelia Koslow, a German Fräulein, or rather a half-breed between German and Russian. She is eighteen years of age, and has been sent to Brussels to finish her education; she is of middle size, stiffly made, body long, legs short, bust much developed but not compactly moulded, waist disproportionately compressed by an inhumanly braced corset, dress carefully arranged, large feet tortured into small *bottines*,* head small, hair smoothed, braided, oiled and gummed to perfection; very low forehead, very diminutive and vindictive grey eyes, somewhat Tartar features, rather flat nose, rather high cheekbones – yet the ensemble not positively ugly; tolerably good complexion. So much for person. As to mind, deplorably ignorant and ill-informed; incapable of writing or speaking correctly even German, her native tongue; a dunce in French, and her attempts at learning English a mere farce, yet she has been at school twelve years; but as she invariably gets her exercises, of every description, done by a fellow pupil, and reads her lessons off a book concealed in her lap, it is not wonderful that her progress has been so snail-like. I do not know what Aurelia's daily habits of life are, because I have not the opportunity of observing her at all times; but from what I see of the state of her desk, books and papers, I should say she is slovenly and even dirty; her outward dress, as I have said, is well attended to, but in passing behind her bench I have remarked that her neck is grey for want of washing, and her hair, so glossy with gum and grease, is not such as one feels tempted to pass the hand over, much less to run the fingers through. Aurelia's conduct in class, at least when I am present, is something extraordinary, considered as an index of girlish innocence. The moment I enter the room, she nudges her next neighbour and indulges in a half-suppressed laugh. As I take my seat on the *estrade*, she fixes her eye on me; she seems resolved to attract and, if possible, monopolize my notice: to this end she launches at me all sorts of looks – languishing, provoking, leering, laughing. As I am found quite proof against this sort of artillery – for we scorn what, unasked, is lavishly offered – she has recourse to the expedient of making noises; sometimes she sighs, sometimes groans, sometimes utters inarticulate sounds for which language has no name. If, in walking up the schoolroom, I pass near her, she puts out her foot that it may touch mine; if I do not happen to observe the manoeuvre, and my boot comes in contact with her *brodequin*, she affects to fall into convulsions of suppressed laughter; if I notice the snare and avoid it, she expresses her mortification in sullen muttering, where I hear myself abused in bad French pronounced with an intolerable Low-German accent.

Not far from Mlle Koslow sits another young lady by name Adèle Dronsart: this is a Belgian, rather low of stature, in form heavy, with broad waist, short neck and limbs, good red-and-white complexion, features well-chiselled and regular, well-cut eyes of a clear brown colour, light-brown hair, good teeth, age not much above fifteen, but as full grown as a stout young Englishwoman of twenty. This portrait gives the idea of a somewhat dumpy but good-looking damsel, does it not? Well, when I looked along the row of young heads, my eye generally stopped at this of Adèle's; her gaze was ever waiting for mine, and it frequently succeeded in arresting it. She was an unnatural-looking being – so young, fresh, blooming, yet so Gorgon-like. Suspicion, sullen ill temper were on her forehead, vicious propensities in her eye, envy and panther-like deceit about her mouth. In general she sat very still; her massive shape looked as if it could not bend much, nor did her large head – so broad at the base, so narrow towards the top – seem made to turn readily on her short neck. She had but two varieties of expression: the prevalent one a forbidding, dissatisfied scowl, varied sometimes by a most pernicious and perfidious smile. She was shunned by her fellow pupils, for, bad as many of them were, few were as bad as she.

Aurelia and Adèle were in the first division of the second class; the second division was headed by a *pensionnaire* named Juanna Trista. This girl was of mixed Belgian and Spanish origin; her Flemish mother was dead, her Catalonian father was a merchant residing in the — Isles, where Juanna had been born and whence she was sent to Europe to be educated. I wonder that anyone, looking at the girl's head and countenance, would have received her under their roof. She had precisely the same shape of skull as Pope Alexander the Sixth;* her organs of benevolence, veneration, conscientiousness, adhesiveness, were singularly small; those of self-esteem, firmness, destructiveness, combativeness, preposterously large; her head sloped up in the penthouse shape, was contracted about the forehead, and prominent behind; she had rather good, though large and marked features; her temperament was fibrous and bilious, her complexion pale and dark, hair and eyes black, form angular and rigid but proportionate, age fifteen.

Juanna was not very thin, but she had a gaunt visage, and her *regard* was fierce and hungry; narrow as was her brow, it presented space enough for the legible graving of two words: Mutiny and Hate; in some one of her other lineaments – I think the eye – cowardice had also its distinct cipher. Mlle Trista thought fit to trouble my first lessons with a coarse workday sort of turbulence; she made noises with her mouth like a horse, she ejected her saliva, she uttered brutal expressions; behind and below her were seated a band of very vulgar, inferior-looking *Flamandes*, including two or three examples of that deformity of person and imbecility of intellect whose frequency in the Low Countries would seem to furnish proof that the climate is such as to induce degeneracy of the human mind and body; these, I soon found, were completely under her influence, and with their aid she got up and sustained a swinish tumult, which I was constrained at last to quell by ordering her and two of her tools to rise from their seats and, having kept them standing five minutes, turning them bodily out of the schoolroom – the accomplices into a large place adjoining called the *grande salle*; the principal into a cabinet, of which I closed the door and pocketed the key. This judgement I executed in the presence of Mlle Reuter, who looked much aghast at beholding so decided a proceeding – the most severe that had ever been ventured on in her establishment. Her look of affright I answered with one of composure, and finally with a smile, which perhaps flattered and certainly soothed her. Juanna Trista remained in Europe long enough to repay, by malevolence and ingratitude, all who had ever done her a good turn; and she then went to join her father in the — Isles, exulting in the thought that she should there have slaves – whom, as she said, she could kick and strike at will.

These three pictures are from the life. I possess others, as marked and as little agreeable, but I will spare my reader the exhibition of them.

Doubtless it will be thought that I ought now, by way of contrast, to show something charming – some gentle virgin head, circled with a halo, some sweet personification of innocence, clasping the dove of peace to her bosom. No: I saw nothing of the sort, and therefore cannot portray it. The pupil in the school possessing the happiest disposition was a young girl from the country, Louise Path; she was sufficiently benevolent and obliging, but not well taught nor well mannered; moreover, the plague spot of dissimulation was in her also; honour and principle were unknown to her: she had scarcely heard their names. The least exceptionable pupil was the poor little Sylvie I have mentioned once before. Sylvie was gentle in manners, intelligent in mind; she was even sincere, as far as her religion would permit her to be so, but her physical organization was defective; weak health stunted her growth and chilled her spirits, and then, destined as she was for the cloister, her whole soul was warped to a conventual bias, and in the tame, trained subjection of her manner, one read that she had already prepared herself for her future course of life by giving up her independence of thought and action into the hands of some despotic confessor. She permitted

herself no original opinion, no preference of companion or employment; in everything she was guided by another. With a pale, passive,
automaton air, she went about all day long doing what she was
bid; never what she liked, or what, from innate conviction, she
thought it right to do. The poor little future *religieuse* had been
early taught to make the dictates of her own reason and conscience
quite subordinate to the will of her spiritual director. She was the
model pupil of Mlle Reuter's establishment: pale, blighted image,
where life lingered feebly, but whence the soul had been conjured
by Romish wizard-craft!

A few English pupils there were in this school, and these might be
divided into two classes: first, the Continental English – the daughters
chiefly of broken adventurers, whom debt or dishonour had driven
from their own country. These poor girls had never known the
advantages of settled homes, decorous example or honest Protestant
education; resident a few months now in one Catholic school now
in another, as their parents wandered from land to land – from
France to Germany, from Germany to Belgium – they had picked
up some scanty instruction, many bad habits, losing every notion
even of the first elements of religion and morals, and acquiring an
imbecile indifference to every sentiment that can elevate humanity;
they were distinguishable by a habitual look of sullen dejection, the
result of crushed self-respect and constant browbeating from their
popish fellow pupils, who hated them as English and scorned them
as heretics.

The second class were British English. Of these I did not
encounter half a dozen during the whole time of my attendance at the seminary; their characteristics were clean but careless dress, ill-arranged hair (compared with the tight and trim
foreigners), erect carriage, flexible figures, white and taper hands,
features more irregular, but also more intellectual than those of
the Belgians, grave and modest countenances, a general air of
native propriety and decency; by this last circumstance alone I
could at a glance distinguish the daughter of Albion and nursling
of Protestantism from the foster-child of Rome, the *protégée* of
Jesuitry: proud, too, was the aspect of these British girls; at once
envied and ridiculed by their Continental associates, they warded

off insult with austere civility, and met hate with mute disdain; they eschewed company-keeping, and in the midst of numbers seemed to dwell isolated.

The teachers presiding over this mixed multitude were three in number, all French – their names, Mlles Zéphyrine, Pélagie and Suzette; the two last were commonplace personages enough; their look was ordinary, their manner was ordinary, their temper was ordinary, their thoughts, feelings and views were all ordinary – were I to write a chapter on the subject, I could not elucidate it further. Zéphyrine was somewhat more distinguished in appearance and deportment than Pélagie and Suzette, but in character a genuine Parisian coquette – perfidious, mercenary and dry-hearted. A fourth *maîtresse* I sometimes saw who seemed to come daily to teach needle-work, or netting, or lace-mending, or some such flimsy art; but of her I never had more than a passing glimpse, as she sat in the *carré* with her frames and some dozen of the elder pupils about her; consequently I had no opportunity of studying her character, or even of observing her person much; the latter, I remarked, had a very girlish air for a *maîtresse*, otherwise it was not striking; of character I should think she possessed but little, as her pupils seemed constantly *en révolte* against her authority. She did not reside in the house; her name, I think, was Mlle Henri.

Amidst this assemblage of all that was insignificant and defective, much that was vicious and repulsive (by that last epithet many would have described the two or three stiff, silent, decently behaved, ill-dressed British girls), the sensible, sagacious, affable directress shone like a steady star over a marsh full of Jack-o'-lanthorns;* profoundly aware of her superiority, she derived an inward bliss from that consciousness which sustained her under all the care and responsibility inseparable from her position; it kept her temper calm, her brow smooth, her manner tranquil. She liked – as who would not? – on entering the schoolroom, to feel that her sole presence sufficed to diffuse that order and quiet which all the remonstrances, and even commands, of her underlings frequently failed to enforce; she liked to stand in comparison, or rather contrast, with those who surrounded her, and to know that in personal as well as mental advantages, she bore away the undisputed palm of preference – the three teachers were all plain. Her pupils she managed with such indulgence and address, taking always on herself the office of recompenser and eulogist, and abandoning to her subalterns every invidious task of blame and punishment, that they all regarded her with deference, if not with affection; her teachers did not love her, but they submitted because they were her inferiors in everything; the various masters who attended her school were each and all in some way or other under her influence: over one she had acquired power by her skilful management of his bad temper; over another by little attentions to his petty caprices; a third she had subdued by flattery; a fourth – a timid man – she kept in awe by a sort of austere decision of mien; me, she still watched, still tried by the most ingenious tests – she roved round me, baffled, yet persevering. I believe she thought I was like a smooth and bare precipice, which offered neither jutting stone nor tree root, nor tuft of grass to aid the climber. Now she flattered with exquisite tact, now she moralized, now she tried how far I was accessible to mercenary motives, then she disported on the brink of affection – knowing that some men are won by weakness – anon, she talked excellent sense, aware that others have the folly to admire judgement. I found it at once pleasant and easy to evade all these efforts; it was sweet, when she thought me nearly won, to turn round and to smile in her very eyes, half scornfully, and then to witness her scarcely veiled, though mute mortification. Still she persevered, and at last, I am bound to confess it, her finger, essaying, proving every atom of the casket, touched its secret spring, and for a moment the lid sprung open; she laid her hand on the jewel within; whether she stole and broke it, or whether the lid shut again with a snap on her fingers, read on, and you shall know.

It happened that I came one day to give a lesson when I was indisposed; I had a bad cold and a cough; two hours' incessant talking left me very hoarse and tired. As I quitted the schoolroom, and was passing along the corridor, I met Mlle Reuter; she remarked, with an anxious air, that I looked very pale and tired. "Yes," I said, "I was fatigued." And then, with increased interest, she rejoined, "You shall not go away till you have had some refreshment." She persuaded me to step into the parlour, and was very kind and gentle while I stayed. The next day she was kinder still; she came herself into the class to see that the windows were closed and that there was no draught; she exhorted me with friendly earnestness not to overexert myself; when I went away, she gave me her hand unasked, and I could not but mark, by a respectful and gentle pressure, that I was sensible of the favour, and grateful for it. My modest demonstration kindled a little merry smile on her countenance; I thought her almost charming. During the remainder of the evening, my mind was full of impatience for the afternoon of the next day to arrive, that I might see her again.

I was not disappointed, for she sat in the class during the whole of my subsequent lesson, and often looked at me almost with affection. At four o'clock she accompanied me out of the schoolroom, asking with solicitude after my health, then scolding me sweetly because I spoke too loud and gave myself too much trouble; I stopped at the glass door which led into the garden to hear her lecture to the end; the door was open, it was a very fine day, and while I listened to the soothing reprimand, I looked at the sunshine and flowers and felt very happy. The day scholars began to pour from the schoolrooms into the passage.

"Will you go into the garden a minute or two," asked she, "till they are gone?"

I descended the steps without answering, but I looked back as much as to say,

"You will come with me?"

In another minute I and the directress were walking side by side down the alley bordered with fruit trees, whose white blossoms were then in full blow as well as their tender green leaves. The sky was blue, the air still, the May afternoon was full of brightness and fragrance. Released from the stifling class, surrounded with flowers and foliage, with a pleasing, smiling, affable woman at my side – how did I feel? Why, very enviably. It seemed as if the romantic visions my imagination had suggested of this garden, while it was yet hidden from me by the jealous boards, were more than realized; and, when a turn in the alley shut out the view of the house, and some tall shrubs excluded M. Pelet's mansion and screened us momentarily from the other houses, rising amphitheatre-like round this green spot, I gave my arm to Mlle Reuter and led her to a garden chair, nestled under some lilacs near. She sat down; I took my place at her side. She went on talking to me with that ease which communicates ease, and, as I listened, a revelation dawned in my mind that I was on the brink of falling in love. The dinner bell rang, both at her house and M. Pelet's; we were obliged to part; I detained her a moment as she was moving away.

"I want something," said I.

"What?" asked Zoraïde naively.

"Only a flower."

"Gather it then – or two, or twenty, if you like."

"No – one will do – but you must gather it and give it to me."

"What a caprice!" she exclaimed, but she raised herself on her tiptoes and, plucking a beautiful branch of lilac, offered it to me with grace. I took it and went away, satisfied for the present, and hopeful for the future.

Certainly that May day was a lovely one, and it closed in moonlight night of summer warmth and serenity. I remember this well; for, having sat up late that evening correcting *devoirs*, and feeling weary and a little oppressed with the closeness of my small room, I opened the often-mentioned boarded window, whose boards, however, I had persuaded old Madame Pelet to have removed since I had filled the post of professor in the *pensionnat de demoiselles* – as, from that time, it was no longer "*inconvenant*"* for me to overlook my own pupils at their sports. I sat down in the window seat, rested my arm on the sill and leant out: above me was the clear-obscure of a cloudless night sky – splendid moonlight subdued the tremulous sparkle of the stars – below lay the garden, varied with silvery lustre and deep shade, and all fresh with dew – a grateful perfume exhaled from the closed blossoms of the fruit trees – not a leaf stirred, the night was breezeless. My window looked directly down upon a certain walk of Mlle Reuter's garden called *l'allée défendue** – so named because the pupils were forbidden to enter it on account of its proximity to the boys' school. It was here that the lilacs and laburnums grew especially thick; this was the most sheltered nook in the enclosure; its shrubs screened the garden chair where that afternoon I had sat with the young directress. I need not say that my thoughts were chiefly with her as I leant from the lattice and let my eye roam, now over the walks and borders of the garden, now along the many-windowed front of the house which rose white beyond the masses of foliage. I wondered in what part of the building was situated her apartment; and a single light, shining through the persiennes* of one *croisée*, seemed to direct me to it.

"She watches late," thought I, "for it must be now near midnight. She is a fascinating little woman," I continued in voiceless soliloquy. "Her image forms a pleasant picture in memory; I know she is not what the world calls pretty – no matter, there is harmony in her aspect, and I like it; her brown hair, her blue eye, the freshness of her cheek, the whiteness of her neck, all suit my taste. Then I respect her talent; the idea of marrying a doll or a fool was always abhorrent to me: I know that a pretty doll, a fair fool, might do well enough for the honeymoon; but when passion cooled, how dreadful to find a lump of wax and wood laid in my bosom, a half idiot clasped in my arms, and to remember that I had made of this my equal – nay, my idol – to know that I must pass the rest of my dreary life with a creature incapable of understanding what I said, of appreciating what I thought or of sympathizing with what I felt! Now, Zoraïde Reuter," thought I, "has tact, *caractère*, judgement, discretion; has she heart? What a good, simple little smile played about her lips when she gave me the branch of lilacs! I have thought her crafty, dissembling, interested sometimes, it is true; but may not much that looks like cunning and dissimulation in her conduct be only the efforts made by a bland temper to traverse quietly perplexing difficulties? And as to interest, she wishes to make her way in the world, no doubt, and who can blame her? Even if she be truly deficient in sound principle, is it not rather her misfortune than her fault? She has been brought up a Catholic: had she been born an Englishwoman and reared a Protestant, might she not have added straight integrity to all her other excellences? Supposing she were to marry an English and Protestant husband, would she not – rational, sensible as she is – quickly acknowledge the superiority of right over expediency, honesty over policy? It would be worth a man's while to try the experiment; tomorrow I will renew my observations. She knows that I watch her: how calm she *is* under scrutiny! It seems rather to gratify than annoy her." Here a strain of music stole in upon my monologue and suspended it; it was a bugle, very skilfully played, in the neighbourhood of the park, I thought, or on the Place Royale. So sweet were the tones, so subduing their effect at that hour, in the midst of silence and under the quiet reign of moonlight, I ceased to think, that I might listen more intently. The strain retreated, its sound waxed fainter and was soon gone; my ear prepared to repose on the absolute hush of midnight once more. No. What murmur was that which, low, and yet near and approaching nearer, frustrated the expectation of total silence? It was someone conversing – yes, evidently, an audible though subdued voice spoke in the garden immediately below me. Another answered: the first voice was that of a man, the second that of a woman; and a man and a woman I saw coming slowly down the alley. Their forms were at first in shade: I could but discern a dusk outline of each, but a ray of moonlight met them at the termination of the walk, when they were under my very nose, and revealed very plainly, very unequivocally, Mlle Zoraïde Reuter, arm in arm, or hand in hand (I forget which), with my principal, confidant and counsellor, M. François Pelet. And M. Pelet was saying:

"*A quand donc le jour des noces, ma bien-aimée?*"*

And Mlle Reuter answered:

"*Mais, François, tu sais bien qu'il me serait impossible de me marier avant les vacances.*"*

"June, July, August, a whole quarter!" exclaimed the director. "How can I wait so long? I who am ready, even now, to expire at your feet with impatience!"

"Ah! If you die, the whole affair will be settled without any trouble about notaries and contracts; I shall only have to order a slight mourning dress, which will be much sooner prepared than the nuptial trousseau."

"Cruel Zoraïde! You laugh at the distress of one who loves you so devotedly as I do: my torment is your sport; you scruple not to stretch my soul on the rack of jealousy; for, deny it as you will, I am certain you have cast encouraging glances on that schoolboy Crimsworth; he has presumed to fall in love, which he dared not have done unless you had given him room to hope."

"What do you say, François? Do you say Crimsworth is in love with me?"

"Over head and ears."

"Has he told you so?"

"No – but I see it in his face: he blushes whenever your name is mentioned."

A little laugh of exulting coquetry announced Mlle Reuter's gratification of this piece of intelligence (which was a lie, by the by – I had never been so far gone as that, after all). M. Pelet proceeded to ask . what she intended to do with me, intimating pretty plainly, and not very gallantly, that it was nonsense for her to think of taking such a *blanc-bec* as a husband, since she must be at least ten years older than I (was she then thirty-two? I should not have thought it). I heard her disclaim any intentions on the subject – the director, however, still pressed her to give a definite answer.

"François," said she, "you are jealous," and still she laughed. Then, as if suddenly recollecting that this coquetry was not consistent with the character for modest dignity she wished to establish, she proceeded in a demure voice: "Truly, my dear François, I will not deny that this young Englishman may have made some attempts to ingratiate himself with me; but, so far from giving him any encouragement, I have always treated him with as much reserve as it was possible to combine with civility; affianced as I am to you, I would give no man false hopes; believe me, dear friend."

Still Pelet uttered murmurs of distrust – so I judged, at least, from her reply.

"What folly! How could I prefer an unknown foreigner to you? And then – not to flatter your vanity – Crimsworth could not bear comparison with you either physically or mentally; he is not a handsome man at all; some may call him gentlemanlike and intelligent-looking, but for my part—"

The rest of the sentence was lost in the distance, as the pair, rising from the chair in which they had been seated, moved away. I waited their return, but soon the opening and shutting of a door informed me that they had re-entered the house; I listened a little longer: all was perfectly still; I listened more than an hour – at last I heard M. Pelet come in and ascend to his chamber. Glancing once more towards the long front of the garden house, I perceived that its solitary light was at length extinguished; so, for a time, was my faith in love and friendship. I went to bed, but something feverish and fiery had got into my veins, which prevented me from sleeping much that night.

Chapter 13

NEXT MORNING I ROSE WITH THE DAWN and, having dressed myself and stood half an hour, my elbow leaning on the chest of drawers, considering what means I should adopt to restore my spirits, fagged with sleeplessness, to their ordinary tone – for I had no intention of getting up a scene with M. Pelet, reproaching him with perfidy, sending him a challenge or performing other gambadoes* of the sort – I hit at last on the expedient of walking out in the cool of the morning to a neighbouring establishment of baths and treating myself to a bracing plunge. The remedy produced the desired effect. I came back at seven o'clock steadied and invigorated, and was able to greet M. Pelet, when he entered to breakfast, with an unchanged and tranquil countenance; even a cordial offering of the hand and the flattering appellation of "*mon fils*", pronounced in that caressing tone with which Monsieur had, of late days especially, been accustomed to address me, did not elicit any external sign of the feeling which, though subdued, still glowed at my heart. Not that I nursed vengeance – no; but the sense of insult and treachery lived in me like a kindling, though as yet smothered coal. God knows I am not by nature vindictive; I would not hurt a man because I can no longer trust or like him; but neither my reason nor feelings are of the vacillating order – they are not of that sand-like sort where impressions, if soon made, are as soon effaced. Once convinced that my friend's disposition is incompatible with my own, once assured that he is indelibly stained with certain defects obnoxious to my principles, and I dissolve the connection. I did so with Edward. As to Pelet, the discovery was yet new; should I act thus with him? It was the question I placed before my mind as I stirred my cup of coffee with a half-*pistolet** (we never had spoons), Pelet meantime being seated opposite, his pallid face looking as knowing and more haggard than usual, his blue eye turned now sternly on his boys and ushers and now graciously on me.

"Circumstances must guide me," said I; and meeting Pelet's false glance and insinuating smile, I thanked Heaven that I had last night opened my window and read by the light of a full moon the true meaning of that guileful countenance. I felt half his master, because the reality of his nature was now known to me; smile and flatter as he would, I saw his soul lurk behind his smile, and heard in every one of his smooth phrases a voice interpreting their treacherous import.

But Zoraïde Reuter? Of course her defection had cut me to the quick? That sting must have gone too deep for any consolations of philosophy to be available in curing its smart? Not at all. The night fever over, I looked about for balm to that wound also, and found some nearer home than at Gilead.* Reason was my physician; she began by proving that the prize I had missed was of little value: she admitted that, physically, Zoraïde might have suited me, but affirmed that our souls were not in harmony, and that discord must have resulted from the union of her mind with mine. She then insisted on the suppression of all repining, and commanded me rather to rejoice that I had escaped a snare. Her medicament did me good. I felt its strengthening effect when I met the directress the next day; its stringent operation on the nerves suffered no trembling, no faltering; it enabled me to face her with firmness, to pass her with ease. She had held out her hand to me – that I did not choose to see. She had greeted me with a charming smile – it fell on my heart like light on stone. I passed on to the *estrade*, she followed me; her eye, fastened on my face, demanded of every feature the meaning of my changed and careless manner. "I will give her an answer," thought I; and, meeting her gaze full, arresting, fixing her glance, I shot into her eyes, from my own, a look where there was no respect, no love, no tenderness, no gallantry; where the strictest analysis could detect nothing but scorn, hardihood, irony. I made her bear it, and feel it; her steady countenance did not change, but her colour rose, and she approached me as if fascinated. She stepped onto the *estrade* and stood close by my side; she had nothing to say. I would not relieve her embarrassment, and negligently turned over the leaves of a book.

"I hope you feel quite recovered today," at last she said, in a low tone.

"And I, mademoiselle, hope that you took no cold last night in consequence of your late walk in the garden."

Quick enough of comprehension, she understood me directly; her face became a little blanched – a very little – but no muscle in her rather marked features moved; and, calm and self-possessed, she retired from the *estrade*, taking her seat quietly at a little distance, and occupying herself with netting a purse. I proceeded to give my lesson; it was a "Composition", i.e. I dictated certain general questions, of which the pupils were to compose the answers from memory, access to books being forbidden. While Mlle Eulalie, Hortense, Caroline, etc., were pondering over the string of rather abstruse grammatical interrogatories I had propounded, I was at liberty to employ the vacant half-hour in further observing the directress herself. The green silk purse was progressing fast in her hands; her eyes were bent upon it; her attitude, as she sat netting within two yards of me, was still yet guarded; in her whole person were expressed at once, and with equal clearness, vigilance and repose – a rare union! Looking at her, I was forced, as I had often been before, to offer her good sense, her wondrous self-control, the tribute of involuntary admiration. She had felt that I had withdrawn from her my esteem; she had seen contempt and coldness in my eye – and to her, who coveted the approbation of all around her, who thirsted after universal good opinion, such discovery must have been an acute wound. I had witnessed its effect in the momentary pallor of her cheek – cheek unused to vary; yet how quickly, by dint of self-control, had she recovered her composure! With what quiet dignity she now sat, almost at my side, sustained by her sound and vigorous sense – no trembling in her somewhat lengthened, though shrewd upper lip, no coward shame on her austere forehead!

"There is metal there," I said, as I gazed. "Would that there were fire also, living ardour to make the steel glow – then I could love her."

Presently I discovered that she knew I was watching her, for she stirred not, she lifted not her crafty eyelid; she but glanced down from her netting to her small foot, peeping from the soft folds of her purple merino gown; thence her eye reverted to her hand, ivory-white, with a bright garnet ring on the forefinger and a light frill of lace round the wrist; with a scarcely perceptible movement she turned her head, causing her nut-brown curls to wave gracefully. In these slight signs I read that the wish of her heart, the design of her brain, was to lure back the game she had scared. A little incident gave her the opportunity of addressing me again.

While all was silence in the class – silence but for the rustling of copybooks and the travelling of pens over their pages – a leaf of the large folding door, opening from the hall, unclosed, admitting a pupil who, after making a hasty obeisance, ensconced herself with some appearance of trepidation, probably occasioned by her entering so late, in a vacant seat at the desk nearest the door. Being seated, she proceeded, still with an air of hurry and embarrassment, to open her *cabas*, to take out her books; and, while I was waiting for her to look up, in order to make out her identity – for, short-sighted as I was, I had not recognized her at her entrance – Mlle Reuter, leaving her chair, approached the *estrade*.

"Monsieur Creemsvort," she said, in a whisper – for when the schoolrooms were silent, the directress always moved with velvet tread and spoke in the most subdued key, enforcing order and stillness fully as much by example as by precept – "Monsieur Creemsvort, that young person who has just entered wishes to have the advantage of taking lessons with you in English; she is not a pupil of the house; she is, indeed, in one sense, a teacher, for she gives instruction in lace-mending, and in little varieties of ornamental needlework. She very properly proposes to qualify herself for a higher department of education, and has asked permission to attend your lessons, in order to perfect her knowledge of English, in which language she has, I believe, already made some progress; of course it is my wish to aid her in an effort so praiseworthy; you will permit her, then, to benefit by your instruction – *n'est-ce pas, monsieur?*" And Mlle Reuter's eyes were raised to mine with a look at once naive, benign and beseeching.

I replied, "Of course," very laconically, almost abruptly.

"Another word," she said, with softness. "Mlle Henri has not received a regular education; perhaps her natural talents are not of the highest order, but I can assure you of the excellence of her intentions, and even of the amiability of her disposition. Monsieur will then, I am sure, have the goodness to be considerate with her at first, and not expose her backwardness, her inevitable deficiencies, before the young ladies, who, in a sense, are her pupils. Will Monsieur Creemsvort favour me by attending to this hint?" I nodded. She continued with subdued earnestness:

"Pardon me, monsieur, if I venture to add that what I have just said is of importance to the poor girl; she already experiences great difficulty in impressing these giddy young things with a due degree of deference for her authority, and should that difficulty be increased by new discoveries of her incapacity, she might find her position in my establishment too painful to be retained – a circumstance I should much regret for her sake, as she can ill afford to lose the profits of her occupation here."

Mlle Reuter possessed marvellous tact; but tact the most exquisite, unsupported by sincerity, will sometimes fail of its effect; thus, on this occasion, the longer she preached about the necessity of being indulgent to the governess-pupil, the more impatient I felt as I listened. I discerned so clearly that while her professed motive was a wish to aid the dull, though well-meaning Mlle Henri, her real one was no other than a design to impress me with an idea of her own exalted goodness and tender considerateness; so having again hastily nodded assent to her remarks, I obviated their renewal by suddenly demanding the compositions, in a sharp accent, and, stepping from the *estrade*, I proceeded to collect them. As I passed the governess-pupil, I said to her:

"You have come in too late to receive a lesson today; try to be more punctual next time."

I was behind her, and could not read in her face the effect of my not very civil speech. Probably I should not have troubled myself to do so, had I been full in front; but I observed that she immediately began to slip her books into her *cabas* again; and, presently, after I had returned to the *estrade*, while I was arranging the mass of compositions, I heard the folding door again open and close; and, on looking up, I perceived her place vacant. I thought to myself, "She will consider her first attempt at taking a lesson in English something of a failure" – and I wondered whether she had departed in the sulks, or whether stupidity had induced her to take my words too literally – or, finally, whether my irritable tone had wounded her feelings. The last notion I dismissed almost as soon as I had conceived it, for not having seen any appearance of sensitiveness in any human face since my arrival in Belgium, I had begun to regard it almost as a fabulous quality. Whether her physiognomy announced it I could not tell, for her speedy exit had allowed me no time to ascertain the circumstance. I had, indeed, on two or three previous occasions, caught a passing view of her (as I believe has been mentioned before); but I never stopped to scrutinize either her face or person, and had but the most vague idea of her general appearance. Just as I had finished rolling up the compositions, the four o'clock bell rang; with my accustomed alertness in obeying that signal, I grasped my hat and evacuated the premises.

Chapter 14

I F I WAS PUNCTUAL IN QUITTING Mlle Reuter's domicile, I was at least equally punctual in arriving there; I came the next day at five minutes before two, and on reaching the schoolroom door, before I opened it, I heard a rapid, gabbling sound, which warned me that the *prière du midi** was not yet concluded. I waited the termination thereof; it would have been impious to intrude my heretical presence during its progress. How the repeater of the prayer did cackle and splutter! I never before or since heard language enounced with such steam-engine haste. "*Notre Père qui êtes au ciel*" went off like a shot; then followed an address to Marie "*vierge céleste, reine des anges, maison d'or, tour d'ivoire!*"* and then an invocation to the saint of the day; and then down they all sat, and the solemn (?) rite was over; and I entered, flinging the door wide and striding in fast, as it was my wont to do now; for I had found that in entering with aplomb, and mounting the *estrade* with emphasis, consisted the grand secret of ensuring immediate silence. The folding doors between the two classes, opened for the prayer, were instantly closed; a *maîtresse*, work-box in hand, took her seat at her appropriate desk; the pupils sat still with their pens and books before them; my three beauties in the van, now well-humbled by a demeanour of consistent cool- ness, sat erect with their hands folded quietly on their knees; they had given up giggling and whispering to each other, and no longer ventured to utter pert speeches in my presence; they now only talked to me occasionally with their eyes, by means of which organs they could still, however, say very audacious and coquettish things. Had affection, goodness, modesty, real talent ever employed those bright orbs as interpreters, I do not think I could have refrained from giving a kind and encouraging, perhaps an ardent reply now and then; but as it was, I found pleasure in answering the glance of vanity with the gaze of stoicism. Youthful, fair, brilliant as were many of my pupils,

I can truly say that in me they never saw any other bearing than such as an austere, though just, guardian might have observed towards them. If any doubt the accuracy of this assertion, as inferring more conscientious self-denial or Scipio-like self-control* than they feel disposed to give me credit for, let them take into consideration the following circumstances, which, while detracting from my merit, justify my veracity.

Know, O incredulous reader! that a master stands in a somewhat different relation towards a pretty, light-headed, probably ignorant girl to that occupied by a partner at a ball, or a gallant on the promenade. A professor does not meet his pupil to see her dressed in satin and muslin, with hair perfumed and curled, neck scarcely shaded by aerial lace, round white arms circled with bracelets, feet dressed for the gliding dance. It is not his business to whirl her through the waltz, to feed her with compliments, to heighten her beauty by the flush of gratified vanity. Neither does he encounter her on the smooth-rolled, tree-shaded boulevard, in the green and sunny park, whither she repairs clad in her becoming walking dress, her scarf thrown with grace over her shoulders, her little bonnet scarcely screening her curls, the red rose under its brim adding a new tint to the softer rose on her cheek; her face and eyes, too, illumined with smiles, perhaps as transient as the sunshine of the gala day, but also quite as brilliant; it is not his office to walk by her side, to listen to her lively chat, to carry her parasol, scarcely larger than a broad green leaf, to lead in a ribbon her Blenheim spaniel or Italian greyhound. No: he finds her in the schoolroom, plainly dressed, with books before her. Owing to her education or her nature, books are to her a nuisance, and she opens them with aversion, yet her teacher must instil into her mind the contents of these books; that mind resists the admission of grave information, it recoils, it grows restive, sullen tempers are shown, disfiguring frowns spoil the symmetry of the face, sometimes coarse gestures banish grace from the deportment, while muttered expressions, redolent of native and ineradicable vulgarity, desecrate the sweetness of the voice. Where the temperament is serene, though the intellect be sluggish, an unconquerable dullness opposes every effort to instruct. Where there is cunning but not energy, dissimulation, falsehood, a thousand schemes and tricks are put in play to evade the necessity of application; in short, to the tutor, female youth, female charms are like tapestry hangings of which the wrong side is continually turned towards him; and even when he sees the smooth, neat external surface, he so well knows what knots, long stitches and jagged ends are behind that he has scarce a temptation to admire too fondly the seemly forms and bright colours exposed to general view.

Our likings are regulated by our circumstances. The artist prefers a hilly country because it is picturesque; the engineer a flat one because it is convenient; the man of pleasure likes what he calls "a fine woman" – she suits him; the fashionable young gentleman admires the fashionable young lady – she is of his kind; the toil-worn, fagged, probably irritable tutor, blind almost to beauty, insensible to airs and graces, glories chiefly in certain mental qualities: application, love of knowledge, natural capacity, docility, truthfulness, gratefulness are the charms that attract his notice and win his regard. These he seeks, but seldom meets; these, if by chance he finds, he would fain retain for ever, and when separation deprives him of them, he feels as if some ruthless hand had snatched from him his only ewe lamb.* Such being the case, and the case it is, my readers will agree with me that there was nothing either very meritorious or very marvellous in the integrity and moderation of my conduct at Mlle Reuter's *pensionnat de demoiselles*.

My first business this afternoon consisted in reading the list of places for the month, determined by the relative correctness of the compositions given the preceding day. The list was headed, as usual, by the name of Sylvie, that plain, quiet little girl I have described before as being at once the best and ugliest pupil in the establishment; the second place had fallen to the lot of a certain Léonie Ledru, a diminutive, sharp-featured and parchment-skinned creature of quick wits, frail conscience and indurated feelings; a lawyer-like thing, of whom I used to say that, had she been a boy, she would have made a model of an unprincipled, clever attorney. Then came Eulalie, the proud beauty, the Juno of the school, whom six long years of drilling in the simple grammar of the English language had compelled, despite the stiff phlegm of her intellect, to acquire a mechanical acquaintance with most of its rules. No smile, no trace of pleasure or satisfaction appeared in Sylvie's nun-like passive face as she heard her name read first. I always felt saddened by the sight of that poor girl's absolute quiescence on all occasions, and it was my custom to look at her, to address her, as seldom as possible; her extreme docility, her assiduous perseverance would have recommended her warmly to my good opinion; her modesty, her intelligence would have induced me to feel most kindly – most affectionately towards her, notwithstanding the almost ghastly plainness of her features, the disproportion of her form, the corpse-like lack of animation in her countenance, had I not been aware that every friendly word, every kindly action, would be reported by her to her confessor, and by him misinterpreted and poisoned. Once I laid my hand on her head, in token of approbation; I thought Sylvie was going to smile: her dim eye almost kindled; but, presently, she shrank from me; I was a man and a heretic; she, poor child! a destined nun and devoted Catholic; thus a fourfold wall of separation divided her mind from mine. A pert smirk, and a hard glance of triumph, was Léonie's method of testifying her gratification; Eulalie looked sullen and envious – she had hoped to be first. Hortense and Caroline exchanged a reckless grimace on hearing their names read out somewhere near the bottom of the list; the brand of mental inferiority was considered by them as no disgrace, their hopes for the future being based solely on their personal attractions.

This affair arranged, the regular lesson followed. During a brief interval, employed by the pupils in ruling their books, my eye, ranging carelessly over the benches, observed, for the first time, that the farthest seat in the farthest row – a seat usually vacant – was again filled by the new scholar, the Mlle Henri so ostentatiously recommended to me by the directress. Today I had on my spectacles; her appearance, therefore, was clear to me at the first glance; I had not to puzzle over it. She looked young; yet, had I been required to name her exact age, I should have been somewhat nonplussed; the slightness of her figure might have suited seventeen; a certain anxious and preoccupied expression of face seemed the indication of riper years. She was dressed, like all the rest, in a dark stuff gown and a white collar; her features were dissimilar to any there: not so rounded, more defined, yet scarcely regular. The shape of her head too was different: the superior part more developed, the base considerably less. I felt assured, at first sight, that she was not a Belgian; her complexion, her countenance, her lineaments, her figure, were all distinct from theirs and, evidently, the type of another race – of a race less gifted with fullness of flesh and plenitude of blood; less jocund, material, unthinking. When I first cast my eyes on her, she sat looking fixedly down, her chin resting on her hand, and she did not change her attitude till I commenced the lesson. None of the Belgian girls would have retained one position, and that a reflective one, for the same length of time. Yet, having intimated that her appearance was peculiar, as being unlike that of her Flemish companions, I have little more to say respecting it; I can pronounce no encomiums on her beauty, for she was not beautiful; nor offer condolence on her plainness, for neither was she plain; a careworn character of forehead, and a corresponding moulding of the mouth, struck me with a sentiment resembling surprise, but these traits would probably have passed unnoticed by any less crotchety observer.

Now, reader, though I have spent more than a page in describing Mlle Henri, I know well enough that I have left on your mind's eye no distinct picture of her; I have not painted her complexion, nor her eyes, nor her hair, nor even drawn the outline of her shape. You cannot tell whether her nose was aquiline or retroussé, whether her chin was long or short, her face square or oval; nor could I the first day, and it is not my intention to communicate to you at once a knowledge I myself gained by little and little.

I gave a short exercise, which they all wrote down. I saw the new pupil was puzzled at first with the novelty of the form and language; once or twice she looked at me with a sort of painful solicitude, as not comprehending at all what I meant; then she was not ready when the others were, she could not write her phrases so fast as they did; I would not help her, I went on relentless. She looked at me; her eye said most plainly, "I cannot follow you." I disregarded the appeal, and, carelessly leaning back in my chair, glancing from time to time with a nonchalant air out of the window, I dictated a little faster. On looking towards her again, I perceived her face clouded with embarrassment, but she was still writing on most diligently; I paused a few seconds; she employed the interval in hurriedly re-perusing what she had written, and shame and discomfiture were apparent in her countenance; she evidently found she had made great nonsense of it. In ten minutes more, the dictation was complete and, having allowed a brief space in which to correct it, I took their books; it was with a reluctant hand Mlle Henri gave up hers, but, having once yielded it to my possession, she composed her anxious face, as if, for the present, she had resolved to dismiss regret and had made up her mind to be thought unprecedentedly stupid. Glancing over her exercises, I found that several lines had been omitted, but what was written contained very few faults; I instantly inscribed "*Bon*" at the bottom of the page and returned it to her; she smiled, at first incredulously, then as if reassured, but did not lift her eyes; she could look at me, it seemed, when perplexed and bewildered, but not when gratified; I thought that scarcely fair.

Chapter 15

S OME TIME ELAPSED BEFORE I AGAIN gave a lesson in the first
class; the holiday of Whitsuntide occupied three days, and on the
fourth it was the turn of the second division to receive my instructions. As I made the transit of the *carré* I observed, as usual, the band
of sewers surrounding Mlle Henri; there were only about a dozen
of them, but they made as much noise as might have sufficed for
fifty; they seemed very little under her control; three or four at once
assailed her with importunate requirements; she looked harassed;
she demanded silence, but in vain. She saw me, and I read in her
eye pain that a stranger should witness the insubordination of her
pupils; she seemed to entreat order – her prayers were useless; then I
remarked that she compressed her lips and contracted her brow; and
her countenance, if I read it correctly, said: "I have done my best; I
seem to merit blame notwithstanding; blame me then who will." I
passed on; as I closed the schoolroom door, I heard her say, suddenly
and sharply, addressing one of the eldest and most turbulent of the lot:
"Améba Müllenberg, ask me no question, and request of me no
assistance, for a week to come; during that space of time I will neither
speak to you nor help you."

The words were uttered with emphasis – nay, with vehemence – and
a comparative silence followed; whether the calm was permanent, I
know not; two doors now closed between me and the *carré*.

Next day was appropriated to the first class; on my arrival I found
the directress seated, as usual, in a chair between the two *estrades*,
and before her was standing Mlle Henri, in an attitude (as it seemed
to me) of somewhat reluctant attention. The directress was knitting
and talking at the same time. Amidst the hum of a large schoolroom,
it was easy so to speak in the ear of one person as to be heard by that
person alone, and it was thus Mlle Reuter parleyed with her teacher.
The face of the latter was a little flushed, not a little troubled; there

was vexation in it, whence resulting I know not, for the directress looked very placid indeed; she could not be scolding in such gentle whispers and with so equable a mien: no, it was presently proved that her discourse had been of the most friendly tendency, for I heard the closing words:

"*C'est assez, ma bonne amie; à present je ne veux pas vous retenir davantage.*"*

Without reply, Mlle Henri turned away; dissatisfaction was plainly evinced in her face, and a smile – slight and brief, but bitter, distrustful and, I thought, scornful – curled her lip as she took her place in the class; it was a secret, involuntary smile, which lasted but a second; an air of depression succeeded, chased away presently by one of attention and interest, when I gave the word for all the pupils to take their reading books. In general I hated the reading lesson; it was such a torture to the ear to listen to their uncouth mouthing of my native tongue, and no effort of example or precept on my part ever seemed to effect the slightest improvement in their accent. Today, each in her appropriate key lisped, stuttered, mumbled and jabbered as usual; about fifteen had racked me in turn, and my auricular nerve was expecting with resignation the discords of the sixteenth, when a full, though low, voice read out, in clear, correct English:

"On his way to Perth, the king was met by a Highland woman, calling herself a prophetess; she stood at the side of the ferry by which he was about to travel to the north, and cried with a loud voice, 'My lord the king, if you pass this water you will never return again alive!'" (*vide* the *History of Scotland*).*

I looked up in amazement; the voice was a voice of Albion; the accent was pure and silvery; it only wanted firmness and assurance to be the counterpart of what any well-educated lady in Essex or Middlesex might have enounced, yet the speaker or reader was no other than Mlle Henri, in whose grave, joyless face I saw no mark of consciousness that she had performed any extraordinary feat. No one else evinced surprise either. Mlle Reuter knitted away assiduously; I was aware, however, that at the conclusion of the paragraph, she had lifted her eyelid and honoured me with a glance sideways; she did not know the full excellency of the teacher's style of reading, but she perceived that her accent was not that of the others, and wanted to discover what I thought; I masked my visage with indifference and ordered the next girl to proceed.

When the lesson was over, I took advantage of the confusion caused by breaking up to approach Mlle Henri; she was standing near the window and retired as I advanced; she thought I wanted to look out, and did not imagine that I could have anything to say to her. I took her exercise book out of her hand; as I turned over the leaves, I addressed her:

"You have had lessons in English before?" I asked.

"No, sir."

"No! You read it well; you have been in England?"

"Oh, no!" with some animation.

"You have been in English families?"

Still the answer was "No". Here my eye, resting on the flyleaf of the book, saw written, "Frances Evans Henri."

"Your name?" I asked.

"Yes, sir."

My interrogations were cut short; I heard a little rustling behind me, and close at my back was the directress, professing to be examining the interior of a desk.

"Mademoiselle," said she, looking up and addressing the teacher, "you will have the goodness to go and stand in the corridor while the young ladies are putting on their things, and try to keep some order."

Mlle Henri obeyed.

"What splendid weather!" observed the directress cheerfully, glancing at the same time from the window. I assented and was withdrawing. "What of your new pupil, monsieur?" continued she, following my retreating steps. "Is she likely to make progress in English?"

"Indeed, I can hardly judge. She possesses a pretty good accent; of her real knowledge of the language I have as yet had no opportunity of forming an opinion."

"And her natural capacity, monsieur? I have had my fears about that: can you relieve me by an assurance at least of its average power?"

"I see no reason to doubt its average power, mademoiselle, but really I scarcely know her, and have not had time to study the calibre of her capacity. I wish you a very good afternoon."

She still pursued me. "You will observe, monsieur, and tell me what you think; I could so much better rely on your opinion than on my own; women cannot judge of these things as men can, and, excuse my pertinacity, monsieur, but it is natural I should feel interested about this poor little girl (*pauvre petite*): she has scarcely any relations, her own efforts are all she has to look to, her acquirements must be her sole fortune; her present position has once been mine, or nearly so; it is then but natural I should sympathize with her; and sometimes, when I see the difficulty she has in managing pupils, I feel quite chagrined. I doubt not she does her best, her intentions are excellent, but, monsieur, she wants tact and firmness. I have talked to her on the subject, but I am not fluent, and probably did not express myself with clearness; she never appears to comprehend me. Now, would you occasionally, when you see an opportunity, slip in a word of advice to her on the subject; men have so much more influence than women have – they argue so much more logically than we do; and you, monsieur, in particular, have so paramount a power of making yourself obeyed; a word of advice from you could not but do her good; even if she were sullen and headstrong (which I hope she is not), she would scarcely refuse to listen to you; for my own part, I can truly say that I never attend one of your lessons without deriving benefit from witnessing your management of the pupils. The other masters are a constant source of anxiety to me; they cannot impress the young ladies with sentiments of respect, nor restrain the levity natural to youth: in you, monsieur, I feel the most absolute confidence; try then to put this poor child into the way of controlling our giddy, high-spirited *Brabantoises*. But, monsieur, I would add one word more: don't alarm her *amour-propre*; beware of inflicting a wound there. I reluctantly admit that in that particular she is blamably – some would say ridiculously – susceptible. I fear I have touched this sore point inadvertently, and she cannot get over it."

During the greater part of this harangue my hand was on the lock of the outer door; I now turned it.

"*Au revoir, mademoiselle*," said I, and I escaped. I saw the directress's stock of words was yet far from exhausted. She looked after me; she would fain have detained me longer. Her manner towards me had been altered ever since I had begun to treat her with hardness and indifference: she almost cringed to me on every occasion; she consulted my countenance incessantly and beset me with innumerable little officious attentions. Servility creates despotism. This slavish homage, instead of softening my heart, only pampered whatever was stern and exacting in its mood. The very circumstance of her hovering round me like a fascinated bird seemed to transform me into a rigid pillar of stone; her flatteries irritated my scorn, her blandishments confirmed my reserve. At times I wondered what she meant by giving herself such trouble to win me, when the more profitable Pelet was already in her nets, and when, too, she was aware that I possessed her secret, for I had not scrupled to tell her as much: but the fact is that as it was her nature to doubt the reality and undervalue the worth of modesty, affection, disinterestedness – to regard these qualities as foibles of character – so it was equally her tendency to consider pride, hardness, selfishness, as proofs of strength. She would trample on the neck of humility, she would kneel at the feet of disdain; she would meet tenderness with secret contempt, indifference she would woo with ceaseless assiduities. Benevolence, devotedness, enthusiasm were her antipathies; for dissimulation and self-interest she had a preference – they were real wisdom in her eyes; moral and physical degradation, mental and bodily inferiority, she regarded with indulgence; they were foils capable of being turned to good account as set-offs for her own endowments. To violence, injustice, tyranny, she succumbed – they were her natural masters; she had no propensity to hate, no impulse to resist them; the indignation their behests awake in some hearts was unknown in hers. From all this it resulted that the false and selfish called her wise, the vulgar and debased termed her charitable, the insolent and unjust dubbed her amiable, the conscientious and benevolent generally at first accepted as valid her claim to be considered one of themselves; but ere long the plating of pretension wore off, the real material appeared below, and they laid her aside as a deception.

Chapter 16

IN THE COURSE OF ANOTHER FORTNIGHT I had seen sufficient of Frances Evans Henri to enable me to form a more definite opinion of her character. I found her possessed in a somewhat remarkable degree of at least two good points, viz. perseverance and a sense of duty. I found she was really capable of applying to study, of contending with difficulties. At first I offered her the same help which I had always found it necessary to confer on the others; I began with unloosing for her each knotty point, but I soon discovered that such help was regarded by my new pupil as degrading; she recoiled from it with a certain proud impatience. Hereupon I appointed her long lessons, and left her to solve alone any perplexities they might present. She set to the task with serious ardour, and having quickly accomplished one labour, eagerly demanded more. So much for her perseverance; as to her sense of duty, it evinced itself thus: she liked to learn, but hated to teach; her progress as a pupil depended upon herself, and I saw that on herself she could calculate with certainty; her success as a teacher rested partly, perhaps chiefly, upon the will of others; it cost her a most painful effort to enter into conflict with this foreign will, to endeavour to bend it into subjection to her own; for in what regarded people in general the action of her will was impeded by many scruples; it was as unembarrassed as strong where her own affairs were concerned, and to it she could at any time subject her inclination, if that inclination went counter to her convictions of right; yet when called upon to wrestle with the propensities, the habits, the faults of others – of children especially, who are deaf to reason and, for the most part, insensate to persuasion – her will sometimes almost refused to act; then came in the sense of duty, and forced the reluctant will into operation. A wasteful expense of energy and labour was frequently the consequence; Frances toiled for and with her pupils like a drudge, but it was long ere her conscientious exertions were rewarded by anything like docility on their part, because they saw that they had power over her, inasmuch as by resisting her painful attempts to convince, persuade, control – by forcing her to the employment of coercive measures – they could inflict upon her exquisite suffering. Human beings – human children especially – seldom deny themselves the pleasure of exercising a power which *they* are conscious of possessing, even though that power consist only in a capacity to make others wretched; a pupil whose sensations are duller than those of his instructor, while his nerves are tougher and his bodily strength perhaps greater, has an immense advantage over that instructor, and he will generally use it relentlessly, because the very young, very healthy, very thoughtless, know neither how to sympathize nor how to spare. Frances, I fear, suffered much; a continual weight seemed to oppress her spirits; I have said she did not live in the house, and whether in her own abode, wherever that might be, she wore the same preoccupied, unsmiling, sorrowfully resolved air that always shaded her features under the roof of Mlle Reuter, I could not tell.

One day I gave, as a *devoir*, the trite little anecdote of Alfred tending cakes in the herdsman's hut,* to be related with amplifications. A singular affair most of the pupils made of it; brevity was what they had chiefly studied; the majority of the narratives were perfectly unintelligible; those of Sylvie and Léonie Ledru alone pretended to anything like sense and connection. Eulalie, indeed, had hit upon a clever expedient for at once ensuring accuracy and saving trouble; she had obtained access somehow to an abridged history of England, and had copied the anecdote out fair. I wrote on the margin of her production "Stupid and deceitful", and then tore it down the middle.

Last in the pile of single-leaved *devoirs*, I found one of several sheets, neatly written out and stitched together; I knew the hand, and scarcely needed the evidence of the signature "Frances Evans Henri" to confirm my conjecture as to the writer's identity.

Night was my usual time for correcting *devoirs*, and my own room the usual scene of such task – task most onerous hitherto; and it seemed strange to me to feel rising within me an incipient sense of interest, as I snuffed the candle and addressed myself to the perusal of the poor teacher's manuscript.

"Now," thought I, "I shall see a glimpse of what she really is; I shall get an idea of the nature and extent of her powers – not that she can be expected to express herself well in a foreign tongue, but still, if she has any mind, here will be a reflection of it."

The narrative commenced by a description of a Saxon peasant's hut, situated within the confines of a great, leafless winter forest; it represented an evening in December; flakes of snow were falling, and the herdsman foretold a heavy storm; he summoned his wife to aid him in collecting their flock, roaming far away on the pastoral banks of the Thone;* he warns her that it will be late ere they return. The good woman is reluctant to quit her occupation of baking cakes for the evening meal; but, acknowledging the primary importance of securing the herds and flocks, she puts on her sheepskin mantle; and, addressing a stranger who rests half reclined on a bed of rushes near the hearth, bids him mind the bread till her return.

"Take care, young man," she continues, "that you fasten the door well after us; and, above all, open to none in our absence; whatever sound you hear, stir not, and look not out. The night will soon fall; this forest is most wild and lonely; strange noises are often heard therein after sunset; wolves haunt these glades, and Danish warriors infest the country; worse things are talked of; you might chance to hear, as it were, a child cry, and on opening the door to afford it succour, a great black bull, or a shadowy goblin dog, might rush over the threshold; or, more awful still, if something flapped, as with wings, against the lattice, and then a raven or a white dove flew in and settled on the hearth, such a visitor would be a sure sign of misfortune to the house; therefore, heed my advice, and lift the latchet for nothing."

Her husband calls her away; both depart. The stranger, left alone, listens awhile to the muffled snow-wind, the remote, swollen sound of the river, and then he speaks.

"It is Christmas Eve," says he. "I mark the date; here I sit alone on a rude couch of rushes, sheltered by the thatch of a herdsman's hut; I, whose inheritance was a kingdom, owe my night's harbourage to a poor serf; my throne is usurped, my crown presses the brow of an invader; I have no friends; my troops wander broken in the hills of Wales; reckless robbers spoil my country; my subjects lie prostrate, their breasts crushed by the heel of the brutal

Dane. Fate! Thou hast done thy worst, and now thou standest before me resting thy hand on thy blunted blade. Aye; I see thine eye confront mine and demand why I still live, why I still hope. Pagan demon, I credit not thine omnipotence, and so cannot succumb to thy power. My God, whose Son, as on this night, took on Him the form of man, and for man vouchsafed to suffer and bleed, controls thy hand, and without His behest thou canst not strike a stroke. My God is sinless, eternal, all-wise – in Him is my trust; and though stripped and crushed by thee – though naked, desolate, void of resource – I do not despair, I cannot despair: were the lance of Guthrum* now wet with my blood, I should not despair. I watch, I toil, I hope, I pray; Jehovah, in His own time, will aid."

I need not continue the quotation: the whole *devoir* was in the same strain. There were errors of orthography, there were foreign idioms, there were some faults of construction, there were verbs irregular transformed into verbs regular; it was mostly made up, as the above example shows, of short and somewhat rude sentences, and the style stood in great need of polish and sustained dignity; yet, such as it was, I had hitherto seen nothing like it in the course of my professorial experience. The girl's mind had conceived a picture of the hut, of the two peasants, of the crownless king; she had imagined the wintry forest, she had recalled the old Saxon ghost legends, she had appreciated Alfred's courage under calamity, she had remembered his Christian education, and had shown him, with the rooted confidence of those primitive days, relying on the scriptural Jehovah for aid against the mythological Destiny. This she had done without a hint from me: I had given the subject, but not said a word about the manner of treating it.

"I will find, or make, an opportunity of speaking to her," I said to myself as I rolled the *devoir* up. "I will learn what she has of English in her besides the name of Frances Evans; she is no novice in the language, that is evident, yet she told me she had neither been in England, nor taken lessons in English, nor lived in English families."

In the course of my next lesson, I made a report of the other *devoirs*, dealing out praise and blame in very small retail parcels, according to my custom, for there was no use in blaming severely, and high encomiums were rarely merited. I said nothing of Mlle Henri's exercise, and, spectacles on nose, I endeavoured to decipher in her countenance her sentiments at the omission. I wanted to find out whether in her existed a consciousness of her own talents. "If she thinks she did a clever thing in composing that *devoir*, she will now look mortified," thought I. Grave as usual, almost sombre, was her face; as usual, her eyes were fastened on the *cahier* open before her; there was something, I thought, of expectation in her attitude, as I concluded a brief review of the last *devoir*, and when, casting it from me and rubbing my hands, I bade them take their grammars, some slight change did pass over her air and mien, as though she now relinquished a faint prospect of pleasant excitement: she had been waiting for something to be discussed in which she had a degree of interest; the discussion was not to come on, so expectation sank back, shrunk and sad, but attention, promptly filling up the void, repaired in a moment the transient collapse of feature; still, I felt, rather than saw, during the whole course of the lesson, that a hope had been wrenched from her, and that if she did not show distress, it was because she would not.

At four o'clock, when the bell rang and the room was in immediate tumult, instead of taking my hat and starting from the *estrade*, I sat still a moment. I looked at Frances: she was putting her books into her *cabas*; having fastened the button, she raised her head; encountering my eye, she made a quiet, respectful obeisance, as bidding good afternoon, and was turning to depart.

"Come here," said I, lifting my finger at the same time. She hesitated; she could not hear the words amidst the uproar now pervading both schoolrooms; I repeated the sign; she approached; again she paused within half a yard of the *estrade*, and looked shy, and still doubtful whether she had mistaken my meaning.

"Step up," I said, speaking with decision. It is the only way of dealing with diffident, easily embarrassed characters, and with some slight manual aid I presently got her placed just where I wanted her to be – that is, between my desk and the window, where she was screened from the rush of the second division, and where no one could sneak behind her to listen.

"Take a seat," I said, placing a tabouret; and I made her sit down. I knew what I was doing would be considered a very strange thing – and, what was more, I did not care. Frances knew it also – and, I fear, by an appearance of agitation and trembling, that she cared much. I drew from my pocket the rolled-up *devoir*.

"This is yours, I suppose?" said I, addressing her in English, for I now felt sure she could speak English.

"Yes," she answered distinctly; and as I unrolled it and laid it out flat on the desk before her with my hand upon it, and a pencil in that hand, I saw her moved and, as it were, kindled; her depression beamed as a cloud might behind which the sun is burning.

"This *devoir* has numerous faults," said I. "It will take you some years of careful study before you are in a condition to write English with absolute correctness. Attend: I will point out some principal defects." And I went through it carefully, noting every error, and demonstrating why they were errors, and how the words or phrases ought to have been written. In the course of this sobering process, she became calm. I now went on:

"As to the substance of your *devoir*, Mlle Henri, it has surprised me; I perused it with pleasure, because I saw in it some proofs of taste and fancy. Taste and fancy are not the highest gifts of the human mind, but such as they are you possess them – not probably in a paramount degree, but in a degree beyond what the majority can boast. You may then take courage; cultivate the faculties that God and nature have bestowed on you, and do not fear in any crisis of suffering, under any pressure of injustice, to derive free and full consolation from the consciousness of their strength and rarity."

"Strength and rarity!" I repeated to myself. "Aye, the words are probably true," for, on looking up, I saw the sun had dissevered its screening cloud: her countenance was transfigured; a smile shone in her eyes – a smile almost triumphant; it seemed to say:

"I am glad you have been forced to discover so much of my nature; you need not so carefully moderate your language. Do you think I am myself a stranger to myself? What you tell me in terms so qualified, I have known fully from a child."

She did say this as plainly as a frank and flashing glance could, but in a moment the glow of her complexion, the radiance of her aspect, had subsided; if strongly conscious of her talents, she was equally conscious of her harassing defects, and the remembrance of these obliterated for a single second, now reviving with sudden force, at once subdued the too vivid characters in which her sense of her powers had been expressed. So quick was the revulsion of feeling, I had not time to check her triumph by reproof; ere I could contract my brows to a frown, she had become serious and almost mournful-looking.

"Thank you, sir," said she, rising. There was gratitude both in her voice and in the look with which she accompanied it. It was time, indeed, for our conference to terminate; for, when I glanced around, behold all the boarders (the day scholars had departed) were congregated within a yard or two of my desk, and stood staring with eyes and mouths wide open; the three *maîtresses* formed a whispering knot in one corner, and close at my elbow was the directress, sitting on a low chair, calmly clipping the tassels of her finished purse.

Chapter 17

AFTER ALL, I HAD PROFITED but imperfectly by the opportunity I had so boldly achieved of speaking to Mlle Henri; it was my intention to ask her how she came to be possessed of two English baptismal names, Frances and Evans, in addition to her French surname; also, whence she derived her good accent. I had forgotten both points – or, rather, our colloquy had been so brief that I had not had time to bring them forward; moreover, I had not half tested her powers of speaking English; all I had drawn from her in that language were the words "Yes" and "Thank you, sir". "No matter," I reflected. "What has been left incomplete now shall be finished another day." Nor did I fail to keep the promise thus made to myself. It was difficult to get even a few words of particular conversation with one pupil among so many, but, according to the old proverb, "Where there is a will, there is a way"; and again and again I managed to find an opportunity for exchanging a few words with Mlle Henri, regardless that Envy stared and Detraction whispered whenever I approached her.

"Your book an instant." Such was the mode in which I often began these brief dialogues; the time was always just at the conclusion of the lesson; and, motioning to her to rise, I installed myself in her place, allowing her to stand deferentially at my side; for I esteemed it wise and right in her case to enforce strictly all forms ordinarily in use between master and pupil; the rather because I perceived that in proportion as my manner grew austere and magisterial, hers became easy and self-possessed – an odd contradiction, doubtless, to the ordinary effect in such cases, but so it was.

"A pencil," said I, holding out my hand without looking at her. (I am now about to sketch a brief report of the first of these conferences.) She gave me one, and while I underlined some errors in a grammatical exercise she had written, I observed:

"You are not a native of Belgium?"

"No."

"Nor of France?"

"No."

"Where, then, is your birthplace?"

"I was born at Geneva."

"You don't call Frances and Evans Swiss names, I presume?"

"No, sir; they are English names."

"Just so; and is it the custom of the Genevese to give their children English appellatives?"

"*Non, monsieur; mais*—"

"Speak English, if you please."

"*Mais*—"

"English—"

"But" – slowly and with embarrassment – "my parents were not all the two Genevese."

"Say *both,* instead of 'all the two', mademoiselle."

"Not *both* Swiss; my mother was English."

"Ah! And of English extraction?"

"Yes – her ancestors were all English."

"And your father?"

"He was Swiss."

"What besides? What was his profession?"

"Ecclesiastic – pastor – he had a church."

"Since your mother is an Englishwoman, why do you not speak English with more facility?"

"*Maman est morte, il y a dix ans.*"*

"And you do homage to her memory by forgetting her language? Have the goodness to put French out of your mind so long as I converse with you – keep to English."

"*C'est si difficile, monsieur, quand on n'en a plus l'habitude.*"*

"You had the *habitude* formerly, I suppose? Now answer me in your mother tongue."

"Yes, sir, I spoke the English more than the French when I was a child."

"Why do you not speak it now?"

"Because I have no English friends."

"You live with your father, I suppose?"

"My father is dead."

"You have brothers and sisters?"

"Not one."

"Do you live alone?"

"No – I have an aunt – *ma tante* Julienne."

"Your father's sister?"

"*Justement, monsieur.*"*

"Is that English?"

"No – but I forget—"

"For which, mademoiselle, if you were a child, I should certainly devise some slight punishment; at your age – you must be two- or three-and-twenty, I should think?"

"*Pas encore, monsieur – en un mois j'aurai dix-neuf ans.*"*

"Well, nineteen is a mature age, and, having attained it, you ought to be so solicitous for your own improvement that it should not be needful for a master to remind you twice of the expediency of your speaking English whenever practicable."

To this wise speech I received no answer; and, when I looked up, my pupil was smiling to herself a much-meaning, though not very gay smile; it seemed to say, "He talks of he knows not what"; it said this so plainly that I determined to request information on the point concerning which my ignorance seemed to be thus tacitly affirmed.

"Are you solicitous for your own improvement?"

"Rather."

"How do you prove it, mademoiselle?"

An odd question, and bluntly put; it excited a second smile. "Why, monsieur, I am not inattentive – am I? I learn my lessons well—"

"Oh, a child can do that! And what more do you do?"

"What more can I do?"

"Oh, certainly, not much; but you are a teacher, are you not, as well as a pupil?"

"Yes."

"You teach lace-mending?"

"Yes."

"A dull, stupid occupation; do you like it?"

"No – it is tedious."

"Why do you pursue it? Why do you not rather teach history, geography, grammar, even arithmetic?"

"Is monsieur certain that I am myself thoroughly acquainted with these studies?"

"I don't know; you ought to be at your age."

"But I never was at school, monsieur."

"Indeed! What then were your friends – what was your aunt about? She is very much to blame."

"No, monsieur, no – my aunt is good – she is not to blame – she does what she can; she lodges and nourishes me" (I report Mlle Henri's phrases literally, and it was thus she translated from the French). "She is not rich; she has only an annuity of twelve hundred francs, and it would be impossible for her to send me to school."

"Rather," thought I to myself on hearing this; but I continued, in the dogmatical tone I had adopted:

"It is sad, however, that you should be brought up in ignorance of the most ordinary branches of education; had you known something of history and grammar, you might, by degrees, have relinquished your lace-mending drudgery, and risen in the world."

"It is what I mean to do."

"How? By a knowledge of English alone? That will not suffice; no respectable family will receive a governess whose whole stock of knowledge consists in a familiarity with one foreign language."

"Monsieur, I know other things."

"Yes, yes; you can work with Berlin wools,* and embroider hand-kerchiefs and collars – that will do little for you."

Mlle Henri's lips were unclosed to answer, but she checked herself, as thinking the discussion had been sufficiently pursued, and remained silent.

"Speak," I continued impatiently. "I never like the appearance of acquiescence when the reality is not there, and you had a contradiction at your tongue's end."

"Monsieur, I have had many lessons both in grammar, history, geography and arithmetic. I have gone through a course of each study."

"Bravo! But how did you manage it, since your aunt could not afford to send you to school?"

"By lace-mending; by the thing monsieur despises so much."

"Truly! And now, mademoiselle, it will be a good exercise for you to explain to me in English how such a result was produced by such means."

"Monsieur, I begged my aunt to have me taught lace-mending soon after we came to Brussels, because I knew it was a *métier*, a trade which was easily learnt, and by which I could earn some money very soon. I learnt it in a few days and I quickly got work, for all the Brussels ladies have old lace – very precious – which must be mended all the times it is washed. I earned money a little, and this money I gave for lessons in the studies I have mentioned; some of it I spent in buying books, English books especially; soon I shall try to find a place of governess, or schoolteacher, when I can write and speak English well; but it will be difficult, because those who know I have been a lace-mender will despise me, as the pupils here despise me. *Pourtant j'ai mon projet*,"* she added in a lower tone.

"What is it?"

"I will go and live in England; I will teach French there."

The words were pronounced emphatically. She said "England" as you might suppose an Israelite of Moses's days would have said Canaan.*

"Have you a wish to see England?"

"Yes, and an intention."

And here a voice, the voice of the directress, interposed:

"*Mademoiselle Henri, je crois qu'il va pleuvoir; vous feriez bien, ma bonne amie, de retourner chez vous tout de suite.*"*

In silence, without a word of thanks for this officious warning, Mlle Henri collected her books; she moved to me respectfully, endeavoured to move to her superior, though the endeavour was almost a failure, for her head seemed as if it would not bend, and thus departed.

Where there is one grain of perseverance or wilfulness in the composition, trifling obstacles are ever known rather to stimulate than discourage. Mlle Reuter might as well have spared herself the trouble of giving that intimation about the weather (by the by, her prediction was falsified by the event – it did not rain that evening). At the close of the next lesson I was again at Mlle Henri's desk. Thus did I accost her:

"What is your idea of England, mademoiselle? Why do you wish to go there?"

Accustomed by this time to the calculated abruptness of my manner, it no longer discomposed or surprised her, and she answered with only so much of hesitation as was rendered inevitable by the difficulty she experienced in improvising the translation of her thoughts from French to English.

"England is something unique, as I have heard and read; my idea of it is vague, and I want to go there to render my idea clear, definite."

"Hum! How much of England do you suppose you could see if you went there in the capacity of a teacher? A strange notion you must have of getting a clear and definite idea of a country! All you could see of Great Britain would be the interior of a school – or, at most, of one or two private dwellings."

"It would be an English school; they would be English dwellings."

"Indisputably; but what then? What would be the value of observations made on a scale so narrow?"

"Monsieur, might one not learn something by analogy? An – échantillon – a – a sample often serves to give an idea of the whole; besides, narrow and wide are words comparative, are they not? All my life would perhaps seem narrow in your eyes – all the life of a – that little animal subterranean – *une taupe – comment dit-on?*"

"Mole."

"Yes – a mole, which lives underground, would seem narrow even to me."

"Well, mademoiselle – what then? Proceed."

"*Mais, monsieur, vous me comprenez.*"*

"Not in the least; have the goodness to explain."

"Why, monsieur, it is just so. In Switzerland I have done but little, learnt but little and seen but little; my life there was in a circle; I walked the same round every day; I could not get out of it; had I rested – remained there even till my death, I should never have enlarged it, because I am poor and not skilful, I have not great acquirements; when I was quite tired of this round, I begged my aunt to go to Brussels; my existence is no larger here, because I am no richer or higher; I walk in as narrow a limit, but the scene is changed;

it would change again if I went to England. I knew something of the bourgeois of Geneva; now I know something of the bourgeois of Brussels; if I went to London, I should know something of the bourgeois of London. Can you make any sense out of what I say, monsieur, or is it all obscure?"

"I see, I see – now let us advert to another subject; you propose to devote your life to teaching, and you are a most unsuccessful teacher; you cannot keep your pupils in order."

A flush of painful confusion was the result of this harsh remark; she bent her head to the desk, but soon raising it replied:

"Monsieur, I am not a skilful teacher, it is true, but practice improves; besides, I work under difficulties; here I only teach sewing, I can show no power in sewing, no superiority – it is a subordinate art; then I have no associates in this house, I am isolated; I am, too, a heretic, which deprives me of influence."

"And in England you would be a foreigner; that too would deprive you of influence, and would effectually separate you from all around you; in England you would have as few connections, as little importance, as you have here."

"But I should be learning something; for the rest, there are probably difficulties for such as I everywhere, and if I must contend, and perhaps be conquered, I would rather submit to English pride than to Flemish coarseness; besides, monsieur—"

She stopped – not evidently from any difficulty in finding words to express herself, but because discretion seemed to say, "You have said enough."

"Finish your phrase," I urged.

"Besides, monsieur, I long to live once more among Protestants; they are more honest than Catholics; a Romish school is a building with porous walls, a hollow floor, a false ceiling; every room in this house, monsieur, has eyeholes and ear holes, and what the house is, the inhabitants are – very treacherous; they all think it lawful to tell lies; they all call it politeness to profess friendship where they feel hatred."

"All?" said I. "You mean the pupils – the mere children – inexperienced, giddy things, who have not learnt to distinguish the difference between right and wrong?"

"On the contrary, monsieur – the children are the most sincere; they have not yet had time to become accomplished in duplicity; they will tell lies, but they do it unartificially, and you know they are lying; but the grown-up people are very false; they deceive strangers, they deceive each other—"

A servant here entered:

"*Mlle Henri – Mlle Reuter vous prie de vouloir bien conduire la petite de Dorlodot chez elle; elle vous attend dans le cabinet de Rosalie la portière – c'est que sa bonne n'est pas venue la chercher – voyez-vous.*"*

"*Eh bien! est-ce que je suis sa bonne – moi?*"* demanded Mlle Henri; then smiling, with that same bitter, derisive smile I had seen on her lips before, she hastily rose and made her exit.

Chapter 18

T HE YOUNG ANGLO-SWISS EVIDENTLY DERIVED both pleasure and profit from the study of her mother tongue. In teaching her I did not, of course, confine myself to the ordinary school routine; I made instruction in English a channel for instruction in literature. I prescribed to her a course of reading; she had a little selection of English classics, a few of which had been left her by her mother, and the others she had purchased with her own penny fee.* I lent her some more modern works; all these she read with avidity, giving me, in writing, a clear summary of each work when she had perused it. Composition, too, she delighted in. Such occupation seemed the very breath of her nostrils,* and soon her improved productions wrung from me the avowal that those qualities in her I had termed taste and fancy ought rather to have been denominated judgement and imagination. When I intimated so much, which I did as usual in dry and stinted phrase, I looked for the radiant and exulting smile my one word of eulogy had elicited before; but Frances coloured. If she did smile, it was very softly and shyly; and instead of looking up to me with a conquering glance, her eyes rested on my hand – which, stretched over her shoulder, was writing some directions with a pencil on the margin of her book.

"Well, are you pleased that I am satisfied with your progress?" I asked.

"Yes," said she slowly, gently, the blush that had half subsided returning.

"But I do not say enough, I suppose?" I continued. "My praises are too cool?"

She made no answer and, I thought, looked a little sad. I divined her thoughts, and should much have liked to have responded to them, had it been expedient to do so. She was not now very ambitious of my admiration – not eagerly desirous of dazzling me; a little affection – ever so little – pleased her better than all the panegyrics in the world. Feeling this, I stood a good while behind her, writing on the margin of her book. I could hardly quit my station or relinquish my occupation; something retained me bending there, my head very near hers, and my hand near hers too; but the margin of a copybook is not an illimitable space – so, doubtless, the directress thought; and she took occasion to walk past in order to ascertain by what art I prolonged so disproportionately the period necessary for filling it. I was obliged to go. Distasteful effort – to leave what we most prefer!

Frances did not become pale or feeble in consequence of her sedentary employment; perhaps the stimulus it communicated to her mind counterbalanced the inaction it imposed on her body. She changed – indeed, changed obviously and rapidly; but it was for the better. When I first saw her, her countenance was sunless, her complexion colourless; she looked like one who had no source of enjoyment, no store of bliss anywhere in the world; now the cloud had passed from her mien, leaving space for the dawn of hope and interest, and those feelings rose like a clear morning, animating what had been depressed, tinting what had been pale. Her eyes, whose colour I had not at first known, so dim were they with repressed tears, so shadowed with ceaseless dejection, now, lit by a ray of the sunshine that cheered her heart, revealed irids of bright hazel – irids large and full, screened with long lashes; and pupils instinct with fire. That look of wan emaciation which anxiety or low spirits often communicates to a thoughtful, thin face, rather long than round, having vanished from hers, a clearness of skin almost bloom, and a plumpness almost embonpoint, softened the decided lines of her features. Her figure shared in this beneficial change: it became rounder and, as the harmony of her form was complete and her stature of the graceful middle height, one did not regret (or at least *I* did not regret) the absence of confirmed fullness; in contours – still slight, though compact, elegant, flexible – the exquisite turning of waist, wrist, hand, foot and ankle satisfied completely my notions of symmetry, and allowed a lightness and freedom of movement which corresponded with my ideas of grace.

Thus improved, thus wakened to life, Mlle Henri began to take a new footing in the school; her mental power, manifested gradually but steadily, ere long extorted recognition even from the envious; and when the young and healthy saw that she could smile brightly, converse gaily, move with vivacity and alertness, they acknowledged in her a sisterhood of youth and health, and tolerated her as of their kind accordingly.

To speak truth, I watched this change much as a gardener watches the growth of a precious plant, and I contributed to it too, even as the said gardener contributes to the development of his favourite. To me it was not difficult to discover how I could best foster my pupil, cherish her starved feelings and induce the outward manifestation of that inward vigour which sunless drought and blighting blast had hitherto forbidden to expand. Constancy of attention, a kindness as mute as watchful – always standing by her, cloaked in the rough garb of austerity and making its real nature known only by a rare glance of interest, or a cordial and gentle word – real respect masked with seeming imperiousness, directing, urging her actions, yet helping her too, and that with devoted care: these were the means I used, for these means best suited Frances's feelings, as susceptible as deep vibrating – her nature at once proud and shy.

The benefits of my system became apparent also in her altered demeanour as a teacher; she now took her place amongst her pupils with an air of spirit and firmness which assured them at once that she meant to be obeyed – and obeyed she was. They felt they had lost their power over her. If any girl had rebelled, she would no longer have taken her rebellion to heart; she possessed a source of comfort they could not drain, a pillar of support they could not overthrow: formerly, when insulted, she wept; now, she smiled.

The public reading of one of her *devoirs* achieved the revelation of her talents to all and sundry; I remember the subject – it was an emigrant's letter to his friends at home. It opened with simplicity; some natural and graphic touches disclosed to the reader the scene of virgin forest and great New World river – barren of sail and flag – amidst which the epistle was supposed to be indited. The difficulties and dangers that attend a settler's life were hinted at; and in the few words said on that subject, Mlle Henri failed not to render audible the voice of resolve, patience, endeavour. The disasters which had driven him from his native country were alluded to; stainless honour, inflexible independence, indestructible self-respect there took the word. Past days were spoken of; the grief of parting, the regrets of absence were touched upon; feeling, forcible and fine, breathed eloquent in every period. At the close, consolation was suggested; religious faith became there the speaker, and she spoke well.

The *devoir* was powerfully written in language at once chaste and choice, in a style nerved with vigour and graced with harmony.

Mlle Reuter was quite sufficiently acquainted with English to understand it when read or spoken in her presence, though she could neither speak nor write it herself. During the perusal of this *devoir*, she sat placidly busy, her eyes and fingers occupied with the formation of a *rivière*, or open-work hem round a cambric handkerchief; she said nothing, and her face and forehead, clothed with a mask of purely negative expression, were as blank of comment as her lips. As neither surprise, pleasure, approbation nor interest were evinced in her countenance, so no more were disdain, envy, annoyance, weariness; if that inscrutable mien said anything, it was simply this:

"The matter is too trite to excite an emotion, or call forth an opinion."

As soon as I had done, a hum rose; several of the pupils, pressing round Mlle Henri, began to beset her with compliments; the composed voice of the directress was now heard:

"Young ladies, such of you as have cloaks and umbrellas will hasten to return home before the shower becomes heavier" (it was raining a little). "The remainder will wait till their respective servants arrive to fetch them." And the school dispersed, for it was four o'clock.

"Monsieur, a word," said Mlle Reuter, stepping onto the *estrade*, and signifying, by a movement of the hand, that she wished me to relinquish, for an instant, the castor* I had clutched.

"Mademoiselle, I am at your service."

"Monsieur, it is of course an excellent plan to encourage effort in young people by making conspicuous the progress of any particularly industrious pupil; but do you not think that, in the present instance, Mlle Henri can hardly be considered as a *concurrent** with the other pupils? She is older than most of them, and has had advantages of an exclusive nature for acquiring a knowledge of English; on the other hand, her sphere of life is somewhat beneath theirs; under these circumstances, a public distinction conferred upon Mlle Henri may be the means of suggesting comparisons and exciting feelings such as would be far from advantageous to the individual forming their object. The interest I take in Mlle Henri's real welfare makes me desirous of screening her from annoyances of this sort; besides, monsieur, as I have before hinted to you, the sentiment of *amour-propre* has a somewhat marked preponderance in her character; celebrity has a tendency to foster this sentiment, and in her it should be rather repressed – she rather needs keeping down than bringing forward; and then I think, monsieur – it appears to me that ambition, *literary* ambition especially, is not a feeling to be cherished in the mind of a woman; would not Mlle Henri be much safer and happier if taught to believe that in the quiet discharge of social duties consists her real vocation than if stimulated to aspire after applause and publicity? She may never marry; scanty as are her resources, obscure as are her connections, uncertain as is her health (for I think her consumptive: her mother died of that complaint), it is more than probable she never will; I do not see how she can rise to a position whence such a step would be possible; but even in celibacy it would be better for her to retain the character and habits of a respectable, decorous female."

"Indisputably, mademoiselle," was my answer. "Your opinion admits of no doubt" – and, fearful of the harangue being renewed, I retreated under cover of that cordial sentence of assent.

At the date of a fortnight after the little incident noted above, I find it recorded in my diary that a hiatus occurred in Mlle Henri's usually regular attendance in class. The first day or two I wondered at her absence, but did not like to ask an explanation of it; I thought indeed some chance word might be dropped which would afford me the information I wished to obtain, without my running the risk of exciting silly smiles and gossiping whispers by demanding it. But when a week passed and the seat at the desk near the door still remained vacant, and when no allusion was made to the circumstance by any individual of the class – when, on the contrary, I found that all observed a marked silence on the point – I determined, *coûte que coûte*,* to break the ice of this silly reserve.

I selected Sylvie as my informant, because from her I knew that I should at least get a sensible answer, unaccompanied by wriggle, titter or other flourish of folly.

"*Où donc est Mlle Henri?*"* I said one day as I returned an exercise book I had been examining.

"*Elle est partie, monsieur.*"*

"*Partie! Et pour combien de temps? Quand reviendra-t-elle?*"*

"*Elle est partie pour toujours, monsieur; elle ne reviendra plus.*"*

"Ah!" was my involuntary exclamation; then, after a pause:

"*En êtes-vous bien sûre, Sylvie?*"*

"*Oui, oui, monsieur, mademoiselle la directrice nous l'a dit elle-même il y a deux ou trois jours.*"*

And I could pursue my enquiries no further; time, place and circumstances forbade my adding another word. I could neither comment on what had been said, nor demand further particulars. A question as to the reason of the teacher's departure, as to whether it had been voluntary or otherwise, was indeed on my lips, but I suppressed it: there were listeners all round. An hour after, in passing Sylvie in the corridor as she was putting on her bonnet, I stopped short and asked:

"Sylvie, do you know Mlle Henri's address? I have some books of hers," I added carelessly, "and I should wish to send them to her."

"No, monsieur," replied Sylvie, "but perhaps Rosalie, the portress, will be able to give it you."

Rosalie's cabinet was just at hand; I stepped in and repeated the enquiry. Rosalie – a smart French grisette* – looked up from her work with a knowing smile, precisely the sort of smile I had been so desirous to avoid exciting. Her answer was prepared; she knew nothing whatever of Mlle Henri's address – had never known it. Turning from her with impatience – for I believed she lied and was hired to lie – I almost knocked down someone who had been standing at my back: it was the directress. My abrupt movement made her recoil two or three steps. I was obliged to apologize, which I did more concisely than politely. No man likes to be dogged, and in the very irritable mood in which I then was, the sight of Mlle Reuter thoroughly incensed me. At the moment I turned, her countenance looked hard, dark and inquisitive; her eyes were bent upon me with an expression of almost hungry curiosity. I had scarce caught this phase of physiognomy ere it had vanished; a bland smile played on her features; my harsh apology was received with good-humoured facility.

"Oh, don't mention it, monsieur; you only touched my hair with your elbow; it is no worse, only a little dishevelled." She shook it back and, passing her fingers through her curls, loosened them into more numerous and flowing ringlets. Then she went on with vivacity:

"Rosalie, I was coming to tell you to go instantly and close the windows of the salon; the wind is rising, and the muslin curtains will be covered with dust."

Rosalie departed. "Now," thought I, "this will not do; Mlle Reuter thinks her meanness in eavesdropping is screened by her art in devising a pretext, whereas the muslin curtains she speaks of are not more transparent than this same pretext." An impulse came over me to thrust the flimsy screen aside and confront her craft boldly with a word or two of plain truth. "The roughshod foot treads most firmly on slippery ground," thought I; so I began:

"Mademoiselle Henri has left your establishment – been dismissed, I presume?"

"Ah, I wished to have a little conversation with you, monsieur," replied the directress with the most natural and affable air in the world, "but we cannot talk quietly here; will monsieur step into the garden a minute?" And she preceded me, stepping out through the glass door I have before mentioned.

"There," said she, when we had reached the centre of the middle alley, and when the foliage of shrubs and trees, now in their summer pride, closing behind and around us, shut out the view of the house, and thus imparted a sense of seclusion even to this little plot of ground in the very core of a capital.

"There! One feels quiet and free when there are only pear trees and rose bushes about one. I dare say you, like me, monsieur, are sometimes tired of being eternally in the midst of life; of having human faces always round you, human eyes always upon you, human voices always in your ear. I am sure I often wish intensely for liberty to spend a whole month in the country at some little farmhouse, *bien gentille, bien propre, tout entourée de champs et de bois; quelle vie charmante que le vie champêtre! N'est-ce pas, monsieur?*"*

"*Cela dépend, mademoiselle.*"*

"*Que le vent est bon et frais!*"* continued the directress; and she was right there, for it was a south wind, soft and sweet. I carried my hat in my hand, and this gentle breeze, passing through my hair, soothed my temples like balm. Its refreshing effect, however, penetrated no deeper than the mere surface of the frame; for as I walked by the side of Mlle Reuter, my heart was still hot within me, and while I was musing the fire burned; then spake I with my tongue:*

"I understand Mlle Henri is gone from hence and will not return?"

"Ah, true! I meant to have named the subject to you some days ago, but my time is completely taken up; I cannot do half the things I wish: have you never experienced what it is, monsieur, to find the day too short by twelve hours for your numerous duties?"

"Not often. Mlle Henri's departure was not voluntary, I presume? If it had been, she would certainly have given me some intimation of it, being my pupil."

"Oh, did she not tell you? That was strange. For my part, I never thought of adverting to the subject; when one has so many things to attend to, one is apt to forget little incidents that are not of primary importance."

"You consider Mlle Henri's dismission, then, as a very insignificant event?"

"Dismission? Ah! She was not dismissed; I can say with truth, monsieur, that since I became the head of this establishment no master or teacher has ever been *dismissed* from it."

"Yet some have left it, mademoiselle?"

"Many; I have found it necessary to change frequently – a change of instructors is often beneficial to the interests of a school; it gives life and variety to the proceedings; it amuses the pupils, and suggests to the parents the idea of exertion and progress."

"Yet, when you are tired of a professor or *maîtresse*, you scruple to dismiss them?"

"No need to have recourse to such extreme measures, I assure you. *Allons, monsieur le professeur – asseyons-nous; je vais vous donner une petite leçon dans votre état d'instituteur.*"* (I wish I might write all she said to me in French – it loses sadly by being translated into English.) We had now reached *the* garden chair; the directress sat down and signed to me to sit by her, but I only rested my knee on the seat and stood leaning my head and arm against the embowering branch of a huge laburnum, whose golden flowers, blended with the dusky green leaves of a lilac bush, formed a mixed arch of shade and sunshine over the retreat. Mlle Reuter sat silent for a moment; some novel movements were evidently working in her mind, and they showed their nature on her astute brow; she was meditating some *chef-d'œuvre** of policy. Convinced by several months' experience that the affectation of virtues she did not possess was unavailing to ensnare me – aware that I had read her real nature, and would believe nothing of the character she gave out as being hers – she had determined, at last, to try a new key, and see if the lock of my heart would yield to that: a little audacity, a word of truth, a glimpse of the real. "Yes, I will try," was her inward resolve; and then her blue eye glittered upon me: it did not flash – nothing of flame ever kindled in its temperate gleam.

"Monsieur fears to sit by me?" she enquired playfully.

"I have no wish to usurp Pelet's place," I answered, for I had got the habit of speaking to her bluntly – a habit begun in anger, but continued because I saw that, instead of offending, it fascinated her. She cast down her eyes and drooped her eyelids; she sighed uneasily; she turned with an anxious gesture, as if she would give me the idea of a bird that flutters in its cage and would fain fly from its jail and jailer, and seek its natural mate and pleasant nest.

"Well – and your lesson?" I demanded briefly.

"Ah!" she exclaimed, recovering herself. "You are so young, so frank and fearless, so talented, so impatient of imbecility, so disdainful of vulgarity, you need a lesson; here it is then: far more is to be done in this world by dexterity than by strength; but, perhaps, you knew that before, for there is delicacy as well as power in your character – policy, as well as pride?"

"Go on," said I, and I could hardly help smiling, the flattery was so piquant, so finely seasoned. She caught the prohibited smile, though I passed my hand over my mouth to conceal it; and again she made room for me to sit beside her. I shook my head, though temptation penetrated to my senses at the moment, and once more I told her to go on.

"Well, then, if ever you are at the head of a large establishment, dismiss nobody. To speak truth, monsieur (and to you I will speak truth), I despise people who are always making rows, blustering, sending off one to the right and another to the left, urging and hurrying circumstances. I'll tell you what I like best to do, monsieur, shall I?" She looked up again; she had compounded her glance well this time – much archness, more deference, a spicy dash of coquetry, an unveiled consciousness of capacity. I nodded; she treated me like the great Mogul* – so I became the great Mogul as far as she was concerned.

"I like, monsieur, to take my knitting in my hands and to sit quietly down in my chair; circumstances defile past me; I watch their march; so long as they follow the course I wish, I say nothing, and do nothing; I don't clap my hands and cry out, 'Bravo! How lucky I am!' to attract the attention and envy of my neighbours – I am merely passive; but when events fall out ill – when circumstances become adverse – I watch very vigilantly; I knit on still, and still I hold my tongue; but every now and then, monsieur, I just put my toe out – so – and give the rebellious circumstance a little secret push, without noise, which sends it the way I wish, and I am successful after all, and nobody has seen my expedient. So, when teachers or masters become troublesome and inefficient – when, in short, the interests of the school would suffer from their retaining their places – I mind my knitting, events progress, circumstances glide past; I see one which, if pushed ever so little awry, will render untenable the post I wish to have vacated – the deed is done – the stumbling block removed – and no one saw me: I have not made an enemy – I am rid of an encumbrance."

A moment since, and I thought her alluring; this speech concluded, I looked on her with distaste. "Just like you," was my cold answer. "And in this way you have ousted Mlle Henri? You wanted her office, therefore you rendered it intolerable to her?"

"Not at all, monsieur, I was merely anxious about Mlle Henri's health; no, your moral sight is clear and piercing, but there you have failed to discover the truth. I took – I have always taken a real interest in Mlle Henri's welfare; I did not like her going out in all weathers; I thought it would be more advantageous for her to obtain a permanent situation; besides, I considered her now qualified to do something more than teach sewing. I reasoned with her – left the decision to herself; she saw the correctness of my views and adopted them."

"Excellent! And now, mademoiselle, you will have the goodness to give me her address."

"Her address!" And a sombre and stony change came over the mien of the directress. "Her address? Ah! – well – I wish I could oblige you, monsieur, but I cannot, and I will tell you why; whenever I myself asked her for her address, she always evaded the enquiry. I thought – I may be wrong – but I *thought* her motive for doing so was a natural, though mistaken reluctance to introduce me to some, probably, very poor abode; her means were narrow, her origin obscure; she lives somewhere, doubtless, in the *'basse ville'*."*

"I'll not lose sight of my best pupil yet," said I, "though she were born of beggars and lodged in a cellar; for the rest, it is absurd to make a bugbear of her origin to me – I happen to know that she was a Swiss pastor's daughter, neither more nor less; and, as to her narrow means, I care nothing for the poverty of her purse as long as her heart overflows with affluence."

"Your sentiments are perfectly noble, monsieur," said the directress, affecting to suppress a yawn; her sprightliness was now extinct, her temporary candour shut up; the little, red-coloured, piratical-looking pennon* of audacity she had allowed to float a minute in the air was furled, and the broad sober-hued flag of dissimulation again hung low over the citadel. I did not like her thus, so I cut short the tête-à-tête and departed.

Chapter 19

NOVELISTS SHOULD NEVER ALLOW THEMSELVES to weary of the study of real life. If they observed this duty conscientiously, they would give us fewer pictures chequered with vivid contrasts of light and shade; they would seldom elevate their heroes and heroines to the heights of rapture – still seldomer sink them to the depths of despair; for if we rarely taste the fullness of joy in this life, we yet more rarely savour the acrid bitterness of hopeless anguish; unless, indeed, we have plunged like beasts into sensual indulgence, abused, strained, stimulated, again overstrained and, at last, destroyed our faculties for enjoyment; then, truly, we may find ourselves without support, robbed of hope. Our agony is great, and how can it end? We have broken the spring of our powers; life must be all suffering – too feeble to conceive faith – death must be darkness – God, spirits, religion can have no place in our collapsed minds, where linger only hideous and polluting recollections of vice; and time brings us on to the brink of the grave, and dissolution flings us in – a rag eaten through and through with disease, wrung together with pain, stamped into the churchyard sod by the inexorable heel of despair.

But the man of regular life and rational mind never despairs. He loses his property – it is a blow – he staggers a moment; then, his energies, roused by the smart, are at work to seek a remedy; activity soon mitigates regret. Sickness affects him; he takes patience – endures what he cannot cure. Acute pain racks him; his writhing limbs know not where to find rest; he leans on Hope's anchors. Death takes from him what he loves, roots up, and tears violently away, the stem round which his affections were twined – a dark, dismal time, a frightful wrench – but some morning Religion looks into his desolate house with sunrise, and says that in another world, another life, he shall meet his kindred again. She speaks of that world as a place unsullied by sin – of that life as an era unembittered by suffering; she mightily strengthens her consolation by connecting with it two ideas – which mortals cannot comprehend, but on which they love to repose – Eternity, Immortality; and the mind of the mourner, being filled with an image, faint yet glorious, of heavenly hills all light and peace – of a spirit resting there in bliss – of a day when his spirit shall also alight there, free and disembodied – of a reunion perfected by love, purified from fear – he takes courage – goes out to encounter the necessities and discharge the duties of life; and, though sadness may never lift her burden from his mind, Hope will enable him to support it.

Well – and what suggested all this? And what is the inference to be drawn therefrom? What suggested it is the circumstance of my best pupil – my treasure – being snatched from my hands and put away out of my reach; the inference to be drawn from it is… that, being a steady, reasonable man, I did not allow the resentment, disappointment and grief, engendered in my mind by this evil chance, to grow there to any monstrous size; nor did I allow them to monopolize the whole space of my heart; I pent them, on the contrary, in one strait and secret nook. In the daytime, too, when I was about my duties, I put them on the silent system;* and it was only after I had closed the door of my chamber at night that I somewhat relaxed my severity towards these morose nurslings and allowed vent to their language of murmurs; then, in revenge, they sat on my pillow, haunted my bed and kept me awake with their long midnight cry.

A week passed. I had said nothing more to Mlle Reuter. I had been calm in my demeanour to her, though stony-cold and hard. When I looked at her, it was with the glance fitting to be bestowed on one who I knew had consulted jealousy as an adviser and employed treachery as an instrument – the glance of quiet disdain and rooted distrust. On Saturday evening, ere I left the house, I stepped into the *salle-à-manger,* where she was sitting alone, and, placing myself before her, I asked, with the same tranquil tone and manner that I should have used had I put the question for the first time:

"Mademoiselle, will you have the goodness to give me the address of Frances Evans Henri?"

A little surprised, but not disconcerted, she smilingly disclaimed any knowledge of that address, adding, "Monsieur has perhaps forgotten that I explained all about that circumstance before – a week ago?"

"Mademoiselle," I continued, "you would greatly oblige me by directing me to that young person's abode."

She seemed somewhat puzzled; and, at last, looking up with an admirably counterfeited air of *naïveté*, she demanded, "Does Monsieur think I am telling an untruth?"

Still avoiding to give her a direct answer, I said, "It is not then your intention, mademoiselle, to oblige me in this particular?"

"But, monsieur, how can I tell you what I do not know?"

"Very well; I understand you perfectly, mademoiselle, and now I have only two or three words more to say. This is the last week in July; in another month the vacation will commence; have the goodness to avail yourself of the leisure it will afford you to look out for another English master – at the close of August, I shall be under the necessity of resigning my post in your establishment."

I did not wait for her comments on this announcement, but bowed and immediately withdrew.

That same evening, soon after dinner, a servant brought me a small packet; it was directed in a hand I knew, but had not hoped so soon to see again; being in my own apartment and alone, there was nothing to prevent my immediately opening it; it contained four five-franc pieces, and a note in English.

Monsieur, I came to Mlle Reuter's house yesterday, at the time when I knew you would be just about finishing your lesson, and asked if I might go into the schoolroom and speak to you. Mlle Reuter came out and said you were already gone; it had not yet struck four, so I thought she must be mistaken, but concluded it would be vain to call another day on the same errand. In one sense a note will do as well: it will wrap up the twenty francs, the price of the lessons I have received from you, and if it will not fully express the thanks I owe you in addition – if it will not bid you goodbye as I could wish to have done – if it will not tell you, as I long to do, how sorry I am that I shall probably never see you more – why, spoken words would hardly be more adequate to the task. Had I seen you, I should probably have stammered out something feeble and unsatisfactory – something belying my feelings rather than explaining them; so it is perhaps as well that I was denied admission to your presence.

You often remarked, monsieur, that my devoirs *dwelt a great deal on fortitude in bearing grief – you said I introduced that theme too often; I find indeed that it is much easier to write about a severe duty than to perform it, for I am oppressed when I see and feel to what a reverse fate has condemned me; you were kind to me, monsieur – very kind; I am afflicted – I am heartbroken to be quite separated from you; soon I shall have no friend on earth. But it is useless troubling you with my distresses. What claim have I on your sympathy? None; I will then say no more. – Farewell, monsieur,*

F.E. HENRI

I put up the note in my pocketbook. I slipped the five-franc pieces into my purse – then I took a turn through my narrow chamber.

"Mlle Reuter talked about her poverty," said I, "and she is poor; yet she pays her debts and more. I have not yet given her a quarter's lessons, and she has sent me a quarter's due. I wonder of what she deprived herself to scrape together the twenty francs – I wonder what sort of a place she has to live in, and what sort of a woman her aunt is, and whether she is likely to get employment to supply the place she has lost. No doubt she will have to trudge about long enough from school to school, to enquire here and apply there – be rejected in this place, disappointed in that. Many an evening she'll go to her bed tired and unsuccessful. And the directress would not let her in to bid me goodbye? I might not have the chance of standing with her for a few minutes at a window in the schoolroom and exchanging some half-dozen of sentences – getting to know where she lived – putting matters in train for having all things arranged to my mind? No address on the note" – I continued, drawing it again from the pocketbook and examining it on each side of the two leaves – "women are women, that is certain, and always do business like women; men mechanically put a date and address to their communications. And these five-franc pieces?" – I hauled them forth from my purse – "if she had offered me them herself instead of tying them up with a thread of green silk in a kind of Lilliputian packet, I could have thrust them back into her little hand and shut up the small, taper fingers over them so and compelled her shame, her pride, her shyness, all to yield to a little bit of determined will. Now where is she? How can I get at her?"

Opening my chamber door, I walked down into the kitchen.

"Who brought the packet?" I asked of the servant who had delivered it to me.

"*Un petit commissionnaire, monsieur.*"*

"Did he say anything?"

"*Rien.*"*

And I wended my way up the backstairs, wondrously the wiser for my enquiries.

"No matter," said I to myself, as I again closed the door. "No matter – I'll seek her through Brussels."

And I did. I sought her day by day whenever I had a moment's leisure, for four weeks; I sought her on Sundays all day long; I sought her on the boulevards, in the Allée Verte,* in the park; I sought her in Sainte-Gudule and Saint-Jacques; I sought her in the two Protestant chapels; I attended these latter at the German, French and English services, not doubting that I should meet her at one of them. All my researches were absolutely fruitless; my security on the last point was proved by the event to be equally groundless with my other calculations. I stood at the door of each chapel after the service, and waited till every individual had come out, scrutinizing every gown draping a slender form, peering under every bonnet covering a young head. In vain – I saw girlish figures pass me, drawing their black scarves over their sloping shoulders, but none of them had the exact turn and air of Mlle Henri's – I saw pale and thoughtful faces *encadrées** in bands of brown hair, but I never found her forehead, her eyes, her eyebrows. All the features of all the faces I met seemed frittered away, because my eye failed to recognize the peculiarities it was bent upon – an ample space of brow and a large, dark and serious eye, with a fine but decided line of eyebrow traced above.

"She has probably left Brussels – perhaps is gone to England, as she said she would," muttered I inwardly, as on the afternoon of the fourth Sunday I turned from the door of the chapel royal, which the doorkeeper had just closed and locked, and followed in the wake of the last of the congregation, now dispersed and dispersing over the square. I had soon outwalked the couples of English gentlemen and ladies. (Gracious goodness! Why don't they dress better? My eye is yet filled with visions of the high-flounced, slovenly and tumbled dresses in costly silk and satin; of the large, unbecoming collars in expensive lace; of the ill-cut coats and strangely fashioned pantaloons which every Sunday, at the English service, filled the chairs of the chapel royal, and after it, issuing forth into the square, came into disadvantageous contrast with freshly and trimly attired foreign figures, hastening to attend salut* at the church of Coburg.) I had passed these pairs of Britons, and the groups of pretty British children, and the British footmen and waiting-maids; I had crossed the Place Royale, and got into the Rue Royale, thence I had diverged into the Rue de Louvain – an old and quiet street. I remember that, feeling a little hungry, and not desiring to go back and take my share of the goûter,* now on the refectory table at Pelet's – to wit, *pistolets* and water – I stepped into a baker's and refreshed myself on a *couc* (?)* – it is a Flemish word, I don't know how to spell it – *à Corinthe – anglice,* a currant bun – and a cup of coffee; and then I strolled on towards the Porte de Louvain.* Very soon I was out of the city and, slowly mounting the hill which ascends from the gate, I took my time; for the afternoon, though cloudy, was very sultry, and not a breeze stirred to refresh the atmosphere. No inhabitant of Brussels need wander far to search for solitude; let him but move half a league from his own city and he will find her brooding still and blank over the wide fields, so drear though so fertile, spread out treeless and trackless round the capital of Brabant. Having gained the summit of the hill, and having stood and looked long over the cultured but lifeless campaign,* I felt a wish to quit the high road, which I had hitherto followed, and get in among those tilled grounds – fertile as the beds of a Brobdingnagian kitchen garden – spreading far and wide even to the boundaries of the horizon, where, from a dusk green, distance changed them to a sullen blue and confused their tints with those of the livid and thunderous-looking sky. Accordingly I turned up a by-path to the right; I had not followed it far ere it brought me, as I expected, into the fields, amidst which, just before me, stretched a long and lofty white wall enclosing, as it seemed from the foliage showing above, some thickly planted nursery of yew and cypress, for of that species were the branches resting on the pale parapets, and crowding gloomily about a massive cross, planted doubtless on a central eminence and extending its arms, which seemed of black marble, over the summits of those sinister trees. I approached, wondering to what house this well-protected garden appertained. I turned the angle of the wall, thinking to see some stately residence; I was close upon great iron gates; there was a hut serving for a lodge near, but I had no occasion to apply for the key – the gates were open; I pushed one leaf back – rain had rusted its hinges, for it groaned dolefully as they revolved. Thick planting embowered the entrance. Passing up the avenue, I saw objects on each hand which, in their own mute language of inscription and sign, explained clearly to what abode I had made my way. This was the house appointed for all living; crosses, monuments and garlands of everlastings announced "The Protestant Cemetery, outside the gate of Louvain".

The place was large enough to afford half an hour's strolling without the monotony of treading continually the same path; and, for those who love to peruse the annals of graveyards, here was variety of inscription enough to occupy the attention for double or treble that space of time. Hither people of many kindreds, tongues and nations had brought their dead for interment; and here, on pages of stone, of marble and of brass, were written names, dates, last tributes of pomp or love, in English, in French, in German and Latin. Here the Englishman had erected a marble monument over the remains of his Mary Smith or Jane Brown, and inscribed it only with her name. There the French widower had shaded the grave of his Elmire or Célestine with a brilliant thicket of roses, amidst which a little tablet rising bore an equally bright testimony to her countless virtues. Every nation, tribe and kindred mourned after its own fashion; and how soundless was the mourning of all! My own tread, though slow and upon smooth-rolled paths, seemed to startle, because it formed the sole break to a silence otherwise total. Not only the winds, but the very fitful, wandering airs were that afternoon, as by common consent, all fallen asleep in their various quarters; the north was hushed, the south silent, the east sobbed not, nor did the west whisper. The clouds in heaven were condensed and dull, but apparently quite motionless. Under the trees of this cemetery nestled a warm, breathless gloom, out of which the cypresses stood up straight and mute, above which the willows hung low and still – where the flowers, as languid as fair, waited listless for night dew or thundershower, where the tombs, and those they hid, lay impassible* to sun or shadow, to rain or drought.

Importuned by the sound of my own footsteps, I turned off upon the turf and slowly advanced to a grove of yews; I saw something stir among the stems; I thought it might be a broken branch swinging; my short-sighted vision had caught no form, only a sense of motion, but the dusky shade passed on, appearing and disappearing at the openings in the avenue. I soon discerned it was a living thing, and a human being; and, drawing nearer, I perceived it was a woman, pacing slowly to and fro, and evidently deeming herself alone as I had deemed myself alone, and meditating as I had been meditating. Ere long she returned to a seat which I fancy she had but just quitted, or I should have caught sight of her before. It was in a nook, screened by a clump of trees; there was the white wall before her, and a little stone set up against the wall, and at the foot of the stone was an allotment of turf freshly turned up, a new-made grave. I put on my spectacles and passed softly close behind her; glancing at the inscription on the stone, I read, "Julienne Henri, died at Brussels, aged sixty. August 10th, 18—." Having perused the inscription, I looked down at the form sitting bent and thoughtful just under my eyes, unconscious of the vicinity of any living thing; it was a slim, youthful figure in mourning apparel of the plainest black stuff, with a little, simple, black crape bonnet; I felt, as well as saw, who it was; and, moving neither hand nor foot, I stood for some moments enjoying the security of conviction. I had sought her for a month, and had never discovered one of her traces – never met a hope, or seized a chance of encountering her anywhere. I had been forced to loosen my grasp on expectation; and, but an hour ago, had sunk slackly under the discouraging thought that the current of life and the impulse of destiny had swept her for ever from my reach; and, behold, while bending suddenly earthward beneath the pressure of despondency – while following with my eyes the track of sorrow on the turf of a graveyard – here was my lost jewel dropped on the tear-fed herbage, nestling in the mossy and mouldy roots of yew trees.

Frances sat very quiet, her elbow on her knee and her head on her hand. I knew she could retain a thinking attitude a long time without change; at last, a tear fell; she had been looking at the name on the stone before her, and her heart had no doubt endured one of those constrictions with which the desolate living, regretting the dead, are at times so sorely oppressed. Many tears rolled down, which she wiped away, again and again, with her handkerchief; some distressed sobs escaped her, and then, the paroxysm over, she sat quiet as before. I put my hand gently on her shoulder; no need further to prepare her, for she was neither hysterical nor liable to fainting fits; a sudden push, indeed, might have startled her, but the contact of my quiet touch merely woke attention as I wished; and though she turned quickly, yet so lightning-swift is thought – in some minds especially – I believe the wonder of what – the consciousness of who it was that thus stole unawares on her solitude had passed through her brain and flashed into her heart even before she had effected that hasty movement; at least, Amazement had hardly opened her eyes and raised them to mine, ere Recognition informed their irids with most speaking brightness. Nervous surprise had hardly discomposed her features ere a sentiment of most vivid joy shone clear and warm on her whole countenance. I had hardly time to observe that she was wasted and pale, ere called to feel a responsive inward pleasure by the sense of most full and exquisite pleasure glowing in the animated flush and shining in the expansive light now diffused over my pupil's face. It was the summer sun flashing out after the heavy summer shower; and what fertilizes more rapidly than that beam, burning almost like fire in its ardour?

I hate boldness – that boldness which is of the brassy brow and insensate nerves; but I love the courage of the strong heart, the fervour of the generous blood; I loved with passion the light of Frances Evans's clear hazel eye when it did not fear to look straight into mine; I loved the tones with which she uttered the words:

"*Mon maître! Mon maître!*"*

I loved the movement with which she confided her hand to my hand; I loved her as she stood there, penniless and parentless; for a sensualist charmless, for me a treasure – my best object of sympathy on earth, thinking such thoughts as I thought, feeling such feelings as I felt; my ideal of the shrine in which to seal my stores of love; personification of discretion and forethought, of diligence and perseverance, of self-denial and self-control – those guardians, those trusty keepers of the gift I longed to confer on her – the gift of all my affections; model of truth and honour, of independence and conscientiousness – those refiners and sustainers of an honest life; silent possessor of a well of tenderness, of a flame, as genial as still, as pure as quenchless, of natural feeling, natural passion – those sources of refreshment and comfort to the sanctuary of home. I knew how quietly and how deeply the well bubbled in her heart; I knew how the more dangerous flame burned safely under the eye of reason; I had seen when the fire shot up a moment high and vivid, when the accelerated heat troubled life's current in its channels; I had seen reason reduce the rebel, and humble its blaze to embers. I had confidence in Frances Evans; I had respect for her, and as I drew her arm through mine and led her out of the cemetery, I felt I had another sentiment, as strong as confidence, as firm as respect, more fervid than either – that of love.

"Well, my pupil," said I, as the ominous-sounding gate swung to behind us, "well, I have found you again: a month's search has seemed long, and I little thought to have discovered my lost sheep* straying amongst graves."

Never had I addressed her but as "Mademoiselle" before, and to speak thus was to take up a tone new to both her and me. Her answer apprised me that this language ruffled none of her feelings, woke no discord in her heart:

"*Mon maître,*" she said, "have you troubled yourself to seek me? I little imagined you would think much of my absence, but I grieved bitterly to be taken away from you. I was sorry for that circumstance when heavier troubles ought to have made me forget it."

"Your aunt is dead?"

"Yes, a fortnight since, and she died full of regret, which I could not chase from her mind; she kept repeating, even during the last night of her existence, 'Frances, you will be so lonely when I am gone, so friendless'; she wished, too, that she could have been buried in Switzerland, and it was I who persuaded her in her old age to leave the banks of Lake Leman and to come – only, as it seems, to die – in this flat region of Flanders.

Willingly would I have observed her last wish and taken her remains back to our own country, but that was impossible; I was forced to lay her here."

"She was ill but a short time, I presume?"

"But three weeks. When she began to sink I asked Mlle Reuter's leave to stay with her and wait on her; I readily got leave."

"Do you return to the *pensionnat*?" I demanded hastily.

"Monsieur, when I had been at home a week, Mlle Reuter called one evening, just after I had got my aunt to bed; she went into her room to speak to her, and was extremely civil and affable, as she always is; afterwards she came and sat with me a long time, and just as she rose to go away, she said: 'Mademoiselle, I shall not soon cease to regret your departure from my establishment, though indeed it is true that you have taught your class of pupils so well that they are all quite accomplished in the little works you manage so skilfully, and have not the slightest need of further instruction; my second teacher must in future supply your place, with regard to the younger pupils, as well as she can, though she is indeed an inferior artiste to you, and doubtless it will be your part now to assume a higher position in your calling; I am sure you will everywhere find schools and families willing to profit by your talents.' And then she paid me my last quarter's salary. I asked, as mademoiselle would no doubt think, very bluntly, if she designed to discharge me from her establishment. She smiled at my inelegance of speech and answered that 'our connection as employer and employed was certainly dissolved, but that she hoped still to retain the pleasure of my acquaintance; she should always be happy to see me as a friend'; and then she said something about the excellent condition of the streets, and the long continuance of fine weather, and went away quite cheerful."

I laughed inwardly; all this was so like the directress – so like what I had expected and guessed of her conduct; and then the exposure and proof of her lie, unconsciously afforded by Frances: "She had frequently applied for Mlle Henri's address" – forsooth. "Mlle Henri had always evaded giving it," etc., etc., and here I found her a visitor at the very house of whose locality she had professed absolute ignorance!

Any comments I might have intended to make on my pupil's communication were checked by the plashing of large raindrops on our faces and on the path, and by the muttering of a distant but coming storm. The warning obvious in stagnant air and leaden sky had already induced me to take the road leading back to Brussels, and now I hastened my own steps and those of my companion, and, as our way lay downhill, we got on rapidly. There was an interval after the fall of the first broad drops before heavy rain came on; in the mean time we had passed through the Porte de Louvain, and were again in the city.

"Where do you live?" I asked. "I will see you safe home."

"Rue Notre Dame aux Neiges," answered Frances.

It was not far from the Rue de Louvain, and we stood on the doorsteps of the house we sought ere the clouds, severing with loud peal and shattered cataract of lightning, emptied their livid folds in a torrent – heavy, prone and broad.

"Come in! Come in!" said Frances as, after putting her into the house, I paused ere I followed. The word decided me. I stepped across the threshold, shut the door on the rushing, flashing, whitening storm and followed her upstairs to her apartments. Neither she nor I were wet; a projection over the door had warded off the straight-descending flood; none but the first large drops had touched our garments; one minute more and we should not have had a dry thread on us.

Stepping over a little mat of green wool, I found myself in a small room with a painted floor and a square of green carpet in the middle; the articles of furniture were few, but all bright and exquisitely clean; order reigned through its narrow limits – such order as it soothed my punctilious soul to behold. And I had hesitated to enter the abode, because I apprehended after all that Mlle Reuter's hint about its extreme poverty might be too well founded, and I feared to embarrass the lace-mender by entering her lodgings unawares! Poor the place might be; poor, truly, it was; but its neatness was better than elegance, and had but a bright little fire shone on that clean hearth, I should have deemed it more attractive than a palace. No fire was there, however, and no fuel laid ready to light; the lace-mender was unable to allow herself that indulgence, especially now when, deprived by death of her sole relative, she had only her own unaided exertions to rely on. Frances went into an inner room to take off her bonnet, and she came out a model of frugal neatness, with her well-fitting black-stuff dress so accurately defining her elegant bust and taper waist, with her spotless white collar turned back from a fair and shapely neck, with her plenteous brown hair arranged in smooth bands on her temples and in a large Grecian plait behind: ornaments she had none – neither brooch, ring nor ribbon; she did well enough without them – perfection of fit, proportion of form, grace of carriage agreeably supplied their place. Her eye, as she re-entered the small sitting room, instantly sought mine, which was just then lingering on the hearth; I knew she read at once the sort of inward ruth and pitying pain which the chill vacancy of that hearth stirred in my soul: quick to penetrate, quick to determine and quicker to put in practice, she had in a moment tied a holland apron round her waist; then she disappeared, and reappeared with a basket; it had a cover; she opened it, and produced wood and coal; deftly and compactly she arranged them in the grate.

"It is her whole stock, and she will exhaust it out of hospitality," thought I.

"What are you going to do?" I asked. "Not surely to light a fire this hot evening? I shall be smothered."

"Indeed, monsieur, I feel it very chilly since the rain began; besides, I must boil the water for my tea, for I take tea on Sundays; you will be obliged to try and bear the heat."

She had struck a light; the wood was already in a blaze; and truly, when contrasted with the darkness, the wild tumult of the tempest without, that peaceful glow which began to beam on the now animated hearth seemed very cheering. A low purring sound, from some quarter, announced that another being, besides myself, was pleased with the change; a black cat, roused by the light from its sleep on a little cushioned footstool, came and rubbed its head against Frances's gown as she knelt; she caressed it, saying it had been a favourite with her "*pauvre tante Julienne*".*

The fire being lit, the hearth swept and a small kettle of a very antique pattern, such as I thought I remembered to have seen in old farmhouses in England, placed over the now ruddy flame, Frances's hands were washed, and her apron removed in an instant; then she opened a cupboard and took out a tea tray, on which she had soon arranged a china tea equipage, whose pattern, shape and size denoted a remote antiquity; a little old-fashioned silver spoon was deposited in each saucer; and a pair of silver tongs, equally old-fashioned, were laid on the sugar basin; from the cupboard, too, was produced a tiny silver cream-ewer, not larger than an egg shell. While making these preparations, she chanced to look up and, reading curiosity in my eyes, she smiled and asked:

"Is this like England, monsieur?"

"Like the England of a hundred years ago," I replied.

"Is it truly? Well, everything on this tray is at least a hundred years old: these cups, these spoons, this ewer are all heirlooms. My great-grandmother left them to my grandmother, she to my mother, and my mother brought them with her from England to Switzerland and left them to me; and, ever since I was a little girl, I have thought I should like to carry them back to England, whence they came."

She put some *pistolets* on the table; she made the tea, as foreigners do make tea – i.e. at the rate of a teaspoonful to half a dozen cups; she placed me in a chair and, as I took it, she asked, with a sort of exultation:

"Will it make you think yourself at home for a moment?"

"If I had a home in England, I believe it would recall it," I answered; and, in truth, there was a sort of illusion in seeing the fair-complexioned, English-looking girl presiding at the English meal and speaking in the English language.

"You have then no home?" was her remark.

"None, nor ever have had. If ever I possess a home, it must be of my own making, and the task is yet to begin." And, as I spoke, a pang, new to me, shot across my heart: it was a pang of mortification at the humility of my position and the inadequacy of my means; while with that pang was born a strong desire to do more, earn more, be more, possess more; and in the increased possessions, my roused and eager spirit panted to include the home I had never had, the wife I inwardly vowed to win.

Frances's tea was little better than hot water, sugar and milk; and her *pistolets*, with which she could not offer me butter, were sweet to my palate as manna.

The repast over, and the treasured plate and porcelain being washed and put by, the bright table rubbed still brighter, "*le chat de ma tante Julienne*"* also being fed with provisions brought forth on a plate for its special use – a few stray cinders and a scattering of ashes too being swept from the hearth – Frances at last sat down; and then, as she took a chair opposite to me, she betrayed, for the first time, a little embarrassment; and no wonder, for indeed I had unconsciously watched her rather too closely, followed all her steps and all her movements a little too perseveringly with my eyes, for she mesmerized me by the grace and alertness of her action – by the deft, cleanly and even decorative effect resulting from each touch of her slight and fine fingers; and when, at last, she subsided to stillness, the intelligence of her face seemed beauty to me, and I dwelt on it accordingly. Her colour, however, rising rather than settling with repose, and her eyes remaining downcast, though I kept waiting for the lids to be raised that I might drink a ray of the light I loved – a light where fire dissolved in softness, where affection tempered penetration, where, just now at least, pleasure played with thought – this expectation not being gratified, I began at last to suspect that I had probably myself to blame for the disappointment; I must cease gazing and begin talking, if I wished to break the spell under which she now sat motionless; so, recollecting the composing effect which an authoritative tone and manner had ever been wont to produce on her, I said,

"Get one of your English books, mademoiselle, for the rain yet falls heavily, and will probably detain me half an hour longer."

Released and set at ease, up she rose, got her book and accepted at once the chair I placed for her at my side. She had selected *Paradise Lost* from her shelf of classics, thinking, I suppose, the religious character of the book best adapted it to Sunday. I told her to begin at the beginning, and while she read Milton's invocation to that heavenly muse who on the "secret top of Oreb or Sinai" had taught the Hebrew shepherd how in the womb of chaos the conception of a world had originated and ripened, I enjoyed, undisturbed, the treble pleasure of having her near me, hearing the sound of her voice – a sound sweet and satisfying in my ear – and looking, by intervals, at her face: of this last privilege, I chiefly availed myself when I found fault with an intonation, a pause or an emphasis; as long as I dogmatized, I might also gaze, without exciting too warm a flush.

"Enough," said I, when she had gone through some half-dozen pages (a work of time with her, for she read slowly and paused often to ask and receive information), "enough; and now the rain is ceasing, and I must soon go." For indeed, at that moment, looking towards the window, I saw it all blue; the thunderclouds were broken and scattered, and the setting August sun sent a gleam like the reflection of rubies through the lattice. I got up; I drew on my gloves.

"You have not yet found another situation to supply the place of that from which you were dismissed by Mlle Reuter?"

"No, monsieur; I have made enquiries everywhere, but they all ask me for references; and to speak truth, I do not like to apply to the directress, because I consider she acted neither justly nor honourably towards me; she used underhand means to set my pupils against me, and thereby render me unhappy while I held my place in her establishment; and she eventually deprived me of it by a masked and hypocritical manoeuvre, pretending that she was acting for my good, but really snatching from me my chief means of subsistence, at a crisis when not only my own life, but that of another, depended on my exertions: of her I will never more ask a favour."

"How, then, do you propose to get on? How do you live now?"

"I have still my lace-mending trade; with care it will keep me from starvation, and I doubt not by dint of exertion to get better employment yet; it is only a fortnight since I began to try; my courage or hopes are by no means worn out yet."

"And if you get what you wish, what then? What are your ultimate views?"

"To save enough to cross the Channel: I always look to England as my Canaan."*

"Well, well – ere long I shall pay you another visit; good evening now," and I left her rather abruptly; I had much ado to resist a strong inward impulse urging me to take a warmer, more expressive leave: what so natural as to fold her for a moment in a close embrace, to imprint one kiss on her cheek or forehead? I was not unreasonable – that was all I wanted; satisfied in that point, I could go away content; and Reason denied me even this; she ordered me to turn my eyes from her face, and my steps from her apartment – to quit her as dryly and coldly as I would have quitted old Madame Pelet. I obeyed, but I swore rancorously to be avenged one day. "I'll earn a right to do as I please in this matter, or I'll die in the contest. I have one object before me now – to get that Genevese girl for my wife; and my wife she shall be – that is, provided she has as much or half as much regard for her master as he has for her. And would she be so docile, so smiling, so happy under my instructions if she had not? Would she sit at my side when I dictate or correct, with such a still, contented, halcyon mien?" For I had ever remarked that however sad or harassed her countenance might be when I entered a room, yet after I had been near her, spoken to her a few words, given her some directions, uttered perhaps some reproofs, she would, all at once, nestle into a nook of happiness and look up serene and revived. The reproofs suited her best of all: while I scolded she would chip away with her penknife at a pencil or a pen, fidgeting a little, pouting a little, defending herself by monosyllables; and when I deprived her of the pen or pencil, fearing it would be all cut away, and when I interdicted even the monosyllabic defence, for the purpose of working up the subdued excitement a little higher, she would at last raise her eyes and give me a certain glance, sweetened with gaiety and pointed with defiance, which, to speak truth, thrilled me as nothing had ever done, and made me, in a fashion (though happily she did not know it), her subject, if not her slave. After such little scenes, her spirits would maintain their flow, often for some hours, and, as I remarked before, her health therefrom took a sustenance and vigour which, previously to the event of her aunt's death and her dismissal, had almost recreated her whole frame.

It has taken me several minutes to write these last sentences; but I had thought all their purport during the brief interval of descending the stairs from Frances's room. Just as I was opening the outer door, I remembered the twenty francs which I had not restored; I paused: impossible to carry them away with me; difficult to force them back on their original owner; I had now seen her in her own humble abode, witnessed the dignity of her poverty, the pride of order, the fastidious care of conservatism, obvious in the arrangement and economy of her little home; I was sure she would not suffer herself to be excused paying her debts; I was certain the favour of indemnity would be accepted from no hand, perhaps least of all from mine: yet, these four five-franc pieces were a burden to my self-respect, and I must get rid of them. An expedient – a clumsy one no doubt, but the best I could devise – suggested itself to me. I darted up the stairs, knocked, re-entered the room as if in haste:

"Mademoiselle, I have forgotten one of my gloves; I must have left it here."

She instantly rose to seek it; as she turned her back, I – being now at the hearth – noiselessly lifted a little vase – one of a set of china ornaments, as old-fashioned as the teacups – slipped the money under it, then saying, "Oh, here is my glove! I had dropped it within the fender; good evening, mademoiselle," I made my second exit.

Brief as my impromptu return had been, it had afforded me time to pick up a heartache; I remarked that Frances had already removed the red embers of her cheerful little fire from the grate: forced to calculate every item, to save in every detail, she had instantly on my departure retrenched a luxury too expensive to be enjoyed alone.

"I am glad it is not yet winter," thought I, "but in two months more come the winds and rains of November; would to God that before then I could earn the right, and the power, to shovel coals into that grate *ad libitum*!"

Already the pavement was drying; a balmy and fresh breeze stirred the air, purified by lightning; I left the west behind me, where spread a sky like opal; azure immingled with crimson: the enlarged sun, glorious in Tyrian tints, dipped his brim already; stepping, as I was, eastward, I faced a vast bank of clouds, but also I had before me the arch of an evening rainbow; a perfect rainbow – high, wide, vivid. I looked long; my eye drank in the scene, and I suppose my brain must have absorbed it; for that night, after lying awake in pleasant fever a long time, watching the silent sheet lightning which still played among the retreating clouds and flashed silvery over the stars, I at last fell asleep; and then in a dream were reproduced the setting sun, the bank of clouds, the mighty rainbow. I stood, methought, on a terrace; I leant over a parapeted wall; there was space below me, depth I could not fathom, but hearing an endless dash of waves, I believed it to be the sea – sea spread to the horizon; sea of changeful green and intense blue: all was soft in the distance; all vapour-veiled. A spark of gold glistened on the line between water and air, floated up, approached, enlarged, changed; the object hung midway between heaven and earth, under the arch of the rainbow; the soft but dusk clouds diffused behind. It hovered as on wings; pearly, fleecy, gleaming air streamed like raiment round it: light, tinted with carnation, coloured what seemed face and limbs; a large star shone with still lustre on an angel's forehead; an upraised arm and hand, glancing like a ray, pointed to the bow overhead, and a voice in my heart whispered:

"Hope smiles on Effort!"

Chapter 20

A COMPETENCY WAS WHAT I WANTED; a competency it was
now my aim and resolve to secure; but never had I been farther
from the mark. With August the school year (*l'année scolaire*) closed,
the examinations concluded, the prizes were adjudged, the schools
dispersed, the gates of all colleges, the doors of all *pensionnats* shut,
not to be reopened till the beginning or middle of October. The last
day of August was at hand, and what was my position? Had I advanced
a step since the commencement of the past quarter? On the contrary,
I had receded one. By renouncing my engagement as English master
in Mlle Reuter's establishment, I had voluntarily cut off £20 from my
yearly income; I had diminished my £60 per annum to £40, and even
that sum I now held by a very precarious tenure.

It is some time since I made any reference to M. Pelet. The moonlight walk is, I think, the last incident recorded in this narrative
where that gentleman cuts any conspicuous figure: the fact is, since
that event, a change had come over the spirit of our intercourse. He,
indeed, ignorant that the still hour, a cloudless moon and an open lattice had revealed to me the secret of his selfish love and false friendship,
would have continued smooth and complaisant as ever; but I grew
spiny as a porcupine and inflexible as a blackthorn cudgel; I never had
a smile for his raillery, never a moment for his society; his invitations to
take coffee with him in his parlour were invariably rejected – and very
stiffly and sternly rejected too; his jesting allusions to the directress
(which he still continued) were heard with a grim calm very different
from the petulant pleasure they were formerly wont to excite. For a
long time Pelet bore with my frigid demeanour very patiently; he
even increased his attentions; but finding that even a cringing politeness failed to thaw or move me, he at last altered too; in his turn he
cooled; his invitations ceased; his countenance became suspicious
and overcast, and I read in the perplexed yet brooding aspect of his

brow a constant examination and comparison of premises, and an anxious endeavour to draw thence some explanatory inference. Ere long, I fancy, he succeeded, for he was not without penetration; perhaps, too, Mlle Zoraïde might have aided him in the solution of the enigma; at any rate, I soon found that the uncertainty of doubt had vanished from his manner; renouncing all pretence of friendship and cordiality, he adopted a reserved, formal, but still scrupulously polite deportment. This was the point to which I had wished to bring him, and I was now again comparatively at my ease. I did not, it is true, like my position in his house; but, being freed from the annoyance of false professions and double-dealing, I could endure it, especially as no heroic sentiment of hatred or jealousy of the director distracted my philosophical soul; he had not, I found, wounded me in a very tender point: the wound was so soon and so radically healed, leaving only a sense of contempt for the treacherous fashion in which it had been inflicted, and a lasting mistrust of the hand which I had detected attempting to stab in the dark.

This state of things continued till about the middle of July, and then there was a little change; Pelet came home one night, an hour after his usual time, in a state of unequivocal intoxication, a thing anomalous with him; for if he had some of the worst faults of his countrymen, he had also one at least of their virtues, i.e. sobriety. So drunk, however, was he on this occasion that after having roused the whole establishment (except the pupils, whose dormitory, being over the classes in a building apart from the dwelling house, was consequently out of the reach of disturbance) by violently ringing the hall bell and ordering lunch to be brought in immediately (for he imagined it was noon, whereas the city bells had just tolled midnight), after having furiously rated the servants for their want of punctuality, and gone near to chastise his poor old mother, who advised him to go to bed, he began raving dreadfully about "*le maudit Anglais, Creemsvort.*"* I had not yet retired; some German books I had got hold of had kept me up late; I heard the uproar below, and could distinguish the director's voice exalted in a manner as appalling as it was unusual. Opening my door a little, I became aware of a demand on his part for "Creemsvort" to be brought down to him, that he might cut his throat on the hall table and wash his honour, which he affirmed to be in a dirty condition, in infernal British blood. "He is either mad or drunk," thought I, "and in either case the old woman and the servants will be the better of a man's assistance," so I descended straight to the hall. I found him staggering about, his eyes in a fine frenzy rolling* – a pretty sight he was, a just medium between the fool and the lunatic.

"Come, M. Pelet," said I, "you had better go to bed," and I took hold of his arm. His excitement, of course, increased greatly at sight and touch of the individual for whose blood he had been making application: he struggled and struck with fury – but a drunken man is no match for a sober one; and, even in his normal state, Pelet's worn-out frame could not have stood against my sound one. I got him up upstairs, and, in process of time, to bed. During the operation he did not fail to utter comminations which, though broken, had a sense in them; while stigmatizing me as the treacherous spawn of a perfidious country, he, in the same breath, anathematized Zoraïde Reuter; he termed her "*femme sotte et vicieuse*",* who, in a fit of lewd caprice, had thrown herself away on an unprincipled adventurer; directing the point of the last appellation by a furious blow, obliquely aimed at me. I left him in the act of bounding elastically out of the bed into which I had tucked him; but, as I took the precaution of turning the key in the door behind me, I retired to my own room assured of his safe custody till morning, and free to draw undisturbed conclusions from the scene I had just witnessed.

Now, it was precisely about this time that the directress, stung by my coldness, bewitched by my scorn and excited by the preference she suspected me of cherishing for another, had fallen into a snare of her own laying – was herself caught in the meshes of the very passion with which she wished to entangle me. Conscious of the state of things in that quarter, I gathered, from the condition in which I saw my employer, that his "ladye-love" had betrayed the alienation of her affections – inclinations, rather, I would say; affection is a word at once too warm and too pure for the subject – had let him see that the cavity of her hollow heart, emptied of his image, was now occupied by that of his usher. It was not without some surprise that I found myself obliged to entertain this view of the case; Pelet, with his old-established school, was so convenient, so profitable a match – Zoraïde was so calculating, so interested a woman – I wondered mere personal preference could, in her mind, have prevailed for a moment over worldly advantage: yet, it was evident, from what Pelet said, that not only had she repulsed him, but had even let slip expressions of partiality for me. One of his drunken exclamations was, "And the jade dotes on your youth, you raw blockhead! And talks of your noble deportment, as she calls your accursed English formality – and your pure morals, forsooth! *Des mœurs de Caton a-t-elle dit – sotte!*"* Hers, I thought, must be a curious soul, where, in spite of a strong, natural tendency to estimate unduly advantages of wealth and station, the sardonic disdain of a fortuneless subordinate had wrought a deeper impression than could be imprinted by the most flattering assiduities of a prosperous *chef d'institution.** I smiled inwardly; and strange to say, though my *amour-propre* was excited not disagreeably by the conquest, my better feelings remained untouched. Next day, when I saw the directress, and when she made an excuse to meet me in the corridor and besought my notice by a demeanour and look subdued to helot humility, I could not love – I could scarcely pity her. To answer briefly and dryly some insinuating enquiry about my health – to pass her by with a stern bow – was all I could; her presence and manner had then, and for some time previously and subsequently, a singular effect upon me; they sealed up all that was good, elicited all that was noxious in my nature; sometimes they enervated my senses, but they always hardened my heart. I was aware of the detriment done, and quarrelled with myself for the change. I had ever hated a tyrant; and, behold, the possession of a slave, self-given, went near to transform me into what I abhorred! There was at once a sort of low gratification in receiving this luscious incense from an attractive and still young worshipper; and an irritating sense of degradation in the very experience of the pleasure. When she stole about me with the soft step of a slave, I felt at once barbarous and sensual as a pasha. I endured her homage sometimes; sometimes I rebuked it. My indifference or harshness served equally to increase the evil I desired to check.

"*Que le dédain lui sied bien!*" I once overheard her say to her mother. "*Il est beau comme Apollon quand il sourit de son air hautain.*"*

And the jolly old dame laughed, and said she thought her daughter was bewitched, for I had no point of a handsome man about me, except being straight and without deformity. "*Pour moi,*" she continued, "*il me fait tout l'effet d'un chat-huant, avec ses bésicles.*"*

Worthy old girl! I could have gone and kissed her had she not been a little too old, too fat and too red-faced; her sensible, truthful words seemed so wholesome, contrasted with the morbid illusions of her daughter.

When Pelet awoke on the morning after his frenzy fit, he retained no recollection of what had happened the previous night, and his mother fortunately had the discretion to refrain from informing him that I had been a witness of his degradation. He did not again have recourse to wine for curing his griefs, but even in his sober mood he soon showed that the iron of jealousy had entered into his soul. A thorough Frenchman, the national characteristic of ferocity had not been omitted by nature in compounding the ingredients of his character; it had appeared first in his access of drunken wrath, when some of his demonstrations of hatred to my person were of a truly fiendish character, and now it was more covertly betrayed by momentary contractions of the features and flashes of fierceness in his light-blue eyes when their glance chanced to encounter mine. He absolutely avoided speaking to me; I was now spared even the falsehood of his politeness. In this state of our mutual relations my soul rebelled, sometimes almost ungovernably, against living in the house and discharging the service of such a man; but who is free from the constraint of circumstances? At that time, I was not: I used to rise each morning eager to shake off his yoke and go out with my portmanteau under my arm, if a beggar, at least a freeman; and in the evening, when I came back from the *pensionnat de demoiselles*, a certain pleasant voice in my ear; a certain face, so intelligent, yet so docile, so reflective, yet so soft, in my eyes; a certain cast of character, at once proud and pliant, sensitive and sagacious, serious and ardent, in my head; a certain tone of feeling, fervid and modest, refined and practical, pure and powerful, delighting and troubling my memory – visions of new ties I longed to contract, of new duties I longed to undertake – had taken the rover and the rebel out of me, and had shown endurance of my hated lot in the light of a Spartan virtue.

But Pelet's fury subsided; a fortnight sufficed for its rise, progress and extinction: in that space of time, the dismissal of the obnoxious teacher had been effected in the neighbouring house, and in the same interval I had declared my resolution to follow and find out my pupil, and upon my application for her address being refused, I had summarily resigned my own post. This last act seemed at once to restore Mlle Reuter to her senses; her sagacity, her judgement, so long misled by a fascinating delusion, struck again into the right track the moment that delusion vanished. By the right track I do not mean the steep and difficult path of principle – in that path she never trod – but the plain highway of common sense, from which she had of late widely diverged. When there, she carefully sought, and, having found, industriously pursued the trail of her old suitor, M. Pelet. She soon overtook him. What arts she employed to soothe and blind him I know not, but she succeeded both in allaying his wrath and hoodwinking his discernment, as was soon proved by the alteration in his mien and manner; she must have managed to convince him that I neither was, nor ever had been, a rival of his, for the fortnight of fury against me terminated in a fit of exceeding graciousness and amenity, not unmixed with a dash of exulting self-complacency, more ludicrous than irritating. Pelet's bachelor's life had been passed in proper French style with due disregard to moral restraint, and I thought his married life promised to be very French also. He often boasted to me what a terror he had been to certain husbands of his acquaintance; I perceived it would not now be difficult to pay him back in his own coin.

The crisis drew on. No sooner had the holidays commenced than note of preparation for some momentous event sounded all through the premises of Pelet; painters, polishers and upholsterers were immediately set to work, and there was talk of *"la chambre de Madame"*, *"le salon de Madame"*.* Not deeming it probable that the old duenna at present graced with that title in our house had inspired her son with such enthusiasm of filial piety as to induce him to fit up apartments expressly for her use, I concluded, in common with the cook, the two housemaids and the kitchen scullion, that a new and more juvenile Madame was destined to be the tenant of these gay chambers.

Presently, official announcement of the coming event was put forth. In another week's time M. François Pelet, *directeur*, and Mlle Zoraïde

Reuter, *directrice*, were to be joined together in the bands of matrimony. Monsieur, in person, heralded the fact to me; terminating his
communication by an obliging expression of his desire that I should
continue, as heretofore, his ablest assistant and most trusted friend,
and a proposition to raise my salary by an additional two hundred
francs per annum. I thanked him, gave no conclusive answer at the
time and, when he had left me, threw off my blouse, put on my coat
and set out on a long walk outside the Porte de Flandre, in order, as I
thought, to cool my blood, calm my nerves and shake my disarranged
ideas into some order. In fact, I had just received what was virtually
my dismissal. I could not conceal, I did not desire to conceal from
myself the conviction that, being now certain that Mlle Reuter was
destined to become Madame Pelet, it would not do for me to remain
a dependent dweller in the house which was soon to be hers. Her
present demeanour towards me was deficient neither in dignity nor
propriety, but I knew her former feeling was unchanged. Decorum
now repressed, and Policy masked it, but Opportunity would be too
strong for either of these – Temptation would shiver their restraints.

I was no pope – I could not boast infallibility: in short, if I stayed,
the probability was that, in three months' time, a practical modern
French novel would be in full process of concoction under the roof
of the unsuspecting Pelet. Now, modern French novels are not to my
taste, either practically or theoretically. Limited as had yet been my
experience of life, I had once had the opportunity of contemplating, near at hand, an example of the results produced by a course
of interesting and romantic domestic treachery. No golden halo of
fiction was about this example: I saw it bare and real, and it was
very loathsome. I saw a mind degraded by the practice of mean sub-
terfuge, by the habit of perfidious deception, and a body depraved
by the infectious influence of the vice-polluted soul. I had suffered
much from the forced and prolonged view of this spectacle; those
sufferings I did not now regret, for their simple recollection acted
as a most wholesome antidote to temptation. They had inscribed
on my reason the conviction that unlawful pleasure, trenching on
another's rights, is delusive and envenomed pleasure – its hollow-
ness disappoints at the time, its poison cruelly tortures afterwards,
its effects deprave for ever.

From all this resulted the conclusion that I must leave Pelet's, and that instantly. "But," said Prudence, "you know not where to go, nor how to live"; and then the dream of true love came over me: Frances Henri seemed to stand at my side; her slender waist to invite my arm; her hand to court my hand; I felt it was made to nestle in mine; I could not relinquish my right to it, nor could I withdraw my eyes for ever from hers, where I saw so much happiness, such a correspondence of heart with heart – over whose expression I had such influence – where I could kindle bliss, infuse awe, stir deep delight, rouse sparkling spirit and sometimes waken pleasurable dread. My hopes to win and possess, my resolutions to work and rise, rose in array against me; and here I was about to plunge into the gulf of absolute destitution. "And all this," suggested an inward voice, "because you fear an evil which may never happen!" "It will happen; you *know* it will," answered that stubborn monitor, Conscience. "Do what you feel is right; obey me, and even in the sloughs of want I will plant for you firm footing." And then, as I walked fast along the road, there rose upon me a strange, inly felt idea of some Great Being – unseen, but all present – who in His beneficence desired only my welfare, and now watched the struggle of good and evil in my heart, and waited to see whether I should obey His voice, heard in the whispers of my conscience, or lend an ear to the sophisms by which His enemy and mine – the Spirit of Evil – sought to lead me astray. Rough and steep was the path indicated by divine suggestion; mossy and declining the green way along which Temptation strewed flowers; but whereas, methought, the Deity of Love, the Friend of all that exists, would smile well-pleased were I to gird up my loins and address myself to the rude ascent; so, on the other hand, each inclination to the velvet declivity seemed to kindle a gleam of triumph on the brow of the man-hating, God-defying demon. Sharp and short I turned round; fast I retraced my steps; in half an hour I was again at M. Pelet's: I sought him in his study; brief parley, concise explanation sufficed; my manner proved that I was resolved; he, perhaps, at heart approved my decision. After twenty minutes' conversation, I re-entered my own room, self-deprived of the means of living, self-sentenced to leave my present home, with the short notice of a week in which to provide another.

Chapter 21

D IRECTLY AS I CLOSED THE DOOR, I saw laid on the table two
letters; my thought was that they were notes of invitation from
the friends of some of my pupils; I had received such marks of attention occasionally, and with me, who had no friends, correspondence
of more interest was out of the question; the postman's arrival had
never yet been an event of interest to me since I came to Brussels.
I laid my hand carelessly on the documents and, coldly and slowly
glancing at them, I prepared to break the seals; my eye was arrested
and my hand too; I saw what excited me, as if I had found a vivid
picture where I expected only to discover a blank page; on one cover
was an English postmark; on the other, a lady's clear, fine autograph;
the last I opened first:

> *Monsieur, I found out what you had done the very morning after
> your visit to me; you might be sure I should dust the china every
> day; and, as no one but you had been in my room for a week, and
> as fairy money is not current in Brussels, I could not doubt who left
> the twenty francs on the chimney piece. I thought I heard you stir
> the vase when I was stooping to look for your glove under the table,
> and I wondered you should imagine it had got into such a little cup.
> Now, monsieur, the money is not mine, and I shall not keep it; I will
> not send it in this note because it might be lost – besides, it is heavy;
> but I will restore it to you the first time I see you, and you must make
> no difficulties about taking it; because, in the first place, I am sure,
> monsieur, you can understand that one likes to pay one's debts; that
> it is satisfactory to owe no man anything;* and, in the second place,
> I can now very well afford to be honest, as I am provided with a
> situation. The last circumstance is, indeed, the reason of my writing
> to you, for it is pleasant to communicate good news; and, in these
> days, I have only my master to whom I can tell anything.*

CHAPTER 21

*A week ago, monsieur, I was sent for by Mrs Wharton, an English
lady; her eldest daughter was going to be married, and some rich
relation having made her a present of a veil and dress in costly old
lace– as precious, they said, almost as jewels, but a little damaged
by time – I was commissioned to put them in repair. I had to do it
at the house; they gave me, besides, some embroidery to complete,
and nearly a week elapsed before I had finished everything. While I
worked, Miss Wharton often came into the room and sat with me,
and so did Mrs Wharton; they made me talk English; asked how I had
learnt to speak it so well; then they enquired what I knew besides –
what books I had read; soon they seemed to make a sort of wonder
of me, considering me no doubt as a learned grisette. One afternoon,
Mrs Wharton brought in a Parisian lady to test the accuracy of my
knowledge of French; the result of it was that, owing probably in a
great degree to the mother's and daughter's good humour about the
marriage, which inclined them to do beneficent deeds, and partly,
I think, because they are naturally benevolent people, they decided
that the wish I had expressed to do something more than mend lace
was a very legitimate one; and the same day they took me in their
carriage to Mrs D.'s, who is the directress of the first English school
at Brussels. It seems she happened to be in want of a French lady
to give lessons in geography, history, grammar and composition, in
the French language. Mrs Wharton recommended me very warmly;
and, as two of her younger daughters are pupils in the house, her
patronage availed to get me the place. It was settled that I am to
attend six hours daily (for, happily, it was not required that I should
live in the house; I should have been sorry to leave my lodgings),
and, for this, Mrs D. will give me twelve hundred francs per annum.*

*You see, therefore, monsieur, that I am now rich; richer almost
than I ever hoped to be: I feel thankful for it, especially as my sight
was beginning to be injured by constant working at fine lace; and I
was getting, too, very weary of sitting up late at nights and yet not
being able to find time for reading or study. I began to fear that I
should fall ill and be unable to pay my way; this fear is now, in a
great measure, removed; and, in truth, monsieur, I am very grateful
to God for the relief; and I feel it necessary, almost, to speak of my
happiness to someone who is kind-hearted enough to derive joy*

from seeing others joyful. I could not, therefore, resist the temptation of writing to you; I argued with myself it is very pleasant to me to write, and it will not be exactly painful, though it may be tiresome, to monsieur to read. Do not be too angry with my circumlocution and inelegancies of expression, and, believe me, your attached pupil,

F.E. HENRI

Having read this letter, I mused on its contents for a few moments – whether with sentiments pleasurable or otherwise I will hereafter note – and then took up the other. It was directed in a hand to me unknown – small and rather neat; neither masculine nor exactly feminine; the seal bore a coat of arms, concerning which I could only decipher that it was not that of the Seacombe family; consequently the epistle could be from none of my almost forgotten and certainly quite forgetting patrician relations. From whom, then, was it? I removed the envelope; the note folded within ran as follows:

I have no doubt in the world that you are doing well in that greasy Flanders; living probably on the fat of the unctuous land; sitting like a black-haired, tawny-skinned, long-nosed Israelite by the fleshpots of Egypt; or like a rascally son of Levi near the brass cauldrons of the sanctuary, and every now and then plunging in a consecrated hook and drawing out of the sea of broth the fattest of heave-shoulders and the fleshiest of wave-breasts.* I know this because you never write to anyone in England. Thankless dog that you are! I, by the sovereign efficacy of my recommendation, got you the place where you are now living in clover, and yet not a word of gratitude, or even acknowledgement, have you ever offered in return; but I am coming to see you, and small conception can you, with your addled aristocratic brains, form of the sort of moral kicking I have, ready-packed in my carpet bag, destined to be presented to you immediately on my arrival.

Meantime I know all about your affairs, and have just got information, by Brown's last letter, that you are said to be on the point of forming an advantageous match with a pursy little Belgian school-mistress – a Mlle Zénobie,* or some such name. Won't I have a look at her when I come over? And this you may rely on: if she pleases my taste, or if I think it worthwhile in a pecuniary point of view, I'll *pounce on your prize and bear her away triumphant in spite of your teeth. Yet I don't like dumpies either, and Brown says she is little and stout – the better fitted for a wiry, starved-looking chap like you.*

Be on the lookout, for you know neither the day nor hour when your – (I don't wish to blaspheme, so I'll leave a blank) – cometh.*

Yours truly,

HUNSDEN YORKE HUNSDEN

"Humph!" said I; and ere I laid the letter down, I again glanced at the small, neat handwriting, not a bit like that of a mercantile man – nor, indeed, of any man except Hunsden himself. They talk of affinities between the autograph and the character: what affinity was there here? I recalled the writer's peculiar face and certain traits I suspected, rather than knew, to appertain to his nature, and I answered, "A great deal."

Hunsden, then, was coming to Brussels, and coming I knew not when; coming charged with the expectation of finding me on the summit of prosperity, about to be married, to step into a warm nest, to lie comfortably down by the side of a snug, well-fed little mate.

"I wish him joy of the fidelity of the picture he has painted," thought I. "What will he say when, instead of a pair of plump turtle doves, billing and cooing in a bower of roses, he finds a single lean cormorant, standing mateless and shelterless on poverty's bleak cliff? Oh, confound him! Let him come, and let him laugh at the contrast between rumour and fact. Were he the Devil himself, instead of being merely very like him, I'd not condescend to get out of his way, or to forge a smile or a cheerful word wherewith to avert his sarcasm."

Then I recurred to the other letter: that stuck a chord whose sound I could not deaden by thrusting my fingers into my ears, for it vibrated within; and though its swell might be exquisite music, its cadence was a groan.

That Frances was relieved from the pressure of want, that the curse of excessive labour was taken off her, filled me with happiness; that her first thought in prosperity should be to augment her joy by sharing it with me, met and satisfied the wish of my heart. Two results of her letter were then pleasant, sweet as two draughts of nectar; but applying my lips for the third time to the cup, they were excoriated as with vinegar and gall.

Two persons whose desires are moderate may live well enough in Brussels on an income which would scarcely afford a respectable maintenance for one in London – and that not because the necessaries of life are so much dearer in the latter capital, or taxes so much higher than in the former, but because the English surpass in folly all the nations on God's earth, and are more abject slaves to custom, to opinion, to the desire to keep up a certain appearance than the Italians are to priestcraft, the French to vainglory, the Russians to their Tsar or the Germans to black beer. I have seen a degree of sense in the modest arrangement of one homely Belgian household that might put to shame the elegance, the superfluities, the luxuries, the strained refinements of a hundred genteel English mansions. In Belgium, provided you can make money, you may save it; this is scarcely possible in England; ostentation there lavishes in a month what industry has earned in a year. More shame to all classes in that most bountiful and beggarly country for their servile following of Fashion; I could write a chapter or two on this subject, but must forbear, at least for the present. Had I retained my £60 per annum, I could, now that Frances was in possession of £50, have gone straight to her this very evening and spoken out the words which, repressed, kept fretting my heart with fever; our united income would, as we should have managed it, have sufficed well for our mutual support; since we lived in a country where economy was not confounded with meanness, where frugality in dress, food and furniture was not synonymous with vulgarity in these various points. But the placeless usher, bare of resource and unsupported by connections, must not think of this; such a sentiment as love, such a word as marriage were misplaced in his heart, and on his lips. Now for the first time did I truly feel what it was to be poor; now did the sacrifice I had made in casting from me the means of living put on a new aspect; instead of a correct, just, honourable act, it seemed a deed at once light and fanatical; I took several turns in my room, under the goading influence of most poignant remorse; I walked a quarter of an hour from the wall to the window; and, at the window, self-reproach seemed to face me; at the wall, self-disdain: all at once out spoke Conscience:

"Down, stupid tormentors!" cried she. "The man has done his duty; you shall not bait him thus by thoughts of what might have been; he relinquished a temporary and contingent good to avoid a permanent and certain evil; he did well. Let him reflect now, and when your blinding dust and deafening hum subside, he will discover a path."

I sat down; I propped my forehead on both my hands; I thought and thought an hour – two hours – vainly. I seemed like one sealed in a subterranean vault who gazes at utter blackness – at blackness ensured by yard-thick stone walls around, and by piles of building above – expecting light to penetrate through granite, and through cement firm as granite. But there are chinks, or there may be chinks, in the best adjusted masonry; there was a chink in my cavernous cell; for, eventually, I saw, or seemed to see, a ray – pallid, indeed, and cold, and doubtful, but still a ray, for it showed that narrow path which Conscience had promised. After two, three hours' torturing research in brain and memory, I disinterred certain remains of circumstances, and conceived a hope that by putting them together an expedient might be framed, and a resource discovered. The circumstances were briefly these.

Some three months ago, M. Pelet had, on the occasion of his *fête*, given the boys a treat, which treat consisted in a party of pleasure to a certain place of public resort in the outskirts of Brussels, of which I do not at this moment remember the name, but near it were several of those lakelets called *étangs*; and there was one *étang*, larger than the rest, where on holidays people were accustomed to amuse themselves by rowing round it in little boats. The boys, having eaten an unlimited quantity of *gaufres** and drank several bottles of Louvain beer amid the shades of a garden made and provided for such crams,* petitioned the director for leave to take a row on the *étang*. Half a dozen of the eldest succeeded in obtaining leave, and I was commissioned to accompany them as surveillant. Among the half-dozen happened to be a certain Jean-Baptiste Vandenhuten, a most ponderous young *Flamand*, not tall, but even now, at the early age of sixteen, possessing a breadth and depth of personal development truly national. It chanced that Jean was the first lad to step into the boat; he stumbled, rolled to one side; the boat revolted at his weight and capsized. Vandenhuten sank like lead, rose, sank again.

My coat and waistcoat were off in an instant; I had not been brought up at Eton and boated and bathed and swam there ten long years for nothing; it was a natural and easy act for me to leap to the rescue. The lads and the boatmen yelled; they thought there would be two deaths by drowning instead of one; but as Jean rose the third time, I clutched him by one leg and the collar, and in three minutes more both he and I were safe landed. To speak Heaven's truth, my merit in the action was small indeed, for I had run no risk, and subsequently did not even catch cold from the wetting; but when M. and Madame Vandenhuten, of whom Jean-Baptiste was the sole hope, came to hear of the exploit, they seemed to think I had evinced a bravery and devotion which no thanks could sufficiently repay. Madame, in particular was "certain I must have dearly loved their sweet son, or I would not thus have hazarded my own life to save his". Monsieur, an honest-looking, though phlegmatic man, said very little, but he would not suffer me to leave the room till I had promised that in case I ever stood in need of help I would, by applying to him, give him a chance of discharging the obligation under which he affirmed I had laid him. These words, then, were my glimmer of light; it was here I found my sole outlet; and in truth, though the cold light roused, it did not cheer me; nor did the outlet seem such as I should like to pass through. Right I had none to M. Vandenhuten's good offices; it was not on the ground of merit I could apply to him; no, I must stand on that of necessity: I had no work; I wanted work; my best chance of obtaining it lay in securing his recommendation. This I knew could be had by asking for it; not to ask because the request revolted my pride and contradicted my habits would, I felt, be an indulgence of false and indolent fastidiousness. I might repent the omission all my life; I would not then be guilty of it.

That evening I went to M. Vandenhuten's; but I had bent the bow and adjusted the shaft in vain: the string broke. I rang the bell at the great door (it was a large, handsome house in an expensive part of the town); a manservant opened; I asked for M. Vandenhuten; M. Vandenhuten and family were all out of town – gone to Ostend – did not know when they would be back. I left my card and retraced my steps.

Chapter 22

A WEEK IS SOON GONE; *le jour des noces** arrived; the marriage was solemnized at Saint-Jacques; Mlle Zoraïde became Madame Pelet, née Reuter; and, in about an hour after this transformation, "the happy pair", as newspapers phrase it, were on their way to Paris – where, according to previous arrangement, the honeymoon was to be spent. The next day I quitted the *pensionnat*. Myself and my chattels (some books and clothes) were soon transferred to a modest lodging I had hired in a street not far off. In half an hour my clothes were arranged in a commode, my books on a shelf, and the "flitting" was effected. I should not have been unhappy that day, had not one pang tortured me – a longing to go to the Rue Notre Dame aux Neiges, resisted yet irritated by an inward resolve to avoid that street till such time as the mist of doubt should clear from my prospects.

It was a sweet September evening – very mild, very still; I had nothing to do; at that hour I knew Frances would be equally released from occupation; I thought she might possibly be wishing for her master; I knew I wished for my pupil. Imagination began with her low whispers, infusing into my soul the soft tale of pleasures that might be.

"You will find her reading or writing," said she. "You can take your seat at her side; you need not startle her peace by undue excitement; you need not embarrass her manner by unusual action or language. Be as you always are: look over what she has written; listen while she reads; chide her, or quietly approve; you know the effect of either system; you know her smile when pleased, you know the play of her looks when roused; you have the secret of awakening what expression you will, and you can choose amongst that pleasant variety. With you she will sit silent as long as it suits you to talk alone; you can hold her under a potent spell; intelligent as she is, eloquent as she can be, you can seal her lips and veil her bright countenance with diffidence; yet, you know, she is not all monotonous mildness; you have seen, with a sort of strange pleasure, revolt, scorn, austerity, bitterness lay energetic claim to a place in her feelings and physiognomy; you know that few could rule her as you do; you know she might break, but never bend under the hand of Tyranny and Injustice, but Reason and Affection can guide her by a sign. Try their influence now. Go – they are not passions; you may handle them safely."

"I will *not* go," was my answer to the sweet temptress. "A man is master of himself to a certain point, but not beyond it. Could I seek Frances tonight, could I sit with her alone in a quiet room and address her only in the language of Reason and Affection?"

"No," was the brief, fervent reply of that Love which had conquered and now controlled me.

Time seemed to stagnate; the sun would not go down; my watch ticked, but I thought the hands were paralysed.

"What a hot evening!" I cried, throwing open the lattice; for, indeed, I had seldom felt so feverish. Hearing a step ascending the common stair, I wondered whether the *locataire*,* now mounting to his apartments, were as unsettled in mind and condition as I was, or whether he lived in the calm of certain resources, and in the freedom of unfettered feelings. What! Was he coming in person to solve the problem hardly proposed in inaudible thought? He had actually knocked at the door – at *my* door– a smart, prompt rap; and, almost before I could invite him in, he was over the threshold and had closed the door behind him.

"And how are you?" asked an indifferent, quiet voice, in the English language; while my visitor, without any sort of bustle or introduction, put his hat on the table, and his gloves into his hat, and drawing the only armchair the room afforded a little forward, seated himself tranquilly therein.

"Can't you speak?" he enquired in a few moments, in a tone whose nonchalance seemed to intimate that it was much the same thing whether I answered or not. The fact is, I found it desirable to have recourse to my good friends *les bésicles*,* not exactly to ascertain the identity of my visitor – for I already knew him, confound his impudence! – but to see how he looked, to get a clear notion of his mien and countenance. I wiped the glasses very deliberately, and put them on quite as deliberately, adjusting them so as not to hurt the bridge of my nose or get entangled in my short tufts of dun hair. I was sitting in the window seat, with my back to the light, and I had him vis-à-vis – a position he would much rather have had reversed, for, at any time, he preferred scrutinizing to being scrutinized. Yes, it was *he*, and no mistake, with his six feet of length arranged in a sitting attitude – with his dark travelling surtout with its velvet collar, his grey pantaloons, his black stock and *his* face, the most original one Nature ever modelled, yet the least obtrusively so; not one feature that could be termed marked or odd, yet the effect of the whole unique. There is no use in attempting to describe what is indescribable. Being in no hurry to address him, I sat and stared at my ease.

"Oh, that's your game – is it?" said he at last. "Well, we'll see about which is the soonest tired." And he slowly drew out a fine cigar case, picked one to his taste, lit it, took a book from the shelf convenient to his hand, then, leaning back, proceeded to smoke and read as tranquilly as if he had been in his own room in Grove Street, —shire, England. I knew he was capable of continuing in that attitude till midnight, if he conceived the whim, so I rose and, taking the book from his hand, I said:

"You did not ask for it, and you shall not have it."

"It is silly and dull," he observed, "so I have not lost much." Then, the spell being broken, he went on, "I thought you lived at Pelet's; I went there this afternoon, expecting to be starved* to death by sitting in a boarding-school drawing room, and they told me you were gone, had departed this morning; you had left your address behind you, though, which I wondered at; it was a more practical and sensible precaution than I should have imagined you capable of. Why did you leave?"

"Because M. Pelet has just married the lady whom you and Mr Brown assigned to me as my wife."

"Oh, indeed!" replied Hunsden with a short laugh. "So you've lost both your wife and your place?"

"Precisely so."

I saw him give a quick covert glance all round my room; he marked its narrow limits, its scanty furniture: in an instant he had comprehended the state of matters – had absolved me from the crime of prosperity. A curious effect this discovery wrought in his strange mind; I am morally certain that if he had found me installed in a handsome parlour, lounging on a soft couch with a pretty, wealthy wife at my side, he would have hated me; a brief, cold, haughty visit would in such a case have been the extreme limit of his civilities, and never would he have come near me more, so long as the tide of fortune bore me smoothly on its surface; but the painted furniture, the bare walls, the cheerless solitude of my room relaxed his rigid pride, and I know not what softening change had taken place both in his voice and look ere he spoke again.

"You have got another place?"

"No."

"You are in the way of getting one?"

"No."

"That is bad; have you applied to Brown?"

"No, indeed."

"You had better; he often has it in his power to give useful information in such matters."

"He served me once very well; I have no claim on him, and am not in the humour to bother him again."

"Oh, if you're bashful and dread being intrusive, you need only commission me. I shall see him tonight; I can put in a word."

"I beg you will not, Mr Hunsden; I am in your debt already; you did me an important service when I was at X—— got me out of a den where I was dying: that service I have never repaid, and at present I decline positively adding another item to the account."

"If the wind sits that way, I'm satisfied. I thought my unexampled generosity in turning you out of that accursed counting house would be duly appreciated some day: 'Cast your bread on the waters, and it shall be found after many days,' say the Scriptures.* Yes, that's right, lad – make much of me – I'm a nonpareil: there's nothing like me in the common herd. In the mean time, to put all humbug aside and talk sense for a few moments, you would be greatly the better of a situation – and, what is more, you are a fool if you refuse to take one from any hand that offers it."

"Very well, Mr Hunsden; now you have settled that point, talk of something else. What news from X—?"

"I have not settled that point, or at least there is another to settle before we get to X—. Is this Miss Zénobie" – ("Zoraïde," interposed I) – "well, Zoraïde – is she really married to Pelet?"

"I tell you yes – and if you don't believe me, go and ask the curé of Saint-Jacques."

"And your heart is broken?"

"I am not aware that it is; it feels all right – beats as usual."

"Then your feelings are less superfine than I took them to be; you must be a coarse, callous character to bear such a thwack without staggering under it."

"Staggering under it? What the deuce is there to stagger under in the circumstance of a Belgian schoolmistress marrying a French schoolmaster? The progeny will doubtless be a strange hybrid race; but that's their lookout – not mine."

"He indulges in scurrilous jests, and the bride was his affianced one!"

"Who said so?"

"Brown."

"I'll tell you what, Hunsden – Brown is an old gossip."

"He is; but in the mean time, if his gossip be founded on less than fact – if you took no particular interest in Miss Zoraïde – why, O youthful pedagogue! did you leave your place in consequence of her becoming Madame Pelet?"

"Because—" I felt my face grow a little hot. "Because – in short, Mr Hunsden, I decline answering any more questions," and I plunged my hands deep in my breeches pockets.

Hunsden triumphed: his eyes – his laugh – announced victory.

"What the deuce are you laughing at, Mr Hunsden?"

"At your exemplary composure. Well, lad, I'll not bore you; I see how it is: Zoraïde has jilted you – married someone richer, as any sensible woman would have done if she had had the chance."

I made no reply – I let him think so, not feeling inclined to enter into an explanation of the real state of things, and as little to forge a false account; but it was not easy to blind Hunsden; my very silence, instead of convincing him that he had hit the truth, seemed to render him doubtful about it; he went on:

"I suppose the affair has been conducted as such affairs always are amongst rational people: you offered her your youth and your talents – such as they are – in exchange for her position and money: I don't suppose you took appearance, or what is called *love*, into the account – for I understand she is older than you – and, Brown says, rather sensible-looking than beautiful. She, having then no chance of making a better bargain, was at first inclined to come to terms with you, but Pelet – the head of a flourishing school – stepped in with a higher bid; she accepted, and he has got her: a correct transaction – perfectly so – businesslike and legitimate. And now we'll talk of something else."

"Do," said I, very glad to dismiss the topic, and especially glad to have baffled the sagacity of my cross-questioner – if, indeed, I had baffled it; for though his words now led away from the dangerous point, his eyes, keen and watchful, seemed still preoccupied with the former idea.

"You want to hear news from X—? And what interest can you have in X—? You left no friends there, for you made none. Nobody ever asks after you – neither man nor woman; and if I mention your name in company, the men look as if I had spoken of Prester John,* and the women sneer covertly. Our X— belles must have disliked you. How did you excite their displeasure?"

"I don't know. I seldom spoke to them – they were nothing to me. I considered them only as something to be glanced at from a distance; their dresses and faces were often pleasing enough to the eye: but I could not understand their conversation, nor even read their countenances. When I caught snatches of what they said, I could never make much of it; and the play of their lips and eyes did not help me at all."

"That was your fault, not theirs. There are sensible as well as handsome women in X— – women it is worth any man's while to talk to, and with whom I can talk with pleasure: but you had and have no pleasant address; there is nothing in you to induce a woman to be affable. I have remarked you sitting near the door in a room full of company, bent on hearing, not on speaking; on observing, not on entertaining; looking frigidly shy at the commencement of a party, confusingly vigilant about the middle and insultingly weary towards the end. Is that the way, do you think, ever to communicate pleasure or excite interest? No; and if you are generally unpopular, it is because you deserve to be so."

"Content!" I ejaculated.

"No, you are not content; you see beauty always turning its back on you; you are mortified and then you sneer. I verily believe all that is desirable on earth – wealth, reputation, love – will for ever to you be the ripe grapes on the high trellis: you'll look up at them; they will tantalize in you the lust of the eye; but they are out of reach: you have not the address to fetch a ladder, and you'll go away calling them sour."*

Cutting as these words might have been under some circumstances, they drew no blood now. My life was changed; my experience had been varied since I left X—, but Hunsden could not know this; he had seen me only in the character of Mr Crimsworth's clerk – a dependant amongst wealthy strangers, meeting disdain with a hard front, conscious of an unsocial and unattractive exterior, refusing to sue for notice which I was sure would be withheld, declining to evince an admiration which I knew would be scorned as worthless. He could not be aware that since then youth and loveliness had been to me everyday objects; that I had studied them at leisure and closely and had seen the plain texture of truth under the embroidery of appearance; nor could he, keen-sighted as he was, penetrate into my heart, search my brain and read my peculiar sympathies and antipathies; he had not known me long enough, or well enough, to perceive how low my feelings would ebb under some influences, powerful over most minds; how high, how fast they would flow under other influences, that perhaps acted with the more intense force on me because they acted on me alone. Neither could he suspect for an instant the history of my communications with Mlle Reuter; secret to him and to all others was the tale of her strange infatuation; her blandishments, her wiles had been seen but by me, and to me only were they known; but they had changed me, for they had proved that I *could* impress. A sweeter secret nestled deeper in my heart, one full of tenderness and as full of strength; it took the sting out of Hunsden's sarcasm; it kept me unbent by shame, and unstirred by wrath. But of all this I could say nothing – nothing decisive at least; uncertainty sealed my lips and, during the interval of silence by which alone I replied to Mr Hunsden, I made up my mind to be for the present wholly misjudged by him – and misjudged I was;

he thought he had been rather too hard upon me, and that I was crushed by the weight of his upbraidings; so, to reassure me, he said doubtless I should mend some day; I was only at the beginning of life yet; and since happily I was not quite without sense, every false step I made would be a good lesson.

Just then I turned my face a little to the light; the approach of twilight, and my position in the window seat, had, for the last ten minutes, prevented him from studying my countenance; as I moved, however, he caught an expression which he thus interpreted:

"Confound it! How doggedly self-approving the lad looks! I thought he was fit to die with shame, and there he sits grinning smiles, as good as to say, 'Let the world wag as it will, I've the philosopher's stone in my waistcoat pocket, and the elixir of life in my cupboard;* I'm independent of both Fate and Fortune!'"

"Hunsden – you spoke of grapes; I was thinking of a fruit I like better than your X— hothouse grapes – a unique fruit, growing wild, which I have marked as my own, and hope one day to gather and taste. It is of no use your offering me the draught of bitterness, or threatening me with death by thirst: I have the anticipation of sweetness on my palate, the hope of freshness on my lips; I can reject the unsavoury, and endure the exhausting."

"For how long?"

"Till the next opportunity for effort; and as the prize of success will be a treasure after my own heart, I'll bring a bull's strength to the struggle."

"Bad luck crushes bulls as easily as bullaces;* and, I believe, the fury dogs you: you were born with a wooden spoon in your mouth, depend on it."

"I believe you; and I mean to make my wooden spoon do the work of some people's silver ladles: grasped firmly, and handled nimbly, even a wooden spoon will shovel up broth."

Hunsden rose. "I see," said he. "I suppose you're one of those who develop best unwatched, and act best unaided – work your own way. Now, I'll go." And, without another word, he was going; at the door he turned.

"Crimsworth Hall is sold," said he.

"Sold!" was my echo.

"Yes; you know, of course, that your brother failed three months ago?"

"What! Edward Crimsworth?"

"Precisely; and his wife went home to her father's; when affairs went awry, his temper sympathized with them; he used her ill; I told you he would be a tyrant to her some day; as to him—"

"Aye, as to him – what has become of him?"

"Nothing extraordinary – don't be alarmed; he put himself under the protection of the court, compounded with his creditors – tenpence in the pound; in six weeks set up again, coaxed back his wife and is flourishing like a green bay tree."*

"And Crimsworth Hall – was the furniture sold too?"

"Everything – from the grand piano down to the rolling pin."

"And the contents of the oak dining room – were they sold?"

"Of course; why should the sofas and chairs of that room be held more sacred than those of any other?"

"And the pictures?"

"What pictures? Crimsworth had no special collection that I know of – he did not profess to be an amateur."

"There were two portraits, one on each side of the mantelpiece; you cannot have forgotten them, Mr Hunsden; you once noticed that of the lady—"

"Oh, I know! The thin-faced gentlewoman with a shawl put on like drapery. Why, as a matter of course, it would be sold among the other things. If you had been rich, you might have bought it, for I remember you said it represented your mother: you see what it is to be without a sou."

I did. "But surely," I thought to myself, "I shall not always be so poverty-stricken; I may one day buy it back yet. Who purchased it? Do you know?" I asked.

"How is it likely? I never enquired who purchased anything; there spoke the unpractical man – to imagine all the world is interested in what interests himself. Now, goodnight – I'm off for Germany tomorrow morning; I shall be back here in six weeks, and possibly I may call and see you again; I wonder whether you'll be still out of place!" he laughed, as mockingly, as heartlessly as Mephistopheles* – and so laughing, vanished.

Some people, however indifferent they may become after a considerable space of absence, always contrive to leave a pleasant impression just at parting; not so Hunsden; a conference with him affected one like a draught of Peruvian bark;* it seemed a concentration of the specially harsh, stringent, bitter; whether, like bark, it invigorated, I scarcely knew.

A ruffled mind makes a restless pillow; I slept little on the night after this interview; towards morning I began to doze, but hardly had my slumber become sleep when I was roused from it by hearing a noise in my sitting room, to which my bedroom adjoined – a step, and a shoving of furniture; the movement lasted barely two minutes; with the closing of the door it ceased. I listened; not a mouse stirred; perhaps I had dreamt it; perhaps a *locataire* had made a mistake and entered my apartment instead of his own. It was yet but five o'clock; neither I nor the day were wide awake; I turned, and was soon unconscious. When I did rise, about two hours later, I had forgotten the circumstance; the first thing I saw, however, on quitting my chamber, recalled it; just pushed in at the door of my sitting room, and still standing on end, was a wooden packing case – a rough-deal affair, wide but shallow; a porter had doubtless shoved it forward, but seeing no occupant of the room, had left it at the entrance.

"That is none of mine," thought I, approaching. "It must be meant for somebody else." I stooped to examine the address:

"Wm Crimsworth, Esq., No. —, —— St, Brussels."

I was puzzled, but concluding that the best way to obtain information was to ask within, I cut the cords and opened the case. Green baize enveloped its contents, sewn carefully at the sides; I ripped the packthread with my penknife, and still, as the seam gave way, glimpses of gilding appeared through the widening interstices. Boards and baize being at length removed, I lifted from the case a large picture, in a magnificent frame; leaning it against a chair, in a position where the light from the window fell favourably upon it, I stepped back – already I had mounted my spectacles. A portrait painter's sky (the most sombre and threatening of welkins), and distant trees of a conventional depth of hue, raised in full relief a pale, pensive-looking female face, shadowed with soft dark hair, almost blending with the equally dark clouds; large, solemn eyes looked reflectively into mine; a thin cheek rested on a delicate little hand; a shawl, artistically draped, half hid, half showed a slight figure. A listener (had there been one) might have heard me, after ten minutes' silent gazing, utter the word, "Mother!" I might have said more – but with me, the first word uttered aloud in soliloquy rouses consciousness; it reminds me that only crazy people talk to themselves, and then I think out my monologue, instead of speaking it. I had thought a long while, and a long while had contemplated the intelligence, the sweetness and – alas! – the sadness also of those fine grey eyes, the mental power of that forehead and the rare sensibility of that serious mouth, when my glance, travelling downwards, fell on a narrow billet, stuck in the corner of the picture, between the frame and the canvas. Then I first asked, "Who sent this picture? Who thought of me, saved it out of the wreck of Crimsworth Hall and now commits it to the care of its natural keeper?" I took the note from its niche; thus it spoke:

There is a sort of stupid pleasure in giving a child sweets, a fool his bells, a dog a bone. You are repaid by seeing the child besmear his face with sugar; by witnessing how the fool's ecstasy makes a greater fool of him than ever; by watching the dog's nature come out over his bone. In giving William Crimsworth his mother's picture, I give him sweets, bells and bone all in one; what grieves me is that I cannot behold the result; I would have added five shillings more to my bid if the auctioneer could only have promised me that pleasure.

H.Y.H.

PS: You said last night you positively declined adding another item to your account with me; don't you think I've saved you that trouble?"

I muffled the picture in its green baize covering, restored it to the case and, having transported the whole concern to my bedroom, put it out of sight under my bed. My pleasure was now poisoned by pungent pain; I determined to look no more till I could look at my ease. If Hunsden had come in at that moment, I should have said to him, "I owe you nothing, Hunsden – not a fraction of a farthing: you have paid yourself in taunts."

Too anxious to remain any longer quiescent, I had no sooner breakfasted than I repaired once more to M. Vandenhuten's, scarcely hoping to find him at home – for a week had barely elapsed since my first call – but fancying I might be able to glean information as to the time his return was expected. A better result awaited me than I had anticipated, for though the family were yet at Ostend, M. Vandenhuten had come over to Brussels on business for the day. He received me with the quiet kindness of a sincere though not excitable man. I had not sat five minutes alone with him in his bureau, before I became aware of a sense of ease in his presence, such as I rarely experienced with strangers. I was surprised at my own composure, for, after all, I had come on business to me exceedingly painful – that of soliciting a favour. I asked on what basis the calm rested – I feared it might be deceptive. Ere long I caught a glimpse of the ground, and at once I felt assured of its solidity; I knew where I was.

M. Vandenhuten was rich, respected and influential; I, poor, despised and powerless; so we stood to the world at large as members of the world's society; but to each other, as a pair of human beings, our positions were reversed. The Dutchman (he was not *Flamand*, but pure *Hollandais*) was slow, cool, of rather dense intelligence, though sound and accurate judgement; the Englishman far more nervous, active, quicker both to plan and to practise, to conceive and to realize. The Dutchman was benevolent, the Englishman susceptible; in short, our characters dovetailed, but my mind, having more fire and action than his, instinctively assumed and kept the predominance.

This point settled, and my position well ascertained, I addressed him on the subject of my affairs with that genuine frankness which full confidence can alone inspire. It was a pleasure to him to be so appealed to; he thanked me for giving him this opportunity of using a little exertion on my behalf. I went on to explain to him that my wish was not so much to be helped as to be put into the way of helping myself; of him I did not want exertion – that was to be my part – but only information and recommendation. Soon after I rose to go. He held out his hand at parting – an action of greater significance with foreigners than with Englishmen. As I exchanged a smile with him, I thought the benevolence of his truthful face was better than the intelligence of my own. Characters of my order experience a balm-like solace in the contact of such souls as animated the honest breast of Victor Vandenhuten.

The next fortnight was a period of many alternations; my existence during its lapse resembled a sky of one of those autumnal nights which are specially haunted by meteors and falling stars. Hopes and fears, expectations and disappointments, descended in glancing showers from zenith to horizon; but all were transient, and darkness followed swift each vanishing apparition. M. Vandenhuten aided me faithfully: he set me on the track of several places, and himself made efforts to secure them for me; but for a long time solicitation and recommendation were vain – the door either shut in my face when I was about to walk in, or another candidate, entering before me, rendered my further advance useless. Feverish and roused, no disappointment arrested me; defeat following fast on defeat served as stimulants to will. I forgot fastidiousness, conquered reserve, thrust pride from me: I asked, I persevered, I remonstrated, I dunned. It is so that openings are forced into the guarded circle where Fortune sits dealing favours round. My perseverance made me known; my importunity made me remarked. I was enquired about; my former pupils' parents, gathering the reports of their children, heard me spoken of as talented, and they echoed the word: the sound, bandied about at random, came at last to ears which, but for its universality, it might never have reached; and at the very crisis when I had tried my last effort and knew not what to do, Fortune looked in at me one morning as I sat in drear and almost desperate deliberation on my bedstead, nodded with the familiarity of an old acquaintance – though God knows I had never met her before – and threw a prize into my lap.

In the second week of October 18—, I got the appointment of English professor to all classes of — College, Brussels, with a salary of three thousand francs per annum; and the certainty of being able, by dint of the reputation and publicity accompanying the position, to make as much more by private lessons. The official notice, which

communicated this information, mentioned also that it was the strong
recommendation of M. Vandenhuten, *négociant*,* which had turned
the scale of choice in my favour.

No sooner had I read the announcement than I hurried to
M. Vandenhuten's bureau, pushed the document under his nose and,
when he had perused it, took both his hands and thanked him with
unrestrained vivacity. My vivid words and emphatic gesture moved
his Dutch calm to unwonted sensation. He said he was happy – glad
to have served me, but he had done nothing meriting such thanks.
He had not laid out a centime – only scratched a few words on a
sheet of paper.

Again I repeated to him:

"You have made me quite happy, and in a way that suits me; I do
not feel an obligation irksome, conferred by your kind hand; I do not
feel disposed to shun you because you have done me a favour; from
this day you must consent to admit me to your intimate acquaintance, for I shall hereafter recur again and again to the pleasure of
your society."

"*Ainsi soit-il*,"* was the reply, accompanied by a smile of benignant
content. I went away with its sunshine in my heart.

Chapter 23

I T WAS TWO O'CLOCK WHEN I RETURNED to my lodgings; my dinner, just brought in from a neighbouring hotel, smoked on the table; I sat down, thinking to eat – had the plate been heaped with potsherds and broken glass, instead of boiled beef and haricots, I could not have made a more signal failure: appetite had forsaken me. Impatient of seeing food which I could not taste, I put it all aside into a cupboard, and then demanded, "What shall I do till evening?" for before 6 p.m. it would be vain to seek the Rue Notre Dame aux Neiges; its inhabitant (for me it had but one) was detained by her vocation elsewhere. I walked in the streets of Brussels, and I walked in my own room from two o'clock till six; never once in that space of time did I sit down. I was in my chamber when the last-named hour struck; I had just bathed my face and feverish hands, and was standing near the glass; my cheek was crimson, my eye was flame, still all my features looked quite settled and calm. Descending swiftly the stair and stepping out, I was glad to see twilight drawing on in clouds; such shade was to me like a grateful screen, and the chill of latter autumn, breathing in a fitful wind from the north-west, met me as a refreshing coolness. Still I saw it was cold to others, for the women I passed were wrapped in shawls, and the men had their coats buttoned close.

When are we quite happy? Was I so then? No; an urgent and growing dread worried my nerves, and had worried them since the first moment good tidings had reached me. How was Frances? It was ten weeks since I had seen her, six since I had heard from her, or of her. I had answered her letter by a brief note, friendly but calm, in which no mention of continued correspondence or further visits was made. At that hour my bark hung on the topmost curl of a wave of fate, and I knew not on what shoal the onward rush of the billow might hurl it; I would not then attach her destiny to mine by the slightest thread; if doomed to split on the rock or run aground on the sandbank, I was resolved no other vessel should share my disaster: but six weeks was a long time; and could it be that she was still well and doing well? Were not all sages agreed in declaring that happiness finds no climax on earth? Dared I think that but half a street now divided me from the full cup of contentment – the draught drawn from waters said to flow only in heaven?

I was at the door; I entered the quiet house; I mounted the stairs; the lobby was void and still, all the doors closed; I looked for the neat green mat; it lay duly in its place.

"Signal of hope!" I said, and advanced. "But I will be a little calmer; I am not going to rush in and get up a scene directly." Forcibly staying my eager step, I paused on the mat.

"What an absolute hush! Is she in? Is anybody in?" I demanded to myself. A little tinkle, as of cinders falling from a grate, replied; a movement – a fire was gently stirred; and the slight rustle of life continuing, a step paced equably backwards and forwards, backwards and forwards, in the apartment. Fascinated, I stood, more fixedly fascinated when a voice rewarded the attention of my strained ear – so low, so self-addressed, I never fancied the speaker otherwise than alone; solitude might speak thus in a desert, or in the hall of a forsaken house.

> "And ne'er but once, my son," he said,
>   "Was yon dark cavern trod;
> In persecution's iron days,
>   When the land was left by God.
> From Bewley's bog, with slaughter red,
>   A wanderer hither drew;
> And oft he stopp'd and turn'd his head,
>   As by fits the night winds blew.
> For trampling round by Cheviot edge
>   Were heard the troopers keen;
> And frequent from the Whitelaw ridge
>   The death-shot flash'd between", etc., etc.*

The old Scotch ballad was partly recited, then dropped; a pause
ensued; then another strain followed, in French, of which the purport,
translated, ran as follows:

> I gave, at first, attention close;
>   Then interest warm ensued;
> From interest, as improvement rose,
>   Succeeded gratitude.
>
> Obedience was no effort soon,
>   And labour was no pain;
> If tired, a word, a glance alone
>   Would give me strength again.
>
> From others of the studious band,
>   Ere long he singled me;
> But only by more close demand
>   And sterner urgency.
>
> The task he from another took,
>   From me he did reject;
> He would no slight omission brook,
>   And suffer no defect.
>
> If my companions went astray,
>   He scarce their wanderings blam'd;
> If I but falter'd in the way,
>   His anger fiercely flam'd.*

Something stirred in an adjoining chamber; it would not do to be
surprised eavesdropping; I tapped hastily, and as hastily entered.
Frances was just before me; she had been walking slowly in her room,
and her step was checked by my advent: Twilight only was with her,
and tranquil, ruddy Firelight; to these sisters, the Bright and the Dark,
she had been speaking, ere I entered, in poetry. Sir Walter Scott's
voice, to her a foreign, far-off sound, a mountain echo, had uttered
itself in the first stanzas; the second, I thought, from the style and the

substance, was the language of her own heart. Her face was grave, its expression concentrated; she bent on me an unsmiling eye – an eye just returning from abstraction, just awaking from dreams: well arranged was her simple attire, smooth her dark hair, orderly her tranquil room; but what – with her thoughtful look, her serious self-reliance, her bent to meditation and haply inspiration – what had she to do with love? "Nothing," was the answer of her own sad, though gentle countenance; it seemed to say, "I must cultivate fortitude and cling to poetry; one is to be my support and the other my solace through life. Human affections do not bloom, nor do human passions glow for me." Other women have such thoughts. Frances, had she been as desolate as she deemed, would not have been worse off than thousands of her sex. Look at the rigid and formal race of old maids – the race whom all despise; they have fed themselves, from youth upwards, on maxims of resignation and endurance. Many of them get ossified with the dry diet; self-control is so continually their thought, so perpetually their object, that at last it absorbs the softer and more agreeable qualities of their nature; and they die mere models of austerity, fashioned out of a little parchment and much bone. Anatomists will tell you that there is a heart in the withered old maid's carcass – the same as in that of any cherished wife or proud mother in the land. Can this be so? I really don't know, but feel inclined to doubt it.

I came forward, bade Frances "Good evening" and took my seat. The chair I had chosen was one she had probably just left: it stood by a little table where were her open desk and papers. I know not whether she had fully recognized me at first, but she did so now; and, in a voice soft but quiet, she returned my greeting. I had shown no eagerness; she took her cue from me, and evinced no surprise. We met as we had always met, as master and pupil – nothing more. I proceeded to handle the papers; Frances, observant and serviceable, stepped into an inner room, brought a candle, lit it, placed it by me; then drew the curtain over the lattice and, having added a little fresh fuel to the already bright fire, she drew a second chair to the table and sat down at my right hand, a little removed. The paper on the top was a translation of some grave French author into English, but underneath lay a sheet with stanzas; on this I laid my hands. Frances half rose, made a movement to recover the captured spoil, saying that was nothing – a mere copy of verses. I put my resistance with the decision I knew she never long opposed; but on this occasion her fingers had fastened on the paper. I had quietly to unloose them; their hold dissolved to my touch; her hand shrunk away; my own would fain have followed it, but for the present I forbade such impulse. The first page of the sheet was occupied with the lines I had overheard; the sequel was not exactly the writer's own experience, but a composition by portions of that experience suggested. Thus, while egotism was avoided, the fancy was exercised, and the heart satisfied. I translate as before, and my translation is nearly literal; it continued thus:

> When sickness stay'd awhile my course,
>   He seem'd impatient still,
> Because his pupil's flagging force
>   Could not obey his will.
>
> One day when summoned to the bed
>   Where pain and I did strive,
> I heard him, as he bent his head,
>   Say, "God, she *must* revive!"
>
> I felt his hand, with gentle stress,
>   A moment laid on mine,
> And wished to mark my consciousness
>   By some responsive sign.
>
> But pow'rless then to speak or move,
>   I only felt, within,
> The sense of Hope, the strength of Love,
>   Their healing work begin.
>
> And as he from the room withdrew,
>   My heart his steps pursued;
> I long'd to prove, by efforts new,
>   My speechless gratitude.

When once again I took my place,
    Long vacant, in the class,
Th' unfrequent smile across his face
    Did for one moment pass.

The lessons done, the signal made
    Of glad release and play,
He, as he passed, an instant stay'd,
    One kindly word to say:

"Jane, till tomorrow you are free
    From tedious task and rule;
This afternoon I must not see
    That yet pale face in school.

"Seek in the garden shades a seat,
    Far from the playground din;
The sun is warm, the air is sweet:
    Stay till I call you in."

A long and pleasant afternoon
    I passed in those green bowers;
All silent, tranquil and alone
    With birds and bees and flowers.

Yet, when my master's voice I heard
    Call from the window, "Jane!"
I entered, joyful, at the word,
    The busy house again.

He, in the hall, paced up and down;
    He paused as I passed by;
His forehead stern relaxed its frown:
    He raised his deep-set eye.

"Not quite so pale," he murmured low.
    "Now, Jane, go rest awhile."

And as I smiled, his smoothened brow
   Returned as glad a smile.

My perfect health restored, he took
   His mien austere again;
And, as before, he would not brook
   The slightest fault from Jane.

The longest task, the hardest theme
   Fell to my share as erst,
And still I toiled to place my name
   In every study first.

He yet begrudged and stinted praise,
   But I had learnt to read
The secret meaning of his face,
   And that was my best meed.

Even when his hasty temper spoke
   In tones that sorrow stirred,
My grief was lulled as soon as woke
   By some relenting word.

And when he lent some precious book
   Or gave some fragrant flower,
I did not quail to Envy's look,
   Upheld by Pleasure's power.

At last our school ranks took their ground;
   The hard-fought field I won;
The prize, a laurel wreath, was bound
   My throbbing forehead on.

Low at my master's knee I bent,
   The offered crown to meet;
Its green leaves through my temples sent
   A thrill as wild as sweet.

The strong pulse of Ambition struck
　　In every vein I owned;
At the same instant, bleeding broke
　　A secret, inward wound.

The hour of triumph was to me
　　The hour of sorrow sore;
A day hence I must cross the sea,
　　Ne'er to recross it more.

An hour hence, in my master's room,
　　I with him sat alone,
And told him what a dreary gloom
　　O'er joy had parting thrown.

He little said; the time was brief,
　　The ship was soon to sail,
And while I sobbed in bitter grief,
　　My master but looked pale.

They called in haste; he bade me go,
　　Then snatched me back again;
He held me fast and murmured low,
　　"Why will they part us, Jane?

"Were you not happy in my care?
　　Did I not faithful prove?
Will others to my darling bear
　　As true, as deep a love?

"O God, watch o'er my foster-child!
　　O guard her gentle head
When winds are high and tempests wild
　　Protection round her spread!

"They call again; leave then my breast;
　　Quit thy true shelter, Jane;

But when deceived, repulsed, oppressed,
   Come home to me again!"

I read – then dreamily made marks on the margin with my pencil – thinking all the while of other things; thinking that "Jane" was now at my side; no child, but a girl of nineteen; and she might be mine, so my heart affirmed; Poverty's curse was taken off me; Envy and Jealousy were far away, and unapprised of this our quiet meeting; the frost of the master's manner might melt; I felt the thaw coming fast whether I would or not; no further need for the eye to practise a hard look, for the brow to compress its expanse into a stern fold: it was now permitted to suffer the outward revelation of the inward glow – to seek, demand, elicit an answering ardour. While musing thus, I thought that the grass on Hermon never drank the fresh dews of sunset* more gratefully than my feelings drank the bliss of this hour.

Frances rose, as if restless; she passed before me to stir the fire, which did not want stirring; she lifted and put down the little ornaments on the mantelpiece; her dress waved within a yard of me; slight, straight and elegant, she stood erect on the hearth.

There are impulses we can control; but there are others which control us, because they attain us with a tiger leap and are our masters ere we have seen them. Perhaps, though, such impulses are seldom altogether bad; perhaps Reason, by a process as brief as quiet, a process that is finished ere felt, has ascertained the sanity of the deed Instinct meditates, and feels justified in remaining passive while it is performed. I know I did not reason, I did not plan or intend – yet, whereas one moment I was sitting solus on the chair near the table, the next, I held Frances on my knee, placed there with sharpness and decision, and retained with exceeding tenacity.

"Monsieur!" cried Frances, and was still: not another word escaped her lips; sorely confounded she seemed during the lapse of the first few moments; but the amazement soon subsided; terror did not succeed, nor fury: after all, she was only a little nearer than she had ever been before to one she habitually respected and trusted; embarrassment might have impelled her to contend, but self-respect checked resistance where resistance was useless.

"Frances, how much regard have you for me?" was my demand. No answer; the situation was yet too new and surprising to permit speech. On this consideration, I compelled myself for some seconds to tolerate her silence, though impatient of it: presently, I repeated the same question – probably not in the calmest of tones; she looked at me: my face, doubtless, was no model of composure, my eyes no still wells of tranquillity.

"Do speak," I urged; and a very low, hurried, yet still arch voice said:

"*Monsieur, vous me faites mal; de grâce lâchez un peu ma main droite.*"*

In truth I became aware that I was holding the said "*main droite*" in a somewhat ruthless grasp: I did as desired; and, for the third time, asked more gently:

"Frances, how much regard have you for me?"

"*Mon maître, j'en ai beaucoup,*"* was the truthful rejoinder.

"Frances, have you enough to give yourself to me as my wife? To accept me as your husband?"

I felt the agitation of the heart, I saw "the purple light of love"* cast its glowing reflection on cheeks, temples, neck; I desired to consult the eye, but sheltering lash and lid forbade.

"*Monsieur,*" said the soft voice at last, "*Monsieur désire savoir si je consens – si – enfin, si je veux me marier avec lui?*"*

"*Justement.*"*

"*Monsieur sera-t-il aussi bon mari qu'il a été bon maître?*"*

"I will try, Frances."

A pause; then with a new, yet still subdued inflexion of the voice – an inflexion which provoked while it pleased me – accompanied, too, by a "*sourire à la fois fin et timide*"* in perfect harmony with the tone:

"*C'est-à-dire, monsieur sera toujours un peu entêté, exigeant, volontaire—*"*

"Have I been so, Frances?"

"*Mais oui; vous le savez bien.*"*

"Have I been nothing else?"

"*Mais oui; vous avez été mon meilleur ami.*"*

"And what, Frances, are you to me?"

"*Votre dévouée élève, qui vous aime de tout son cœur.*"*

"Will my pupil consent to pass her life with me? Speak English now, Frances."

Some moments were taken for reflection; the answer, pronounced slowly, ran thus:

"You have always made me happy; I like to hear you speak; I like to see you; I like to be near you; I believe you are very good, and very superior; I know you are stern to those who are careless and idle, but you are kind, very kind to the attentive and industrious, even if they are not clever. Master, I should be *glad* to live with you always," and she made a sort of movement, as if she would have clung to me, but restraining herself she only added with earnest emphasis: "Master, I consent to pass my life with you."

"Very well, Frances."

I drew her a little nearer to my heart; I took a first kiss from her lips, thereby sealing the compact, now framed between us; afterwards she and I were silent, nor was our silence brief. Frances's thoughts, during this interval, I know not, nor did I attempt to guess them; I was not occupied in searching her countenance, nor in otherwise troubling her composure. The peace I felt, I wished her to feel; my arm, it is true, still detained her; but with a restraint that was gentle enough, so long as no opposition tightened it. My gaze was on the red fire; my heart was measuring its own content; it sounded and sounded, and found the depth fathomless.

"Monsieur," at last said my quiet companion, as stirless in her happiness as a mouse in its terror. Even now in speaking she scarcely lifted her head.

"Well, Frances?" I like unexaggerated intercourse; it is not my way to overpower with amorous epithets any more than to worry with selfishly importunate caresses.

"*Monsieur est raisonnable, n'est-ce pas?*"*

"Yes; especially when I am requested to be so in English; but why do you ask me? You see nothing vehement or obstrusive in my manner; am I not tranquil enough?"

"*Ce n'est pas cela*—"* began Frances.

"English!" I reminded her.

"Well, monsieur, I wished merely to say that I should like, of course, to retain my employment of teaching. You will teach still, I suppose, monsieur?"

"Oh, yes! It is all I have to depend on."

"*Bon!* – I mean, good. Thus we shall have both the same profession. I like that; and my efforts to get on will be as unrestrained as yours – will they not, monsieur?"

"You are laying plans to be independent of me," said I.

"Yes, monsieur; I must be no encumbrance to you – no burden in any way."

"But, Frances, I have not yet told you what my prospects are. I have left M. Pelet's; and after nearly a month's seeking, I have got another place, with a salary of three thousand francs a year, which I can easily double by a little additional exertion. Thus you see it would be useless for you to fag yourself by going out to give lessons; on six thousand francs you and I can live, and live well."

Frances seemed to consider. There is something flattering to man's strength, something consonant to his honourable pride, in the idea of becoming the providence of what he loves – feeding and clothing it, as God does the lilies of the field.* So, to decide her resolution, I went on:

"Life has been painful and laborious enough to you so far, Frances; you require complete rest; your twelve hundred francs would not form a very important addition to our income, and what sacrifice of comfort to earn it! Relinquish your labours: you must be weary, and let me have the happiness of giving you rest."

I am not sure whether Frances had accorded due attention to my harangue; instead of answering me with her usual respectful promptitude, she only sighed and said:

"How rich you are, monsieur!" and then she stirred uneasily in my arms. "Three thousand francs!" she murmured. "While I get only twelve hundred!" She went on faster. "However, it must be so for the present; and, monsieur, were you not saying something about my giving up my place? Oh, no! I shall hold it fast," and her little fingers emphatically tightened on mine.

"Think of my marrying you to be kept by you, monsieur! I could not do it; and how dull my days would be! You would be away teaching in close, noisy schoolrooms from morning till evening, and I should be lingering at home, unemployed and solitary; I should get depressed and sullen, and you would soon tire of me."

"Frances, you could read and study – two things you like so well."

"Monsieur, I could not; I like a contemplative life, but I like an active life better; I must act in some way, and act with you. I have taken notice, monsieur, that people who are only in each other's company for amusement never really like each other so well, or esteem each other so highly, as those who work together, and perhaps suffer together."

"You speak God's truth," said I at last, "and you shall have your own way, for it is the best way. Now, as a reward for such ready consent, give me a voluntary kiss."

After some hesitation, natural to a novice in the art of kissing, she brought her lips into very shy and gentle contact with my forehead; I took the small gift as a loan, and repaid it promptly, and with generous interest.

I know not whether Frances was really much altered since the time I first saw her; but, as I looked at her now, I felt that she was singularly changed for me – the sad eye, the pale cheek, the dejected and joyless countenance I remembered as her early attributes, were quite gone, and now I saw a face dressed in graces: smile, dimple and rosy tint rounded its contours and brightened its hues. I had been accustomed to nurse a flattering idea that my strong attachment to her proved some particular perspicacity in my nature; she was not handsome, she was not rich, she was not even accomplished, yet was she my life's treasure; I must then be a man of peculiar discernment. Tonight my eyes opened on the mistake I had made; I began to suspect that it was only my tastes which were unique, not my power of discovering and appreciating the superiority of moral worth over physical charms. For me, Frances had physical charms: in her there was no deformity to get over; none of those prominent defects of eyes, teeth, complexion, shape which hold at bay the admiration of the boldest male champions of intellect (for women can love a downright ugly man if he be but talented); had she been either *édentée, myope, rugueuse, ou bossue,** my feelings towards her might still have been kindly, but they could never have been impassioned; I had affection for the poor little misshapen Sylvie, but for her I could never have had love. It is true Frances's mental points had been the first to interest me, and they still retained the strongest hold on my preference; but I liked the graces of her person too. I derived a pleasure, purely material, from contemplating the clearness of her brown eyes, the fairness of her fine skin, the purity of her well-set teeth, the proportion of her delicate form; and that pleasure I could ill have dispensed with. It appeared, then, that I too was a sensualist, in my temperate and fastidious way.

Now, reader, during the last two pages I have been giving you honey fresh from flowers, but you must not live entirely on food so luscious; taste then a little gall – just a drop, by way of change.

At a somewhat late hour I returned to my lodgings: having temporarily forgotten that man had any such coarse cares as those of eating and drinking, I went to bed fasting. I had been excited and in action all day, and had tasted no food since eight that morning; besides, for a fortnight past, I had known no rest either of body or mind; the last few hours had been a sweet delirium; it would not subside now and, till long after midnight, broke with troubled ecstasy the rest I so much needed. At last I dozed, but not for long; it was yet quite dark when I awoke, and my waking was like that of Job when a spirit passed before his face, and, like him, "the hair of my flesh stood up". I might continue the parallel, for in truth, though I saw nothing, yet, "a thing was secretly brought unto me, and mine ear received a little thereof; there was silence, and I heard a voice",* saying: "In the midst of life we are in death."*

That sound, and the sensation of chill anguish accompanying it, many would have regarded as supernatural; but I recognized it at once as the effect of reaction. Man is ever clogged with his mortality, and it was my mortal nature which now faltered and plained – my nerves which jarred and gave a false sound – because the soul, of late rushing headlong to an aim, had overstrained the body's comparative weakness. A horror of great darkness fell upon me;* I felt my chamber invaded by one I had known formerly, but had thought for ever departed. I was temporarily a prey to hypochondria.

She had been my acquaintance – nay, my guest – once before in boyhood; I had entertained her at bed and board for a year; for that space of time I had her to myself in secret; she lay with me, she ate with me, she walked out with me, showing me nooks in woods, hollows in hills where we could sit together and where she could drop her drear veil over me, and so hide sky and sun, grass and green tree; taking me entirely to her death-cold bosom and holding me with arms of bone. What tales she would tell me at such hours! What songs she would recite in my ears! How she would discourse to me of her own country – the grave – and again and again promise to conduct me there ere long; and, drawing me to the very brink of a black, sullen river, show me, on the other side, shores unequal with mound, monument and tablet, standing up in a glimmer more hoary than moonlight. "Necropolis!" she would whisper, pointing to the pale piles, and add, "It contains a mansion prepared for you."

But my boyhood was lonely, parentless, uncheered by brother or sister; and there was no marvel that, just as I rose to youth, a sorceress, finding me lost in vague mental wanderings, with many affections and few objects, glowing aspirations and gloomy prospects, strong desires and slender hopes, should lift up her illusive lamp to me in the distance and lure me to her vaulted home of horrors. No wonder her spells *then* had power; but *now*, when my course was widening, my prospect brightening – when my affections had found a rest – when my desires, folding wings, weary with long flight, had just alighted on the very lap of fruition and nestled there warm, content, under the caress of a soft hand – why did hypochondria accost me now?

I repulsed her as one would a dreaded and ghastly concubine coming to embitter a husband's heart towards his young bride; in vain: she kept her sway over me for that night and the next day, and eight succeeding days. Afterwards, my spirits began slowly to recover their tone; my appetite returned, and in a fortnight I was well. I had gone about as usual all the time, and had said nothing to anybody of what I felt; but I was glad when the evil spirit departed from me* and I could again seek Frances and sit at her side, freed from the dreadful tyranny of my demon.

Chapter 24

ONE FINE, FROSTY SUNDAY IN NOVEMBER, Frances and I took a long walk; we made the tour of the city by the boulevards; and, afterwards, Frances being a little tired, we sat down on one of those wayside seats placed under the trees, at intervals, for the accommodation of the weary. Frances was telling me about Switzerland; the subject animated her; and I was just thinking that her eyes spoke full as eloquently as her tongue, when she stopped and remarked:

"Monsieur, there is a gentleman who knows you."

I looked up: three fashionably dressed men were just then passing – Englishmen, I knew by their air and gait as well as by their features; in the tallest of the trio I at once recognized Mr Hunsden; he was in the act of lifting his hat to Frances; afterwards, he made a grimace at me and passed on.

"Who is he?"

"A person I knew in England."

"Why did he bow to me? He does not know me."

"Yes, he does know you, in his way."

"How, monsieur?" (She still called me "monsieur"; I could not persuade her to adopt any more familiar term.)

"Did you not read the expression of his eyes?"

"Of his eyes? No. What did they say?"

"To you they said, 'How do you do, Wilhelmina Crimsworth?' To me, 'So you have found your counterpart at last; there she sits, the female of your kind!'"

"Monsieur, you could not read all that in his eyes: he was so soon gone."

"I read that and more, Frances; I read that he will probably call on me this evening, or on some future occasion shortly; and I have no doubt he will insist on being introduced to you; shall I bring him to your rooms?"

"If you please, monsieur – I have no objection; I think, indeed, I should rather like to see him nearer; he looks so original."

As I had anticipated, Mr Hunsden came that evening. The first thing he said was:

"You need not begin boasting, Monsieur le Professeur; I know about your appointment to — College, and all that; Brown has told me." Then he intimated that he had returned from Germany but a day or two since; afterwards, he abruptly demanded whether that was Madame Pelet-Reuter with whom he had seen me on the boulevards. I was going to utter a rather emphatic negative, but on second thoughts I checked myself and, seeming to assent, asked what he thought of her.

"As to her, I'll come to that directly; but first I've a word for you. I see you are a scoundrel; you've no business to be promenading about with another man's wife. I thought you had sounder sense than to get mixed up in foreign hodge-podge of this sort."

"But the lady?"

"She's too good for you evidently; she is like you, but something better than you – no beauty, though; yet when she rose (for I looked back to see you both walk away) I thought her figure and carriage good. These foreigners understand grace. What the devil has she done with Pelet? She has not been married to him three months – he must be a spoon!"*

I would not let the mistake go too far; I did not like it much.

"Pelet? How your head runs on Mons. and Madame Pelet! You are always talking about them. I wish to the gods you had wed Mlle Zoraïde yourself!"

"Was that young gentlewoman not Mlle Zoraïde?"

"No – nor Madame Zoraïde either."

"Why did you tell a lie, then?"

"I told no lie; but you are in such a hurry... She is a pupil of mine – a Swiss girl."

"And of course you are going to be married to her? Don't deny that."

"Married! I think I shall – if Fate spares us both ten weeks longer. That is my little wild strawberry, Hunsden, whose sweetness made me careless of your hothouse grapes."

"Stop! No boasting – no heroics; I won't bear them. What is she? To what *caste* does she belong?"

I smiled. Hunsden unconsciously laid stress on the word "caste" – and, in fact, republican, lord-hater as he was, Hunsden was as proud of his old —shire blood, of his descent and family standing, respectable and respected through long generations back, as any peer in the realm of his Norman race and Conquest-dated title. Hunsden would as little have thought of taking a wife from a *caste* inferior to his own as a Stanley would think of mating with a Cobden.* I enjoyed the surprise I should give; I enjoyed the triumph of my practice over his theory; and, leaning over the table and uttering the words slowly but with repressed glee, I said concisely:

"She is a lace-mender."

Hunsden examined me. He did not *say* he was surprised, but surprised he was; he had his own notions of good breeding. I saw he suspected I was going to take some very rash step; but repressing declamation or remonstrance, he only answered:

"Well, you are the best judge of your own affairs. A lace-mender may make a good wife as well as a lady; but of course you have taken care to ascertain thoroughly that since she has not education, fortune or station, she is well furnished with such natural qualities as you think most likely to conduce to your happiness. Has she many relations?"

"None in Brussels."

"That is better. Relations are often the real evil in such cases. I cannot but think that a train of inferior connections would have been a bore to you to your life's end."

After sitting in silence a little while longer, Hunsden rose and was quietly bidding me good evening; the polite, considerate manner in which he offered me his hand (a thing he had never done before) convinced me that he thought I had made a terrible fool of myself, and that, ruined and thrown away as I was, it was no time for sarcasm or cynicism, or indeed for anything but indulgence and forbearance.

"Goodnight, William," he said, in a really soft voice, while his face looked benevolently compassionate. "Goodnight, lad. I wish you and your future wife much prosperity; and I hope she will satisfy your fastidious soul."

I had much ado to refrain from laughing as I beheld the magnanimous pity of his mien; maintaining, however, a grave air, I said:

"I thought you would have liked to have seen Mlle Henri?"

"Oh, that is the name! Yes – if it would be convenient, I should like to see her – but—." He hesitated.

"Well?"

"I should on no account wish to intrude."

"Come, then," said I. We set out. Hunsden no doubt regarded me as a rash, imprudent man, thus to show my poor little grisette sweetheart in her poor little unfurnished *grenier*;* but he prepared to act the real gentleman, having, in fact, the kernel of that character under the harsh husk it pleased him to wear by way of mental mackintosh. He talked affably, and even gently, as we went along the street; he had never been so civil to me in his life. We reached the house, entered, ascended the stair; on gaining the lobby, Hunsden turned to mount a narrower stair which led to a higher storey; I saw his mind was bent on the attics.

"Here, Mr Hunsden," said I quietly, tapping at Frances's door. He turned; in his genuine politeness he was a little disconcerted at having made the mistake; his eye reverted to the green mat, but he said nothing.

We walked in, and Frances rose from her seat near the table to receive us; her mourning attire gave her a recluse, rather conventual, but withal very distinguished look; its grave simplicity added nothing to beauty, but much to dignity; the finish of the white collar and *manchettes** sufficed for a relief to the merino gown of solemn black; ornament was forsworn. Frances curtsied with sedate grace, looking, as she always did when one first accosted her, more a woman to respect than to love; I introduced Mr Hunsden, and she expressed her happiness at making his acquaintance in French. The pure and polished accent, the low yet sweet and rather full voice produced their effect immediately; Hunsden spoke French in reply; I had not heard him speak that language before; he managed it very well. I retired to the window seat; Mr Hunsden, at his hostess's invitation, occupied a chair near the hearth; from my position I could see them both, and the room too, at a glance. The room was so clean and bright, it looked like a little polished cabinet; a glass filled with flowers in the centre of the table, a fresh rose in each china cup on the mantelpiece gave it an air of *fête*. Frances was serious, and Mr Hunsden subdued, but both mutually polite; they got on at the French swimmingly: ordinary topics were discussed with great state and decorum; I thought I had never seen two such models of propriety, for Hunsden (thanks to the constraint of the foreign tongue) was obliged to shape his phrases, and measure his sentences with a care that forbade any eccentricity. At last England was mentioned, and Frances proceeded to ask questions. Animated by degrees, she began to change, just as a grave night sky changes at the approach of sunrise: first it seemed as if her forehead cleared, then her eyes glittered, her features relaxed and became quite mobile; her subdued complexion grew warm and transparent; to me, she now looked pretty; before, she had only looked ladylike.

She had many things to say to the Englishman just fresh from his island country, and she urged him with an enthusiasm of curiosity, which ere long thawed Hunsden's reserve as fire thaws a congealed viper. I use this not very flattering comparison because he vividly reminded me of a snake waking from torpor as he erected his tall form, reared his head, before a little declined, and, putting back his hair from his broad Saxon forehead, showed unshaded the gleam of almost savage satire which his interlocutor's tone of eagerness and look of ardour had sufficed at once to kindle in his soul and elicit from his eyes: he was himself, as Frances was herself, and in none but his own language would he now address her.

"You understand English?" was the prefatory question.

"A little."

"Well, then, you shall have plenty of it; and first, I see you've not much more sense than some others of my acquaintance" – indicating me with his thumb – "or else you'd never turn rabid about that dirty little country called England; for rabid, I see, you are: I read Anglophobia in your looks, and hear it in your words. Why, mademoiselle, is it possible that anybody with a grain of rationality should feel enthusiasm about a mere name, and that name England? I thought you were a lady abbess five minutes ago, and respected you accordingly; and now I see you are a sort of Swiss sibyl, with High Tory and High Church principles!"

"England is your country?" asked Frances.

"Yes."

"And you don't like it?"

"I'd be sorry to like it! A little corrupt, venal, lord-and-king-cursed nation, full of mucky pride (as they say in —shire) and helpless pauperism; rotten with abuses, worm-eaten with prejudices!"

"You might say so of almost every state; there are abuses and prejudices everywhere, and I thought fewer in England than in other countries."

"Come to England and see. Come to Birmingham and Manchester; come to St Giles's in London,* and get a practical notion of how our system works. Examine the footprints of our august aristocracy; see how they walk in blood, crushing hearts as they go. Just put your head in at English cottage doors; get a glimpse of Famine crouched torpid on black hearthstones; of Disease lying bare on beds without coverlets, of Infamy wantoning viciously with Ignorance, though indeed Luxury is her favourite paramour and princely halls are dearer to her than thatched hovels—"

"I was not thinking of the wretchedness and vice in England; I was thinking of the good side – of what is elevated in your character as a nation."

"There is no good side – none at least of which you can have any knowledge; for you cannot appreciate the efforts of industry, the achievements of enterprise or the discoveries of science: narrowness of education and obscurity of position quite incapacitate you from understanding those points; and as to historical and poetical associations, I will not insult you, mademoiselle, by supposing that you alluded to such humbug."

"But I did, partly."

Hunsden laughed – his laugh of unmitigated scorn.

"I did, Mr Hunsden. Are you of the number of those to whom such associations give no pleasure?"

"Mademoiselle, what is an association? I never saw one. What is its length, breadth, weight, value – aye, *value*? What price will it bring in the market?"

"Your portrait, to anyone who loved you, would, for the sake of association, be without price."

That inscrutable Hunsden heard this remark and felt it rather acutely, too, somewhere; for he coloured – a thing not unusual with him, when hit unawares on a tender point. A sort of trouble momentarily darkened his eye, and I believe he filled up the transient pause succeeding his antagonist's home-thrust by a wish that someone did love him as he would like to be loved – someone whose love he could unreservedly return.

The lady pursued her temporary advantage.

"If your world is a world without associations, Mr Hunsden, I no longer wonder that you hate England so. I don't clearly know what paradise is, and what angels are; yet, taking it to be the most glorious region I can conceive, and angels the most elevated existences – if one of them – if Abdiel the Faithful* himself" – she was thinking of Milton – "were suddenly stripped of the faculty of association, I think he would soon rush forth from 'the ever-during gates', leave heaven and seek what he had lost in hell. Yes, in the very hell from which he turned 'with retorted scorn'."*

Frances's tone in saying this was as marked as her language, and it was when the word "hell" twanged off from her lips with a somewhat startling emphasis that Hunsden deigned to bestow one slight glance of admiration. He liked something strong, whether in man or woman; he liked whatever dared to clear conventional limits. He had never before heard a lady say "hell" with that uncompromising sort of accent, and the sound pleased him from a lady's lips; he would fain have had Frances to strike the string again, but it was not in her way. The display of eccentric vigour never gave her pleasure, and it only sounded in her voice or flashed in her countenance when extraordinary circumstances – and those generally painful – forced it out of the depths where it burned latent. To me, once or twice, she had, in intimate conversation, uttered venturous thoughts in nervous language; but when the hour of such manifestation was past, I could not recall it; it came of itself and of itself departed. Hunsden's excitations she put by soon with a smile, and, recurring to the theme of disputation, said:

"Since England is nothing, why do the Continental nations respect her so?"

"I should have thought no child would have asked that question," replied Hunsden, who never at any time gave information without reproving for stupidity those who asked it of him. "If you had been my pupil, as I suppose you once had the misfortune to be that of a deplorable character not a hundred miles off, I would have put you in the corner for such a confession of ignorance. Why, mademoiselle, can't you see that it is our *gold* which buys us French politeness, German goodwill and Swiss servility?" And he sneered diabolically.

"Swiss!" said Frances, catching the word "servility". "Do you call my countrymen servile?" And she started up. I could not suppress a low laugh; there was ire in her glance and defiance in her attitude. "Do you abuse Switzerland to me, Mr Hunsden? Do you think I have no associations? Do you calculate that I am prepared to dwell only on what vice and degradation may be found in Alpine villages, and to leave quite out of my heart the social greatness of my countrymen, and our blood-earned freedom, and the natural glories of our mountains? You're mistaken – you're mistaken!"

"Social greatness? Call it what you will, your countrymen are sensible fellows; they make a marketable article of what to you is an abstract idea; they have, ere this, sold their social greatness and also their blood-earned freedom to be the servants of foreign kings."*

"You never were in Switzerland?"

"Yes – I have been there twice."

"You know nothing of it."

"I do."

"And you say the Swiss are mercenary, as a parrot says 'Poor Poll', or as the Belgians here say the English are not brave, or as the French accuse them of being perfidious: there is no justice in your dictums."

"There is truth."

"I tell you, Mr Hunsden, you are a more unpractical man than I am an unpractical woman, for you don't acknowledge what really exists; you want to annihilate individual patriotism and national greatness as an atheist would annihilate God and his own soul, by denying their existence."

"Where are you flying to? You are off at a tangent – I thought we were talking about the mercenary nature of the Swiss."

"We were – and if you proved to me that the Swiss are mercenary tomorrow (which you cannot do), I should love Switzerland still."

"You would be mad, then – mad as a March hare – to indulge in a passion for millions of shiploads of soil, timber, snow and ice."

"Not so mad as you who love nothing."

"There's a method in my madness;* there's none in yours."

"Your method is to squeeze the sap out of creation and make manure of the refuse by way of turning it to what you call use."

"You cannot reason at all," said Hunsden. "There is no logic in you."

"Better to be without logic than without feeling," retorted Frances, who was now passing backwards and forwards from her cupboard to the table, intent, if not on hospitable thoughts,* at least on hospitable deeds, for she was laying the cloth and putting plates, knives and forks thereon.

"Is that a hit at me, mademoiselle? Do you suppose I am without feeling?"

"I suppose you are always interfering with your own feelings and those of other people, and dogmatizing about the irrationality of this, that and the other sentiment, and then ordering it to be suppressed because you imagine it to be inconsistent with logic."

"I do right."

Frances had stepped out of sight into a sort of little pantry; she soon reappeared.

"You do right? Indeed, no! You are much mistaken if you think so. Just be so good as to let me get to the fire, Mr Hunsden; I have something to cook." An interval occupied in settling a casserole on the fire; then, while she stirred its contents: "Right! as if it were right to crush any pleasurable sentiment that God has given to man, especially any sentiment that, like patriotism, spreads man's selfishness in wider circles" (fire stirred, dish put down before it).

"Were you born in Switzerland?"

"I should think so, or else why should I call it my country?"

"And where did you get your English features and figure?"

"I am English, too; half the blood in my veins is English; thus I have a right to a double power of patriotism, possessing an interest in two noble, free and fortunate countries."

"You had an English mother?"

"Yes, yes; and you, I suppose, had a mother from the moon or from Utopia, since not a nation in Europe has a claim on your interest?"

"On the contrary, I'm a universal patriot, if you could understand me rightly: my country is the world."

"Sympathies so widely diffused must be very shallow: will you have the goodness to come to table? Monsieur" – to me, who appeared to be now absorbed in reading by moonlight – "Monsieur, supper is served."

This was said in quite a different voice to that in which she had been bandying phrases with Mr Hunsden – not so short: graver and softer.

"Frances, what do you mean by preparing supper? We had no intention of staying."

"Ah, monsieur, but you have stayed, and supper is prepared; you have only the alternative of eating it."

The meal was a foreign one, of course; it consisted in two small but tasty dishes of meat prepared with skill and served with nicety; a salad and *fromage français* completed it. The business of eating interposed a brief truce between the belligerents, but no sooner was supper disposed of than they were at it again. The fresh subject of dispute ran on the spirit of religious intolerance which Mr Hunsden affirmed to exist strongly in Switzerland, notwithstanding the professed attachment of the Swiss to freedom. Here Frances had greatly the worst of it, not only because she was unskilled to argue, but because her own real opinions on the point in question happened to coincide pretty nearly with Mr Hunsden's, and she only contradicted him out of opposition. At last she gave in, confessing that she thought as he thought, but bidding him take notice that she did not consider herself beaten.

"No more did the French at Waterloo," said Hunsden.

"There is no comparison between the cases," rejoined Frances. "Mine was a sham fight."

"Sham or real, it's up with you."

"No; though I have neither logic nor wealth of words, yet in a case where my opinion really differed from yours, I would adhere to it when I had not another word to say in its defence; you should be baffled by dumb determination. You speak of

Waterloo; your Wellington ought to have been conquered there, according to Napoleon; but he persevered in spite of the laws of war, and was victorious in defiance of military tactics. I would do as he did."

"I'll be bound for it you would; probably you have some of the same sort of stubborn stuff in you."

"I should be sorry if I had not; he and Tell were brothers, and I'd scorn the Swiss, man or woman, who had none of the much enduring nature of our heroic William in his soul."*

"If Tell was like Wellington, he was an ass."

"Does not ass mean *baudet*?" asked Frances, turning to me.

"No, no," replied I, "it means an *esprit-fort;** and now," I continued, as I saw that fresh occasion of strife was brewing between these two, "it is high time to go."

Hunsden rose. "Goodbye," said he to Frances. "I shall be off for this glorious England tomorrow, and it may be twelve months or more before I come to Brussels again. Whenever I do come, I'll seek you out, and you shall see if I don't find means to make you fiercer than a dragon. You've done pretty well this evening, but next interview you shall challenge me outright. Meantime you're doomed to become Mrs William Crimsworth, I suppose; poor young lady! But you have a spark of spirit; cherish it, and give the Professor the full benefit thereof."

"Are you married, Mr Hunsden?" asked Frances, suddenly.

"No. I should have thought you might have guessed I was a Benedict* by my look."

"Well, whenever you marry, don't take a wife out of Switzerland; for if you begin blaspheming Helvetia and cursing the cantons – above all, if you mention the word ass in the same breath with the name Tell (for ass *is baudet*, I know; though monsieur is pleased to translate it *esprit-fort),* your mountain maid will some night smother her *Breton-bretonnant,** even as your own Shakespeare's Othello smothered Desdemona."

"I am warned," said Hunsden, "and so are you, lad" (nodding to me). "I hope yet to hear of a travesty of the Moor and his gentle lady, in which the parts shall be reversed according to the plan just sketched – you, however, being in my nightcap. Farewell, mademoiselle!" He bowed on her hand, absolutely like Sir Charles Grandison on that of Harriet Byron,* adding: "Death from such fingers would not be without charms."

"*Mon Dieu!*" murmured Frances, opening her large eyes and lifting her distinctly arched brows. "*C'est qu'il fait des compliments! Je ne m'y suis pas attendu.*"* She smiled, half in ire, half in mirth, curtsied with foreign grace, and so they parted.

No sooner had we got into the street than Hunsden collared me.

"And that is your lace-mender?" said he. "And you reckon you have done a fine, magnanimous thing in offering to marry her? You, a scion of Seacombe, have proved your disdain of social distinctions by taking up with an *ouvrière*!* And I pitied the fellow, thinking his feelings had misled him, and that he had hurt himself by contracting a low match!"

"Just let go my collar, Hunsden."

On the contrary, he swayed me to and fro; so I grappled him round the waist. It was dark; the street lonely and lampless. We had then a tug for it; and after we had both rolled on the pavement, and with difficulty picked ourselves up, we agreed to walk on more soberly.

"Yes, that's my lace-mender," said I, "and she is to be mine for life – God willing."

"God is not willing – you can't suppose it; what business have you to be suited so well with a partner? And she treats you with a sort of respect, too, and says 'Monsieur', and modulates her tone in addressing you, actually, as if you were something superior! She could not evince more deference to such a one as I, were she favoured by fortune to the supreme extent of being my choice instead of yours."

"Hunsden, you're a puppy. But you've only seen the title page of my happiness; you don't know the tale that follows; you cannot conceive the interest and sweet variety and thrilling excitement of the narrative."

Hunsden – speaking low and deep, for we had now entered a busier street – desired me to hold my peace, threatening to do something dreadful if I stimulated his wrath further by boasting. I laughed till my sides ached. We soon reached his hotel; before he entered it, he said:

"Don't be vainglorious. Your lace-mender is too good for you, but not good enough for me; neither physically nor morally does she come up to my ideal of a woman. No; I dream of something far beyond that pale-faced, excitable little Helvetian (by the by, she has infinitely more of the nervous mobile Parisienne in her than of the robust *jungfrau*).* Your Mlle Henri is in person *chétive*, in mind *sans caractère*, compared with the queen of my visions. You, indeed, may put up with that *minois chiffonné*;* but when I marry I must have straighter and more harmonious features, to say nothing of a nobler and better developed shape than that perverse, ill-thriven child can boast."

"Bribe a seraph to fetch you a coal of fire from heaven,* if you will," said I, "and with it kindle life in the tallest, fattest, most boneless, fullest-blooded of Rubens's painted women – leave me only my Alpine peri, and I'll not envy you."

With a simultaneous movement, each turned his back on the other. Neither said "God bless you", yet on the morrow the sea was to roll between us.

Chapter 25

I N TWO MONTHS MORE, FRANCES HAD FULFILLED the time
of mourning for her aunt. One January morning – the first
of the New Year holidays – I went in a fiacre, accompanied
only by M. Vandenhuten, to the Rue Notre Dame aux Neiges,
and having alighted alone and walked upstairs, I found Frances
apparently waiting for me, dressed in a style scarcely appropriate to that cold, bright, frosty day. Never till now had I seen her
attired in any other than black or sad-coloured stuff; and there
she stood by the window, clad all in white, and white of a most
diaphanous texture; her array was very simple, to be sure, but
it looked imposing and festal because it was so clear, full and
floating; a veil shadowed her head and hung below her knee; a
little wreath of pink flowers fastened it to her thickly tressed
Grecian plait, and thence it fell softly on each side of her face.
Singular to state, she was or had been crying; when I asked her
if she were ready, she said "Yes, monsieur" with something very
like a checked sob; and when I took a shawl which lay on the
table and folded it round her, not only did tear after tear course
unbidden down her cheek, but she shook to my ministration
like a reed. I said I was sorry to see her in such low spirits, and
requested to be allowed an insight into the origin thereof. She
only said, "It was impossible to help it," and then voluntarily,
though hurriedly, putting her hand into mine, accompanied me
out of the room and ran downstairs with a quick, uncertain step,
like one who was eager to get some formidable piece of business
over. I put her into the fiacre. M. Vandenhuten received her and
seated her beside himself; we drove all together to the Protestant
chapel, went through a certain service in the Common Prayer
Book, and she and I came out married. M. Vandenhuten had
given the bride away.

We took no bridal trip; our modesty, screened by the peaceful obscurity of our station, and the pleasant isolation of our circumstances, did not exact that additional precaution. We repaired at once to a small house I had taken in the *faubourg** nearest to that part of the city where the scene of our avocations lay.

Three or four hours after the wedding ceremony, Frances, divested of her bridal snow and attired in a pretty lilac gown of warmer materials, a piquant black silk apron and a lace collar with some finishing decoration of lilac ribbon, was kneeling on the carpet of a neatly furnished though not spacious parlour, arranging on the shelves of a chiffonnière some books, which I handed to her from the table. It was snowing fast out of doors; the afternoon had turned out wild and cold; the leaden sky seemed full of drifts, and the street was already ankle-deep in the white downfall. Our fire burned bright, our new habitation looked brilliantly clean and fresh, the furniture was all arranged, and there were but some articles of glass, china, books, etc., to put in order. Frances found in this business occupation till teatime, and then, after I had distinctly instructed her how to make a cup of tea in rational English style, and after she had got over the dismay occasioned by seeing such an extravagant amount of material put into the pot, she administered to me a proper British repast, at which there wanted neither candles nor urn, firelight nor comfort.

Our week's holiday glided by, and we readdressed ourselves to labour. Both my wife and I began in good earnest with the notion that we were working people, destined to earn our bread by exertion, and that of the most assiduous kind. Our days were thoroughly occupied; we used to part every morning at eight o'clock, and not meet again till 5 p.m.; but into what sweet rest did the turmoil of each busy day decline! Looking down the vista of memory, I see the evenings passed in that little parlour like a long string of rubies circling the dusk brow of the past. Unvaried were they as each cut gem, and like each gem brilliant and burning.

A year and a half passed. One morning (it was a *fête,* and we had the day to ourselves) Frances said to me, with a suddenness peculiar to her when she had been thinking long on a subject and at last, having came to a conclusion, wished to test its soundness by the touchstone of my judgement:

"I don't work enough."

"What now?" demanded I, looking up from my coffee, which I had been deliberately stirring while enjoying, in anticipation, a walk I purposed to take with Frances, that fine summer day (it was June), to a certain farmhouse in the country where we were to dine. "What now?" And I saw at once, in the serious ardour of her face, a project of vital importance.

"I am not satisfied," returned she. "You are now earning eight thousand francs a year" – it was true: my efforts, punctuality, the fame of my pupils' progress, the publicity of my station had so far helped me on – "while I am still at my miserable twelve hundred francs. I *can* do better, and I *will*."

"You work as long and as diligently as I do, Frances."

"Yes, monsieur, but I am not working in the right way, and I am convinced of it."

"You wish to change – you have a plan for progress in your mind; go and put on your bonnet; and, while we take our walk, you shall tell me of it."

"Yes, monsieur."

She went – as docile as a well-trained child; she was a curious mixture of tractability and firmness: I sat thinking about her and wondering what her plan could be, when she re-entered.

"Monsieur, I have given Minnie" – our *bonne* – "leave to go out too, as it is so very fine; so will you be kind enough to lock the door and take the key with you?"

"Kiss me, Mrs Crimsworth," was my not very apposite reply; but she looked so engaging in her light summer dress and little cottage bonnet, and her manner in speaking to me was then, as always, so unaffectedly and suavely respectful, that my heart expanded at the sight of her, and a kiss seemed necessary to content its importunity.

"There, monsieur."

"Why do you always call me 'Monsieur'? Say 'William'."

"I cannot pronounce your 'W'; besides, 'Monsieur' belongs to you; I like it best."

Minnie having departed in clean cap and smart shawl, we, too, set out, leaving the house solitary and silent – silent, at least, but for the ticking of the clock. We were soon clear of Brussels; the fields received

us, and then the lanes, remote from carriage-resounding *chaussées*.*
Ere long we came upon a nook, so rural, green and secluded it might
have been a spot in some pastoral English province; a bank of short
and mossy grass, under a hawthorn, offered a seat too tempting to be
declined; we took it, and when we had admired and examined some
English-looking wild flowers growing at our feet, I recalled Frances's
attention and my own to the topic touched on at breakfast.

"What was her plan?" A natural one – the next step to be mounted
by us – or, at least, by her – if she wanted to rise in her profession.
She proposed to begin a school. We already had the means for com-
mencing on a careful scale, having lived greatly within our income.
We possessed, too, by this time, an extensive and eligible connection,
in the sense advantageous to our business; for, though our circle of
visiting acquaintance continued as limited as ever, we were now
widely known in schools and families as teachers. When Frances
had developed her plan, she intimated, in some closing sentences,
her hopes for the future. If we only had good health and tolerable
success, we might, she was sure, in time realize an independency; and
that, perhaps, before we were too old to enjoy it; then both she and I
would rest; and what was to hinder us from going to live in England?
England was still her Promised Land.

I put no obstacle in her way; raised no objection; I knew she was
not one who could live quiescent and inactive, or even comparatively
inactive. Duties she must have to fulfil, and important duties; work to
do – and exciting, absorbing, profitable work; strong faculties stirred
in her frame, and they demanded full nourishment, free exercise: mine
was not the hand ever to starve or cramp them; no, I delighted in
offering them sustenance, and in clearing them wider space for action.

"You have conceived a plan, Frances," said I, "and a good plan;
execute it; you have my free consent, and wherever and whenever my
assistance is wanted, ask and you shall have."

Frances's eyes thanked me almost with tears; just a sparkle or two,
soon brushed away; she possessed herself of my hand too, and held
it for some time very close clasped in both her own, but she said no
more than, "Thank you, monsieur."

We passed a divine day, and came home late, lighted by a full
summer moon.

Ten years rushed now upon me with dusty, vibrating, unresting wings; years of bustle, action, unslacked endeavour; years in which I and my wife, having launched ourselves in the full career of progress, as progress whirls on in European capitals, scarcely knew repose, were strangers to amusement, never thought of indulgence – and yet, as our course ran side by side, as we marched hand in hand, we neither murmured, repented nor faltered. Hope indeed cheered us; health kept us up; harmony of thought and deed smoothed many difficulties, and, finally, success bestowed every now and then encouraging reward on diligence. Our school became one of the most popular in Brussels, and as by degrees we raised our terms and elevated our system of education, our choice of pupils grew more select, and at length included the children of the best families in Belgium. We had, too, an excellent connection in England, first opened by the unsolicited recommendation of Mr Hunsden, who having been over, and having abused me for my prosperity in set terms, went back, and soon after sent a leash* of young —shire heiresses – his cousins – as he said, "to be polished off by Mrs Crimsworth".

As to this same Mrs Crimsworth, in one sense she was become another woman, though in another she remained unchanged. So different was she under different circumstances, I seemed to possess two wives. The faculties of her nature, already disclosed when I married her, remained fresh and fair; but other faculties shot up strong, branched out broad and quite altered the external character of the plant. Firmness, activity and enterprise, covered with grave foliage, poetic feeling and fervour; but these flowers were still there, preserved pure and dewy under the umbrage of later growth and hardier nature: perhaps I only in the world knew the secret of their existence, but to me they were ever ready to yield an exquisite fragrance and present a beauty as chaste as radiant.

In the daytime my house and establishment were conducted by Madame the directress, a stately and elegant woman, bearing much anxious thought on her large brow, much calculated dignity in her serious mien; immediately after breakfast I used to part with this lady; I went to my college, she to her schoolroom; returning for an hour in the course of the day, I found her always in class, intently occupied – silence, industry, observance, attending on her presence.

When not actually teaching, she was overlooking and guiding by eye and gesture; she then appeared vigilant and solicitous. When communicating instruction, her aspect was more animated; she seemed to feel a certain enjoyment in the occupation. The language in which she addressed her pupils, though simple and unpretending, was never trite or dry; she did not speak from routine formulas – she made her own phrases as she went on, and very nervous* and impressive phrases they frequently were; often, when elucidating favourite points of history, or geography, she would wax genuinely eloquent in her earnestness. Her pupils, or at least the elder and more intelligent amongst them, recognized well the language of a superior mind; they felt too, and some of them received the impression of elevated sentiments; there was little fondling between mistress and girls, but some of Frances's pupils in time learnt to love her sincerely, all of them beheld her with respect; her general demeanour towards them was serious, sometimes benignant when they pleased her with their progress and attention, always scrupulously refined and considerate. In cases where reproof or punishment was called for, she was usually forbearing enough; but if any took advantage of that forbearance, which sometimes happened, a sharp, sudden and lightning-like severity taught the culprit the extent of the mistake committed. Sometimes a gleam of tenderness softened her eyes and manner, but this was rare; only when a pupil was sick, or when it pined after home, or in the case of some little motherless child, or of one much poorer than its companion, whose scanty wardrobe and mean appointments brought on it the contempt of the jewelled young countesses and silk-clad misses. Over such feeble fledglings the directress spread a wing of kindliest protection: it was to their bedside she came at night to tuck them warmly in; it was after them she looked in winter to see that they always had a comfortable seat by the stove; it was they who by turns were summoned to the salon to receive some little dole of cake or fruit – to sit on a footstool at the fireside – to enjoy home comforts, and almost home liberty, for an evening together – to be spoken to gently and softly, comforted, encouraged, cherished – and when bedtime came, dismissed with a kiss of true tenderness. As to Julia and Georgiana G——, daughters of an English baronet, as to Mlle Mathilde de ——, heiress of a Belgian count, and sundry other children of patrician race, the directress was careful of them as of the others, anxious for their progress as for that of the rest – but it never seemed to enter her head to distinguish them by a mark of preference; one girl of noble blood she loved dearly – a young Irish baroness – Lady Catherine —, but it was for her enthusiastic heart and clever head, for her generosity and her genius: the title and rank went for nothing.

My afternoons were spent also in college, with the exception of an hour that my wife daily exacted of me for her establishment, and with which she would not dispense. She said I must spend that time amongst her pupils to learn their characters, to be *au courant** with everything that was passing in the house, to become interested in what interested her, to be able to give her my opinion on knotty points when she required it, and this she did constantly, never allowing my interest in the pupils to fall asleep, and never making any change of importance without my cognizance and consent. She delighted to sit by me when I gave my lessons (lessons in literature), her hands folded on her knee, the most fixedly attentive of any present. She rarely addressed me in class; when she did, it was with an air of marked deference; it was her pleasure, her joy to make me still the master in all things.

At six o'clock p.m. my daily labours ceased. I then came home, for my home was my heaven; ever at that hour, as I entered our private sitting room, the lady directress vanished from before my eyes, and Frances Henri, my own little lace-mender, was magically restored to my arms; much disappointed she would have been if her master had not been as constant to the tryst as herself, and if his truthful kiss had not been prompt to answer her soft "*Bonsoir, monsieur*".

Talk French to me she would, and many a punishment she has had for her wilfulness. I fear the choice of chastisement must have been injudicious, for instead of correcting the fault, it seemed to encourage its renewal. Our evenings were our own: that recreation was necessary to refresh our strength for all the due discharge of our duties; sometimes we spent them all in conversation, and my young Genevese, now that she was thoroughly accustomed to her English professor, now that she loved him too absolutely to fear him much, reposed in him a confidence so unlimited that topics of conversation could no more be wanting with him than subjects for communion with her own heart. In those moments, happy as a bird with its mate, she would show me what she had of vivacity, of mirth, of originality in her well-dowered nature. She would show, too, some stores of raillery, of *malice*,* and would vex, tease, pique me sometimes about what she called my *"bizarreries anglaises"*, my *"caprices insulaires"*,* with a wild and witty wickedness that made a perfect white demon of her while it lasted. This was rare, however, and the elfish freak was always short: sometimes when driven a little hard in the war of words – for her tongue did ample justice to the pith, the point, the delicacy of her native French, in which language she always attacked me – I used to turn upon her with my old decision and arrest bodily the sprite that teased me. Vain idea! No sooner had I grasped hand or arm than the elf was gone; the provocative smile quenched in the expressive brown eyes, and a ray of gentle homage shone under the lids in its place. I had seized a mere vexing fairy, and found a submissive and supplicating little mortal woman in my arms. Then I made her get a book and read English to me for an hour by way of penance. I frequently dosed her with Wordsworth in this way, and Wordsworth steadied her soon; she had a difficulty in comprehending his deep, serene and sober mind; his language, too, was not facile to her; she had to ask questions, to sue for explanations, to be like a child and a novice, and to acknowledge me as her senior and director. Her instinct instantly penetrated and possessed the meaning of more ardent and imaginative writers. Byron excited her; Scott she loved; Wordsworth only she puzzled at, wondered over and hesitated to pronounce an opinion upon.

But whether she read to me, or talked with me, whether she teased me in French or entreated me in English, whether she jested with wit, or enquired with deference, narrated with interest or listened with attention, whether she smiled *at* me or *on* me, always at nine o'clock I was left... abandoned. She would extricate herself from my arms, quit my side, take her lamp and be gone. Her mission was upstairs; I have followed her sometimes and watched her. First she opened the door of the *dortoir* (the pupils' chamber), noiselessly she glided up the long room between the two rows of white beds, surveyed all the sleepers; if any were wakeful, especially if any were sad, spoke to them and soothed them; stood some minutes to ascertain that all was safe and tranquil; trimmed the watch-light which burned in the apartment all night, then withdrew, closing the door behind her without sound. Thence she glided to our own chamber; it had a little cabinet within; this she sought; there, too, appeared a bed, but one, and that a very small one; her face (the night I followed and observed her) changed as she approached this tiny couch; from grave it warmed to earnest; she shaded with one hand the lamp she held in the other; she bent above the pillow and hung over a child asleep; its slumber (that evening at least, and usually, I believe) was sound and calm; no tear wet its dark eyelashes; no fever heated its round cheek; no ill dream discomposed its budding features. Frances gazed, she did not smile, and yet the deepest delight filled, flushed her face; feeling, pleasurable, powerful, worked in her whole frame, which still was motionless. I saw, indeed, her heart heave; her lips were a little apart, her breathing grew somewhat hurried; the child smiled; then at last the mother smiled too, and said in low soliloquy, "God bless my little son!" She stooped closer over him, breathed the softest of kisses on his brow, covered his minute hand with hers and at last started up and came away. I regained the parlour before her. Entering it two minutes later, she said quietly as she put down her extinguished lamp:

"Victor rests well: he smiled in his sleep; he has your smile, monsieur."

The said Victor was of course her own boy, born in the third year of our marriage: his Christian name had been given him in honour of M. Vandenhuten, who continued always our trusty and well-beloved friend.

Frances was then a good and dear wife to me, because I was to her a good, just and faithful husband. What she would have been had she married a harsh, envious, careless man – a profligate, a prodigal, a drunkard or a tyrant – is another question, and one which I once propounded to her. Her answer, given after some reflection was:

"I should have tried to endure the evil or cure it for awhile; and when I found it intolerable and incurable, I should have left my torturer suddenly and silently."

"And if law or might had forced you back again?"

"What, to a drunkard, a profligate, a selfish spendthrift, an unjust fool?"

"Yes."

"I would have gone back; again assured myself whether or not his vice and my misery were capable of remedy; and if not, have left him again."

"And if again forced to return, and compelled to abide?"

"I don't know," she said hastily. "Why do you ask me, monsieur?"

I would have an answer, because I saw a strange kind of spirit in her eye, whose voice I determined to waken.

"Monsieur, if a wife's nature loathes that of the man she is wedded to, marriage must be slavery. Against slavery all right thinkers revolt, and though torture be the price of resistance, torture must be dared: though the only road to freedom lie through the gates of death, those gates must be passed, for freedom is indispensable. Then, monsieur, I would resist as far as my strength permitted; when that strength failed, I should be sure of a refuge. Death would certainly screen me both from bad laws and their consequences."

"Voluntary death, Frances?"

"No, monsieur. I'd have courage to live out every throe of anguish fate assigned me, and principle to contend for justice and liberty to the last."

"I see you would have made no patient Grizzle.* And now, supposing fate had merely assigned you the lot of an old maid, what then? How would you have liked celibacy?"

"Not much, certainly. An old maid's life must doubtless be void and vapid – her heart strained and empty. Had I been an old maid, I should have spent existence in efforts to fill the void and ease the aching. I should have probably failed, and died weary and disappointed, despised and of no account, like other single women. But I'm not an old maid," she added quickly. "I should have been, though, but for my master. I should never have suited any man but Professor Crimsworth – no other gentleman, French, English or Belgian, would have thought me amiable or handsome; and I doubt whether I should have cared for the approbation of many others, if I could have obtained it. Now, I have been Professor Crimsworth's wife eight years, and what is he in my eyes? Is he honourable, beloved—" She stopped; her voice was cut off; her eyes suddenly suffused. She and I were standing side by side; she threw her arms round me, and strained me to her heart with

226

passionate earnestness: the energy of her whole being glowed in her dark and then dilated eye, and crimsoned her animated cheek; her look and movement were like inspiration; in one there was such a flash, in the other such a power. Half an hour afterwards, when she had become calm, I asked where all that wild vigour was gone which had transformed her erewhile and made her glance so thrilling and ardent – her action so rapid and strong. She looked down, smiling softly and passively:

"I cannot tell where it is gone, monsieur," said she, "but I know that, whenever it is wanted, it will come back again."

Behold us now at the close of the ten years, and we have realized an independency. The rapidity with which we attained this end had its origin in three reasons: firstly, we worked so hard for it; secondly, we had no encumbrances to delay success; thirdly, as soon as we had capital to invest, two well-skilled counsellors – one in Belgium, one in England, viz. Vandenhuten and Hunsden – gave us each a word of advice as to the sort of investment to be chosen. The suggestion made was judicious; and, being promptly acted on, the result proved gainful – I need not say how gainful; I communicated details to Messrs Vandenhuten and Hunsden; nobody else can be interested in hearing them.

Accounts being wound up, and our professional connection disposed of, we both agreed that, as Mammon was not our master, nor his service that in which we desired to spend our lives – as our desires were temperate and our habits unostentatious – we now had abundance to live on – abundance to leave our boy; and should, besides, always have a balance on hand, which, properly managed by right sympathy and unselfish activity, might help Philanthropy in her enterprises and put solace into the hand of Charity.

To England we now resolved to take wing; we arrived there safely; Frances realized the dream of her lifetime. We spent a whole summer and autumn in travelling from end to end of the British islands, and afterwards passed a winter in London. Then we thought it high time to fix our residence. My heart yearned towards my native county of —shire; and it is in —shire I now live; it is in the library of my own home I am now writing. That home lies amid a sequestered and rather hilly region, thirty miles removed from X— – a region whose verdure the smoke of mills has not yet sullied, whose waters still run pure, whose swells of moorland preserve in some ferny glens that lie between them the very primal wildness of nature: her moss, her bracken, her blue-bells, her scents of reed and heather, her free and fresh breezes. My house is a picturesque and not too spacious dwelling, with low and long windows, a trellised and leaf-veiled porch over the front door, just now, on this summer evening, looking like an arch of roses and ivy. The garden is chiefly laid out in lawn, formed of the sod of the hills, with herbage short and soft as moss, full of its own peculiar flowers, tiny and star-like, embedded in the minute embroidery of their fine foliage. At the bottom of the sloping garden there is a wicket, which opens upon a lane as green as the lawn, very long, shady and little frequented; on the turf of this lane generally appear the first daisies of spring – whence its name, Daisy Lane, serving also as a distinction to the house.

It terminates (the lane I mean) in a valley of wood; which wood – chiefly oak and beech – spreads shadowy about the vicinage of a very old mansion, one of the Elizabethan structures, much larger, as well as more antique than Daisy Lane, the property and residence of an individual familiar both to me and to the reader. Yes, in Hunsden Wood – for so are those glades and that grey building, with many gables and more chimneys, named – abides Yorke Hunsden, still unmarried; never, I suppose, having yet found his ideal, though I know at least a score of young ladies, within a circuit of forty miles, who would be willing to assist him in the search.

The estate fell to him by the death of his father, five years since; he has given up trade, after having made by it sufficient to pay off some encumbrances by which the family heritage was burdened. I say he abides here, but I do not think he is resident about five months out of the twelve; he wanders from land to land, and spends some part of each winter in town; he frequently brings visitors with him when he comes to —shire, and these visitors are often foreigners; sometimes he has a German metaphysician, sometimes a French savant; he had once a dissatisfied and savage-looking Italian, who neither sang nor played, and of whom Frances affirmed that he had *"tout l'air d'un conspirateur."**

What English guests Hunsden invites are all either men of Birmingham or Manchester – hard men, seemingly knit up in one thought, whose talk is of free trade.* The foreign visitors, too, are politicians; they take a wider theme – European progress – the spread of liberal sentiments over the Continent; on their mental tablets, the names of Russia, Austria and the Pope are inscribed in red ink.* I have heard some of them talk vigorous sense – yea, I have been present at polyglot discussions in the old, oak-lined dining room at Hunsden Wood, where a singular insight was given of the sentiments entertained by resolute minds respecting old northern despotisms and old southern superstitions; also, I have heard much twaddle, enounced chiefly in French and Deutsch, but let that pass. Hunsden himself tolerated the drivelling theorists; with the practical men he seemed leagued hand and heart.

When Hunsden is staying alone at the Wood (which seldom happens), he generally finds his way two or three times a week to Daisy Lane. He has a philanthropic motive for coming to smoke his cigar on our porch on summer evenings: he says he does it to kill the earwigs amongst the roses – with which insects, but for his benevolent fumigations, he intimates we should certainly be overrun. On wet days, too, we are almost sure to see him; according to him, it gets on time to work me into lunacy by treading on my mental corns, or to force from Mrs Crimsworth revelations of the dragon within her by insulting the memory of Hofer* and Tell.

We also go frequently to Hunsden Wood, and both I and Frances relish a visit there highly. If there are other guests, their characters are an interesting study; their conversation is exciting and strange; the absence of all local narrowness both in the host and his chosen society gives a metropolitan, almost a cosmopolitan freedom and largeness to the talk. Hunsden himself is a polite man in his own house: he has, when he chooses to employ it, an inexhaustible power of entertaining guests; his very mansion too is interesting, the rooms look storied, the passages legendary, the low-ceiled chambers, with their long rows of diamond-paned lattices, have an old-world, haunted air; in his travels he has collected stores of articles of *vertu*,* which are well and tastefully disposed in his panelled or tapestried rooms: I have seen there one or two pictures and one or two pieces of statuary which many an aristocratic connoisseur might have envied.

When I and Frances have dined and spent an evening with Hunsden, he often walks home with us. His wood is large, and some of the timber is old and of huge growth. There are winding ways in it which, pursued through glade and brake, make the walk back to Daisy Lane a somewhat long one. Many a time, when we have had the benefit of a full moon, and when the night has been mild and balmy – when, moreover, a certain nightingale has been singing, and a certain stream, hid in alders, has lent the song a soft accompaniment – the remote church bell of the one hamlet in a district of ten miles has tolled midnight ere the lord of the wood left us at our porch. Free-flowing was his talk at such hours, and far more quiet and gentle than in the daytime and before numbers. He would then forget politics and discussion, and would dwell on the past times of his house, on his family history, on himself and his own feelings – subjects each and all invested with a peculiar zest, for they were each and all unique. One glorious night in June, after I had been taunting him about his ideal bride and asking him when she would come and graft her foreign beauty on the old Hunsden oak, he answered suddenly:

"You call her ideal; but see, here is her shadow; and there cannot be a shadow without a substance."

He had led us from the depth of the "winding way" into a glade from whence the beeches withdrew, leaving it open to the sky; an unclouded moon poured her light into this glade, and Hunsden held out under her beam an ivory miniature.

Frances, with eagerness, examined it first; then she gave it to me – still, however, pushing her little face close to mine, and seeking in my eyes what I thought of the portrait. I thought it represented a very handsome and very individual-looking female face, with, as he had once said, "straight and harmonious features". It was dark; the hair, raven-black, swept not only from the brow, but from the temples – seemed thrust away carelessly, as if such beauty dispensed with, nay, despised arrangement. The Italian eye looked straight into you, and an independent, determined eye it was; the mouth was as firm as fine; the chin ditto. On the back of the miniature was gilded "Lucia".

"That is a real head," was my conclusion.

Hunsden smiled.

"I think so," he replied. "All was real in Lucia."

"And she was somebody you would have liked to marry – but could not?"

"I should certainly have liked to marry her, and that I *have* not done so is a proof that I *could* not."

He repossessed himself of the miniature, now again in Frances's hand, and put it away.

"What do *you* think of it?" he asked of my wife, as he buttoned his coat over it.

"I am sure Lucia once wore chains and broke them," was the strange answer. "I do not mean matrimonial chains," she added, correcting herself, as if she feared misinterpretation, "but social chains of some sort. The face is that of one who has made an effort, and a successful and triumphant effort, to wrest some vigorous and valued faculty from insupportable constraint; and when Lucia's faculty got free, I am certain it spread wide pinions and carried her higher than—" She hesitated. ˈ

"Than what?" demanded Hunsden.

"Than *les convenances** permitted you to follow."

"I think you grow spiteful – impertinent."

"Lucia has trodden the stage," continued Frances. "You never seriously thought of marrying her; you admired her originality, her fearlessness, her energy of body and mind; you delighted in her talent, whatever that was – whether song, dance or dramatic representation – you worshipped her beauty, which was of the sort after your own heart, but I am sure she filled a sphere from whence you would never have thought of taking a wife."

"Ingenious," remarked Hunsden. "Whether true or not is another question. Meantime, don't you feel your little lamp of a spirit wax very pale, beside such a *girandole** as Lucia's?"

"Yes."

"Candid, at least; and the professor will soon be dissatisfied with the dim light you give?"

"Will you, monsieur?"

"My sight was always too weak to endure a blaze, Frances," and we had now reached the wicket.

I said, a few pages back, that this is a sweet summer evening; it is – there has been a series of lovely days, and this is the loveliest;

the hay is just carried from my fields, its perfume still lingers in the air. Frances proposed to me, an hour or two since, to take tea out on the lawn; I see the round table, loaded with china, placed under a certain beech; Hunsden is expected – nay, I hear he is come – there is his voice, laying down the law on some point with authority; that of Frances replies; she opposes him, of course. They are disputing about Victor, of whom Hunsden affirms that his mother is making a milksop. Mrs Crimsworth retaliates:

"Better a thousand times he should be a milksop than what he, Hunsden, calls 'a fine lad'; and, moreover, she says that if Hunsden were to become a fixture in the neighbourhood and were not a mere comet, coming and going no one knows how, when, where or why, she should be quite uneasy till she had got Victor away to a school at least a hundred miles off; for that, with his mutinous maxims and unpractical dogmas, he would ruin a score of children."

I have a word to say of Victor ere I shut this manuscript in my desk – but it must be a brief one, for I hear the tinkle of silver on porcelain.

Victor is as little of a pretty child as I am of a handsome man or his mother of a fine woman: he is pale and spare, with large eyes, as dark as those of Frances, and as deeply set as mine. His shape is symmetrical enough, but slight; his health is good. I never saw a child smile less than he does, nor one who knits such a formidable brow when sitting over a book that interests him, or while listening to tales of adventure, peril or wonder narrated by his mother, Hunsden or myself. But, though still, he is not unhappy – though serious, not morose; he has a susceptibility to pleasurable sensations almost too keen, for it amounts to enthusiasm.* He learnt to read in the old-fashioned way out of a spelling book at his mother's knee, and as he got on without driving by that method, she thought it unnecessary to buy him ivory letters, or to try any of the other inducements to learning now deemed indispensable. When he could read, he became a glutton of books, and is so still. His toys have been few, and he has never wanted more. For those he possesses, he seems to have contracted a partiality amounting to affection; this feeling, directed towards one or two living animals of the house, strengthens almost to a passion.

Mr Hunsden gave him a mastiff cub, which he called Yorke, after the donor; it grew to a superb dog, whose fierceness, however, was much modified by the companionship and caresses of its young master. He would go nowhere, do nothing without Yorke; Yorke lay at his feet while he learnt his lessons, played with him in the garden, walked with him in the lane and wood, sat near his chair at meals, was fed always by his own hand, was the first thing he sought in the morning, the last he left at night. Yorke accompanied Mr Hunsden one day to X—, and was bitten in the street by a dog in a rabid state. As soon as Hunsden had brought him home and had informed me of the circumstance, I went into the yard and shot him where he lay licking his wound: he was dead in an instant; he had not seen me level the gun; I stood behind him. I had scarcely been ten minutes in the house, when my ear was struck with sounds of anguish: I repaired to the yard once more, for they proceeded thence. Victor was kneeling beside his dead mastiff, bent over it, embracing its bull-like neck and lost in a passion of the wildest woe; he saw me.

"Oh, Papa, I'll never forgive you! I'll never forgive you!" was his exclamation. "You shot Yorke – I saw it from the window. I never believed you could be so cruel – I can love you no more!"

I had much ado to explain to him, with a steady voice, the stern necessity of the deed; he still, with that inconsolable and bitter accent which I cannot render, but which pierced my heart, repeated:

"He might have been cured – you should have tried – you should have burnt the wound with a hot iron, or covered it with caustic. You gave no time; and now it is too late – he is dead!"

He sank fairly down on the senseless carcass; I waited patiently a long while, till his grief had somewhat exhausted him; and then I lifted him in my arms and carried him to his mother, sure that she would comfort him best. She had witnessed the whole scene from a window; she would not come out for fear of increasing my difficulties by her emotion, but she was ready now to receive him. She took him to her kind heart, and onto her gentle lap; consoled him but with her lips, her eyes, her soft embrace, for some time; and then, when his sobs diminished, told him that Yorke had felt no pain in dying, and that if he had been left to expire naturally, his end would have been most horrible; above all, she told him that I was not cruel (for that idea seemed to give exquisite pain to poor Victor), that it was my affection for Yorke and him which had made me act so, and that I was now almost heartbroken to see him weep thus bitterly.

Victor would have been no true son of his father had these considerations, these reasons, breathed in so low, so sweet a tone – married to caresses so benign, so tender, to looks so inspired with pitying sympathy – produced no effect on him. They did produce an effect: he grew calmer, rested his face on her shoulder and lay still in her arms. Looking up, shortly, he asked his mother to tell him over again what she had said about Yorke having suffered no pain, and my not being cruel; the balmy words being repeated, he again pillowed his cheek on her breast and was again tranquil.

Some hours after, he came to me in my library, asked if I forgave him and desired to be reconciled. I drew the lad to my side, and there I kept him a good while, and had much talk with him, in the course of which he disclosed many points of feeling and thought I approved of in my son. I found, it is true, few elements of the "good fellow" or the "fine fellow" in him, scant sparkles of the spirit which loves to flash over the wine cup, or which kindles the passions to a destroying fire, but I saw in the soil of his heart healthy and swelling germs of compassion, affection, fidelity. I discovered in the garden of his intellect a rich growth of wholesome principles: reason, justice, moral courage promised, if not blighted, a fertile bearing. So I bestowed on his large forehead, and on his cheek – still pale with tears – a proud and contented kiss, and sent him away comforted. Yet I saw him the next day laid on the mound under which Yorke had been buried, his face covered with his hands; he was melancholy for some weeks, and more than a year elapsed before he would listen to any proposal of having another dog.

Victor learns fast. He must soon go to Eton – where, I suspect, his first year or two will be utter wretchedness: to leave me, his mother and his home will give his heart an agonized wrench; then, the fagging will not suit him – but emulation, thirst after knowledge, the glory of success will stir and reward him in time. Meantime, I feel in myself a strong repugnance to fix the hour which will uproot my sole olive branch* and transplant it far from me; and, when I speak to Frances on the subject, I am heard with a kind of patient pain, as though I alluded to some fearful operation, at which her nature shudders, but from which her fortitude will not permit her to recoil. The step must, however, be taken, and it *shall* be; for, though Frances will not make a milksop of her son, she will accustom him to a style of treatment, a forbearance, a congenial tenderness he will meet with from none else. She sees, as I also see, a something in Victor's temper – a kind of electrical ardour and power – which emits, now and then, ominous sparks; Hunsden calls it his spirit, and says it should not be curbed. I call it the leaven of the offending Adam, and consider that it should be, if not *whipped* out of him, at least soundly disciplined;* and that he will be cheap of* any amount of either bodily or mental suffering which will ground him radically in the art of self-control. Frances gives this *something* in her son's marked character no name; but when it appears in the grinding of his teeth, in the glittering of his eye, in the fierce revolt of feeling against disappointment, mischance, sudden sorrow or supposed injustice, she folds him to her breast, or takes him to walk with her alone in the wood; then she reasons with him like any philosopher, and to reason Victor is ever accessible; then she looks at him with eyes of love, and by love Victor can be infallibly subjugated; but will reason or love be the weapons with which in future the world will meet his violence? Oh, no! For that flash in his black eye – for that cloud on his bony brow – for that compression of his statuesque lips, the lad will some day get blows instead of blandishments – kicks instead of kisses; then for the fit of mute fury which will sicken his body and madden his soul; then for the ordeal of merited and salutary suffering, out of which he will come (I trust) a wiser and a better man.

I see him now: he stands by Hunsden, who is seated on the lawn under the beech; Hunsden's hand rests on the boy's collar, and he is instilling God knows what principles into his ear. Victor looks well just now, for he listens with a sort of smiling interest; he never looks so like his mother as when he smiles – pity the sunshine breaks out so rarely! Victor has a preference for Hunsden, full as strong as I deem desirable, being considerably more potent, decided and indiscriminating than any I ever entertained for that personage myself. Frances, too, regards it with a sort of unexpressed anxiety; while her son leans on Hunsden's knee or rests against his shoulder, she roves with restless movement round, like a dove guarding its young from a hovering hawk; she says she wishes Hunsden had children of his own, for then he would better know the danger of inciting their pride and indulging their foibles.

Frances approaches my library window, puts aside the honeysuckle which half covers it and tells me tea is ready; seeing that I continue busy, she enters the room, comes near me quietly and puts her hand on my shoulder.

"*Monsieur est trop appliqué.*"*

"I shall soon have done."

She draws a chair near and sits down to wait till I have finished; her presence is as pleasant to my mind as the perfume of the fresh hay and spicy flowers, as the glow of the westering sun, as the repose of the midsummer eve are to my senses.

But Hunsden comes; I hear his step, and there he is, bending through the lattice, from which he has thrust away the woodbine with unsparing hand, disturbing two bees and a butterfly.

"Crimsworth! I say, Crimsworth! Take that pen out of his hand, mistress, and make him lift up his head."

"Well, Hunsden? I hear you."

"I was at X— yesterday! Your brother Ned is getting richer than Croesus by railway speculations; they call him in the Piece Hall a stag of ten,* and I have heard from Brown. M. and Madame Vandenhuten and Jean-Baptiste talk of coming to see you next month. He mentions the Pelets too; he says their domestic harmony is not the finest in the world, but in business they are doing "*on ne peut mieux*"* – which circumstance, he concludes, will be a sufficient consolation to both for any little crosses in the affections. Why don't you invite the Pelets to —shire, Crimsworth? I should so like to see your first flame, Zoraïde. Mistress, don't be jealous, but he loved that lady to distraction; I know it for a fact. Brown says she weighs twelve stones now; you see what you've lost, Mr Professor. Now, monsieur and madame, if you don't come to tea, Victor and I will begin without you."

"Papa, come!"

Note on the Text

The text in this volume is based on the first edition of *The Professor* (1857), incorporating some of the corrections made in the Oxford University Press edition of 1987, as well as some additional corrections by the present editors. The spelling and punctuation have been standardized, modernized and made consistent throughout.

Notes

p. 3, *"the Hill of Difficulty"*: In John Bunyan's *Pilgrim's Progress*, Christian ascends this hill and finds an arbour halfway up, created for weary travellers to rest there for a short period.

p. 3, *Adam's doom*: Genesis 3:19. "In the sweat of thy face shalt thou eat bread, till thou return unto the ground; for out of it wast thou taken: for dust thou art, and unto dust shalt thou return."

p. 5, *Pylades and Orestes*: The nephew and son of Agamemnon, King of Mycenae or Argos, respectively, and famed for their loyal friendship.

p. 7, *Croesus*: The last king of Lydia (from 560–46 BC), famed for his wealth. Hence the expression "rich as Croesus".

p. 10, *no man can serve two masters*: Matthew 6:24.

p. 15, *laden with pieces*: A piece was a standard length in which cloth was woven.

p. 17, *I will place my cup... it will run over of itself*: A reference to Psalms 23:5, "my cup runneth over".

p. 17, *a strait gate*: Matthew 7:13–14; Luke 13:24.

p. 19, *posed*: Perplexed.

p. 23, *bumps of ideality... conscientiousness*: Phrenological terms.

p. 24, *turban*: A headdress made to resemble the oriental turban, fashionable in the late eighteenth and early nineteenth centuries.

p. 24, *mushroom-place... knew his own grandfather*: A reference to the mass movement of workers from the countryside into the manufacturing towns during the Industrial Revolution.

p. 25, *quiz*: An eccentric person.

p. 28, *Just so must Lot have left Sodom... brass clouds*: Genesis 19:15–26.

p. 28, *meditating in the field... camel's hump*: Genesis 24:30–63.

p. 29, *happed*: Covered over or wrapped, often for the sake of warmth.

p. 29, *Thiers... Richter*: Adolphe Thiers (1797–1877); Abel-François Villemain (1790–1870); Charles Paul de Kock (1793–1871); George Sand (1804–76), the pseudonym of Amantine Aurore Lucile Dupin; Eugène, or Marie-Joseph Sue (1804–57); Johann Wolfgang von Goethe (1749–1832); Friedrich Schiller (1759–1805); Heinrich Zschokke (1771–1848); Johann Paul Friedrich Richter (1763–1825), known as Jean Paul.

p. 32, *interested*: I.e. self-interested.

p. 32, *Juggernaut*: A title of the Hindu god Krishna's. An image of the god is dragged through Puri every year on a processional car, and devotees used to throw themselves underneath it.

p. 36, *just men made perfect*: Hebrews 12:23.

p. 36, *the Israelite... tale of bricks*: Exodus 5:6–19.

p. 38, *fugleman*: A well-drilled and expert soldier formerly placed in front of a company as a model for the others to follow.

p. 42, *glass of toast-and-water*: Water which has had toast steeped in it.

p. 46, *organ of caution*: Another phrenological term.

p. 49, *diligence*: A public stagecoach.

p. 49, *fiacre*: A small carriage.

p. 50, *croisées*: Casements.

p. 53, *General Belliard*: Augustin-Daniel Belliard (1769–1832) was a French general during the Revolutionary Wars. He later became the French ambassador to Brussels.

p. 53, *externats*: Day girls.

p. 55, *Messieurs... livres de lectures*: "Gentlemen, take out your reading books" (French). All subsequent translations will be from French unless otherwise stated.

p. 55, *The Vicar of Wakefield*: An extremely popular novel (1766) written by Oliver Goldsmith (1728–74).

p. 56, *voix de poitrine*: "Voice from the chest."

p. 56, *Comme c'est affreux*: "How frightful!"

p. 56, *C'est assez... ira bien*: "That's enough for today, gentlemen; tomorrow we will carry on, and I hope that everything will go well."

p. 56, *C'est bien... que le savoir*: "Good, very good! I see that you, sir, have skill; that appeals to me, because in teaching skill does as much as knowledge."

p. 57, *Light not being taxed*: A reference to the Window Tax introduced in England and Wales in 1696.

p. 57, *La fenêtre... monsieur*: "The closed window overlooks the garden of a young ladies' boarding school, and propriety demands... well, you understand... don't you, sir?"

p. 57, *pas de géant*: Literally "giant's step"; this was a structure often found in playgrounds, consisting of ropes attached to a crown that pivots about a fixed point and allows one to take long strides.

p. 58, *Zoraïde*: The name of a young Moorish woman in *Don Quixote* who elopes with her lover.

p. 58, *Brabant*: The central province of Belgium, which included Brussels.

p. 59, *Sainte-Gudule*: Saints-Michel-et-Gudule is a cathedral in Brussels. It was a church when Charlotte Brontë was in Brussels, but it was given cathedral status in 1962.

p. 59, *The boy is father to the man*: An echoing of William Wordsworth's (1770–1850) 'My Heart Leaps Up', in which the poet states, "The Child is father of the Man".

p. 59, *political history of their ancestors*: Before the Belgian Revolution of 1830–31, the Belgians had been ruled by a series of foreign powers.

p. 60, *Ce ne... allez!*: "They are just Flemings – come!"

p. 62, *Plaît-il?*: "I beg your pardon?"

p. 62, *Salle of the Grande Harmonie*: The hall in which the society La Grande Harmonie gave concerts.

p. 63, *fauteuil*: Armchair.

p. 63, *fermière*: Farmer's wife.

p. 63, *maîtresse d'auberge*: A female innkeeper.

p. 63, *directrice de pensionnat*: Headteacher of a boarding school.

p. 64, *petit verre*: Literally "little glass", but generally meaning a glass of liqueur.

p. 64, *Pourvu que... bien l'air*: "As long as you are well behaved, and, to tell the truth, it looks that you are."

p. 65, *Quel charmant jeune homme!*: "What a charming young man!"

p. 65, *car Zoraïde... maîtresse-femme*: "Because Zoraïde does everything like a queen; she truly is the woman in charge."

p. 65, *C'est absolument comme mon fils!*: "That's exactly like my son!"

p. 65, *Comment... allez déjà?*: "What! You are going already?"

p. 65, *Prenez encore... une tasse de café?*: "Have something more, sir; a baked apple, biscuits, another cup of coffee?"

p. 68, *pendule*: A small clock with a pendulum.

p. 68, *chiffonnière*: A small cupboard.

p. 68, *Monsieur Creemsvort, n'est-ce pas?*: "Mr Creemsvort, is it not?"

p. 69, *Du reste*: Besides.

p. 70, *Ah! C'est comme tous les Anglais*: "Ah! It's the same with all English people."

p. 71, *Comme vous avez... donc passé*: "You look radiant! I have never seen you so cheerful. What has happened?"

p. 71, *Apparemment... les changements*: "Apparently I like changes."

p. 71, *Ah! Je comprends... savez-vous?*: "Ah! I understand – so that's it – only be wise. You are very young – too young for the role you are going to play; you must take care – you know?"

p. 71, *Mais quel danger y a-t-il?* "But what danger is there?"

p. 71, *Je n'en sais rien... voilà tout*: "I don't know – do not indulge in vivid impressions – that's all."

p. 72, *mousseline-de-laine*: A light fabric used primarily for dresses.

p. 72, *manchettes*: Ornamental cuffs.

p. 72, *brodequins*: Boots that reached quite high up the leg.

p. 72, *sanctum sanctorum*: "Holy of Holies" (Latin).

p. 72, *estrade*: A dais.

p. 73, *Prenez vos cahiers... mesdemoiselles*: "Take out your dictation books, young ladies."

p. 73, *Eulalie... rire*: "Eulalie, I am ready to faint with laughter."

p. 73, *Comme... en parlant*: "How he blushed when speaking!"

p. 73, *Oui... blanc-bec*: "Yes, he's a real novice."

p. 73, *Tais-toi... il nous écoute*: "Be quiet, Hortense – he's listening to us."

p. 74, *figure de Vierge*: Face of the Virgin.

p. 75, *Dictez-nous... monsieur*: "Dictate something easy to us to start with, sir."

p. 75, *de sa façon*: "In her own way."

p. 75, *Pauline Borghese*: Pauline Borghese (1780–1825) was a famous beauty whose elder brother was Napoleon Bonaparte (1769–1821).

p. 75, *Lucrèce de Borgia*: Lucrezia Borgia (1480–1519) was notorious for her lack of morality.

p. 75, *Comment dit-on...monsieur?*: "How do you say *point et virgule* in English, sir?"

p. 75, *Simi-collong... c'est drôle!*: "Simi-collong? Ah, how funny!"

p. 75, *J'ai une si... d'écrire!*: "I have such a bad pen – it's impossible to write!"

p. 75, *Mais, monsieur... si vite*: "But, sir – I can't follow – you go so fast."

p. 75, *Je n'ai rien compris, moi!*: "I haven't understood anything!"

p. 75, *C'est si difficile, l'Anglais!*: "English is so difficult!"

p. 75, *Je déteste la dictée*: "I hate dictation."

p. 75, *Quel ennui... l'on ne comprend pas!*: "What a bore to write something you don't understand!"

p. 75, *Donnez-moi votre cahier*: "Give me your exercise book."

p. 76, *Et vous... donnez-moi le vôtre*: "And you, young lady – give me yours."

p. 76, *C'est honteux!*: "It's shameful!"

p. 76, *C'est bien... de vous*: "Good – I am pleased with you."

p. 76, *salle à manger*: Dining room.

p. 76, *beaufet... armoire vitrée*: A sideboard and a glazed cupboard respectively.

p. 76, *cabas*: A small satchel.

p. 77, *Et les trois... premier banc?*: "And the three young ladies on the first bench?"

p. 77, *Ah! Tout va au mieux!*: "Ah! Everything is going well!"

p. 78, *Talleyrand*: Charles-Maurice de Talleyrand-Périgord (1754–1838) was a French statesman famed for his diplomacy.

p. 79, *maigre day*: A day on which abstinence from meat is required.

p. 79, *Eh bien... un peu*: "Well, you worthless person! Where are you going? Come to the dining room so that I can scold you a little."

p. 80, *C'est... la surveillance*: "It's a great responsibility, keeping watch."

p. 80, *Plaît-il?*: "I beg your pardon?"

p. 80, *Des bêtes de somme... de somme*: "Beasts of burden... beasts of burden."

p. 80, *Servez-vous, mon garçon*: "Help yourself, my boy."

p. 80, *C'est joli – cela*: "That's nice – that is."

p. 80, *Honi soit qui mal y pense*: "Shame on him who thinks evil of it." The motto of the Order of the Garter, an order of chivalry founded by Edward III (1312–77) in 1348.

p. 80, *Je connais... voyez-vous?*: "I know something of my little neighbour – you see?"

p. 81, *elle est... supérieurement?*: "She is still young, older than you perhaps, but just enough to unite the tenderness of a young mother and the love of a devoted wife; would this not go excellently with you?"

p. 82, *bonnet-grec*: A soft hat with a tassel.

p. 82, *et dîtes-moi... dans l'autre*: "And tell me if there is not the cat in one and the fox in the other."

p. 82, *patte de velours*: "Velvet paw."

p. 82, *N'y a-t-il… jeunes têtes?*: "Are there not some beautiful studies among those young heads?"

p. 83, *Je les connais… une belle brune*: "I know them! They are always among the front ranks at the cathedral and on walks; a superb blonde, a pretty little mischievous one and a beautiful brunette."

p. 84, *Béranger's*: Pierre-Jean de Béranger (1780–1857) was a poet and writer of popular songs.

p. 85, *demoiselles de magasins*: "Shopgirls."

p. 86, *bottines*: Light boots worn by women and children.

p. 88, *the same shape of skull as Pope Alexander the Sixth*: Rodrigo Borgia (1431–1503), Pope Alexander VI, was, like his daughter Lucrezia, reputed to have been a poisoner. His alleged womanizing was one of the reasons his surname became synonymous with infamy and libidinousness. The majority of the ensuing description of Juanna makes use of phrenological descriptions.

p. 91, *Jack-o'-lanthorns*: A phosphorescent light sometimes visible at night on marshy ground.

p. 94, *inconvenant*: "Improper."

p. 94, *l'allée défendue*: "The forbidden path."

p. 95, *persiennes*: "Shutters."

p. 96, *A quand donc… ma bien-aimée?*: "And when is the wedding day, my beloved?"

p. 96, *Mais… avant les vacances*: "But, François, you know well that it would be impossible for me to marry before the holidays."

p. 98, *gambadoes*: Sudden and unexpected actions.

p. 98, *pistolet*: A small Belgian bread roll.

p. 99, *balm… Gilead*: Jeremiah 8:22; 46:11.

p. 104, *prière du midi*: Midday prayer.

p. 104, *Notre Père… tour d'ivoire!*: "Our Father who art in heaven… Mary, heavenly virgin, queen of angels, house of gold, tower of ivory!"

p. 105, *Scipio-like self-control*: Publius Cornelius Scipio Africanus (236 BC–183 BC), often known simply as Scipio Africanus, was a famous Roman general and consul. He defeated Hannibal at the Battle of Zama in 202 BC. It is said that when his soldiers brought a beautiful princess to him following the capture of New Carthage (modern Cartagena in Spain), Scipio sent her back to her fiancé.

p. 106, *his only ewe lamb*: 2 Samuel 12:1–7.

p. 111, *C'est assez... retenir davantage*: "That is enough, my good friend; I don't want to detain you any longer at present."

p. 111, *On his way to Perth... vide the History of Scotland*: The reading is taken from Sir Walter Scott's (1771–1832) *Tales of a Grandfather* (1827–31).

p. 116, *Alfred tending cakes in the herdsman's hut*: A famous legend: during a retreat in his defence against the Viking invasion of Britain, King Alfred the Great (849–99) is said to have stayed incognito in a peasant's hut, where he was scolded by the wife for letting cakes burn on the fire.

p. 117, *Thone*: The River Tone in Somerset. The legend of Alfred and the burnt cakes was said to have taken place in the Somerset Levels.

p. 118, *Guthrum*: Guthrum (d. c.890) led a Danish invasion of England, and proclaimed himself King of East Anglia. He waged war against Alfred the Great (849–899).

p. 123, *Maman est morte... dix ans*: "Mother died ten years ago."

p. 123, *C'est si difficile... a plus l'habitude*: "It is so difficult, sir, when one is no longer used to it."

p. 124, *Justement, monsieur*: "Exactly, sir."

p. 124, *Pas encore... dix-neuf ans*: "Not yet, sir – in one month I will be nineteen years old."

p. 125, *Berlin wools*: Fine dyed wool.

p. 126, *Pourtant... mon projet*: "Yet, I have my plan."

p. 126, *Israelite of Moses's days*: The Israelites at that time were enslaved in Egypt. Canaan was the land promised by God to Abraham (Genesis 17:8).

p. 126, *Mademoiselle... tout de suite*: "Miss Henri, I believe it is going to rain; you would do well, my good friend, to return home immediately."

p. 127, *Mais… comprenez*: "But, sir, you understand me."

p. 129, *Mlle Henri… voyez-vous*: "Miss Henri – Miss Reuter wishes that you would be so good as to take the little Dorlodot girl home, she is waiting for you in the portress Rosalie's room – it is because her maid is not coming to get her – you see."

p. 129, *Eh bien… moi?*: "Well! Am I her maid – me?"

p. 130, *penny fee*: Wages.

p. 130, *breath of her nostrils*: Isaiah 2:22.

p. 133, *castor*: Fur hat.

p. 133, *concurrent*: Competitor.

p. 134, *coûte que coûte*: At all costs.

p. 135, *Où… Mlle Henri?*: "Where is Miss Henri, then?"

p. 135, *Elle est partie, monsieur*: "She has left, sir."

p. 135, *Partie… reviendra-t-elle?*: "Left! For how long? When will she return?"

p. 135, *Elle… ne reviendra plus*: "She has left for ever, sir: she is not returning."

p. 135, *En êtes-vous… Sylvie?*: "Are you quite sure, Sylvie?"

p. 135, *Oui, oui… trois jours*: "Yes, yes, sir, the headmistress told us herself two or three days ago."

p. 135, *grisette*: A young working-class French woman.

p. 136, *bien gentille… N'est-ce pa, monsieur?*: "Very nice, very clean, surrounded by fields and woods; what a charming life rural life is! Isn't it so, sir?"

p. 137, *Cela dépend, mademoiselle*: "That depends, madam."

p. 137, *Que le vent… frais!*: "How lovely and fresh the wind is!"

p. 137, *while I was musing… my tongue*: Psalms 39:3.

p. 137, *Allons… votre état d'instituteur*: "Come, Professor, let us sit; I will give you a little lesson in your roles as teacher."

p. 138, *chef-d'oeuvre*: Masterpiece.

p. 139, *the great Mogul*: The Mogul or Mughal Empire covered much of the Indian Subcontinent by the early eighteenth century. Its emperors were often referred to as "the great Mogul".

p. 140, *basse ville*: "Lower town." This part of Brussels was a poor district.

p. 140, *pennon*: "Flag."

p. 142, *silent system*: A penal system in which prisoners worked in total silence.

p. 145, *Un petit commissionnaire, monsieur*: "A little messenger, sir."

p. 145, *Rien*: "Nothing."

p. 145, *Allée Verte*: A country lane that ran along the side of the Willebroek Canal and joined Brussels and Laeken. It was a famous processional and promenading route.

p. 145, *encadrées*: "Framed."

p. 146, *salut*: An evening service of Benediction.

p. 146, *goûter*: Afternoon tea.

p. 146, *couc (?)*: "*Koek*" is the Flemish for cake.

p. 146, *anglice*: "In plain English."

p. 146, *Porte de Louvain*: One of the gates to the city.

p. 146, *campaign*: Open country.

p. 148, *impassible*: Insensible.

p. 149, *Mon maître! Mon maître!*: "My master! My master!"

p. 150, *lost sheep*: Matthew 18:11–13.

p. 153, *pauvre tante Julienne*: "Poor Aunt Julienne."

p. 155, *le chat de ma tante Julienne*: "My aunt Julienne's cat."

p. 156, *my Canaan*: See second note to p. 126.

p. 161, *le maudit Anglais, Creemsvort*: "The confounded Englishman, Crimsworth."

p. 162, *fine frenzy rolling*: See *A Midsummer Night's Dream*, Act v, Sc. 1, l. 7.

p. 162, *femme sotte et vicieuse*: "A foolish and licentious woman."

p. 163, *Des mœurs... sotte!*: "The morals of Cato she said – fool!" Cato the Elder (*c*.234 BC–149 BC) was famed for his distaste for luxury, which he thought corrupted Roman morals.

p. 163, *chef d'institution*: Head of a school.

p. 163, *Que le dédain... air hautain*: "How well disdain becomes him! He is as beautiful as Apollo when he smiles with a haughty air."

p. 164, *Pour moi... avec ses bésicles*: "For me, he looks like an owl with his glasses on."

p. 165, *la chambre... de Madame*: "Madam's bedroom", "Madam's sitting room".

p. 168, *owe no man anything*: Romans 13:8. "Owe no man anything, but to love one another: for he that loveth another hath fulfilled the law."

p. 170, *heave-shoulders... wave-breasts*: Leviticus 10:14–15.

p. 170, *Zénobie*: Zenobia, Countess of Northangerland, a strong-minded and intellectual woman, features in much of the Brontës' youthful writings.

p. 171, *Be on the lookout... cometh*: Matthew 25:13.

p. 173, *gaufres*: "Waffles."

p. 173, *crams*: Densely crowded parties.

p. 175, *le jour des noces*: "The day of the wedding."

p. 176, *locataire*: "Lodger."

p. 176, *les bésicles*: "The glasses."

p. 177, *starved*: Frozen to death.

p. 178, *Cast your bread... say the Scriptures*: Ecclesiastes 11:1.

p. 180, *Prester John*: A legendary Christian king said to rule a nation in the East.

p. 181, *ripe grapes... calling them sour*: A reference to 'The Fox and the Grapes', one of Aesop's fables.

p. 182, *the philosopher's stone... in my cupboard*: Medieval alchemical terms. The philosopher's stone was believed to turn base metals into gold, while the elixir of life was a potion that could grant the drinker eternal life.

p. 182, *bullaces*: Wild plums.

p. 183, *flourishing... bay tree*: Psalms 37:35.

p. 183, *Mephistopheles*: A demon in the Faust legend.

p. 184, *Peruvian bark*: Quinine is extracted from the cinchona tree, which is native to Peru and western South America.

p. 188, *négociant*: Merchant.

p. 188, *Ainsi soit-il*: "So it shall be."

p. 190, *And ne'er... flash'd between*: See Sir Walter Scott's 'The Shepherd's Tale' (1799).

p. 191, *I gave... flam'd*: These lines were probably written by the author while she was studying in Brussels.

p. 197, *the grass on Hermon... of sunset*: Psalms 133:3.

p. 198, *Monsieur... main droite*: "Sir, you are hurting me; for mercy's sake let go of my right hand a little."

p. 198, *Mon maître... ai beaucoup*: "My master, I have a lot."

p. 198, *the purple light of love*: From Thomas Gray's (1716–71) 'The Progress of Poesy'.

p. 198, *Monsieur... avec lui?*: "Sir, sir desires to know if I consent – if – in a word, I would like to marry him?"

p. 198, *Justement*: "Exactly."

p. 198, *Monsieur... bon maître?*: "Will sir be as a good a husband as he has been a master?"

p. 198, *sourire... et timide*: "A smile both subtle and timid."

p. 198, *C'est-à-dire... volontaire?*: "That is to say, sir will always be a little stubborn, demanding and wilful—?"

p. 198, *Mais oui... savez bien*: "Of course; you know it well."

p. 198, *Mais oui... meilleur ami*: "Why yes; you have been my best friend."

p. 198, *Votre dévouée élève... tout son cœur*: "Your devoted pupil, who loves you with all her heart."

p. 199, *Monsieur est raisonnable, n'est-ce pas?*: "Monsieur is reasonable, isn't he?"

p. 199, *Ce n'est pas cela—*: "It is not that—"

p. 200, *lilies of the field*: Matthew 6:28.

p. 201, *édentée... bossue*: "Toothless, short-sighted, rough or hunchbacked."

p. 202, *the hair of my flesh... heard a voice*: Job 4:13–16.

p. 202, *In the midst of life we are in death*: From the *Book of Common Prayer*, and used in Anglican funeral services.

p. 202, *A horror of great darkness fell upon me*: Genesis 15:12.

p. 203, *the evil spirit departed from me*: 1 Samuel 16:23.

p. 205, *spoon*: A foolish person.

p. 206, *Stanley... Cobden*: Edward Smith-Stanley (1799–1869), 14th Earl of Derby, and Richard Cobden (1804–65) were parliamentary opponents at the time of the repeal of the Corn Laws (1846).

p. 207, *grenier*: "Attic".

p. 207, *manchettes*: See second note to p. 72.

p. 209, *St Giles's*: St Giles was a deprived part of London. William Hogarth's (1697–1764) infamous 'Gin Lane' etching depicts the squalor that characterized the area.

p. 210, *Abdiel the Faithful*: *Paradise Lost*, V, 896.

p. 210, *ever-during gates... retorted scorn*: *Paradise Lost*, VII, 206; V, 906.

p. 211, *the servants of foreign kings*: The Swiss had a long history of providing mercenaries.

p. 212, *there's a method in my madness*: See *Hamlet*, Act II, Sc. 2, l. 20.

p. 212, *intent... hospitable thoughts*: *Paradise Lost*, V, 332.

p. 214, *he and Tell... our heroic William in his soul*: William Tell was a legendary folk hero of Switzerland. He was a symbol of liberty and the rejection of tyranny as a result of his assassination of the despotic bailiff Albrecht Gessler in Altdorf, Switzerland.

p. 214, *esprit-fort*: A strong-minded person.

p. 214, *a Benedict*: A confirmed bachelor.

p. 214, *Breton-bretonnant*: A Breton-speaking Breton.

p. 215, *Sir Charles Grandison... Harriet Byron*: The protagonists of Samuel Richardson's (1689–1761) *The History of Sir Charles Grandison* (1753).

p. 215, *Mon Dieu... pas attendu*: "My God! He pays compliments! I did not expect it."

p. 215, *ouvrière*: "Working woman."

p. 216, *jungfrau*: "Maiden" (German).

p. 216, *chétive... sans caractère... minois chiffonné*: "Puny... characterless... charming imperfections."

p. 216, *a seraph... coal of fire from heaven*: Isaiah 6:6.

p. 218, *faubourg*: "Suburb."

p. 220, *chaussées*: "Roads."

p. 221, *leash*: A set of three.

p. 222, *nervous*: Strong.

p. 223, *au courant*: "Familiar."

p. 224, *malice*: "Mischievousness."

p. 224, *bizarreries anglaises... caprices insulaires*: "English strangeness... island whims."

p. 226, *no patient Grizzle*: In William Combe's (1742–1823) satirical poem *The Tour of Dr Syntax in Search of the Picturesque* (1812), the Doctor travels with his patient and ill-used old steed Grizzle.

p. 228, *tout l'air... conspirateur*: "Exactly the air of a conspirator."

p. 229, *free trade*: A much debated topic, particularly in relation to the Corn Laws (tariffs and restrictions on the import and export of grain), which were repealed in 1846.

p. 229, *Russia, Austria and the Pope... red ink*: Tsarist Russia and the Austrian Empire were both infamous for the oppression of their people, while Pope Gregory XVI (r. 1831–46) was a conservative and traditionalist who opposed modernizing reforms throughout Europe and was a particularly ardent proponent of papal infallibility.

p. 229, *Hofer*: Andreas Hofer (1767–1810) was the leader of the Tyrolean Rebellion in 1809 during the War of the Fifth Coalition.

p. 229, *vertu*: "Quality."

p. 231, *les convenances*: "Propriety."

p. 231, *girandole*: A type of firework; an ornamental candlestick, often supporting numerous candles.

p. 232, *enthusiasm*: A passionate and fervent intensity of feeling far stronger than that implied by the word today.

p. 234, *sole olive branch*: Psalms 128:3.

p. 235, *the offending Adam... soundly disciplined*: A reference to *Henry V*, Act 1, Sc. 1, ll. 29–30.

p. 235, *he will be cheap of*: He will not be overpaid.

p. 236, *Monsieur est trop appliqué*: "Monsieur is too industrious."

p. 236, *Piece Hall a stag of ten*: A piece hall is a cloth exchange, and a stag of ten is a stag whose antlers are made up of ten branches. They were particularly prized by hunters.

p. 236, *on ne peut mieux*: The meaning here is "as well as could be".

Extra Material

on

Charlotte Brontë's

The Professor

Charlotte Brontë's Life

Charlotte Brontë was born on 21st April 1816 in her father's parsonage in Thornton, Yorkshire. She was the third child of Revd Patrick Brontë and Maria, née Branwell. Patrick Brontë was a Cambridge-educated Irish expatriate and Anglican clergyman who had published several volumes of poems and prose, but later devoted most of his energies to his parishioners and to various aspects of public and religious life. *Birth and Early Life*

In June 1817 Charlotte's brother Branwell was born, the son Patrick and Maria had been longing for. The highest hopes of the family came to rest on his shoulders, an expectation he would go on bitterly and notoriously to disappoint. Emily Brontë was born in July 1818 and Anne in January 1820. Later in 1820, Patrick was appointed as perpetual curate at Haworth, where the Brontë family would spend the majority of their lives. In September 1821 Charlotte's mother Maria, after over seven months of illness, died of cancer. Her sister Elizabeth moved from Cornwall to live with the family in Haworth on a permanent basis, acting as a mother figure to the Brontë children.

In 1824 the Brontë girls – with the exception of Anne, who was too young – entered the Clergy Daughters' School at Cowan Bridge, having previously been educated at home by their father. In the school's register for the year 1824, the following entry can be found: "Charlotte Brontë... Reads tolerably – Writes indifferently – Ciphers a little and works neatly. Knows nothing of Grammar, Geography, History or Accomplishments. Altogether clever of her age but knows nothing systematically." Charlotte famously portrayed the school as Lowood in *Jane Eyre*, condemning its brutal regime, which aroused a great deal of controversy at the time. It is difficult, in retrospect, to see how much of what she wrote was a fair description of the establishment, but biographers have pointed to evidence that the *Early Schooling* school's founder, Revd Carus Wilson, considered the ideas of death and hell to be essential to children's development, and physical punishment vital to "save their souls". It has also been claimed that the school heating was inadequate and food was poor. In 1825, first Maria, and then Elizabeth – Charlotte's elder sisters – left the school due to ill health, and died of tuberculosis in Haworth the same year. As soon as he saw the signs of tuberculosis in Elizabeth, Patrick withdrew Charlotte and Emily from the school.

Glass Town, Angria and Gondal   One night in 1826, Patrick brought home some model soldiers for Branwell. Each of the children adopted one, and they all started to invent stories about them, initially consisting of wars and battles based on the Napoleonic campaigns. These tales gradually evolved into the fantasy sagas of Glass Town, Angria and Gondal. Angria was Charlotte and Branwell's domain (while Anne and Emily were the creators of Gondal), and its central character, the Duke of Zamorna, is in some respects a prefiguration of Mr Rochester in *Jane Eyre*. One of the curiosities of these juvenile writings is that they were all written out in miniscule, almost undecipherable handwriting, bound up in tiny booklets, perhaps for love of secrecy or because of the scarcity of ink and paper.

Roe Head   In January 1831, Charlotte was sent to Roe Head School in Mirfield, where she met Ellen Nussey and Mary Taylor, who became lifelong friends of hers. Roe Head was an entirely different kind of school to Cowan Bridge: there were only a very small number of pupils, and the school was run and owned by Miss Margaret Wooler under a disciplined but compassionate regime. Though on first arriving at the school Charlotte found it difficult to mix with her fellow students, in time they came to respect her intellect and integrity. At the end of her first half-year, Charlotte won three prizes. After three successful half-years, she left Roe Head in July 1832.

After some time spent at Haworth indulging in her private pursuits, Charlotte returned to Roe Head towards the end of July 1835 to take up a position as a teacher. Emily went with her to attend Roe Head as a pupil, but the school proved uncongenial to her temperament, and she went back home after only three months. Anne took her place in January 1836. For the first few months at Roe Head, it seems that Charlotte was desperately unhappy; she continued writing her Angrian tales and felt keenly the disparity between this dream world and day-to-day work at the school – she did not appear to be very fond of the children either, and the job offered no real prospect of future advancement. In December 1836, Charlotte wrote to the poet Robert Southey, who warned her about the dangers of indulging in daydreams, and explained to her that literature could not be a woman's business – advice for which Charlotte thanked him. In 1837, Roe Head School was relocated to Dewsbury Moor. Charlotte was unhappy about the new location and the ever-increasing responsibilities she had to take on. When Anne left the school towards the end of the year due to ill health, Charlotte felt her solitude even more keenly, and in May 1838 she moved back to Haworth on the advice of her doctor.

In March 1839, Charlotte received a marriage proposal from Revd *Marriage Proposals and* Henry Nussey, Ellen's brother, but rejected it politely: "I have no *Life as a Governess* personal repugnance to the idea of a union with you – but I feel convinced that mine is not the sort of disposition calculated to form the happiness of a man like you… I am not the serious, grave, cool-headed individual you suppose – you would think me romantic and eccentric – you would say I was satirical and severe." In May, Charlotte took up a position as a governess to the Sidgwick family, at Stonegappe near Skipton, but the circumstances there were intolerable to her: she was overburdened with work, had no time to herself and found the children unruly. Having resigned her position two months later, she returned home, where in August she received a second marriage proposal, this time from Revd James Pryce, a young Irish clergyman.

After a break from work of more than eighteen months, in March 1841 Charlotte took up a position as a governess with the White family of Upperwood House, Rawdon, near Leeds. This was, in some respects, a much more positive experience than her previous stay with the Sidgwick family, but Charlotte still was not entirely happy there, tired of the everyday drudgery of her duties, feeling "such a strong wish for wings – wings such as wealth can furnish – such an urgent thirst to see – to know, to learn".

In the summer of the same year, Charlotte discussed with Emily *Brussels and the* the idea of setting up their own school. In September they formed a *Pensionnat Heger* plan to go abroad for a few months to improve their foreign languages and increase their teaching credentials, and Aunt Branwell agreed to finance the venture. Having left her position at Rawdon in December, she arrived with Emily at the Pensionnat Heger in Brussels in February 1842. Charlotte's friend Mary Taylor had been travelling in Belgium and Holland, and was based nearby in the Château de Koekelberg. Initially Charlotte enjoyed her time at the Heger school and liked Brussels as a city, relishing the opportunity of being a pupil again, rather than working as a teacher or a governess. The school was efficiently run by Constantin Heger and his wife Zoë. Heger had a reputation as an exceptionally fine teacher of literature, with a keen intelligence and commitment to the pupils' interests. The two sisters had to face the difficulty, however, of all the lessons being conducted in French, with no concession made to their lack of knowledge of the language: Charlotte, having learnt a little, was in a better position than Emily, who knew virtually none. Nevertheless, Charlotte and Emily focused on their work to the exclusion of everything else, and they quickly adapted – despite not being very popular among their fellow pupils – in part due to M. Heger offering them private tuition. Heger taught the girls to write in French in a variety of imitative styles, with an extreme attention to detail: this instruction in the craft of writing would greatly benefit them both later on. The environment was in many ways perfect for Charlotte to flourish, and the two Brontës decided not to return home in September as originally planned, but to remain at the Pensionnat for another half-year in different capacities: Emily to teach music, and Charlotte to teach English. They were to receive no salaries, but would have board and tuition free of charge.

Death of Aunt Branwell   However, these plans were abandoned when Aunt Branwell died on 29th October. The sisters felt it was their duty to return home immediately, even if they could not make it back in time for the funeral. They were given a letter by M. Heger for Patrick Brontë, recommending that Charlotte and Emily should return to Brussels for a further year to complete their studies, at the end of which a position at the school could probably be offered to at least one of them.

Teaching in Brussels   Accordingly, in January 1843 Charlotte returned to Brussels, but without Emily, who stayed at the Parsonage to look after her father. It was now arranged for Charlotte to provide some tuition in return for free board and a small salary. However, just like at Roe Head, she found the transition from pupil to teacher uncongenial to her nature: disciplining pupils proved to be particularly difficult for her because of her sensitivity and a slightly eccentric physical appearance (even when fully grown, she was remarkably short and very near-sighted); there were no more private lessons given to her by M. Heger, and she disliked the other teachers. Furthermore, Mme Heger seemed to turn against her, probably because she suspected Charlotte had fallen in love with her husband – a fact attested to by her subsequent passionate letters to him. This experience, though deeply painful to Charlotte at the time, furnished her with the material for her first novel, *The Professor*.

In January 1844, Charlotte left Brussels and returned home. *Return to Haworth and* There she looked after her father, whose eyesight was failing, and *Visit to Hathersage* revived the idea of a school, but the lack of prospective pupils made the project unviable. When Anne returned to Haworth after her latest attempt at being a governess, Charlotte was able to take a short holiday in Hathersage, Derbyshire, with her friend Ellen Nussey. The scenery of this part of the Peak District would later provide inspiration for the landscape surrounding the Rivers' cottage in *Jane Eyre*. It is also probable that the name of the novel's heroine originates from the area, as Hathersage Church contains four medieval brasses of the Eyre family. North Lees Hall, the fifteenth-century home of the Eyre family, which lay two miles from Hathersage, may have provided material for the novel's Thornfield Hall. The flat moorlands between Sheffield and Hathersage resemble the setting for Jane's flight from Thornfield, and Hathersage may have inspired the fictional village of Morton.

On returning to Haworth, Charlotte found Branwell at home, *Anne, Branwell and* giving in to alcoholism after a disastrous episode in his professional *the Robinsons* life. Branwell had been engaged as a tutor to the son of the Robinson family at Thorp Green near York – Anne had already been working for them as a governess for almost three years – but had recently been relieved of his duties and ordered to cease all communication with any member of the family. There has been much speculation about what exactly led to Branwell's dismissal. Recent scholarship shows that, as Branwell claimed, there was almost certainly some kind of affair between him and Mrs Robinson – but the exact nature of that affair, and how it was discovered, remain unanswered questions. Anne resigned her position before Branwell was dismissed, and it remains unclear whether she did so because she didn't wish to become entangled with Branwell's situation or for other reasons. In any case, this scandal completed the ruin of Branwell – who, having already seen his aspirations as a poet and painter frustrated, took even more heavily to drink and opium. Patrick and Charlotte were unsympathetic to his plight, and this lack of sympathy may have further contributed to his downfall. Branwell went on to run up debts, write wild letters and generally behave in such an irresponsible way that he brought constant turbulence and distress to the Parsonage. This also may have put an end to any plans for the Brontës' own school.

Publication of Poems   It was at this time, in the latter half of 1845, when all the Brontë siblings were at home, having failed to maintain employment and independence, that the three sisters took their first step towards submitting their literary endeavours to the public eye. Charlotte chanced upon a notebook containing Emily's poems, was greatly impressed by their quality and proposed that they should be published. Emily was initially incensed by this perceived intrusion on her privacy, since Gondal and its related poems were a creation that she had shared only with Anne. But thanks to the insistence of Charlotte, and Anne's mediation, Emily gradually warmed to the idea of publishing some of her verse jointly with her sisters', under the condition that they use pseudonyms and keep their identities secret. After spending the end of 1845 collating their various poems into one manuscript and editing out all the explicit Gondal and Angria references, Charlotte obtained a positive reply from the small London publisher Alyott & Jones in January 1846 – with the proviso that they must pay for publication themselves – and in May of the same year the sisters received the advance copies of *Poems* by Currer, Ellis and Acton Bell. Although there were some favourable reviews, they managed to sell only two copies of the book.

The Professor and   Still, seeing their work in print must have acted as a strong incen-
Jane Eyre tive to the Brontë sisters as they devoted all their energies to writing their first novels: Anne's *Agnes Grey*, Emily's *Wuthering Heights* and Charlotte's *The Professor* were soon completed and submitted to London publishers. *Agnes Grey* and *Wuthering Heights* were accepted in July 1847 by Thomas Cautley Newby of 72 Mortimer Street, Cavendish Square, on condition that the authors pay a deposit of fifty pounds. Charlotte, on the other hand, received a number of rejections for *The Professor*, including one from Smith, Elder & Co., which encouraged her to submit more work. As Charlotte later wrote: "It declined... to publish that tale for business

reasons, but it discussed its merits and demerits so courteously, so considerately, in a spirit so rational, with a discrimination so enlightened, that this very refusal cheered the author better than a vulgarly expressed acceptance would have done. It was added that a work in three volumes would meet with careful attention." Charlotte, keen to seize the opportunity, quickly finished and submitted the other novel she had been working on over the past year, *Jane Eyre*. This was read with great enthusiasm by Smith, Elder & Co., and published in October 1847 to immediate success and critical acclaim.

Jane Eyre: An Autobiography was published under the pseudonym of Currer Bell, just as Charlotte's poetry had been, and the author fiercely guarded her anonymity. However, given the popularity of the novel, people inevitably started speculating about the identity of its mysterious author. The publication of *Wuthering Heights* by Ellis Bell and *Agnes Grey* by Acton Bell naturally added to the buzz, and the association of these initially less well-received novels with *Jane Eyre* helped their commercial success. There were even rumours that the three novels were all the work of a single hand, a fact the publishers did not fail to capitalize on, although the Brontë sisters were sufficiently upset by this false rumour to travel to London (with the exception of Emily, and much to her chagrin) and present themselves to the publishers as proof of their separate identities. Slowly, Charlotte's and her sisters' authorship of the works became known, although they continued the deception of publishing their books under the old pseudonyms for the rest of their lives. *Speculation regarding Currer Bell*

If 1847 was full of promise for the sisters' literary prospects, the following two years again brought death and tragedy into the Brontë household. In September 1848 Branwell, by now a broken man in the grip of alcoholism and depression, suddenly died of consumption. Emily, who had been tirelessly caring for her dying brother, also showed symptoms of tuberculosis soon after his funeral. She refused to rest or see a doctor, and died on 19th December. Shortly after this, Anne, who had shared a bedroom with Emily, also caught the disease and, although she travelled to Scarborough on the Yorkshire coast with Charlotte in a desperate bid to restore her ailing health, died there on 28th May. Deeply shocked by this series of deaths, Charlotte nevertheless carried on working on her next novel, *Shirley*, under the constant encouragement of her publisher. *Deaths of Branwell, Emily and Anne*

Shirley was eventually published in October 1849, but did not meet with quite as much critical and commercial success as *Jane Eyre*. The stress of writing under such adverse circumstances took its toll, but Charlotte found catharsis in this task. As she later wrote: "Whatever now becomes of the work, the occupation of writing it has been a boon to me. It took me out of dark and desolate reality into an unreal but happier region."

The London Literary Scene As concealing her identity was becoming more and more difficult, Charlotte started making appearances in London society. There she mixed with critics and writers such as her literary hero William Makepeace Thackeray (to whom she had dedicated the second edition of *Jane Eyre*), visited art galleries, theatres, monuments, and had her portrait drawn by George Richmond. But her enjoyment of these occasions was thwarted by her extreme shyness and lack of conversational ease and urban sophistication: once again she found that she did not fit in, and was perceived as slightly gauche, whilst still commanding respect as a writer. After an event organized by Thackeray to meet the mysterious author of *Jane Eyre*, his daughter described Charlotte as appearing "in mittens, in silence, in seriousness".

Meeting Elizabeth Gaskell In 1850, during a summer holiday in the Lake District, Charlotte met the novelist Elizabeth Gaskell, and the two formed a lasting friendship. The following year, Charlotte received a third marriage proposal, this time from James Taylor, the managing clerk of her publishers. Once again, she rejected the proposal, confiding to her friend Ellen Nussey: "Could I ever feel for him enough love to accept of him as a husband? Friendship, gratitude, esteem I have – but each moment he came near me, and that I could see his eyes fastened on me, my veins ran ice." That year, she also tried again – as she had done before embarking on *Shirley* – to convince Smith, Elders and Co. that *The Professor* might be publishable, with some revision. However, they were not to be persuaded, and Charlotte's first novel was not published until after her death.

Villette Charlotte's time was now divided between the aching silence left behind at Haworth by the untimely departure of her siblings and a busy life in London. She continued work on her next novel, *Villette*, throughout 1852, but progress was slow and troubled. On the one hand she seemed to have lost confidence in her artistic abilities, and on the other the pressure of the public's increased expectations and her publisher's tight deadlines plunged her into a state of anxiety and depression: "I don't get on – I feel fettered – incapable – sometimes very low." In order to finish the novel, she cloistered herself away in Haworth, declining any social invitations. The final volume of *Villette* was delivered to Smith, Elder and Co. in November 1852, and the book was published two months later.

Just before the publication of *Villette*, Charlotte had received a *Arthur Bell Nicholls* fourth marriage proposal, this time from Revd Arthur Bell Nicholls, who had been curate of Haworth since 1845. He was a reserved, serious and grave man of strong convictions, and highly conscientious in the performance of his duties. Ellen Nussey had shown early suspicions of his inclinations for Charlotte, teasingly encouraging a potential match. Charlotte responded to her in a letter: "I cannot for my life see those interesting germs of goodness in him you discovered. His narrowness of mind always strikes me chiefly – I fear he is indebted to your imagination for his hidden treasures." Charlotte also resented the village rumour that she was "going to be married to her papa's curate". She did, however, gradually warm to Nicholls, especially after he roared with laughter over the depiction of the curacy in *Shirley*. When she received his proposal, Charlotte asked if he had obtained her father's permission, and he answered that he had not dared to do so, perhaps anticipating a negative response. Indeed, on hearing the news, Patrick was furious: he was outraged that a mere curate should want to marry his now famous daughter, and refused even to consider the idea. This outright refusal drove Nicholls to despair: he stopped eating and drinking, shut himself up in his lodgings and, at one point, appeared to break down in the middle of a communion service. He volunteered as a missionary to Australia, but then reconsidered, and instead took a curacy at Kirk Smeaton in North Yorkshire.

However, at this point Charlotte seemed to have developed a *Marriage to Nicholls* much stronger sympathy for Nicholls, perhaps as a reaction to her father's harsh treatment of him. After some time, Charlotte confessed to her father that she had been corresponding with Nicholls, and demanded the right to become better acquainted with him. Patrick reluctantly gave her permission to continue the correspondence and meet with him, and was finally persuaded by a belligerent Charlotte to sanction their marriage. By April 1854, Charlotte and Arthur were engaged.

It was then arranged that Arthur should return to Haworth as Patrick's curate and live in the Parsonage with Charlotte and her father, whose deteriorating eyesight made it impossible for him to live alone. On 29th June 1854, the couple were married by Arthur's friend, Revd Sutcliffe Sowden, vicar of Hebden Bridge. The wedding was attended by only a small number of people: Ellen Nussey and Miss Wooler from among Charlotte's acquaintances, and probably only a few other household friends and servants. Patrick, however, pleading ill health, was not there. As the bride could be given away by a friend in the absence of a father, it was decided that this task be fulfilled by Miss Wooler.

The couple's honeymoon was spent first in North Wales and then in Ireland, where Nicholls had grown up. Having expressed, in letters around this time, some reservations about her marriage, it seems that Charlotte was now impressed by Arthur's relatives. In her eyes, they were all very civilized, well educated and perfectly embodying "Englishness" – as she put it – and this led her to revise her opinion of her husband as a humble curate.

Married Life   On returning to the Parsonage, Charlotte became absorbed in her new domestic role, and on the whole seemed to be happy with her situation, although in a letter to Ellen Nussey she hinted at some initial difficulties in adapting to married life: "It is a solemn and strange and perilous thing for a woman to become a wife." It was at this time that Arthur chanced upon another intimate – and in his eyes unguarded – letter from Charlotte to Ellen, which alarmed him to the danger that her reputation might be damaged if her private correspondence were to fall into the wrong hands. His solution to this problem was to offer Ellen a choice: either she would promise to burn Charlotte's letters after reading them, or they would have to pass his censorship before being sent out. Ellen reluctantly agreed to burn Charlotte's letters, but then refrained from doing so, perhaps convinced that Arthur was censoring her friend's letters anyway.

Willie Ellin and Emma   Fully absorbed by the great changes in her private life, Charlotte did not write anything of consequence for some time, although she tried to rework 'Willie Ellin', a story she had begun in the spring of 1853. This became the fragment now known as 'Emma', and is probably the last piece she ever wrote.

Straight after her marriage, Charlotte's health improved signifi- *Pregnancy and Illness*
cantly: in a letter to Miss Wooler, she reported with satisfaction
that she had not been suffering from "headache, sickness and
indigestion" for a long time. However, falling pregnant at the age
of thirty-eight, she experienced severe morning sickness, which
confined her to her bed. When Arthur consulted a doctor on the
matter, he was told that the illness might last some time, but was
not dangerous. Yet Charlotte's condition worsened – she became
emaciated, feverish, exhausted and too sick even to answer letters
– which Arthur and Patrick were obliged to take care of.

On 17th February, Charlotte made her will, bequeathing everything to her husband. On the same day, Tabby Aykroyd, a beloved
servant to the Brontës for over thirty years, died at the age of
eighty-four. Charlotte grew inexorably weaker and eventually
delirious. Gaskell relates the story that when Charlotte recognized
her husband's "woe-worn face and caught the sound of some murmured words of prayer that God would spare her", she exclaimed,
"Oh!... I'm not going to die, am I? He will not separate us, we
have been so happy."

On Saturday morning, 31st March 1855, Charlotte Brontë died, *Death*
three weeks before her thirty-ninth birthday. The cause of death
was certified as being "Phthisis", or tuberculosis of the lungs. It is
virtually certain that what had worn her down more than anything
else was the pregnancy and the violent nausea resulting from it. The
baby died with her: there would be no descendants of the Brontës
of Haworth, of which only Patrick now remained. He would die
in 1861, at the age of eighty-four.

Charlotte Brontë's life began to be mythologized almost immedi- *Posthumous Reputation*
ately after her death. Her friend Harriet Martineau wrote a tribute
to her which contained most of the half-truths and misconceptions
that have come to be essential to the Brontë legend – that Patrick
was "simple and unworldly" and "too much absorbed in his studies
to notice [Charlotte's] occupations", that Branwell was "a young
man of once splendid promise which was early blighted" and that
their home was among "wild Yorkshire hills... in a place where
newspapers were never seen". Similar claims were developed further
as Charlotte's death was reported in the press, along with stories
about how the harsh regime at Cowan Bridge School had killed

her sisters and stunted her growth, and about the sisters' secluded life at Haworth.

Gaskell's The Life of   Having read a particularly misleading article in *Sharpe's London*
Charlotte Brontë *Magazine*, Ellen Nussey urged Arthur and Patrick to commission Elizabeth Gaskell, an established author and a friend of Charlotte's, to write an authorized biography in order to set the record straight. Gaskell, who had already been considering a similar project, quickly accepted. She gained access to Charlotte's letters and interviewed those who had been close to her – Ellen Nussey being the most eager to assist her.

Patrick's attitude towards this project may have been slightly naive, expecting the plain unvarnished truth to speak for itself and immediately prevent any falsehood spreading. Arthur's understanding of it was more realistic, though he did demand to be consulted about the material used in the book. Both of them heard almost nothing from Gaskell while she was researching her subject, and were reluctant to offer her anything more than was absolutely necessary in terms of personal letters and stories relating to Charlotte, not realizing the disproportionate amount of material Gaskell was receiving from Ellen Nussey. There is also evidence that Ellen was selective in what she chose to show the biographer. Gaskell managed to track down Mary Taylor, Charlotte's schoolfriend at Roe Head, in New Zealand: she had destroyed all of the letters Charlotte had written to her, but was able to supply an account of their schooldays based on memory. In the early summer of 1856, Gaskell visited the Pensionnat Heger in Brussels, where she was assisted in her endeavours by M. Heger, but received with coldness by Mme Heger – possibly because of the recent publication of *Villette* in French and the thinly disguised, unflattering portrayal of her in the book.

The *Life of Charlotte Brontë* was published in March 1857 to immediate success. Yet, written from the outset with the clear intention of protecting Charlotte from the accusations of "coarseness" that had been made against her, the work was part panegyric, part hagiography, passing over anything that may have been considered unedifying by the Victorian reading public, such as the letters Charlotte wrote to the married M. Heger. While suppressing aspects of Charlotte's character and life, the work indulged in unsubstantiated gossip concerning Patrick, Branwell and several others. In fact, Gaskell's claims regarding Branwell and Mrs Robinson, now Lady Scott, resulted in her being sued for libel, and the first and second printings of the book being withdrawn. Immediately after publication, Gaskell had left for Italy, and was therefore unaware of these complications until her return, by which time her husband and her lawyers had published an unconditional retraction of any claims made against Lady Scott. Just as this was dealt with, however, another libel case threatened to emerge from Revd Carus Wilson's son, on account of Gaskell's comments about the Clergy Daughters' School at Cowan Bridge, upon which Charlotte had largely based her fictional Lowood. The dispute generated a raging exchange of letters in the press which lasted for months on end. In September 1857, the third edition of Gaskell's biography – which omitted all the contentious passages – was finally published, putting an end to the public disputes.

In the same year, Charlotte's first novel, *The Professor*, was published posthumously, by approval of Nicholls, who took it upon himself to edit parts of the novel deemed vulgar, "unfeminine" and "open to misinterpretation". *Posthumous Publication of The Professor*

Charlotte Brontë's Works

Charlotte's apprenticeship to the art of writing began at a very early age, in the form of plays, poems, novelettes and various other fragmentary pieces which she co-created with her siblings. Part of this body of work survives and is commonly known as the "Angrian saga", in reference to Angria, a fictional world created by Charlotte and her brother Branwell, although in fact it encompasses writings which relate to associated imaginary worlds. It all originated in the "young men plays", in which Branwell, Charlotte, Emily and Anne imagined stories about an African colony initially called Glass Town and then Verdopolis. The resulting narratives, each one purportedly written by one of their fictional protagonists, were penned into small booklets in tiny script. Charlotte continued writing Angrian pieces until she was at least twenty-three. Anne and Emily also developed *Glass Town and Angria* their own fantasy sagas, set in the fictional land of Gondal, but unfortunately none of the Gondal writings – with the exception of a few poems – have survived.

Readers only familiar with Charlotte Brontë's novels tend to see her as an earnest and unselfconscious writer, and her Angrian juvenilia is often regarded as the product of naive escapism. However, her novelettes, especially her later ones, are in fact replete with irony, topical detail, deliberate intertextual play and awareness of political and economic realities. Not only are elements of various popular Victorian prose genres clearly visible in her Angrian compositions – from the "silver fork" novel and its tales of urban fashionable life to the "Newgate" novel and its lurid depiction of working-class criminality, as well as the supernatural flair of Gothic fiction and the exotic and adventurous appeal of contemporary travelogues – but, imitating her favourite contemporary journals such as *Blackwood's Magazine* and *Fraser's Magazine*, she actively lampooned and questioned the conventions she drew upon.

The chronicles of Angria and those of related realms do not constitute a coherent, linear narrative, but can be read as stand-alone sketches revolving around recurring characters, such as the Byronic Duke of Zamorna, the foppish Castlereagh, the rogue Alexander Percy and the dashing opera singer and mistress Louisa Vernon, all of whom also appear under various pseudonyms. The stories span a wide range of intrigues, duels, adulterous relationships, lovers' complaints and high-society scandals.

As well as prose, Angria inspired Charlotte to write poems, which were more often than not also reflections of her own personal state of mind. Although this poetry was restricted to her private circle, Charlotte did, for a while at least, harbour ambitions to become a famous poet, as evidenced by her letter to the Poet Laureate Robert Southey (29th December 1836), in which she sent samples of her verse and requested his advice. His response was less than encouraging: whilst acknowledging her "faculty for verse", he added that this gift was not a rare occurrence these days and advised against the pursuit of poetry as a profession. Posterity has to a certain extent agreed with Southey's appraisal – although it must be noted that he seemed to be dismissive of any poetic faculty in a woman – as nowadays Charlotte Brontë the poet is not considered on a par with Charlotte Brontë the novelist.

At any rate, as has been mentioned above, Charlotte did finally *Poetry* make her verse available to the public when in the autumn of 1845 she persuaded her sisters Emily and Anne to find a publisher for a joint collection of their poetry. At Emily's request, they decided to adopt the pseudonyms of Currer, Ellis and Acton Bell and remove any Angria or Gondal references from their work. Alyott & Jones, a small London publisher, accepted to publish the volume as long as the sisters paid for the venture themselves, and the book was printed in May 1846. Although reportedly only selling two copies, there were some encouraging reviews – significantly, these lavished most praise on "Ellis Bell" (Emily) while gently dismissing the efforts of "Currer" and "Acton". This may be due to the fact that Charlotte had by this time more or less abandoned poetry as her preferred mode of expression – no more than three of the nineteen compositions she contributed to the collection were recent ones – and her correspondence suggests that she would have preferred it if her poems had been omitted altogether. Nevertheless, Charlotte's publisher for her novels, Smith, Elder & Co., bought *Poems by Currer, Ellis and Acton Bell* from Alyott & Jones and reissued the collection in November 1848 on the back of *Jane Eyre*'s success.

The Professor, the first novel written by Charlotte Brontë, but also *The Professor* the only one never to appear during her lifetime, was completed and originally submitted for publication to various publishers in 1846, along with her sisters' novels *Wuthering Heights* and *Agnes Grey*. Even at the height of *Jane Eyre*'s success, Charlotte was unable to get it published. It was rejected nine times in total, including three times by Smith, Elder & Co., the publisher of the rest of her fiction, who eventually published it in 1857, two years after her death. Charlotte Brontë always maintained a high opinion of her first novel: "My feeling towards it can only be paralleled by those of a doting parent towards an idiot child. Its merit – I plainly perceive – will never be owned by anybody but... me."

The Professor tells the story of William Crimsworth, the son of a bankrupt mill owner, who after leaving Eton is offered both a rectorship and marriage to one of his despised cousins by his wealthy and aristocratic uncles, both of whom had loathed William's manufacturer father and thus disowned their sister, William's mother, who died shortly after giving birth to him. William refuses this offer and chooses to join his brother Edward's mill as a clerk. But life there is difficult, as his tyrannical brother treats him with disdain, and his efforts go unthanked and unrewarded. Having received a letter of introduction to a prominent Englishman in Brussels from the eccentric mill owner Mr Hunsden, William decides to relocate to the Belgian capital, where after some initial difficulties he manages to secure a position at M. Pelet's school for boys. After impressing in this role, he is invited to teach at a neighbouring girls' boarding school, under the directorship of the unscrupulous, manipulative and coquettish Mlle Zoraïde Reuter.

He soon realizes that M. Pelet and Mlle Reuter are secretly betrothed, yet in his subsequent proud and scornful treatment of Zoraïde, he unwittingly imbues her with a fervent desire for him, and M. Pelet rages at William when Mlle Reuter breaks off their betrothal due to her feelings for William. However, it is a newly appointed sewing teacher, Frances Evans Henri, the impoverished, orphaned daughter of a Swiss pastor, who is the object of William's affections. She joins his class to improve her English, and his stern yet encouraging methods reveal her dormant skill in the language, learnt while her English mother was still alive. William and Frances both live for the brief moments at the end of the lesson when they can communicate while the students bustle in and out, but their burgeoning friendship is cut short by Mlle Reuter's abrupt dismissal of Mlle Henri. Having tried in vain to obtain the details of her whereabouts from Mlle Reuter, William resigns his position at the *pensionnat* and ceaselessly searches Brussels for her. When he finally finds her at her aunt's grave, Frances invites William to her humble lodgings in a poor district of Brussels. Friendless and without family or employment, Frances longs for England, her mother's homeland, and wishes to become an accomplished teacher and advance in life. Thanks to her assiduousness, natural intelligence and William's teaching, she soon gains a position at a new English school in Brussels.

William longs to ask her to be his wife, but having left his teaching posts, he is in no position to do so until he finds employment. With the help of the father of a pupil he once saved from drowning, William is appointed English professor at a prestigious college in Brussels. He asks Frances to marry him, and she accepts. The married pair eventually open their own school, and then, having made enough money to give up teaching, they move to England with their son Victor, and settle near to Hunsden in the English countryside.

The Professor's critical reception at the time was not entirely enthusiastic: it was generally seen as valuable for the light it shed on Charlotte's literary development, but not comparable to her later works – sales were consequently lacklustre. It caused much consternation to Gaskell, Nicholls and George Smith, Charlotte's publisher, due to its supposed coarseness, and as such Nicholls made several deletions. In fact, Gaskell later wrote that she wished Nicholls had "altered more". The novel was viewed as a forerunner of *Villette*, a sort of apprenticeship in the writing of the latter novel. It is clear, though, that this was not the case. Charlotte wrote to Smith stating that parts of the novel were "as good as I can write", and that it "contains more pith, more substance, more reality, in my judgement, than much of *Jane Eyre*". Despite the fame and success that *Jane Eyre* and subsequent works brought, Charlotte continued to spend much of her time editing and working on the rejected manuscript of *The Professor*, submitting it again and again, and believing unequivocally in its merits. Thankfully, there has been a reappraisal of *The Professor* in recent years, with many critics pointing to the acuity of its social and political insights, and its power as the poignant story of a self-made man.

By mid-1847, having failed to get *The Professor* published, but *Jane Eyre* at the same time arousing the interest of Smith, Elder & Co. in her as a writer, Charlotte quickly completed a novel she had begun working on since around August 1846. As we have seen above, the new novel, *Jane Eyre: An Autobiography*, was accepted enthusiastically by the publisher and printed in October 1847, under the pseudonym of Currer Bell.

It was an immediate success with the reading public, gaining the approval of such luminaries as Thackeray, who reportedly read the book from cover to cover in a single day, and to whom Charlotte would dedicate the second edition of the novel.

The plot of the novel centres on the eponymous heroine and her development from childhood to maturity. Jane is an orphan living under the care of her uncle and aunt, the Reeds. After the death of Mr Reed, Mrs Reed – who, along with her spoilt children, shows no sympathy or affection towards the child – resolves to send Jane to Lowood, a school for orphans, in which the pupils are subjected to abhorrent and inhumane conditions. Despite the hardships, and the horrors of a typhus epidemic, Jane becomes a model pupil and, completing her education, remains at the institution for two years as a teacher.

Finding life at the school too limiting, Jane secures a position as a governess at Thornfield Hall. There she takes charge of the education of Adèle Varens, a ten-year-old French girl. Her new employer is Edward Fairfax Rochester, a dark-haired, moody and taciturn man. Despite his volatile, passionate nature, Jane gradually grows fond of him. Believing that Mr Rochester is going to marry the beautiful Blanche Ingram, Jane is consumed by pangs of jealousy, and she realizes she has fallen in love with him. She reveals her feelings to him and they become engaged to be married. In the month leading to the wedding, Jane is troubled by disquieting events, such as the appearance of a mysterious woman in her room who tears her wedding veil apart. When Rochester and Jane are at the altar exchanging vows, the wedding is interrupted by a man who announces an impediment to the marriage, claiming that Rochester is already married. It emerges that Rochester had been duped into a union with a beautiful Creole woman, Bertha Mason, who would soon show symptoms of the mental illness running in her family. Now he keeps the madwoman locked in a room in the attic under the scarcely reliable supervision of Grace Poole.

Jane runs away from Thornfield in the middle of the night, and is offered hospitality by the clergyman St John Rivers and his two sisters Diana and Mary. St John offers Jane a job as schoolmistress at the parish school for poor girls, which she gladly accepts. Eventually St John discovers her true identity, which reveals her to be the Rivers' long-lost cousin. It also emerges that Jane has inherited twenty thousand pounds from her uncle, John Eyre, who had cut the Rivers out of his will because of an argument with their father. Jane insists on splitting her inheritance equally with her cousins, and St John – whose heart is set on becoming a missionary in India

– tries to persuade Jane to accompany him and become his wife. She refuses to marry him, since it is clear that the love he feels for her is that of a cousin and not of a husband.

One night, Jane hears a preternatural voice calling out to her from afar. Jane leaves immediately for Thornfield, which she finds burnt to the ground. She discovers that Bertha Mason was responsible for the fire, and that Rochester lost a hand and his eyesight while trying in vain to save his first wife. On learning that he has moved to nearby Ferndean, she seeks him out. There she is joyfully reunited with him, and they marry at last.

After the success of *Jane Eyre*, Charlotte Brontë – like many other writers – faced the challenge of producing a worthy follow-up. As her publisher was reluctant to reconsider *The Professor*, she looked to some unfinished Angrian material for inspiration and began writing what would later become *Shirley*, submitting the first volume – which had been completed in September 1848, probably before Branwell's death on the 24th – to her publisher in February 1849. As Smith, Elder & Co. were aware of the author's extremely difficult personal circumstances during the composition of her new work, they reacted encouragingly and did not express any reservations they might have had. Charlotte labouredly managed to complete the novel, which was published in October 1849, with the author refusing to revise some of the imperfections highlighted by her editors, such as its lack of focus (the eponymous heroine only appears at the end of the first volume) and its disparaging treatment of the British clergy in the opening chapter. There was also surprise that Charlotte chose the Luddite revolts as her subject matter, having little direct knowledge of working-class life. The decision to move away from the timeless romance and drama of *Jane Eyre* to a more sober, historical type of novel-writing was deliberate, the opening chapter of *Shirley* revealing that she wanted to write "something unromantic as Monday morning". Whilst reviews were mixed (Charlotte famously cried over the *Times* review of 7 December 1849), Charlotte received an appreciative letter from fellow novelist Elizabeth Gaskell, who had a year earlier published a novel, *Mary Barton*, dealing with similar issues.

The novel is set in early-nineteenth-century Yorkshire, a period marked by the Napoleonic Wars and the Luddite revolts. Two of

Shirley

the central characters are Robert Moore, the owner of a struggling mill, and Caroline Helstone, the daughter of a conservative reverend. Caroline is in love with Robert, but is unable to command his attention as he is too preoccupied with the future of his business. She is also frustrated by her father's animosity towards her beloved and his refusal to allow her to undertake governessing work. Towards the end of the first volume, Caroline meets Shirley Keeldar, a stoical and unconventional heiress – Charlotte's loving tribute to her sister Emily, who had recently died – and the two, although very different in nature and outlook, strike up an unlikely friendship. Meanwhile Robert decides to acquire new machinery for his factory, causing outrage among his workers, who – fearing for their jobs – launch an attack on the mill. In the middle of this unrest, Caroline, believing Robert has designs on Shirley, falls gravely ill, but is brought back to health by the news that the woman who has been caring for her, Mrs Pryor, is in fact her long-lost mother. Shirley gradually falls in love with Robert's brother Louis, while the reinvigorated Caroline ends up nursing Robert himself, who has been shot in an ambush by a mysterious attacker. Both couples end up declaring their love for each other and getting married.

Villette   Having started to write a new novel sometime in 1850, Charlotte sent the first two volumes of *Villette* to Smith, Elder & Co. in October 1852. The publisher raised a number of issues, but Charlotte, as was her habit, refused to revise her work, and felt encouraged to press on with the third volume, which she delivered on 20th November 1852. Smith, Elder & Co. were still not entirely pleased with it – their criticism mainly focusing on the unsympathetic nature of the novel's female protagonist, Lucy Snowe, and the lack of romance in the ending. They were also reluctant to publish the new novel pseudonymously. In the end, they relented and published *Villette* in January 1853. Its reception was on the whole favourable, although her friend Harriet Martineau launched into a personal attack on Charlotte Brontë in her review of the book for the *Daily News*. Charlotte was greatly upset by it and, as a result, ceased all communication with her. Thackeray privately disliked the work, but Charlotte was never to learn of this. Others were more enthusiastic, however, such as George Eliot, who exclaimed: "Villette! Villette! Have you read it?... It is a still more wonderful book than *Jane Eyre*. There is something almost preternatural in its power."

The novel, which can be seen to some extent as a reworking of *The Professor*, draws on Charlotte's experience in Brussels. Similarly to *Jane Eyre*, it chronicles the personal journey towards adulthood and maturity of its female protagonist, who looks back at her life from old age.

The novel opens with fourteen-year-old Lucy Snowe staying at the town house of her wealthy godmother Mrs Bretton and her son John Graham. During her stay, a second guest arrives, the young Pauline Home, daughter of a friend and distant relative of Mrs Bretton's late husband. A few weeks after Paulina's departure and relocation to the Continent, Lucy leaves the Bretton household and is reunited with her relatives. Eight years pass and, bereaved of her family, Lucy takes on a position as the carer of Miss Marchmont, a wealthy, crippled old maid. When her employer suddenly dies, Lucy, again destitute and friendless, uses the little money she possesses to travel to London and, despite her poor knowledge of French, boards a ship for the kingdom of Labassecour (a fictitious country based on Belgium). Upon the recommendation of fellow passenger Ginevra Fanshawe, she journeys to the capital Villette, where she secures a position as a nanny and governess for the daughters of Mme Beck, the directress of a boarding school for girls. Lucy gradually wins the respect of Mme Beck and is appointed as the replacement of one of the school's English teachers. Mme Beck – an acerbic portrait of the real-life Mme Heger – is described as a "little Bonaparte in a mouse-coloured silk gown" whose watchwords are "surveillance" and "espionage". Manipulative, meddling and tyrannical, she interferes with the lives, affections and relationships of all the people who fall under her influence. Nevertheless, Lucy is initially satisfied with her new life as a teacher, but during a school vacation she sinks into depression out of loneliness and, after trying in vain to confide her problems to Père Silas, a Jesuit priest, she ends up collapsing in the street. When she reawakens, she finds that she has been taken in and cared for by the young physician Dr John, a regular visitor to Mme Beck's establishment. Dr John turns out to be none other than John Graham, the son of Mrs Bretton, who has also recently relocated to Villette. Lucy falls in love with Dr John, but he does not reciprocate her feelings, as he is infatuated with the flirtatious Ginevra Fanshawe. But having discovered Ginevra's true nature, Dr John's affections shift towards his childhood playmate Paulina Home – now revealed to be Countess de Bassompierre – and, despite her father's initial opposition, he ends up marrying her. Lucy is left heartbroken, but she finds herself drawn to the fiery and moody English literature teacher Paul Emanuel, Mme Beck's cousin. The two fall in love, but a "secret junta" of enemies – Mme Beck, Père Silas and Mme Walravens, the grandmother of M. Paul's long-deceased fiancée, Justine Marie – conspire to keep the couple apart, and persuade M. Paul to leave for Guadeloupe to look after a friend's interests. Before his departure, Paul declares his love for Lucy and, anticipating his return in around three years' time, sets her up as the headmistress of a girls' school in Villette. The ending strongly suggests that M. Paul's vessel is shipwrecked by storm on its journey back from the West Indies, and Lucy – her fate mirroring that of Miss Marchmont – is destined to a long life of solitude and bereavement.

Willie Ellin and Emma   In the spring of 1853, Charlotte had started work on a new story, 'Willie Ellin', which she would later revisit and expand – her untimely death in 1855, however, prevented her from completing it. The fragment, now known as 'Emma', is set in a finishing school and centres around a young girl, Matilda, who is exposed as an impostor when her pretensions to nobility are revealed to be false. George Smith of Smith, Elder & Co. convinced the widowed Revd Nicholls to publish 'Emma' in his newly founded *Cornhill Magazine*, with an introduction by Thackeray. Since its first publication, there have been attempts by other writers to continue the narrative, such as *Emma Brown* by Clare Boylan (2004).

Select Bibliography

Biographies:
Bentley, Phyllis, *The Brontës* (London: Thames and Hudson, 1969)
Barker, Juliet, *The Brontës* (London: Weidenfeld and Nicolson, 1994)
Fraser, Rebecca, *Charlotte Brontë*, 2nd ed. (London: Vintage, 2003)
Gaskell, Elizabeth, *The Life of Charlotte Brontë* (London: Penguin, 1997)
Gérin, Winifred, *Charlotte Brontë: The Evolution of Genius*, 2nd ed. (Oxford: Oxford University Press, 1969)
Winnifrith, Tom, *A New Life of Charlotte Brontë* (Basingstoke: Macmillan, 1988)

Additional Recommended Background Material:
Barker, Juliet, *The Brontës: A Life in Letters* (London: Penguin, 1997)
Gilbert, Sandra M. and Gubar, Susan S., *The Madwoman in the Attic: The Woman Writer and the Nineteenth-Century Lit-erary Imagination,* 2nd ed. (New Haven, CT: Yale University Press, 2000)
Glen, Heather, ed., *The Cambridge Companion to the Brontës* (Cambridge: Cambridge University Press, 2002)
Winnifrith, Tom, *The Brontës and their Background* (London: Macmillan, 1988)

On the Web:
www.bronte.org.uk
www.lang.nagoya-u.ac.jp/~matsuoka/Bronte.html

ALMA CLASSICS

ALMA CLASSICS aims to publish mainstream and lesser-known European classics in an innovative and striking way, while employing the highest editorial and production standards. By way of a unique approach the range offers much more, both visually and textually, than readers have come to expect from contemporary classics publishing.

LATEST TITLES PUBLISHED BY ALMA CLASSICS

www.almaclassics.com